Thin Ice

by Frieda Korobkin

D1215744

RoseDog Books

PITTSBURGH, PENNSYLVANIA 15238

RoseDog Books
585 Alpha Drive, Suite 103
Pittsburgh, PA 15238
Visit our website at *www.rosedogbookstore.com*

ISBN: 978-1-4809-7374-9
eISBN: 978-1-4809-7397-8

Also by the author:

Throw Your Feet Over Your Shoulders
(Beyond the Kindertransport)

Outlaw Inlaws
(or how to get along with your children's inlaws)
Written under the pseudonym Friddles

For my daughter, Jennifer

A woman of great courage and even greater faith

Acknowledgments

≫⋘

I am profoundly grateful to Dr. Steven Lowenstein, who graciously and generously spent hours with me, going over historical and geographical details about German Jewry of the 1930's in general, and the Frankfurt Jewish community in particular. His professional expertise in these areas, together with his fluency in the German language, formed the background for the first part of the novel. Any errors I have made in transposing Dr. Lowenstein's facts are mine alone.

Thank you to my son, Rabbi Daniel Korobkin, for explaining certain Jewish laws; and to Rabbi Kalman Topp, who gave me the commentary about wicked Haman. If I have not conveyed either or both of their words accurately, the fault is all mine.

If my novel is at all readable it is largely due to the brilliant editing and insights of my dear friend, Rachelle Needle. Thank you, Rachelle, for giving so generously of your time and talent.

Thanks also to my good friend, school-teacher Elaine Reiman, for reading more than one draft and correcting my grammar and anachronisms.

Saul Turteltaub, television writer-producer and good friend, also read an early draft, and his critique was extremely helpful.

To my children Jennifer Niman and Dr. Samuel Korobkin: your constant encouragement and support mean the world to me. Ditto for my amazing grandchildren, especially Zeke Korobkin, who read an early draft and made very helpful suggestions.

Special thanks to Leslie Zurla, the artist responsible for the cover art. Leslie is not only a very talented and professional artist, she is a pleasure to work with, a real mensch.

Without my rock and strength and biggest fan, not one word would have been written. As always, thank you Len.

Author's Disclaimer

⟫⟪

Although the names of various historical figures are mentioned, as are historical events, this novel is strictly a work of fiction. And although the Frankfurt synagogues I have attempted to describe actually did exist, to the best of my knowledge, a Rabbi Gutfreund did not. His character arose purely from my imagination, as did all the other non-historical characters in the novel. Any resemblance to any person, whether living or dead, is entirely coincidental.

Zechut Avot LeOlam Kayemet

The good deeds of ancestors reverberate forever

(Talmud Yerushalmi, Tractate Sanhedrin, Chapter 10)

Part One

✦

Frankfurt, Germany 1935

Chapter 1

⇒⋘

The day begins badly for Herr Gustav Mayer, and only gets worse as it progresses. It should have been an ordinary day, an ordinary winter's day, seasonably cold, with the usual meetings with customers, the usual hassles with deliveries and suppliers, And, but for the scheduled meeting in Berlin that afternoon, which has been gnawing at him for days, it might well have been an ordinary day like any other.

It is only much later that he is reminded wryly of his late father's favorite rhymed bon mot: *Es konnte immer schlimmer zein*. Things can always be worse.

How much worse, is impossible for him to imagine.

The night has been a restless one, with dreams invading Herr Mayer's sleep like a legion of Prussian mercenaries. It irks him that he was prevented from traveling to Berlin the previous day. The extra time would have given him a solid night's rest in his hotel bed, after enjoying a leisurely supper at his favorite restaurant in the Jewish quarter near the Alexanderplatz. In the morning, he would have had time to eat a late *Frühstück*, to read the newspapers in peace without the telephone or the children interrupting, and later, weather permitting, he might have taken an unhurried mid-morning stroll through the Tiergarten, as he often does during his routine visits to the capital. Most important of all, the extra time might have given him the opportunity to prepare for the meeting. As if it were possible to prepare for a meeting for which no agenda or purpose has been given. It is not only the prospect of the meeting, but the manner in which he was summoned, that have made him so uneasy.

Hence the dreams.

An emergency at the plant, and previously scheduled appointments with foreign buyers who had traveled to Frankfurt for the express purpose of meeting with him, made it impossible for him to leave the day before as he would have liked, certainly not on such short notice. Another of his father's favorite sayings pops into his head. *Der Mensch tracht und Gott lacht.* Man plans, but God has other ideas.

He has instructed Gertrud to book him into his usual suite at the Adlon; his driver Hans will stay, as he always does, in the nearby *pension*. Herr Mayer has no idea how long the meeting will last, but regardless of when it ends it will be too late to attempt the long drive back to Frankfurt on the same day.

It seems to him that he has finally just drifted off, when the shriek of the alarm clock jolts him awake on the dot of six. Immediately alert, he stretches his arm to silence the clock, which stands on the mahogany nightstand that separates his bed from Frau Mayer's. Slipping on the glasses that lie beside the clock, he swings his legs out from under the warm *Daunendecke* and slides his feet directly into the fur-lined leather slippers that have been waiting for him all night, like two sentries at attention. He shrugs on the robe laid out on the bench at the foot of his bed. Nearby, draped across a wooden valet, is the suit he chose so carefully the previous evening. The choice was not an easy one to make, and he had to ponder many minutes before finally selecting the charcoal gray worsted with black waistcoat, a crisp white shirt with stiff collar stays, a grey and black striped tie. And a single pearl *Krawatte* pin. He is confident that he will present a conservative appearance, one that will show his worth without screaming 'opulent' in the manner of some of the *Ost-Juden*, those vulgar, loud-mouthed Polish Jews, who are moving into the neighborhood in alarming numbers and are soon in danger of taking over the *Synagoge*.

Not only is Herr Mayer anxious about the meeting, he is puzzled. Why was he specifically told, no, *ordered*, to attend the meeting alone, without any member of his staff? Even more disturbing is the word that was used: *Verboten*. The voice on the phone, a harsh guttural baritone, specifically forbade it. The exact address for the meeting was also not revealed. Hans is to drop him off on the corner of a small side street opposite the Tiergarten. A car will pick him up at four o'clock. *Pünktlich*.

Herr Mayer takes the three prescribed steps to the commode in the corner, tying the belt of his robe on the way. There, prepared by Inge the evening before, is a blue and white Delft bowl and matching pitcher filled with water, ready for him to make the initial ablutions of the day. He pours water in generous amounts over each fisted hand by turn: three times over the right, then three over the left. He shivers involuntarily when the icy liquid accosts his skin, but he welcomes this frigid wake-up call as an impetus to start the day. He lifts the crisp white linen towel lying folded neatly beside the bowl. The raised initial in the center, a cursive *M*, emits a pleasant sheen in the early morning gloom. He recites the first prescribed blessing of the day as he wipes his hands: *Thank you,* mein Gott, *for restoring my soul in Your abundant goodness and mercy.*

He pulls aside the heavy brocade *Vorhang* that covers the windows. He sees that it is no longer snowing. It is still dark outside, but the sky is clear and luminous with an early morning moon and a sprinkling of stars that light up the courtyard onto which the bedroom faces. The flurries that started the previous night just before Herr Mayer retired have merely left a slight dusting of white powder on the cobblestones, and a shimmering of frost that reflects the starry sky. There should be no problem getting to Berlin on time. The drive should take no more than five hours, six at most. If they start out promptly at eight, as planned, they should reach Berlin no later than two in the afternoon, giving them plenty of time to spare, even enough time to stop for a light lunch. He can depend on Hans to be up early, to make sure the Daimler's motor turns over readily and the heater is working properly, so that Herr Mayer will enter a warm and smoothly humming machine.

He drops the curtain, turns away from the window, and makes his way across the room toward the bathroom. He walks in the semi-darkness without

switching on any lights. It might be thought that Herr Mayer is being considerate about not disturbing Frau Mayer, still sleeping in the other bed. But this
is not so. Herr Mayer was taught to be parsimonious, and electricity is not
cheap. He is forever lecturing the children on the need to turn off lights before
leaving their rooms. Only a few days ago he finally made good on his
umpteenth warning to Fritz and withheld his allowance. He hopes his son has
learned his lesson, just as he, Gustav, had to when he was about Fritz's age.
But given the boy's phlegmatic nature, Herr Mayer is not optimistic. Aside
from this, Herr Mayer has no need to move quietly for he knows that Frau
Mayer, as is her habit every day except on Shabbat, is already up; that she has
her own internal alarm clock, is already in the kitchen, preparing his first cup
of coffee of the day before he leaves for *shul*. He savors that first cup in anticipation, brewed just the way he likes it: hot, but not too hot to drink, strong,
but not too strong, with a dollop of *Schlag*, no sugar.

But wait. He senses there is something not quite right. He stops, he
frowns, he listens. He hears nothing. The absence of sound is not unusual for
the kitchen lies at the other end of the sprawling apartment and Inge, Hans's
wife, is not due to arrive until eight o'clock. But something is amiss. It takes
him a moment to realize what it is. There is no *Kaffee* in the air. By this time
the fragrance of freshly brewed coffee should be suffusing the apartment, as-
saulting him with its aroma, pulling him into the kitchen by the *Nase*. Yet, this
morning there is nothing; not a hint of coffee in the air. He is suddenly filled
with unease. He will never be sure what makes him turn. Is it a sound, perhaps
the rustle of linen, a breath, a sigh? But turn he does, only to discern in the
early morning gloom the shadowy contour of his wife's form, fetally coiled, in
the bed that lies across from his own, on the other side of the nightstand.

Momentarily he just stands there perplexed, his astonishment outweighing
his unease. Has he mistaken the day? Is it possible that he is confused and that
today is the Sabbath? Surely not. No, no it cannot be. For one thing, he would
never set the alarm to ring on Shabbat and, besides, hadn't they just celebrated
Shabbat three or four days' ago? Isn't today *Mittwoch*, Wednesday, the day of

his Berlin meeting, something it would be impossible for him to forget? His momentary confusion and unease are promptly replaced by annoyance. Collecting himself, he switches on the lamp that stands on the second nightstand on the other side of Frau Mayer's bed. She doesn't move but he thinks he has detected another sound, perhaps a moan? He notices, for the first time, that the tendrils of hair escaping from beneath her white night cap are gray. He has trouble remembering the original color: wasn't her hair dark brown? Or, perhaps, auburn? By day, when her hair is covered with a turban or wig, the gray is undetectable. He bends over her, about to touch her shoulder. He hesitates. He tries to recall the last time he had physical contact with his wife, but is unable to remember. He detects a sour odor and draws back, repulsed.

"Frau Mayer," he says loudly, unable to mask his irritation. "*Was ist den los?* What is wrong with you?"

For a split second he has trouble recalling his wife's name. It was shortly after Henrietta was born that he started calling her Frau Mayer, or occasionally *Mutti*. It seemed natural to address her in this way in the presence of the children, as terms of respect, and it soon became a habit. He knows that this practice is a source of amusement to some of their acquaintances. One day he overheard two men talking about him in the *shul* cloakroom. Obviously, they didn't realize he was there, and he had not meant to eavesdrop. He was hidden behind a row of coats, searching for his *Regenmantel*. He did not hear the beginning of their conversation, but then one of the men said, "I would lay a bet that he even calls her Frau Mayer in their *Schlafzimmer,* maybe even when, you know…" followed by laughter. There could be no mistaking whom they were talking about, nor what they meant.

"Marga", he says, more calmly this time, suppressing his irritation by a great effort of will. "Can you hear me? *Bist du krank?* Are you ill?"

Today of all days, he can't help thinking.

Another moan, more pronounced this time, escapes Frau Mayer's lips and now there is no mistaking the sour smell Herr Mayer detected previously. Barely able to control his revulsion, he is nevertheless beginning to be alarmed.

At the same moment he feels his bladder signaling that it is about to erupt, reminding him that he was on his way to the bathroom when he was sidetracked. With the self-discipline that governs all his actions, he commands his bladder to be still, forces himself to sit on the side of his wife's bed, and lifts the hand lying limply on the counterpane. The hand feels hot and clammy to his touch.

"Can you hear me? Can you talk? What is the matter? Shall I summon Herr Doktor Graff?"

He cannot recall Frau Mayer ever being ill. Even in childbirth she was not incapacitated. At any event, that is how he remembers things. Henrietta is seventeen; Fritz almost sixteen. Their births happened so long ago, in a different era, almost as if to different people, almost as if in another country.

He catches another moan from his wife's lips, then a rumbling of sound, but his bladder informs him it can no longer obey, and sends him dashing to the bathroom where he finally finds relief. As he washes his hands he looks at his image in the mirror above the sink. Always punctilious, some might say vain, about his appearance, he peers near-sightedly into the mirror and cannot help noticing that his hairline has receded further. Just the other day his barber, Luigi, (*geborn* Ludwig), using his hands expressively as if he were really Italian, and speaking in the affected Italian accent he acquired along with his name, mentioned that some of his customers were sporting fake hair pieces. Might not Herr Mayer consider getting one of those *toupées*? "They are very comfortable, *mein* Herr, and impossible to detect", the barber added, "and the new, more expensive kinds even stay on in bad *Wetter*." Unbidden, a line from Ovid pops into Herr Mayer's head. In his Latin class in *Gymnasium* they had studied *Ars Amatoria* and even then young Gustav Mayer was struck by Ovid's opinion of *calvus*, baldness. An eyesore, the poet had called it. But surely it must have been the French who came up with the word *toupée*. You can always rely on the French for such frivolous inventiveness. Herr Mayer doesn't go in for such *Dummheit*, and conveyed his opinion to his ersatz Italian barber in no uncertain terms.

He shakes his head and the image in the mirror does the same. Such contemplation goes against Herr Mayer's nature. And why on earth is he diverted by such nonsense when he has this important day ahead of him and his wife is lying unmoving and in apparent distress in the next room? With wet hands, he tames back the thinning hair on his head and smoothes the trim 'salt and pepper' *Schnurrbart* on his lip. He spends an extra minute to brush his teeth. While he seems to have inherited his mother's near-sightedness, he has been fortunate to inherit the evenness and whiteness of his teeth from his father. Certainly more fortunate than his brother Heinz, the famous *Rechtsanwalt* whose mouth is so crowded with overlapping teeth and so stained with tobacco that Gustav always finds himself looking away, slightly repelled, when his brother speaks, and unable to suppress a shiver of distaste when the man displays the full horror of his teeth in a smile. That his brother is a successful lawyer, with a clientele that includes the famous and infamous not only of Frankfurt, but of international repute, is a mystery to him. He often wonders how Heinz was able to snag a wife, considering this very visible shortcoming, and such a beauty to boot, although Bertha seems happy enough with him despite their disparate backgrounds …

But that is an *andere Geschichte*. Another story entirely.

Herr Mayer wipes his hands, then hurries back to his wife's side. She is still lying as he left her, eyes closed, not moving, but making little moaning sounds. For the first time he notices beads of sweat on her forehead, but reassured that she is breathing, he re-ties the belt of his robe and makes for the telephone in his study down the hallway.

He will telephone the doctor, rouse the children, then get dressed. After which he will summon Hans to bring the car round. He must leave for Berlin as planned. No matter what.

Chapter 2

⇒✦⇐

The Gutmans, Samuel and Hannah, occupy the apartment next door to the Mayers. The two apartments are the only ones on the top floor of the three-storey building located on the corner of Schutzenstrasse. It is one of the more prestigious buildings in this part of town, overlooking the River Main. The Gutman dwelling is similar in size to the Mayers' apartment but seems smaller as a result of the clutter created by the Gutmans' five children, ranging in age from seventeen down to the four-year-old twins, and Hannah's widowed mother, Oma Fleissig, who lives with them. The children are quite a boisterous bunch. Just ask Herr Mayer, who has often complained of the noise made by the Gutman children who seem always to be jumping and thumping and chasing each other and creating such a racket that it often sounds as if they are about to break through the very walls separating the two apartments. Even though the building is a solid structure, and even though the Gutmans have deep, lush carpeting in every room, some of it covered with extra rugs of Persian origin, the pounding caused by little Gutman feet and their owners' high spirits are never muted to Herr Mayer's satisfaction.

Samuel Gutman is unfailingly apologetic when Herr Mayer complains of the noise (it must be noted that it is never Frau Mayer who complains), yet he cannot help being mildly amused by Herr Mayer's proper demeanor, his *echt Deutsch* mannerisms. Samuel wonders why the man doesn't just knock on the wall with a broom handle or *Spazierstock*. That is what Samuel might have done if he wanted to send a not-so-subtle message to his noisy neighbors. Instead, Herr Mayer presents himself at the Gutmans' door, rigid and formal, and he could not be more shocked at Samuel's walking stick-broom handle suggestion if Samuel had proposed he light a fire on the Sabbath. It has also not escaped Samuel's notice that Herr Mayer's visits always occur when Samuel is at home. After all, it would not do to confront Hannah Gutman with his complaints. Such weighty matters are best handled man to man, *nicht wahr?*

Wearing a three-piece, pin-striped black suit, his shoes gleaming so brilliantly that Samuel is momentarily blinded by their radiance, Herr Mayer tips his homburg in solemn greeting when Samuel opens the door.

"*Gnädig* Herr Gutman," he begins. "*Es tut mir wirklich Leid*, it really pains me to complain once again, but is it not possible for you to control your children a little better? After a long day at my business, surely you understand that I need some peace and *Ruhe.*"

"Of course, of course, *natürlich*. I am so sorry Herr Mayer that my children are sometimes so *ausgelassen* and wild. I assure you that we do our utmost to keep them quiet. But please, *Ich bitte ihnen*, won't you come in and have some refreshments? Perhaps a cup of tea and a slice of my mother-in-law's delicious *Schwartzwald Kuchen?*" At the same time, Samuel Gutman turns and calls to the unseen culprits whose raised childish and high-spirited voices can clearly be heard in another room, accompanied by a lot of clumping and thumping. "*Kinder, Kinder*, I beg of you, please. You are making much too much noise." Either the children have not heard their father, or simply choose to ignore him. Samuel Gutman spreads his arms in a helpless gesture and shrugs his shoulders sheepishly, apologizing all over again to the man standing on his doorstep.

Herr Mayer invariably refuses Herr Gutman's invitation. He has not set foot in the Gutmans' apartment since they moved in several months ago. With a slight bow, and a military clicking of heels, he departs. Samuel Gutman politely accompanies Herr Mayer half way down the corridor until he sees him safely, from a distance, into the Mayers' apartment, all the while trying to engage the man in conversation. But to no avail. Herr Mayer doesn't even respond to Samuel's hesitant observations about the weather, but walks stiffly, staring straight ahead until he reaches his door. There, he turns the handle and enters, without so much as a backward glance at his neighbor; no further parting nod or acknowledgment. At least, Samuel consoles himself wryly, the man didn't slam the door in my face.

⇒⇐

Unlike the Mayers, whose German origins date back to the 16th century, Samuel Gutman and his sister Judith are the first Gutmans to be born in Germany, while his wife, Hannah, came to the country as an infant when her family immigrated from Poland. The Gutmans are considered, by their new German Jewish *Landsmannin*, to be *Ost-Juden*, a pejorative term for east European Jews, a species that is looked down upon with disdain and condescension by *Yekkes* like Herr Mayer.

Samuel Gutman's late father, Izaak Gutman, came from Odessa in the Ukraine, where he and *his* father, Samuel's grandfather, became successful grain merchants who hobnobbed and traded with the illustrious Efrussis, and, it is rumored, with the most important leaders of governments and crowned heads of Europe. After the death of his parents, Izaak Gutman left Odessa in the 1880's, in large part because of the pogroms directed against the Jewish population; pogroms that were occurring with more and more frequency and with increasing savagery. Izaak and his new bride Rivka, instead of settling in Paris as the Efrussis did, or in any of the other European capitals they might have chosen, moved to Frankfurt *am* Main, where there was known to be a thriving and growing Orthodox Jewish community.

Izaak Gutman's friends and co-religionists were aghast when he confided his plans.

"You have a thriving business here in Odessa," said his close friend Zalman Schwartz, "not to mention a beautiful home. How can you give it all up and start over again? And with those *Yekkes* in Frankfurt yet, who are more German than the Germans and walk with their noses in the air."

But Izaak could not be persuaded to stay. "Zalman, my *chaver*," he said, "I know you mean well, but you don't understand. If the Almighty should bless Rivka and me with children, I don't want to bring them up here in Odessa where the next pogrom is lurking around the corner, and where they will not be allowed in the universities, courtesy of our dear Tsar, may his name be extinguished. Yes, I know what you're going to say," he held up his hand to prevent Zalman from interrupting, "everything is quiet and looks to remain so for the foreseeable future, and perhaps by the time we have children there may be a new Tsar and a change of policy. But there are no guarantees, and I don't want to take a chance. Besides," he added, "you know how much I'm taken with the Hirsh philosophy: *Torah im Derech Eretz*. We've discussed it many times, and you've always agreed with me and said you feel the same way. I want our children to have all the advantages of the German *Kultur* combined with a sound Jewish education. I want them to learn German, which will surely be of more use to them than Yiddish and Russian. I want them to be able to converse in French and English, and what would be so terrible if they had a smattering of the classics, of Latin and Greek?" He put his hand on his friend's shoulder for emphasis. "Surely you understand, Zalman? I just want my children to have better opportunities than we have here. And those opportunities are nowhere more available to Jews than in Germany. Opportunities that are practically unheard of here in Odessa. You know that as well as I do."

The two men sat for several minutes in silence, the kind of silence that only two men who have been friends since childhood can enjoy, as Zalman absorbed Izaak's words. They continued to debate back and forth, each presenting his case, one for going, one for staying, with Zalman's arguments becoming weaker by the minute and less convincing, even to himself.

"Don't think," said Izaak, "that this is an easy decision for me. As you know, my father of blessed memory built a successful business and, let's face it, despite all the anti-Semitism and pogroms, despite the taxes, and all the bribes we have to pay, we have prospered. And don't think I haven't taken into account that because Odessa is a port city, it has been much easier for us to import and export than if we were somewhere inland. Which is why I've decided to give up the grain business."

"Give up the grain business?" Zalman Schwartz echoed, horrified. He stared at his friend in disbelief and began to stutter. "B-but your family has been in the grain business for generations. That is all you know. All you have ever known, since you were this high." He measured with his palm the height of a small boy.

Izaak sighed. "Yes, that's very true." He laughed self-deprecatingly. "Who knows what I'll end up doing? Perhaps I'll even open a retail shop. At any rate, I have enough put by for a rainy day so that whatever I decide to do in the way of business, we should be fine. Whatever happens," he added in a more serious vein, "I feel in my bones it's time for us to move on."

Finally, when Zalman saw that Izaak's mind was made up and that he could not dissuade his friend, he put his arm around Izaak's shoulders. "I will miss you, my *chaver*," he said simply.

The philosophy of Jewish neo-Orthodoxy first expounded by Rabbi Samson Rafael Hirsch in the mid 1800's that Izaak found so appealing, was a simple yet revolutionary departure from prevailing Orthodox thinking. Hirsch declared that religious Jews were not only *allowed* to study secular subjects alongside their immersion in the holy books, but that, indeed, they were *obligated* to do so, that Jews had a responsibility to participate in their surrounding *Kultur*, to be able to answer the arguments of the *maskilim*, those 'enlightened' Jews who had wandered away from the teachings of their ancestors.

Before emigrating, Izaak Gutman hedged his bets, so to speak, by purchasing parcels of real estate in Europe. He also made what was considered by some of his friends a foolish investment. In fact, when his *chevra*, the men of his daily prayer *minyan* heard about it, they were not only shocked, but many, even his friend Zalman, thought he was losing his touch, even losing his mind. One of his business associates actually laughed in his face and mocked him outright. "*Bist du meshugge?*" he asked, in the Yiddish they spoke among themselves. Have you gone crazy?

For among Izaak Gutman's purchases, was a strip of desolate, uninhabited land in Palestine, on the outskirts of Jerusalem.

><

In Frankfurt, Izaak Gutman did indeed enter the retail business by opening a woman's clothing shop on *Der Zeil*, one of Frankfurt's busiest shopping streets. Samuel believes that his father may have named the shop *Chez Gutman* as a whimsical nod to the Paris he had passed up. And now, after Izaak's untimely death, Samuel finds himself the director of a flourishing retail emporium. For a while, until her marriage, Samuel's sister Judith was involved in the running of the business. Now, Judith and her husband, Bruno Ehrlich, an antiques dealer, live in Berlin. Samuel's widowed mother Rivka Gutman spends part of the year with her daughter's family in Berlin. Often, the Ehrlichs, their two children and Oma Gutman travel to Frankfurt to celebrate the Passover and Tabernacles festivals with Samuel and Hannah and their family. At other times the Gutmans and the Ehrlichs gather in Berlin, but less often since the arrival of the Gutman twins.

><

"*Schatzie*," Samuel calls out when he re-enters the apartment, at the same time loosening the cravat around his neck which he hastily slipped on when he realized Herr Mayer was at the door. "*Wo bist du?* Where are you? Herr Mayer has left."

Samuel calls Hannah and each of their children by the same pet name, or a variation thereof. *Schatzie, Schatzilein, mein kleiner Schatz.* My little treasure. It takes a really naughty misdeed by one of the children to prompt their father to address him or her by name. And when he does, which is very rarely, the miscreant knows he means business. Sometimes, to be sure, when Samuel is 'Schatzing' it is difficult to know whom he is addressing. This can and does lead to confusion, if not outright obfuscation on the part of the older boys who are wily enough to take advantage of their father's tender habit.

"But Papa, you didn't tell me to finish my homework," fourteen-year-old Izaak might answer with wide-eyed innocence to a mild rebuke from his father. "I thought you were talking to Josh."

Izaak was, of course, named for Samuel's father, while ten-year-old Joshua bears the name of Hannah's late father.

Hannah emerges from the kitchen where she and her mother took refuge as soon as they heard Herr Mayer's voice at the door. The two women, assisted by the housekeeper, Liesl, have been busy with supper preparations and getting the twins ready for bed, the latter task being a nightly challenge and the noise producer that so upsets Herr Mayer. The twins, Simon and Benny, are the two most active and rambunctious little boys imaginable, and each evening it is a battle to get them in and out of the bath, into their pajamas, and into bed. They chase each other from room to room, from one end of the apartment to the other, screaming and shouting and laughing at the top of their lungs like little banshees. It's impossible for their parents to be angry at them, or even to be very firm; they are such bewitching little angels with their blonde locks, big blue eyes and rosy cheeks. The twins are identical but for a small mole on the neck of little Simon. In looks, they favor their mother who covers her blonde hair during the day with a variety of scarves fastened fetchingly at the nape of her neck. Benny is somewhat quieter and gentler than Simon, but needs only to be enticed into mischief by his brother, the natural leader, until, as Samuel likes to say, they begin to *reissen Stücke*. In other words, until all hell breaks loose.

"I don't like to say it," Hannah tells her husband, "but that Herr Mayer makes me feel rather uncomfortable."

"I think that's the unkindest thing I've ever heard you say about anyone," Samuel says, smiling at his wife, and at the same time tucking back a wisp of blonde hair that has escaped from her head scarf.

"I wonder if he realizes that his wife sometimes comes in to visit and *kaffeklatsch* with me and Oma."

"I doubt it. He would probably think it beneath her. He might even forbid it if he knew."

"Actually, I think she's just lonely. I feel sorry for her and have come to like her. The other day I suggested that we stop addressing each other so formally, that we stop *Frau*-ing and *Sie*-ing each other. She was so touched, I thought she was going to cry. Her name is Marga, by the way."

"I hope you're not making a mistake, *mein Schatz*," says Samuel, putting his arm around his wife's waist and leading her toward the kitchen. "You know how that *echt Yekke* crowd feel about us. By the way, didn't Naomi mention the other day that she's in the same class as the Mayers' daughter? Or am I mistaken?"

"Yes, with Henrietta. The girls have become quite close, I think. Which is actually what I wanted to talk to you about. I got the feeling from something Marga said that she's a bit worried about Henrietta, that she feels the girl has become secretive. If that's the case, I'm concerned that she might not be the right influence for Naomi."

"Mmm, you may be right. But I think we can trust Naomi not to be so easily influenced and, besides, *Schatzie*, if the Mayer girl is having problems it may be good for her to have a friend like Naomi to confide in. I can imagine," Samuel adds, "that it isn't easy for any girl to have such a strict Teutonic father. But she's probably just going through the usual rebellious teenage phase we all went through at that age, when we were convinced our parents were *Idioten*, total imbeciles."

"I don't think I ever went through a rebellious phase," says Hannah dreamily remembering. "In fact, when I look back on it, I think perhaps I was too compliant."

"You are the exception that proves the rule, *Schatzilein*," he teases her. "But you are being too hard on yourself, as usual. Remember, you were very young when your father died and it was only natural that you would try not to make life more difficult for your mother. But come, let's go join the children for supper." He sniffs the air, stretching his neck this way and that with deliberately exaggerated movements. "Is that Oma Fleissig's *Kalbfleisch Schnitzel* that is making my mouth water? I've suddenly developed a ravenous appetite."

"Wait a minute, Samuel," says Hannah, holding her husband's arm to detain him as he is about to open the door to the kitchen. "I haven't told you everything." Husband and wife, arms linked, move back into the formal dining room. The room is furnished in a very un-Germanic style: none of the heavy pieces usually found in the homes of the *Yekkes* who, ever since the first Jew set foot in Germany, have been scrabbling to emulate their non-Jewish neighbors. Hannah, whose taste dictates the furnishing of the Gutman home, would have none of that bulky, gloomy look that includes thick draperies so beloved by the Mayers and their whole *echt-Deutsch* co-religionists. "I find that so depressing," she told Samuel. The result is a room that has an airy, cheerful, eclectic look, part French, - Louis XVI dining chairs, and part English, - a Queen Anne dining table, and the more modern Edwardian look in the sleek sideboard, with a touch of art deco in the lamps and other accessories. The only concession to the fashion of the day is in the china services. The more formal Sabbath 'meat' set consists of an elegant gold-rimmed Rosenthal pattern. For less formal 'dairy' meals, a more cheerful design, also Rosenthal, white china covered with delicate little blue forget-me-nots.

Samuel looks at his wife questioningly. "Yesterday," Hannah says, "when Frau Mayer, I mean Marga, was visiting, I felt something was bothering her, apart from her daughter, that is. Of course, I didn't want to pry, but just as she was leaving and I was about to close the door, she turned suddenly and said, 'Hannah, I'm at my wits' end. I have nowhere else to turn. It embarrasses me, but I must ask you to do me *ein Gefallen*.' I asked her to come back inside so we could discuss the 'favor' she wanted. She was clearly reluctant until I told her that Oma was in her room, resting. We sat in the kitchen for several minutes without her saying a word. She seemed quite agitated, and wouldn't look at me, just kept staring at the floor and wringing her hands. I realized she was having difficulty voicing whatever it was she wanted to ask. So I took her hand and said, 'Marga, whatever it is, you know you can ask and I will do my best to help you.' Finally, she raised her eyes and haltingly explained the 'favor' she wanted."

Samuel is all ears by now. He can't believe that anyone in the Mayer family would come to anyone in the Gutman family for a favor. "What on earth...?" he begins.

Hannah interrupts. "Oh Samuel, you will feel as sorry for her as I do when you hear what she asked of me, of us, actually. And she was so ashamed and embarrassed. She just didn't know where to look while she was talking. Apparently the son, Fritz, is frightened to walk to and from school on his own, especially since the recent 'incidents'. Apart from the constant threat from the Hitler *Jugend*, some of his own classmates bully him and call him names because he has bad acne and is such a gentle, serious boy. The other day, some of the boys roughed him up on his way home from school, and he came home in a terrible state. But Herr Mayer refuses to provide any protection for him. Even when he might be able to spare the chauffeur to drive the boy to school, he won't allow it. Marga says her husband feels Fritz is a *Waschlappen*, that he has to stop being such a sissy and learn to defend himself like a man."

Samuel groans in disbelief. They have been sitting at the dining room table. Now he jumps up in anger and begins pacing the room. "That poor boy," he says, punching the palm of one hand with the fist of the other. "I don't blame him for being frightened. I feel like taking that Herr Mayer and giving him a good shaking." Then he turns, and sits down again next to his wife. "But, *Schatzie*, what has that to do with us, what can we do...?"

"Well," says Hannah, "Somehow Marga heard that we now have a car service to take Izaak and Josh to and from school. She asked me if her son could join them. As you know, they attend the same school, although Fritz is older and is in a higher form."

"But *natürlich*," replies Samuel immediately. "Poor boy," he says again. "And poor Frau Mayer. I assume you told her that of course he is more than welcome to ride with our boys."

"Yes, of course I did. She said she wants to pay her share for the service, but I got the impression, even though she didn't actually come right out and say so, that she doesn't want her husband to know about the arrangement and so paying might be a problem for her."

"Don't worry, *Schatzie*," he says grimly. "He certainly won't hear it from me. And as to payment, please assure her that there is no need to concern herself on that score."

In complete agreement with each other, husband and wife, arm in arm, make their way to the kitchen, the large, cozy room in which the Gutman family gather for all *Wochentag* meals - that is, every day except on the Sabbath and Festivals and other special occasions - when two little whirlwinds come barreling through the door toward them, partially clad for bed, but showing no inclination to sleep. To the contrary, they are in high spirits. Each one is an airplane: arms outstretched, diving, waving, dipping their little wings this way and that, and making appropriate zooming sounds to accompany the airplanes' maneuvers. A bedraggled grandmother hobbles after them, holding her cane in one hand and those parts of their sleepwear that she has not managed to get them into in her other hand.

"Poor Oma," says Hannah. "I know it's a thankless task, especially with your bad hip. You should let Liesl see to them. Here, let me have the pajamas. Perhaps I'll be more successful." At the same time Samuel blocks the little boys in their tracks and scoops them up, one in each arm. The twins squeal with delight and loop their arms around their father's neck, grinding their faces into his flesh.

Frau Fleissig, a woman in her early seventies, looks totally beaten and exhausted. "*Dank Gott*," she says, relinquishing the pajamas to her daughter with a sigh of relief. "They are like little animals, completely *ausgelassen*. Quite impossible to control."

The two little animals, in answer to the tickles they are receiving from their father, squirm out of his grasp and resume chasing each other up and down the corridor and in and out of all the rooms of the apartment, expecting the adults to run after them until they are caught.

"*Achtung, achtung!*" screams Simon, "*achtung Juthen, achtung Juthen, achtung Juthen.*" and Benny echoes him. "*Achtung, achtung Juthen, achtung Juthen!* The boys' pronunciation of the word *Juden* comes out with a sweet lisping sound, so that it takes Samuel a split second to decode what they are screaming at the top of their lungs. He has been playing along, following them, pretending to be unable to catch them. Now he stops in his tracks. His eyes meet Hannah's over the children's heads. "*Um Gottes Willen.* Where on earth...?" But they both know where the children heard that phrase. And it is as if an icy cloud has passed over their heads and settled in the apartment.

"Come, *meine Schätze*, no more games now," says Samuel. "If you behave yourselves and go quietly into your beds I'll come in and read you a story."

Chapter 3

⇒•⇐

Gustav Mayer's family has been in the metals and armaments business seemingly forever. He has documents showing that a Gustaf Mayer in the 16th century, in Bavaria, had dealings with Emperor Maximilian I, an unusually
benevolent monarch to the Jews in an era when accusations of ritual murder
were pervasive, and when Jews were being expelled or banished from German
communities at the drop of a hat. Or, more often than not, as the easiest way to
avoid paying debts owed them by the Christian ruling powers. The 16th century
Gustaf was a swordsmith in Maximilian's army, a specialist in forging the *Zwei-
händer*, the two-handed sword that was the most popular weapon of its day.
There is a vacuum in the information Herr Mayer has been able to glean, leading
him to believe that Gustaf and his family may have been expelled from Bavaria
by a subsequent and less benign monarch. Or, perhaps, that the upheaval caused
in Germany by Martin Luther and the Reformation resulted in Gustaf's move -
whether voluntarily or involuntarily is unclear - to another state.

The next clue Gustav Mayer has been able to unearth about his ancestry
does not emerge until late in the 17th century, in the state of Hesse, when the
firm Mayer Metallgesellschaft G.m.b.H., registered to a Heinz Mayer, first
appears in the city of Frankfurt's official business records.

Since that time, from 1699 to be exact, there is a straight line of Mayers
who have owned and operated EmEm, as it is popularly known, and who have

managed to navigate and survive waves of anti-Semitism, internecine strife, and wider wars, while still maintaining their Jewish identity among the communities in which they lived. In some cases, this perversely resulted in the level of religious observance practiced today by Gustav Mayer and his family. However, such Orthodoxy seems to have by-passed Gustav Mayer's younger brother Heinz, the lawyer, who lives with his wife Bertha in the upscale and more secular *westlich* part of town and whose Jewish allegiance is tied to the relatively new Reform movement that sprang up in Germany in the late 1880's and has been rapidly gaining in popularity.

Gustav Mayer's great-grandfather was an intimate friend of Otto von Bismarck when the Count was Frederick William IV's emissary in the 1850's to the federal Diet in Frankfurt. At that time, according to the business records, EmEm was awarded a huge and exclusive armaments contract to supply the military stationed not only in the state of Hesse but also in other provinces across the country. It was those transactions that put the firm Mayer Metallgesellschaft G.m.b.H. on the same map as the Krupp family's industrial empire and the Mauser brothers' munitions conglomerate. And EmEm has been manufacturing and supplying all kinds of materiel and armaments to the German ruling powers ever since.

One of Gustav Mayer's most prized possessions is a framed medal centered prominently on the wall behind his office desk, the Iron Cross First Class awarded to his late father, Julius Mayer, for 'brave and *patriotisch* service' to the Weimar Republic in the Prussian war. The black medal with its silver border is embedded in a background of royal blue velvet. Depending on the angle of light streaming through the office window and hitting the frame just so, it sometimes seems to Herr Mayer that his father's medal illuminates the whole office. Surrounding the medal, and covering the rest of the wall are portraits of his early ancestors, some painted before the era of photography, when EmEm was still manufacturing swords, followed by photographs of more recent forebears. There are oil portraits of an assortment of Gustafs, Heinzes, Fritzes and Juliuses; one of the oil portraits is of a Mayer ancestor posed holding one of the famous two-handed swords manufactured by EmEm in its early days.

But Gustav Mayer's favorite image is not a painting but a black and white photograph showing Kaiser Wilhelm II in the act of pinning the Iron Cross to *Ober-leutnant* Julius Mayer's uniform. The photograph holds a magnetic pull for Gustav Mayer; he would not be able to explain its fascination, but hardly a day goes by that he doesn't stop to gaze at it, as if paying obeisance. What a moment that must have been! His father, not yet married, young and handsome, and still in possession of all his thick, dark hair, precisely parted off-center as if with a ruler, slicked back and glistening in the sun. He stands stiff and unsmiling, his military bearing ramrod straight, his chest slightly puffed out with pride, his eyes wide and unblinking, focused on an invisible distance, his left hand resting lightly on the pommel of his sword. The Kaiser bends over in front of him, his *Schnur-rbart* almost grazing the left side of Julius' uniformed chest where the medal will reside. If he gazes at the image long enough, Herr Mayer can almost imagine that the uniformed man in the photograph is not his father at all, but Gustav himself receiving the medal from the Kaiser, and sometimes that sensation is so overpowering that he has to scratch the spot on his chest where he feels the bristly hairs of the Kaiser's outsize mustache brushing against him.

Before his untimely death from a massive heart attack, Julius Mayer taught his son Gustav EmEm's business. He taught the young Gustav how to handle suppliers and customers with tact and patience, how to negotiate the best price, when to give ground and when to stand firm, and, most important of all, - and this his father drilled into him over and over again -, he was to be scrupulously honest in all his dealings and was never to compromise on the quality of EmEm's products.

Gustav's brother Heinz showed no proclivity for the family business. Though disappointing to Julius, it allowed the younger brother to find his way into the law.

Often, when he has a difficult business decision to make, Herr Mayer finds himself communing with his father's photograph. And, sometimes, just by staring at his father's image and putting the problem into words, he is inspired to reach a decision, a decision that he feels his father himself would have made. Yesterday, he confided to the photograph that he is troubled by the forthcoming meeting in Berlin. "I was ordered, *Vater, ordered*. I have no choice. What can be the meaning of it? Do you have any ideas?" But this time there were no stirrings of inspiration, no messages from his father, no clue as to why he has been summoned so peremptorily to Berlin.

⇒⇐

Herr Mayer has no difficulty waking Fritz up. The boy is his mother's favorite, and is strongly attached to her. Too attached, in Herr Mayer's opinion. Fritz wakes up the moment Herr Mayer flicks the light on in his son's room and announces without preamble, "Your mother is ill. I have telephoned for Doktor Graff. Get up and get dressed."

Fritz is almost as tall as his father, and still growing. He has a face that might be called handsome were it not covered with the pimples common to boys his age and which make him self-conscious about his appearance. So self-conscious has he become that he often makes excuses for not going to school. Usually it's his stomach, although sometimes he complains of headaches. Doktor Graff has examined him more than once and found nothing physically wrong with him. The doctor has given his considered opinion that the boy likes to, as he puts it, *sich krank stellen*, that he is malingering. Frau Mayer, for once shedding her usual diffidence, came to her son's defense and protested the doctor's diagnosis. "How can Doktor Graff say that," she asked her husband, "when nothing could be further from the truth? You know as well as I do that Fritz is conscientious and is getting good marks in school. He is merely sensitive, that's all." She went on to suggest that Herr Mayer engage private tutors for the boy to shield him from the daily torment at the hands of his classmates. "It will only be temporary," she hastened to add. "Eventually his face will clear up, and he can go back to school." But Herr Mayer would not hear of it. He emphatically resisted what he calls his wife's tendency to *verzartein* the boy. "*Quatsch*, Frau Mayer," he said. "What nonsense. Stop mollycoddling him. It's high time you stopped treating him like a baby or he will never become a man." And that was the last word ever heard on the subject of tutors.

Fritz regularly begs his mother to find a salve or lotion, anything to take away those ugly sores for which Herr Doktor Graff has found no remedy; she, in turn, reprimands him for squeezing the pimples until they bleed. "You are only making them worse, *mein liebes Kind*," she tells him, gently. Of course, he doesn't listen, and the pimples continue to erupt and proliferate, sometimes turning into boils or crusting up into scabs, sometimes becoming oozing, screaming sores, that only annoy and frustrate him more. Herr Mayer, over-hearing Fritz complain, tells his son to stop whining. "If you ignore them and leave them alone, they will go away on their own. They are hardly the *schwarze Pest*, the Black Plague." And Herr Mayer gives his usual little snort of annoy-ance, a sound that resembles a laugh, but isn't. He has no patience for these self-indulgent complaints. And no patience for Frau Mayer who, he feels, en-courages them.

"What's wrong with Mutti?," asks Fritz, sitting up in bed, a worried frown on his pimpled face. "She seemed alright last night at *Abendessen*."

But Herr Mayer has already left his son's room and is out of earshot. He is down the hallway at Henrietta's door, his hand raised, about to knock. He hesitates. He can't help remembering the last time he entered his daughter's room, some months before, and how unwelcome he was...

He remembers that, nearing her room, he was greeted by the quiet strains of music coming from her phonograph - the birthday present he gave her - was it four, five years ago? She has already pronounced it too cumbersome and outmoded, that she would like one of those new Decca machines that have just come on the market. As he came closer he recognized the mellow string section from Schubert's Unfinished. He remembers thinking, *grossartig*, excel-lent. Henrietta is finally knuckling down, doing her homework, and he said a silent *danken Gott* that, though his daughter seems uninterested in any other of her school subjects, at least she loves music, one pastime of which he can wholeheartedly approve. Given his own love of the music of Wagner and Bach and Mozart, he felt that here was an interest they could share, father and daughter; however, when he invited her into his study to listen to a Fritz Kreizler concert on the wireless, or when he asked her to accompany him to the Opernhaus where they were presenting *Lohengrin*, she churlishly declined both invitations, not even bothering to invent an excuse.

He remembers thinking she might not be able to hear his knock above the music, and so he turned the door knob, without knocking, and walked into her room. The memory of the look on Henrietta's face as she slowly raised her head from whatever she was writing at her desk, is impossible to forget. It was a look of unmistakable disdain. He can no longer recall the purpose of his visit to her room, but he is convinced that the look on his daughter's face is chiseled in his memory forever. He also remembers how casually, but deliberately, she turned over the sheet of paper on which she had been writing as if to make quite sure that her father understood that he had disturbed her in the midst of a private activity, that his was an unwelcome intrusion. Certainly, she was not engaged in homework.

Now he knocks on Henrietta's door, and waits. He knocks again. Once, twice, then again, louder. There is no answer; no sign that she is even in the room. He tries the *Knopf.* The door is locked. How often has he warned Frau Mayer to confiscate the keys to the children's bedrooms, that it is dangerous for them to lock themselves in. What would happen if, *Gott behüte*, there was a fire? Apart from that, what great secrets can either of the children possibly have that prompt locked doors?

It seems to him that his daughter has become not only a stranger, but a stranger who harbors a deep and inexplicable animosity toward him. He has trouble recalling that she was once an enchanting, precocious child, though admittedly tending to rebel against his rules. He remembers sometimes dandling her on his knee; he thinks he once or twice may even have read some Grimm stories to her at bedtime. On the other hand, his strict but necessary rules about bed times, punctual arrival at synagogue on the Sabbath, and the importance of good marks at school, have in recent years been the source of increasing friction. Because her love of music manifested itself at a very young age, Herr Mayer was convinced Henrietta would do well on the piano. But, after taking lessons for a few weeks, during which time she refused to practice, Henrietta stamped her foot and announced that she would never again take another piano lesson.

Herr Mayer rarely raises his voice, but now he does. "Henrietta, open this door *sofort*. Immediately."

He hears a mumbling, then a movement, and a barely awake Henrietta opens the door a crack, peering out with eyes that are barely open. "What is all the *Getue* about so early in the morning? I was fast asleep." Her voice is hoarse from sleep and indignation. Only with great effort does he manage to control himself. Quietly he says, "This is no time to complain, Henrietta. Your mother is ill and I have to leave for Berlin within the hour. Get dressed. I have sent for Doktor Graff." And he strides away, not waiting or wanting to see or hear his daughter's reaction. Or, for that matter, if she will obey him.

Chapter 4

⇒⇐

It is barely a five-minute walk from the Borneplatz *shul* to the apartment building. Samuel has participated, as he does regularly, in the early morning *Shacharit* service. This is the same prayer service attended by Herr Mayer, when he is in town, that is. It is well-known that Herr Mayer travels extensively on business and so his absence today is not noteworthy. On those days when Herr Mayer does attend, he slips away the minute the service is over. Samuel suspects that this may have something to do with Herr Mayer not wishing to walk back to the apartment building in Samuel's company. Occasionally, he has observed Herr Mayer just a few paces ahead of him or glimpsed him from a distance, entering the building. On some days, Herr Mayer's Daimler is waiting for him outside the synagogue, his chauffeur at the wheel, its motor purring, ready to whisk him away to an unknown destination the moment he appears.

The air is cold and penetrating on this overcast February morning. The trees lining the streets are bare of leaves, except for the occasional evergreen, the *Tannenbaüme* that interrupt the bleakness here and there; the sun is nowhere to be seen. Samuel walks along the Mainkai, the stretch that runs parallel with the river. Today the water is black and forbidding, its surface filled with floating patches of dark and dirty ice floes. A wind has whipped up, stirring white-crested waves in the river, and sending blocks of ice crashing noisily against each other and against the embankment, creating muffled explosions that send puffs of smoke up into the frigid air. With his right gloved hand, he tightens the *Schal* around his neck and ears, and with his left hand holds tightly onto his fedora. He is thankful to be almost home where a hearty breakfast always awaits him: usually *Pfannkuchen*, thin little crepes that he relishes, stuffed with apples or blueberries, accompanied by his mother-in-law's homemade warm *Brötchen* slathered in butter and marmalade. All washed down with a cup of piping hot *Kaffee* that only Hannah knows how to prepare, some of which she sends along with him in a *Thermosflasche* to fortify him during the morning at *Chez Gutman*, until one o'clock, when he comes home for *Mittagessen*.

As soon as he turns the corner into his street he is shocked to see and hear the ambulance pulling away from the curb in front of the apartment building, its siren beginning a mournful wail. He notices some of the neighbors standing outside the building: the widower Herr Sulzbacher, whose wife died shortly after Samuel and Hannah moved into the building and whom they have be-friended; the childless Frau Prager who lives on the second floor with her re-cently retired husband. He detects other neighbors watching more discreetly from behind partially drawn curtains. He hastens his step, suddenly filled with foreboding, praying silently that the ambulance not be for his mother-in-law, Frau Fleissig, or, *Gott behüte*, one of the children. But then he recognizes the unmistakable black Opel, the model driven by almost all the physicians in the area, and at the same time recognizes the man behind the wheel. *Gott sei dank*, he says to himself, relieved that Herr Doktor Graff could not possibly have been summoned for any member of his family. The Gutmans' medical needs are attended by a different physician, Doctor Moishe (Moses to the *Yekkes*) Schwartz, the son of Zalman, who was the late Izaak Gutman's best friend in Odessa. But then Samuel's anxiety rises again as he recognizes the Mayer chil-dren, whose names escape him, entering the open rear door of the Opel. His relief once again turns to concern.

Doktor Graff is an old-time board member of the Borneplatz *shul* who, like Gustav Mayer, comes from old German Jewish stock. He looks to be in his early sixties, close to retirement, a man who carries himself in the very correct and erect fashion of most of the *echt Deutsch* Jewish men whose families have lived in Germany for centuries. The doctor, like Herr Mayer, is always impeccably groomed and outfitted in a conservative suit and black homburg. Samuel recently experienced an unpleasant *Konfrontation* with the doctor. It happened at the conclusion of the Friday night service. One of the other old-timers had noticed Samuel swaying to and fro, with his eyes closed during the *Amidah* prayer, a practice called *schockling* in Yiddish. East-European Jews claim that *schockling* not only helps them focus their devotion and attention when praying, but keeps their thoughts from the profane. Doktor Graff, barely able to contain his outrage, confronted Samuel with gnashed teeth and informed him that this appalling "*shtetl* custom would not be tolerated in the Borneplatz *Synagoge*." *Eklig*, he had called it. Repulsive.

When Samuel came home and related the incident to Hannah she urged him, not for the first time, to "resign from that *Yekkische* club. You are not comfortable there, and you never will be. Why not go to a smaller *shul* or *stiebel* where you'll be welcomed with open arms." This is the only bone of contention between them, and he resists, as he has done many times in the past. "The Borneplatz *shul* is one of the reasons my father, of blessed memory, gave up everything in Odessa to move here. I won't let myself be intimidated by that crowd. Besides, there is now a considerable *Ost-Juden* presence in the *shul*, and it's growing all the time."

Samuel forces himself to approach the Opel. "*Guten Morgen*, Herr Doktor, may I inquire what is wrong? Can I be of any help?"

Stiffly, and with ill-concealed distaste, the doctor acknowledges Samuel Gutman's greeting by opening the driver's side window a crack, and, without looking directly at him, answers brusquely, "I have no time to talk, Herr Gutman. I must be on my way to the hospital."

"But who is it, then, who is ill? Is it Herr Mayer?" presses Samuel, even as Doktor Graff rolls up the window again and begins to maneuver the Opel away from the curb.

Samuel steps away from the car. He thinks the doctor may have mouthed something and made a negative motion with his hand. He wishes he might have spoken to the two children in the rear seat before they were driven off. It seems to him that they were sitting as far apart from each other as possible, the girl behind Herr Doktor Graff, the bottom half of her face hidden under a red muffler, her shoulders slumped, her head turned toward the window; her brother behind the passenger seat, wearing his peaked school cap, his head down and his right hand scrabbling furiously at his face. The small crowd has dispersed. There is nobody outside who might have answered his questions. Those poor children, he thinks, as he bounds up the three flights to his apartment.

He has hardly managed to turn the key in the lock when the door is flung open by his daughter Naomi, her face, - a face so precious to him and a reflection of his own features, a face that is almost always smooth and sunny -, now contorted and tearstained. "Oh Papa, did you hear what happened. It's *furchtbar*. Just awful." And Naomi throws herself into her father's arms and bursts into tears.

Chapter 5

The unlikely friendship that has blossomed in recent months between Naomi Gutman and Henrietta Mayer has come about through an accident of geography. For no two seventeen-year old girls could be more dissimilar. The Gutmans have not long been living in the apartment building, where the Mayers have lived for many years. The birth of the twins four years ago made their prior quarters too cramped, forcing them to find a more spacious dwelling. Both families, the Mayers and the Gutmans, can well afford the more upscale *westen* district, but remain in the *Ostern* because of the Hirsch *shul* located nearby on Borneplatz. The previous occupants of the Gutman apartment were Herr Mayer's younger brother, the lawyer Heinz and his beautiful wife, Bertha.

Rumor has it that from the first day that Heinz and Bertha Mayer, then newlyweds, took up residence next door to Gustav and Marga Mayer, Bertha did not stop complaining. First it was about her sister-in-law Marga. Bertha has tried, oh how she has tried, but the woman is *unmöglich*, impossible to befriend. After that, the complaints became more bitter, more frequent, and directed at the encroaching Orthodox Jewish population. The *Nachbarschaft* has become too filled with those distasteful *Ost-Juden* and their repulsive habits; you can spot them a mile away, just by the way they talk with their hands. They have ruined the whole neighborhood. Bertha clamored and nagged until finally Heinz, who secretly agreed with her, gave in. Now they live *am westen*, or, as

Samuel Gutman might say mischievously and with a deliberate Yiddish intonation, the *hoche Fenster* district, the rich 'high window' district, closer to the Reform *Neue Synagoge*, where they have been members for many years.

In this way does the geographical accident come about, planting Naomi Gutman right next door to Henrietta Mayer, their two apartments separated merely by the span of a man-made wall. At first, the girls barely acknowledge each other's existence, merely nodding shyly when bumping into each other in the hallway or on the stairs. Each curious about the other, they inspect each other surreptitiously from beneath hooded eyes. Perhaps Henrietta notices that Naomi is dressed in the latest woolen skirts and twinsets; not surprising since her father is the owner of *Chez Gutman*. She will have observed also that Naomi walks with a slight limp, and will naturally wonder about it. Henrietta doesn't shop in department stores; Herr Mayer won't permit it, and certainly looks down on a commercial establishment like *Chez Gutman*. He insists that his wife and daughter patronize the exclusive boutiques of the Westside. It is more than likely that Naomi, for her part, notices that Henrietta is tall, with a slim, shapely figure, that everything she wears looks casually elegant and simply smashing, and that she has the most beautiful thick, long curly blonde hair Naomi has ever seen.

Since last August, when they found themselves both attending the Lyzeum, the Jewish *Gymnasium*, the girls have been walking to and from school together. This has happened naturally, without any planning; one morning, they just fell in step with each other and have been walking together ever since. In bad weather, Herr Mayer has Hans drive Henrietta in the Daimler. When Henrietta sees Naomi trudging along with her uneven gait through the rain or snow, she bids Hans stop the car and beckons Naomi to hop in. Usually they ride in almost complete silence; the girls find little in common to talk about. They are rarely in the same class, except for such subjects as music and gym.

Naomi is a star student, a talented, conscientious girl who loves to read; she is particularly enthralled with poetry, with the works of Rilke and Goethe, and always hands in her homework on time. She has also been taking piano lessons for many years and is conscientious about practicing. Henrietta, on the other hand, is just the opposite: she hates school, detests her teachers, and is always delinquent with homework assignments. The only subjects for which she can find any enthusiasm are music (she sings in the school choir), and gymnastics. She loves to ice-skate, and is serious about practicing her figure eights and lutzes. She dreams of being on the German skating team for next winter's Olympics games in Garmisch, though she doubts her father will allow it. She knows that her mother, who was in her youth a fairly good skater herself, wouldn't mind at all.

Not long after the Gutmans moved into their new apartment, Herr Mayer's complaints about the noise began.

On the morning after Herr Mayer's latest visit to the Gutmans' door, the two girls walk to school together as usual. It is a cold, gloomy day with a distinct possibility of snow in the air. Naomi's auburn, unruly hair is tucked into a red woolen hat that also covers her ears; it was knitted for her by Oma Fleissig. The hood of her beige woolen toggle coat is pulled over the hat for extra warmth. Henrietta is similarly protected from the cold by a black coat and woolen cap that hides the blonde locks that Naomi admires so much. Both girls have leather satchels attached to their backs in rucksack style, so that their gloved hands are free. Naomi's satchel is bulging with books, weighing her down and accentuating her limp; Henrietta's satchel is flat and almost empty.

"My father doesn't like small children very much," says Henrietta without preamble. "He's an idiot."

Naomi is so shocked to hear anyone speak about their father in this way, she can barely stutter a reply. "B-but he's not entirely wrong, Henrietta. The twins are really impossibly *ausgelassen*. I can never even start doing my homework until they're in bed. I can't concentrate when they're around. Still," she adds, not wishing Henrietta to get the wrong impression, "I love them to pieces. They're really sweet, despite everything. Especially when they're asleep!"

"I've decided never to have children," says Henrietta emphatically. "I think my Aunt Bertha has the right idea. She says children are just too much trouble. Don't you agree?"

"I know what you mean," replies Naomi, as always trying to be agreeable. "Especially with what's going on lately. My father says it will soon not be safe for us to walk to school by ourselves anymore."

"Oh, *Dummheit*. I'm not afraid. And I wish *my* father wouldn't insist on sending the car for me the minute he feels a few drops of *Regen*. He still thinks I'm a baby, that I'll melt."

"Well," says Naomi, "my father has hired a car to take my brothers to and from their school every day. He won't let them ride their bicycles anymore. There have been *Zwischenfalls*, you know, in that neighborhood. Jewish boys being beaten up on their way home from school."

"Rubbish!" says Henrietta, "There've always been so-called 'incidents'. I'm sure they're exaggerated. I'd love to ride to school on a bicycle, but my impossible father refuses to buy me one. He says it is not *angebracht* for Jewish girls to ride bicycles. Not appropriate, my foot!" Suddenly, she stops walking, pulls Naomi's arm, and apropos of nothing, bursts out, "Naomi, let's not go to school today. Let's *schwänzen die Schule*! Let's play truant. Don't you sometimes feel like doing something, you know, something different? Something daring?"

Naomi is horrified. "O-oh, I couldn't possibly," she stutters. "Besides, I have an important grammar test today and ..."

Henrietta interrupts. "I knew you wouldn't," she says, letting go of Naomi's arm and waving her hands in disgust as she walks rapidly ahead of Naomi. "You are such a *Musterkind*, a real goody-goody. I'm sure my father would love to have you for a daughter instead of me."

Naomi limps awkwardly as fast as she can to catch up to Henrietta. She is miserable, without knowing why. Trying to be conciliatory, she says, "So, what would you do if you weren't in school today?"

Henrietta doesn't have to think. She throws back her head joyfully, claps her gloved hands together and says, "I would be on the ice, of course. I want to skate around and around the rink and never stop. Besides, there's this dreamy *Kerl* there. He's an instructor who's been giving me lessons. You can't believe how handsome he is." Once again, she stops walking, takes Naomi's arm, making her stop, too. She says, "Naomi, can you keep a secret? I'll burst if I don't tell someone."

Naomi is so shocked by now, that she can only give a tiny nod, which is all the encouragement Henrietta needs.

"Oh Naomi. You can't imagine what it feels like when Otto, that's his name, takes my hand and skates around the rink with me. When he demonstrates how I should position myself for a jump, he sometimes puts his hand on my shoulder or leg, and then.... Oh Naomi, I get shivers through my whole body, and it's not from the cold ice, I assure you!"

"B-but Henrietta..." is all Naomi manages to get out.

"I know, I know. It's wrong I know. We are religious and Otto's not even Jewish. But I can't seem to help myself. He's so unbelievably *schön*. So beautiful! Can you say that about a man? I can't keep my eyes off him. And he tells me *I'm* beautiful. Can you believe that? Oh Naomi, I can't wait to see him again. Just thinking about him gives me goose bumps all over."

Naomi is relieved that they have reached the school. "I...I don't know what to say Henrietta," she says. "What do you want me to say? I think you're incorrigible. Totally *unverbesserlich*. Think what your parents would say if they knew."

"You mean if my father knew that the instructor he's paying to give his daughter skating lessons is ..... Oh, but what's the use. Don't say anything. There's nothing you can say to me that I haven't told myself."

Chapter 6

≫﹡≪

Berlin.

Gustav Mayer leaves the meeting, his body trembling, his mind in a state of turmoil. Usually able to control his emotions, to control situations, to control business meetings, at this moment he feels only confusion and disorientation.

Actually, he feels ill.

Once again he is blindfolded, pushed into the back of a car, and then unceremoniously dropped off a few minutes later on the same corner where they picked him up. Hans is waiting for him next to the parked Daimler. The cold air hits Herr Mayer forcefully but he welcomes it after the over-heated office where the meeting took place. Hans holds the car door open for him and he slides his weary body into the back seat. He can't wait to leave the vicinity. He wishes he had been able to take notes of the meeting; notes he would now be able to take out and peruse. But this too was *verboten*. There will be no *Protokoll* of this meeting, he was told; in fact there was no meeting, *verstehen Sie*? Do you understand? Now, in the car, he doesn't even dare remove from his pocket the one piece of paper that was given to him. *Die Liste*. He is afraid to look at it. While there is nothing to stop him from going over the meeting in his mind, he resists the temptation. He recognizes that he is too agitated to think clearly. He will wait until he is in his room at the Adlon. He will order a drink, a double *Whisky*. Then he will take a hot bath; soaking in warm water always relaxes him.

Because of the unexpected delay in leaving Frankfurt, there was no time to stop off to eat when they reached the capital. Herr Mayer has eaten nothing all day, but he has no appetite. Hans asks if he would like to be dropped off at one of the kosher restaurants Herr Mayer likes to patronize, but the mere thought of food nauseates him. He bids Hans to drive directly to the hotel.

He has not thought of Frau Mayer all afternoon, had not had an opportunity to do so. But now, the memory of this morning's events strikes him with almost physical force. Was it only a few hours ago that his wife was taken to hospital? It has been a long, long day. He must telephone Frankfurt as soon as he arrives at the hotel.

It is nearly six o'clock and already dark as they drive along the boulevard snaking past the Tiergarten. The streets are brightly lit, and though it is bitterly cold, there are many people in the park, strolling along, talking and laughing, as if without a care in the world. The park is brightly lit, and the air so clear that Herr Mayer can even detect the minute tendrils of smoke bursting from the lips of the talkers and laughers. Although he cannot hear them, he can see their mouths, even their bared teeth, as they gyrate in silent speech and laughter, and the sight stirs in him the memory of a mime performance he once saw years ago as a teenager. In another life.

The whole scene creates an air of everyday normalcy that is belied by the swastikas hanging from every window and crevice, from every lamppost and flagpole, with the ubiquitous picture of the Chancellor pasted on billboards and on building facades, in every direction Herr Mayer turns his head.

Light rain begins to fall as they turn down Unter der Linden and pass the Brandenburg Gate. Hans pulls up outside the imposing building that is the Adlon, and jumps out of the car to remove Herr Mayer's small valise from the trunk together with the black umbrella that is always kept there. The Adlon's uniformed doorman appears, carrying an unfurled umbrella, and opens the Daimler's rear door for Herr Mayer to exit. However, before Herr Mayer has a chance to extricate himself, he recognizes Schmidt, one of the Adlon's young assistant managers, running toward them through the rain, his face flushed and flustered, both hands outstretched, palms outward in a pushing motion, as if barring Herr Mayer from leaving the vehicle, and at the same time waving the doorman away from the scene.

Herr Mayer has one foot on the ground, the other still inside the car, with the stooped form of Schmidt, his usually impeccably groomed blonde hair falling in damp disarray over his forehead, hovering above the open door.

"The Adlon extends its *herzlich* and sincere apologies to Herr Mayer, but we regret we are unable to accommodate you."

Even as Herr Mayer tries to absorb this shocking message it is clear to him that young Schmidt doesn't seem the slightest bit regretful. On the contrary, there is an unmistakable smirk on his face. Or is Herr Mayer imagining things? Is he being paranoid? After the events of this afternoon, it is entirely possible.

Such a thing has never happened before. Surely there must be some mistake. "Did not my secretary telephone to reserve my usual suite for tonight?"

"*Ja, Ja.* She did. However, we have strict orders from the Chancellor's office. We regret the Adlon can no longer accommodate Jews."

Herr Mayer's mind is working in slow motion. "But I have just come from... I have just met with... Surely I would have been told..." He catches himself in time. He has met no-one, there was no meeting. His voice trails off, his mind slowly beginning to comprehend.

Schmidt's face is still half way into the rear of the Daimler, his body bent over in an awkward position but acting as a barrier to prevent Herr Mayer from exiting the car. He continues his message as if Herr Mayer has not spoken: "The Adlon has taken the liberty of reserving a suite for Herr Mayer at the Esplanade. They have assured us that they are still accommodating *Juden* and that Herr Mayer will be made most comfortable."

With that, the young man removes his face and body from the car, and Herr Mayer automatically pulls his foot back into the vehicle. For the first time he notices the young man's swastika armband, and remembers now that the Adlon is the Chancellor's favorite watering spot in Berlin. The fog lifts completely. All is now clear.

He notices Schmidt saying something to Hans, who is in the act of replacing Herr Mayer's valise and umbrella into the trunk; presumably he is giving the chauffeur directions to the Esplanade. Then Schmidt stands at attention and gives Hans the Heil Hitler salute before wheeling smartly around and heading back inside the hotel. Somewhere, in the back of his mind, in spite of the conflicting thoughts and emotions racing through it, Herr Mayer registers that Hans did not return Schmidt's salute, but kept his head inside the trunk of the car, busying himself with its contents.

Herr Mayer has no memory of the drive along the Potsdamer Platz, and has only a vague impression of an ornamental building of Belle Epoque design. He does not recall checking into the Esplanade, of signing his name in the hotel register, although he must have done so. He does not recall entering his suite. Never in all his forty-eight years does he remember being so out of control. Even as a mere child, not much older than Bar Mitzvah age, when disciplined by teachers or by his father, young Gustav nearly always managed the situation, giving such rational reasons against the proposed punishment that all his elders' arguments were completely neutralized, leaving them scratching their heads and wondering how they had been out-maneuvered by a mere boy.

He has no recollection of getting undressed, no memory of running a bath. It is only when he finds himself soaking in the hot water, that he finally begins to relax and get his bearings, to collect his thoughts; that he is finally able to reconstruct and face the events of the last few hours…

Chapter 7

Samuel Gutman puts his arm around his daughter's shoulders and guides her into the kitchen. He has always been more protective of Naomi than of the other children, not only because she is his first-born and the only girl, but more so because she was born with one leg slightly shorter than the other, a defect that was not apparent until she took her first steps. This she did not do until she was almost two years old, causing him and Hannah many sleepless nights. The doctors later surmised that her handicap had held the child back from walking earlier. Once they became aware of it, Samuel and Hannah consulted every known specialist, took every measure they were instructed. They had the poor child suffer through all kinds of tests, some quite painful, had her pulled and massaged this way and that, had her perform all sorts of physical exercises, go through all kinds of treatments. All to no avail. In the end, the only thing that has helped is a small corrective wedge built into all of Naomi's left shoes. Even so, she still walks with a slight limp, which is scarcely noticeable except when she is tired after walking a long stretch or if she is weighed down by her bulging satchel.

Hannah and Liesl are with the twins, getting them washed and dressed. The commotion they cause during this daily struggle can be heard through closed doors: muffled laughter intermingled with gentle scoldings. The older boys have already left for school. Frau Fleissig has not yet emerged from her room. She is having difficulty sleeping; as a result she doesn't fall asleep until the early hours of the morning and then doesn't get up until quite late, sometimes not until noon.

"Come, *Schatzilein*," Samuel says, all the while holding Naomi close. "Let's have a cup of hot *Kakao* together. Just the two of us, like we used to when you were little. And you can tell me *was ist passiert*, what happened."

Naomi's father has always had the ability to calm her fears. Even as a small child, when hurt by her brothers, or by other children who teased her and made cruel remarks about her deformity, Samuel was able to wipe her tears, smooth her ruffled feelings, and make her laugh. Today is no different. Before they reach the kitchen, Naomi's sobs have subsided and she is wiping her eyes.

The Gutman kitchen is the hub of all the family's activities. It is a large, cheerful room overlooking the street, and beyond it the river. Hannah has hung white *broderie anglais* curtains on the windows; they are usually tied back, as they are today, so as not to block the view. The walls of the kitchen are a glossy white with matching white stove and the latest white model of the new refrigerators that have become the rage. Hanging on one wall is the only splash of color: a full size Edouard Manet still-life, two very large and very yellow lemons that strike a dramatic contrast to the white background. Samuel had wanted to hang a blown up photograph of Jerusalem's Wailing Wall on that spot, but Hannah had gently protested. It is she who is the art connoisseur, she the one who visits museums and galleries, and he has always deferred to her taste in art and furnishings. Besides, he can never refuse his Hannale, his *über-Schatzie*, anything.

Now Samuel learns that the ambulance he saw a little while ago took Frau Mayer to the Rothschild hospital.

"Do you know what's wrong with her?" he asks Naomi.

"I'm not sure," She is red-eyed, but no longer agitated. "But I managed to say a couple of words to Henrietta before they left and she said that Herr Doktor Graff thinks it's appendicitis. It must be really bad for her to have been taken to hospital, don't you think, Papa?"

"Well," he says, "*Blinddarmentzundung*. It's no joke, of course, but appendicitis shouldn't be dangerous in this day and age. I'm sure she'll have the finest medical attention. Anyway, we will pray for her, *Schatzie, nicht wahr?*"

Naomi brightens somewhat. "Of course, Papa. But I don't understand something. There was no sign of Henrietta's father this morning. He didn't go to with Frau Mayer in the ambulance. And Henrietta didn't say anything more, except that she wasn't going to be in school today."

"Mmm," he says. "Well, he wasn't in *shul* this morning, so perhaps he went separately, for some reason, in his own car. Does Mutti know what's happened?"

"Yes, she's very upset. She said as soon as the boys are dressed she'll go to the hospital. She said Liesl can give them their breakfast."

"In that case," says Samuel, "I will order a car for her, and she can drop you off at school on the way. That is, *Schatzie*, unless you feel too upset to go to school and want to stay home today. After all the commotion this morning, it would be quite understandable. It will give you the opportunity to practice the Chopin etude you said has been giving you trouble."

Samuel says this only half-seriously; he knows his Naomi well, and is not surprised when she heatedly objects. "Papa, how can you even suggest such a thing! Today of all days when I have my first Shakespeare class with Fraulein Schloss." Then her face, animated just a moment before, falls. "Of course, perhaps I should go with Mutti to the hospital. Henrietta may need me to keep her company."

Samuel doesn't comment. He wants her to arrive at her own decision.

"You know," she continues enthusiastically, "we are going to be learning Hamlet. I'm so excited. I've even been reading it ahead of the class, on my own. It's just so incredible, totally *unglaublich*. I can't believe the original English can be any better than the German. Oh, Papa, what shall I do? I hate to miss the first class."

"I remember studying Hamlet when I was in *Gymnasium*," Samuel says. "The only part I remember is the beginning of the famous speech: '*Sein oder nicht sein*'. I don't even remember the rest of the quotation. Of course, I was never the student that you are, *mein Schatz*, and I found it tough going. Still, I admit, from what I remember it's a very powerful play."

"*Sein oder nicht sein. Das ist die Frage,*" says Naomi.

"That's it! Of course. *Dummkopf* that I am," Samuel says, hitting his forehead with his hand in mock exasperation. "How could I forget that line. *To be or not to be. That is the question.* You see, *Schatzie*, I told you I wasn't a good student."

"Oh, Papa, you're so silly," says Naomi, and impulsively gets up, puts her arms around his neck and kisses him. Her face, so much like his own, but with much finer, smaller features, brightens again. "I know what I'll do, Papa" she says, "I'll go to school and the minute I come home I'll knock on Henrietta's door and spend all evening with her if she wants me to. If necessary, I won't even do my homework or practice piano."

"That's a fine solution," he tells her, giving her a hug. "And if Mutti finds Henrietta when she arrives at the hospital she will be sure to tell her to expect you later. How does that sound?"

With her spirits restored, Naomi doesn't even finish the hot cocoa Samuel poured for her, but runs to her room to fetch her satchel.

Chapter 8

Hans makes good time and they reach Berlin without mishap. But because of the delay caused by Frau Mayer's *Episode* Herr Mayer was unable to attend the early morning service at the Borneplatz *shul*. He keeps an extra set of *tefillin* in the car, just for emergencies, and does a quick recitation of the morning prayers during the long drive. By now, Hans is used to seeing Herr Mayer with the phylacteries strapped to his head and left arm. Often, an early business appointment causes him to pray in the car en route to their destination. During his prayers, Herr Mayer keeps the curtains on the rear windows drawn to avoid the stares of curious, and very likely anti-Semitic, gawkers. After he has neatly packed away the *tefillin* in their black velvet pouch, Herr Mayer opens the curtains and asks Hans to turn on the radio. He is proud to be one of the first owners of a car radio; the Ideal Blaupunkt cost him a small fortune, but it was more than worth it. At first Hans grumbled about having to sacrifice so much of the dashboard to accommodate the radio, but Herr Mayer thinks he is getting used to it. From the way Hans sometimes taps the steering wheel in time to a particular *brio* or *allegro* piece, Herr Mayer suspects he enjoys the music, though he will never admit it. Herr Mayer is now looking into getting a telephone installed; he has heard from a business associate that in Sweden an engineer by the name of Eriksson has invented such a device. It is rumored that the Chancellor has one in his car. Herr Mayer doesn't know how much space a telephone might take up or how much installation is involved. But one thing he can be sure of: he will be in for more grumbling from Hans.

Herr Mayer is thus able to peruse some business papers and files while listening to Wagner's *Tannhauser* Overture. The reception is not terribly good, but the full-blooded sound of one of his favorite pieces by his favorite composer helps him concentrate on the documents and distracts him from thinking about the forthcoming meeting. And keeps him from the occasional pangs of guilt that have assailed him off and on all day over deserting Frau Mayer. Even though he knows he had no choice in the matter.

They stop at an inn for *Benzin*, a cup of coffee, and a chance to relieve themselves. During this, their only stop, Herr Mayer uses the inn's telephone to call Doktor Graff to ascertain Frau Mayer's condition. But he is unable to reach the doctor.

They arrive at the outskirts of the city at three thirty-five; the appointment has been called for four o'clock, *pünktlich*. On the dot. The events of the morning and the prospect of the forthcoming meeting have robbed Herr Mayer of any appetite; he doesn't even remember that the *Episode* caused him to skip breakfast, that all he has put into his mouth all day is a cup of coffee at a wayside inn.

Hans drops him off at the designated corner, and then drives off as instructed. The whole day has been sunless, gloomy and cold, and dusk is rapidly settling over the city. A biting, almost gale force wind, whips the corner where Herr Mayer stands, and nearly knocks him off his feet. He is barely able to save his homburg from being carried away. However, he has barely waited one minute before a sleek black sedan pulls up noiselessly in front of him. Before he realizes what is happening, a man jumps out from the passenger seat, grabs him and pushes him into the rear seat where another man roughly removes Herr Mayer's glasses and ties a blindfold around his eyes. Herr Mayer tries to protest but is quickly silenced. "*Schweigen*. No talking," one of the men orders sharply. The car starts to move but doesn't travel very far. Herr Mayer is pulled out, still blindfolded.

Everything has happened so quickly and so silently that Herr Mayer has not even been able to register the features of the two men. He only remembers the flashes of swastika armbands. He is led blindly up some stairs, prevented from stumbling by the men holding him, one by each arm. The blindfold is removed, and his glasses thankfully returned to him. Never has he felt so vulnerable and defenseless. Now, with his glasses restored, he finds himself in a small windowless room where a severe-looking, middle-aged woman, wearing the ubiquitous armband, awaits him. With one gesture and the one word, '*bitte*,' she both relieves him of his coat and homburg and at the same time indicates that he is to be seated on one of several upright chairs lining the room. She retreats in silence, and he is left to cool his heels for the best part of an hour.

The room is oppressively overheated, unbearably hot. The walls are stark and bare, except for a huge framed photograph of the Chancellor. It portrays him in a double-breasted light gray suit, his right forearm encircled by a swastika band, bent at the elbow and raised, palm outward, in his signature casual *heil* salute. He looks stern and statesmanlike despite the truncated mustache, a *Schnurrbart* Herr Mayer finds a trifle ridiculous. He feels stifled by the heat; he realizes the waistcoat was a mistake, an unnecessary vanity. His hands are wet from perspiration and his glasses feel glued to the bridge of his nose. He removes them, takes out his *Taschentuch*, a white crisp handkerchief lightly starched by Inge to his specification, wipes his hands and dries the area around his nose. He holds the glasses up to the light and notices a filmy residue; he polishes them before putting them on again, then carefully re-folds the handkerchief and replaces it in his pocket. He is tempted to loosen his tie and unbutton his stiff shirt collar, but he doesn't dare. He looks around the room. There is no reading matter to be seen, nor even a table that might have held a magazine or newspaper. He was specifically forbidden to bring any papers or documents of any kind with him. Again, the word *verboten* was used. He was cautioned specifically against carrying an attaché case. As a result, he cannot even use this waiting time to go over any business files; he has had to leave them in the car. He considers walking up and down the small room to stretch his limbs after the long drive, but decides against it; it occurs to him that it is not impossible that he is being watched. He nervously checks and re-checks the Tissot fob watch he inherited from his father; puts it to his ear to make sure it is working properly, re-winds it, just in case.

At precisely five o'clock an inner door opens and a tall young man enters. Blonde, blue-eyed, unmistakably Aryan, he is dressed in the uniform of the increasingly visible Brownshirts: shiny black boots, the requisite armband, and a bandolier-type strap across his chest that holds a black holstered pistol. He approaches Herr Mayer without a word and indicates that he is to stand and lift his arms. Once again, Herr Mayer's inclination is to protest, but he knows it is useless; he has no choice but to allow himself to be patted down. He swallows his humiliation. The Waterman fountain pen that he keeps in the inside pocket of his suit jacket is immediately confiscated. The youth hesitates over the watch, but leaves it in Herr Mayer's vest pocket. Then, just as the woman had, the young Nazi utters the one word 'bitte,' and indicates that Herr Mayer is to follow him.

Herr Mayer is led down a wide corridor and past several doors each of which is guarded by Brownshirt replicas, each similarly outfitted and armed. Then the youth opens a door at the end of the corridor and silently ushers Herr Mayer into another windowless room. This is a much larger room than the one in which he was kept waiting. There, sprawling in deep comfortable leather armchairs in front of an enormous desk, are two men, both wearing military uniforms, each of which is plastered with rows upon rows of colored ribbons and medals. Both men are wearing the swastika armbands that Herr Mayer is learning to expect. One of the men is corpulent, with a round, multi-chinned face and ruddy complexion, his girth taking up the whole chair. The other man, dark-haired and mustached, is much thinner than his companion; he wears a monocle and a severe expression. There is a third armchair, unoccupied, behind the desk. The men do not stand to greet Herr Mayer, and no introductions are made. Herr Mayer has the feeling that he recognizes at least one of the men, possibly both. He may have seen photographs of them in the *Frankfurter Zeitung*. The youth remains near the door, standing stiffly at attention.

One of the men, once again with the utterance of the one word '*bitte*', indicates to Herr Mayer the upright chair on the other side of the room. Herr Mayer sits, and the man begins to speak. Herr Mayer immediately detects a common, unrefined dialect, *bayerisch* perhaps?

"The Chancellor has expressed a wish to meet with you. He will be here in a few minutes. We are sure you understand what a tremendous honor this is. *Nicht wahr?*" he sneers. "The Chancellor does not make a habit of meeting with Jews."

Herr Mayer merely inclines his head. Fortunately, he is not expected to say anything.

The man continues. "When the Chancellor enters, you are to stand at attention, like so, raise your right arm, like so, and exclaim 'Heil Hitler' in a strong voice, like so." The man stands and demonstrates. Then he commands Herr Mayer to rehearse the greeting, "So we can be sure you know how to say it correctly, *nicht wahr?*"

Herr Mayer stands, forces himself to raises his right arm. He feels the words lodging in the back of his throat. But he manages a tolerable 'Heil Hitler' at the precise moment that there is a commotion at the door, which is flung open and the subject of the portrait in the waiting room, Adolf Hitler himself, strides into the room.

The two uniformed men immediately spring to attention, the young man at the door stiffens his already stiff spine, they all click their heels in unison and with one voice exclaim "Heil Hitler!" Herr Mayer is caught with his arm arrested in midair, but the Chancellor, with an affable smile, extends his right hand, plucks Herr Mayer's hand from midair to shake it in greeting, and with his left hand gives Herr Mayer a friendly slap on the back.

"*Ach so*," says Herr Hitler. "Herr Mayer, I presume. I have been looking forward to meeting you. It is very good of you to come all the way from Frankfurt to see me. I trust you had a pleasant *Reise*, a good trip?" Not waiting for a reply, he continues, "I see you have already met *Standatenführer* Von Ribbentrop and *Kommissar* Göring. *Sehr gut*. I hope they have been treating you well. *Also*, we can get right down to business."

With that, Herr Hitler walks around the desk and sits in the empty armchair. Herr Mayer's immediate impression is that the Chancellor is not very tall, not the slightest bit imposing. He doesn't know what he expected, certainly a man with more stature. Certainly not a man who, when sitting in a deep armchair seems almost to disappear. Herr Hitler's face looks just as it does in the portrait; his dark hair precisely parted on the right side, with a small tuft falling over his forehead. He even seems to be wearing the same light gray double-breasted suit with, of course, the swastika armband. In real life the mustache doesn't seem quite so silly. Herr Mayer is suddenly possessed with a ridiculous thought: could that little clump of hair suspended over the Chancellor's forehead be the work of Herr Mayer's barber Luigi, perhaps one of his toupée creations? He dismisses the thought as quickly as it arrived. He is feeling a little light-headed, perhaps from not having eaten all day.

Von Ribbentrop and Göring resume their seats, and Hitler motions for Herr Mayer to do the same.

Herr Hitler pulls himself up in the armchair, leans forward and sits erectly so that he no longer looks so small; he wastes no time getting to the point. He fixes his steely blue eyes on Herr Mayer.

"I have asked you here, Herr Mayer, for a *bestimmt* purpose. The *Vaterland* needs your services, or, to be more specific, the services of Mayer Metallgesellschaft G.m.b.H., or EmEm as I understand you call it. Am I right?" Not waiting for confirmation from Herr Mayer, he continues, with a sneer in his voice. "It is not my habit to do business with you people. But, it has come to my attention that EmEm manufactures certain, er, let us say certain *Erzeugnisse*, products that Germany needs. Von Ribbentrop will give you *eine Liste* and the quantities required. It is possible that there are some items on the list that EmEm does not now manufacture. In that case, I assume you have the capacity to do so in the future. On the list there are also delivery schedules and locations. I expect them to be strictly adhered to."

Herr Hitler clears his throat, straightens the pristine blotter on his desk and continues: "Let me be clear about one thing." Here he shakes his right index finger in Herr Mayer's direction. "It will soon be *verboten* for a Jewish *Gesellschaft* such as yours to continue employing Aryan workers. However, I am making an exception in your case. I know your father fought for the Fatherland and was awarded a medal for bravery, from the Kaiser, no less." A sarcastic, derisive tone has crept into Herr Hitler's tone when speaking of the Kaiser. His voice rises by several decibels. "This means nothing to me. *Nichts*, I tell you. *Nichts*." With that, Herr Hitler pounds the desk with his fist for emphasis, partially raising his body from the chair so that he leans vertically over the desk; flecks of spittle come sailing across the room, dispersing in all directions. "So, consider yourself fortunate, not only that we are honoring you with the opportunity of being of service to the *Vaterland*, but that we are allowing you to continue your operations uninterrupted."

Herr Mayer is given no opportunity to reply. Not that he wants to. He cannot even begin to absorb the shocking diatribe he has just heard. He feels beads of sweat running down his face and inside the back of his shirt. He wishes he could wipe his forehead, but doesn't dare take out the *Taschentuch* from his pocket. He wonders, unaccountably, why the young Nazi who searched him didn't confiscate the handkerchief at the same time as the fountain pen. Probably, he thinks wryly, he found no value in my handkerchief. But why did he leave the watch?

"One thing more," Herr Hitler continues in a quieter tone, settling back in his chair. "We certainly do not expect you to work for nothing. *Nein, nein. Sicher nicht.* Of course not. However, we expect to be charged no more than the cost price. Not one *Pfennig* more. None of your Jewish usurious practices, none of the *schmutzige Geschäfte.* the shady dealings that you people are so famous for. The huge profits you make from your other customers will, I am sure, more than compensate you. Göring," he turns to the more substantial of the two uniformed men, "you know some Yiddish, don't you? Didn't you once tell me what the letters 'G.m.b.H.' stand for?"

"Ach, what a memory *mein* Führer has!" Göring exclaims admiringly. "I have heard the letters stand for the Yiddish phrase '*Genuvim mit beider hent*'.

Which means 'Thieves with both hands'". Göring collapses with laughter, his generous paunch jumping up and down in syncopation with the sounds emitting from his throat. Von Ribbentrop, first making sure that Hitler is enjoying the joke, belatedly joins in. Hitler's loud "ha, ha, ha," sounds forced, but very soon all three Nazis are slapping their thighs and rolling around in their chairs with mirth. Even the young sentry at the door cannot keep from smiling.

Herr Mayer sits in his chair, not moving. It is not so much that he is afraid to move; he is paralyzed, rooted to his chair, incapable of moving, incapable of grasping what he has just heard, what is happening. A minute ago he was sweating. Now he begins to feel cold. Then hot. Cold and hot by turns. He wonders if he is coming down with something. He puts his hand on his right knee to stop it from shaking. He hopes the three Nazis have not noticed.

Herr Hitler gets up to leave, still laughing. Göring and Von Ribbentrop jump to their feet with a resounding 'Heil Hitler'. Herr Mayer, too, automatically stands. Before the door closes behind him, Hitler turns, and now he is no longer laughing. He points his finger at Herr Mayer. "Don't think for one minute," he says, his voice low and ominous, and there is no mistaking the threat in his parting words. "Don't think that I don't know the real meaning of G.m.b.H. *Gesellschaft mit beschränkter Haftung*. A company with limited liability. As far as we are concerned, Mayer Metallgesellschaft G.m.b.H. has full and total liability. So, remember," he says lowering his voice even more and once again wagging his finger menacingly; his blue eyes are like flint and contain no hint of amusement. "We are counting on you and EmEm. Do not let us down."

⇒≪

Herr Mayer dries himself off. He dons the plush white bathrobe provided by the Esplanade. He is beginning to collect his thoughts, beginning to think more clearly. He still has no appetite, but will call down for that double *Whisky* he promised himself earlier. He has been afraid to look at the list. It is still residing in the pocket of his suit jacket, which he doesn't even recall taking off and discarding on the bed together with the rest of his clothes. First, he will try to reach Herr Doktor Graff again; it is entirely possible the doctor has telephoned him at the Adlon, not realizing that he is not staying there. It occurs to him that perhaps he ought to also telephone his children.

He lifts each garment from the bed to hang, one by one, in the wardrobe, and discovers that his watch, the precious heirloom inherited from his father, is still hanging from his vest pocket, its gold chain still attached to the top buttonhole. *Vielleicht*, he muses, perhaps this is why that young Nazi didn't take it: he couldn't work out how to detach the chain. Or, *vielleicht*, unlike the fountain pen, which was not returned to him, he didn't consider the watch a likely weapon. He can think of no other reason.

Then he takes out *die Liste*.

Chapter 9

The sister and brother sit in opposite corners of the private hospital room. Like two contestants in a boxing ring. A young nurse in a crisp white uniform has just finished making up the metal bed with white sheets and blankets tucked in rigidly with military precision. The bed has iron bars around it. So different from the bed their mother is used to sleeping in, with its expanse of down pillows and soft, silky sheets spun from the finest Egyptian percale. Herr Mayer told Doktor Graff to spare no expense in Frau Mayer's medical care; money is no object. The doctor has instructed the children to wait here, in the room to which Frau Mayer will be wheeled after her operation. It is almost noon and they are still waiting.

Both children are miserable, each completely absorbed in their own thoughts. Now and then Henrietta jumps up impatiently and paces back and forth a few times before flopping herself down again in her chair. Both had no opportunity to eat anything before being rushed to the hospital in the doctor's car, although Fritz feels more nauseous than hungry.

The source of each child's misery is not the same. Fritz is miserable because he loves his Mutti and is frightened. He chanced to see his mother before she was carried down the stairs on a stretcher and then placed in the ambulance. Her eyes were closed and she was moaning with pain. Her face was as white as the coats worn by the men carrying the stretcher. He barely recognized her.

He tried to approach her, but the Herr Doktor pulled him back with a harsh '*nein, nein*', and then bundled him and Henrietta into the back seat of his car. Fritz has not seen or heard from his father since Herr Mayer woke him so urgently this morning. He has since been told that his father is on his way to Berlin on urgent business.

Now, Fritz cowers in the corner of the hospital room near the window, picking at his face, which has become mottled, red and oozy. Every now and then a little sob escapes him, and once he cries out, "Oh Mutti, my poor Mutti," at which Henrietta, as if suddenly aware of her brother's presence in the room, tells him scathingly to shut up. "Don't be such a wimp," she says with undisguised contempt. "*Um Gottes Willen.* For heaven's sake. Must you snivel like that? And stop picking at your pimples. It's disgusting. Mutti will be fine."

Fritz pulls himself further into the corner, trying to make himself invisible. He resembles a tortoise retracting its head. He can't stand it when Henrietta is so *gemein* to him. He longs for them to be friends, but lately it seems that his sister is getting meaner and meaner, angrier and angrier by the day. He possesses no weapons with which to fight her, doesn't even have a clue how to answer her. As to his father's absence, he doesn't know what to think. What urgent business can possibly be more important than Mutti's illness?

Henrietta's misery is for an entirely different reason. It's not that she doesn't care that her mother is ill, even though she despises her almost as much as she despises her father. But her mind is occupied with more pressing matters. The first being, what is keeping Tante Bertha? According to Herr Doktor Graff, Tante Bertha is supposed to be here with them at the hospital. She is supposed to stay with Henrietta and Fritz until Frau Mayer is wheeled in from the recovery room and the private nurse comes on duty. Then they are to go with their aunt to her apartment where they will spend the night.

So far, there is no sign of Tante Bertha. Henrietta loves her aunt, but knows she is not very dependable. As for Onkel Heinz, he intimidates her; she sees him rarely as he is always busy. Instinctively, she senses that Tante Bertha understands her. She is longing to tell her about Otto. She is almost sure Tanta

Bertha will be sympathetic. She imagines her saying, "Have fun, my child, I know exactly how you feel, I was young once, too." Or words to that effect. But how can she be certain?

When she was a little girl, and Tante Bertha and Onkel Heinz lived next door in the apartment now occupied by the Gutmans, Henrietta was more often to be found in their apartment than in her own. Tante Bertha allowed her to do all kinds of things that she wasn't allowed to do in her own home, such as play with the perfume bottles on Tante Bertha's *Friesiertisch*. Little Henrietta delighted in arranging and re-arranging all those little bottles on her aunt's dressing table; she was enchanted with the different shapes and sizes and hues. She would hold them up and marvel at the way they caught the light and shone and sparkled, like fairy nectar. And, every now and then, Tante Bertha actually took some of the precious fairy nectar and, to the child's delight, dabbed it behind little Henrietta's ears. At other times they'd listen to music together on Tante Bertha's new gramophone, usually the Italian operas her aunt adored. Tante Bertha would accompany the sopranos in their arias, singing in a lower key and slightly off tune. She would act along with the music, deliberately exaggerating all her movements as she sang about unrequited love, or pretended to be on her death bed, making little Henrietta shriek with laughter. She entrusted the child with the task of cranking up the gramophone when it started to run down, a job Henrietta loved. Eventually, as Henrietta became familiar with the arias, the two of them would have a grand time singing together and then collapsing with laughter on Tante Bertha's *chaise longue*. Tante Bertha would then envelope Henrietta in her arms, kiss and tickle her, making the child laugh and laugh and kick and scream for help.

It was because of her aunt's absorption with opera and the popular songs of the day, that Henrietta realized as she grew older that she herself possessed a tolerable soprano voice. By now, she has, on her own, accumulated an impressive collection of recordings of famous symphonic and operatic performances, like those of Enrico Caruso and Amelita Galli-Curci. Caruso's recording of *La Donna è Mobile* is one of her favorites and she never tires of listening to it over and over again.

Bertha and Heinz are childless, supposedly by choice. In many ways Henrietta has taken the place of the daughter Bertha never had. Over the years, when adults talked and gossiped, as they will, not realizing that little ears are listening, Henrietta overheard an assortment of rumors about Tante Bertha: that she and Onkel Heinz are not even legally married, that Bertha was married previously to another man, that there was no proper divorce. Or something along those lines. Another rumor has it that Tanta Bertha is not Jewish.

Henrietta couldn't care less about the rumors. To her mind, they just add to the glamour and excitement that radiates from Tante Bertha. She admires the way her aunt carries herself, her head held high as if she hasn't a care in the world. She admires the way she laughs off the rumors with a toss of her head, for not seeming to mind what people think of her. She admires the way Tante Bertha dresses with color and flair, and a panache that Henrietta does not see in any other woman, certainly not in her own mother. In Henrietta's eyes, all women look drab and colorless next to Tante Bertha. Who but Tanta Bertha would dare to wear a bright orange lipstick? Or the thick, dark eye shadow that makes her appear so alluring and mysterious, and wickedly *seksi*?

No, Henrietta's main concern is not her mother. What a waste of time, she fumes. She had it all planned. She would have had to involve Naomi for her plan to succeed, but that was unavoidable. Now, all she can think is, how *ironisch* this is, how crazily ironic. I was going to play truant today anyway, yet here I am, for once with an honest excuse for being absent from school, but still unable to go to the *Eisbahn*. Where Otto must be waiting for me. She stamps her foot in frustration. To be stuck in this horrible hospital room with that horrible hospital smell, and with her horrible little snot of a brother! It is just not *gerecht*, not fair at all…

There is a knock on the door. Henrietta jumps up eagerly and runs to open it. Her face, which for a mere second was eager and animated with relief that Tante Bertha has arrived, immediately drops with disappointment when she sees who it is.

"I hope I'm not intruding," says Hannah Gutman. Henrietta's crestfallen look has not escaped her; the girl was obviously expecting and hoping to see someone else. Hannah speaks in the same slightly tentative way as her daughter. "B-but, you see, I was worried about your mother and…" Her voice trails off.

Henrietta cannot hide her disappointment even though she quite likes Frau Gutman. She has only met her a few times on the stairs of their apartment building, but the woman has always greeted her with a friendly smile; once she even asked Henrietta to give "*ein Gruss* to your mother."

Fritz automatically stands up at the sight of Hannah Gutman. The good manners that have been drilled into him since he was a small child, now come to the rescue. Besides, he is relieved that an adult has arrived, that he no longer has to be alone with his *gemeine* sister.

Hannah hastens to cover up the awkward moment. "I telephoned the hospital earlier but was unable to get any information," she explains, "so, I thought I would come over in person to see if I can be of any help. At the desk downstairs they told me your mother should be out of the operating room very soon." She walks over to the little table near the hospital bed, and puts down the basket she has brought with her. "I..I do hope you're both hungry. I've brought you sandwiches and some of my mother's homemade *Streusel Kuchen*. I hope you like Swiss cheese and mashed egg with *Gurken*. After all, it was so early when you left and I thought you might not have had a chance…"

Hannah uncovers the basket to reveal an abundance of food and a thermos flask containing hot chocolate; the children's mouths begin to water despite their misery. Only good manners stop Fritz from attacking the sandwiches; in fact he remembers to wash his hands ritually at the sink in the room, before eating. Henrietta has no such reservations. She mutters a curt "*Danke schön, Frau Gutman,*" and at the same time grabs one of the sandwiches, each of which has been lovingly wrapped in *Pergamentpapier* and a white cloth napkin. Fritz recites the requisite blessing under his breath before biting into his cheese sandwich. Hannah is impressed with the boy's restraint and devotion to religious ritual, especially in such stressful circumstances. She gives him a warm smile of approval and is touched to see the boy's pock-marked face, which just a moment ago was tearstained and miserable, become momentarily alive and flushed with pleasure. It occurs to Hannah that compliments must be a rarity in this boy's life.

The brother and sister eat in a silence interrupted only by muffled hospital sounds coming from outside the room: the padded footsteps of the staff, the wheels of medicine carts and beds being trundled from place to place, the clank of instruments being dropped into bowls. The room is pervaded with a pungent hospital odor, a mixture of antiseptic and carbolic and something unidentifiable. Hannah Gutman is at a loss for words. She is surprised to have found the children waiting alone in this room. She doesn't know what to make of it. Where is their father? And what about their aunt and uncle? Surely they have been informed? She doesn't even know how much the children have been told about their mother's condition. She is afraid to ask; and it is not her place to question them.

Both Henrietta and Fritz are beginning to feel better, their spirits revived somewhat by the food. Hannah has poured the hot chocolate into mugs for them, and the two children gulp down the sweet hot liquid greedily, not hiding their obvious thirst.

"I didn't realize I was so thirsty," says Henrietta, her good manners finally surfacing. "Thank you, Frau Gutman."

"Thank you, Frau Gutman," Fritz echoes shyly. "The sandwiches were very good, and so was the *Kuchen*."

"I'm so glad you enjoyed them," Hannah says, as she folds up the used napkins and greaseproof paper and places them in the empty basket. "By the way, Henrietta, Naomi sends you her love. She says to tell you that if you wish she will come over to keep you company this evening."

"Oh, that won't be necessary, Frau Gutman," Henrietta replies. "We're not spending the night at home. We're going to be sleeping at our aunt's apartment."

The girl pointedly consults her wristwatch. "As a matter of fact, she should be here at any moment."

Hannah takes this information and the airy and deliberate way in which it was delivered as an unmistakable hint that Henrietta wishes her gone. There has been no mention of where the father is, or when he is expected. She gathers the mugs and thermos flask, removing all traces of the refreshments, and picks up her basket. "Please give your mother my fondest wishes for a speedy recovery." She walks to the door, then turns and adds, "A-and please remember, should you need anything, anything at all, we are just next door, and we are only too happy…" She sees the children have already forgotten her: the boy in his corner staring out the window, his hand already at his face, the girl pacing the hospital room, obviously absorbed in her own world. Hannah closes the door softly behind her.

Chapter 10

Henrietta is in heaven. At least, she thinks this is what heaven must be like. She is so happy she can barely breathe. Otto has his left arm around her waist, and together they are gliding seamlessly over the ice, in perfect symmetry. Her feet, encased in white leather skates, are moving of their own volition, first the right, then the left, in flawless synchronicity with her partner. She feels weightless, floating over the ice. Henrietta's ill mother is forgotten, her father and brother are non-existent. It is a blissful Thursday afternoon, with very few skaters on the rink. After spending the night at Tante Bertha's apartment, their aunt has given both children permission to stay out of school. "With your mother in hospital," she tells them, "don't you think it would show a lack of feeling if you turned up at school today as if nothing has happened?"

Unlike Henrietta, Fritz is a conscientious student, but not at all interested in sports, which makes him a perfect target for the bullies in his class. He is relieved not to have to face them today. Yet Aunt Bertha's pronouncement doesn't fill him with joy. In a moment of unusual candor he once confided shyly to Onkel Heinz, in answer to his uncle's question, that the subjects he likes best in school are *Biologie* and *Chemie*. When his uncle didn't laugh at his choices, as Fritz feared he might, he was emboldened to confide further that he had hopes of becoming a physician when he grew up. "Or, perhaps," he said, "I will become a research scientist and find a cure for *Krebs*." Onkel Heinz put his arm around his nephew's shoulders, and bent his head to equalize their disparate heights. "*Wunderbar! Wunderbar!*" he exclaimed enthusiastically. "If anyone can find a cure for cancer, it will be you, my boy. Go for it! Of course," he continued, "my brother, that is to say, your father, is surely depending on you to go into EmEm, and, personally, I was secretly hoping that you might have an interest in the law…" Here Onkel Heinz, without removing his arm from Fritz's shoulders, turned to face the boy with a smile that displayed the stained and crooked teeth his brother finds so abhorrent, but which his clients not only overlook but apparently find confidence-inducing. With his right hand he took the boy's hand and shook it, man to man. "Good luck, dear boy," he said. "I know whatever field you choose you will be a huge success."

Fritz turned away at this rare praise and words of encouragement to hide the tears that, embarrassingly, suddenly welled up behind his eyes.

Now Fritz expresses to his aunt his desire to visit his mother in the hospital. "I'll take my school books with me and do my homework there, but I want to be with Mutti when she wakes up." Henrietta gives her brother a withering look. Behind her aunt's back, she puts her index finger deep into her throat, and makes a gagging sound to show her disgust. She has other plans. She has no difficulty persuading her aunt to drop her off at the *Eisbahn*. She has decided it might not be such a good idea to confide in Tante Bertha about Otto just yet. With her mother ill, why take a chance that Tanta Bertha might not be as understanding as she has thought. "Mutti would be the first one to encourage me to keep practicing," she says piously. "It's been several days since I've been on the ice and already I feel stiff and rusty. Besides, I can go to the hospital later in the day when Vater comes home from Berlin. He's bound to be back by then."

Henrietta arrives at the skating rink a little before noon. She doubts Otto can be expecting her. They have no lesson scheduled for today. She changes into her skates and the ski outfit her father insists she wear on the ice ("none of those shameless little skirts for you, *mein liebes Mädchen*"). She walks out of the locker room to the edge of the rink in search of him. She spots him immediately; the rink is almost empty except for Otto, who is giving a lesson to a young woman with long dark hair and a slender figure. Even from a distance Henrietta can see she is very pretty and older, perhaps in her twenties. Otto is holding her hand and she is wearing one of those 'shameless little skirts' so scorned by Herr Mayer, a skirt that shows off her shapely legs to great advantage. She is obviously a beginner on the ice, stumbling and sliding all over the place, which gladdens Henrietta's heart. Until she sees Otto mouthing something into the young woman's ear, making her throw back her head with laughter, and then Otto joins in and the two of them are laughing uncontrollably, as if sharing a hilarious joke. The sound of their laughter bounces off the ice and reaches Henrietta all the way at the other end of the rink. She suddenly feels ill; there is a sinking feeling at the bottom of her stomach. The eager anticipation that filled her just moments ago, has been snatched away. She berates herself. Why on earth did she insist on coming today? What could have possessed her? Is this her punishment for not going to school? For 'appropriating' a powder compact and rouge from her mother's dressing table? Or worse, for not going to the hospital to visit her mother? Her head droops and she turns to go back into the building.

But then she hears someone shouting her name; the sound echoes hollowly off the ice, rising above the sprightly music pouring from the loudspeakers. She turns back to see Otto waving; she hears him yelling her name from the other end of the rink. "Hen-ri-etta, Hen-ri-etta." Otto has noticed her! He bends to say something to the young woman, then guides her to safety off the ice. Now he is skating speedily and urgently over to Henrietta, reaching her in just a few strokes of his skates. The point of his right skate digs into the ice as he swivels to a sudden, crunching halt, sending little chips of ice up into the air. Then, bowing to Henrietta with exaggerated gallantry and a flourish of his arm, he reaches for her hand, turns it over and presses his mouth to the palm, all the while looking directly into her eyes. "*Mein liebes schönes Fraulein*, my beautiful Henrietta," he says, keeping her hand against his lips. "How I have been waiting and longing for this moment. I have been so *trostlos*, absolutely desolate, not knowing if I will see you today. You can't begin to imagine how wretched I've been feeling."

Henrietta can't help laughing at his antics even as she snatches her hand back from his grasp. She hopes he hasn't noticed the blush that she feels suffusing her cheeks, that he can't sense how her legs have become weak and wobbly at the touch of his lips on her palm. "What nonsense!" she says, with a toss of her head, a movement she has picked up unconsciously from Tante Bertha. "You didn't look at all wretched a few minutes ago. I'm glad to see you had other lessons to keep you from missing me too much."

"Are you jealous, my sweet, beautiful Henrietta? How pretty you look when you're cross and do that with your head," teases Otto. "Do you mean my eleven o'clock lesson?" He waves dismissively toward the other end of the rink where he was skating with the pretty, dark-haired girl just a moment before. "What an ordeal. Absolute torture. That one will never learn to keep her balance on the ice. You can't believe how relieved I was when I saw you. I was afraid you weren't coming today." He takes her hand once more. "Oh, Henrietta, my sweet Henrietta. You rescued me just in the nick of time. I came this close to *Selbstmord*," and he demonstrates with his thumb and index finger just how close he came to committing suicide.

"Oh please, Otto, I don't believe a word you say," says Henrietta with another toss of her head, but this time making no attempt to remove her hand from his. "Anyway, wild horses couldn't keep me away. From the ice, that is. You know how I love to skate."

"Of course," replies Otto, smiling. "From the ice. I didn't think I was the *Anreiz*, the inducement." Holding her hand, he leads her onto the ice, just at the same moment that Henrietta notices the small pin attached to the lapel of his jacket. She frowns. "I don't remember seeing that before," she says, drawing back a little. Otto looks down at his collar with a puzzled frown, as if he has just discovered the miniature swastika pin and can't imagine how it got there. "Oh, this little thing," he says, flipping the collar with his free hand. "It doesn't mean anything, it's not important, believe me. The boss told me I have to wear it if I want to keep my job; I'm scared he'll fire me if I refuse."

Otto is a 23-year old, very Aryan German of average intelligence and above average height and looks, of which he is very conscious, just as he not unmindful of the effect his deep blue eyes, wavy blonde hair, and practiced charm have on the opposite sex. Not only do young girls like Henrietta find him captivating, but even older women are enticed by his looks and physique. His frame is lithe and loose, advertising his athleticism, and his manner so engaging that he is almost irresistible. He holds Henrietta's hand and again gazes deeply into her eyes; she, in turn, signals to him her willingness – no, her eagerness – to be led by him. Now, with his other arm around her waist, they glide onto the ice just as the first sweeping, rhythmic notes of a Strauss waltz fill the arena.

Round and round the rink the two skate in perfect unison. They do not speak; speech has become superfluous. Henrietta has never felt so graceful, so alive, yet at the same time so filled with a feeling that this cannot be happening. She is skimming effortlessly over the icy surface, then floating as if in a dream. Otto's hand tightens around her waist, and he turns his head to smile conspiratorially at her, making her turn her head and return his smile. They skate for several seconds in this fashion, looking into each other's eyes. Henrietta doesn't know how she is able to continue skating without stumbling, but she does. Her legs move automatically, robot-like. Finally, she looks away, but not before Otto has read and interpreted correctly the look of trust and longing in her eyes. Without Henrietta realizing it, Otto's hand, which has been clasping her waist, has slowly inched higher until it is almost completely…

She is paralyzed with shock but incapable of protesting, incapable of stopping him. She feels his eyes still on her, but now she keeps hers focused straight ahead, as if she has not noticed anything amiss, as if what he is doing is the most natural thing in the world. Her feet are still sailing automatically over the ice, but her heart is racing wildly, she can scarcely breathe. A tremor that is entirely foreign to her travels throughout her whole body. A part of her mind tells her that this is wrong, that she cannot allow this. But another part tells her that it is too late, that Otto's hand belongs where it is, in that place, near her heart.

And there it stays.

Chapter 11

≫≪

They reach the outskirts of Frankfurt a little after four o'clock on Thursday afternoon, and Herr Mayer instructs Hans to drive straight to the Rothschild hospital on Unterweg. It is hard to believe it is only twenty-four hours since his meeting with Herr Hitler and his henchmen; an eternity seems to have elapsed. The journey back from Berlin was hampered by a detour from the main road, making them lose time. No explanation was given for the sudden diversion of traffic, which was directed by men in black uniforms and swastika armbands. Their return was further delayed by sleeting rain and then, with the oncoming dusk, an unusual fog descended suddenly, without warning, smothering the approach into Frankfurt, and then the city itself, with a thick, tenebrous blanket.

During the drive back from Berlin, even the Goldberg Variations are unable to keep Herr Mayer's mind from returning over and over again to the meeting, or to his conversation with Doktor Graff. The doctor seemed somewhat guarded on the phone, hemming and hawing in a way that is not like him at all and then abruptly cutting the conversation off with the excuse that they had a bad connection. But the temptation to return to yesterday's events overrides Herr Mayer's concern for his wife, and makes it impossible for him to keep to his resolve not to think about the meeting.

The meeting that was not a meeting, the meeting that never took place.

After Bach, the melodic, passionate chords of Mendelssohn's violin concerto, though often interrupted by static, help to keep his thoughts at bay for a while. And, now that he has had a few hours' sleep and has eaten, he finds he is able to view the whole affair more calmly, with more detachment than the previous evening. He goes over in his mind the Chancellor's words, and the words of his two lieutenants, Göring and von Ribbentropp. How badly do they need EmEm's products? He is certain that most of the items on the list, such as the rifle with the new recoil mechanism, are not manufactured by any other German company. But why are they not approaching foreign manufacturers, such as the French, or even the Americans? It cannot be purely a matter of price. He remembers the Chancellor's warning not to charge one *Pfennig* above cost, and he doesn't know whether to laugh or cry. Even without discussing this with his comptroller he knows that EmEm will never be able to meet this condition for long. And still survive.

Once more he goes over the list. To be sure, there are items on it that EmEm has never manufactured before. Not because they do not have the capacity to do so, but because... And then, in a flash, it dawns on him, the reason Herr Hitler has apparently not approached any foreign company. Of course! How could he have been so *dumm*! He now sees why Herr Hitler needs EmEm's cooperation. Perhaps the Chancellor has also approached Krupp and Mauser and other German manufacturers, companies that are larger than EmEm and have international branches, companies that are owned by gentiles. But perhaps not. In fact, certainly not. The more Herr Mayer thinks about it, the more he is convinced that Herr Hitler has not approached any other company. Not yet, anyway. The Chancellor has had no hesitation about intimidating him, a Jew, a Jew whom he knows he can threaten with imprisonment, or worse, if he is not obeyed, and if the rumors are to be believed. Perhaps the Chancellor is not so confident about coercing the Krupp family. Can it be that he is not sure of their cooperation? Can it be that he is afraid they may resist his plans, perhaps even rebel? Or that they will leak his plans to the press before he is ready to make them known? And a foreign manufacturer, if approached, would certainly inform the press.

These thoughts and questions and many others battle around in Herr Mayer's head during the drive back to Frankfurt. The Mendelssohn ends, as does the journey, without providing any satisfactory answers.

During the return journey, he becomes conscious, more than once, of Hans looking at him repeatedly through his rearview mirror. He doesn't recall noticing this kind of attention from Hans before; it is a speculative, measuring gaze. He wonders what Hans is thinking, what he suspects; it is only natural for the man to be curious about the secrecy surrounding the drop-off and pick-up location, to wonder at the strict and unusual orders he received from Herr Mayer to leave him on that windy corner and drive off immediately. It would be only natural for Hans to wonder where Herr Mayer went after he dropped him off, to wonder whom he was meeting, to wonder at the identity of the driver of the black sedan with darkened windows that returned Herr Mayer to the same corner two hours later.

Hans and Inge Bauer are church-going Lutherans. Somewhere in Hans's German ancestry there must have been *Bauers*, farmers, who adopted the name. Herr Mayer recalls Hans telling him that there are Bauer relatives – perhaps an older brother? – working the old family farmstead somewhere in a rural area not far from Frankfurt. Hans is built like a *Bauer*, tall, with massive shoulders and large, strong hands made for digging the soil. The couple has worked for Herr Mayer's family ever since the Mayers' marriage, just as an assortment of prior Bauers served prior generations of Mayers, in a long, unbroken chain of faithful and devoted service. But these are turbulent times. How can Herr Mayer be certain where Hans's loyalties lie? The relationship between Herr Mayer and his chauffeur has always been *korrekt* and proper. Herr Mayer has never engaged in a political discussion with him. But then, he ruefully reflects, he realizes he has never had a discussion with Hans on any subject other than the weather, the workings of the Daimler, and polite inquiries about his health. He now recalls that the Bauers' only child died several years ago. From some sort of blood disease perhaps? At the time, Frau Mayer was very attentive toward them, had even cooked food and brought it to them herself, to their small *Wohnung* in the working district of the city. Naturally, he and Frau Mayer gave Hans and Inge several days off to mourn their son. Or was it a daughter?

There was no discussion with Hans and Inge when Adolf Hitler was elected Chancellor in 1933, when cheering, hysterical mobs poured onto the streets. Herr Mayer cannot recall any reaction on their part to the book burnings. Perhaps the Bauers do not follow politics closely; perhaps they have never even heard of the book burnings. That Hans did not return a Heil Hitler salute - what does that mean? Perhaps Hans didn't even see Schmidt's salute, or hear Schmidt's 'Heil Hitler'. It may be as simple as that.

As planned, Herr Doktor Graff is waiting for Herr Mayer at the hospital, outside Frau Mayer's room, his face somber as the two men shake hands.

"I wish I had better news for you, Gustav," the doctor says. "There was no point in alarming you while you were in Berlin, so I tried not to be too *deutlich* over the telephone, though I did try to prepare you." He clears his throat. He is visibly uncomfortable, a reluctant messenger. "I'm afraid by the time we got Frau Mayer onto the operating table her appendix had burst."

Herr Mayer stares at the doctor blankly.

"But you operated, *nein*? So she will recover, *nicht wahr?*"

The doctor cannot meet Herr Mayer's eyes.

"I'm sorry to say that peritonitis seems to have set in. I was in the operating room during the surgery. We had the best surgeon, as you know, Herr Doktor Friedmann, who, you may remember, removed Henrietta's tonsils a few years ago. He was unable to contain the infection, it had already spread. Frau Mayer has not regained consciousness. Of course, we are doing everything humanly possible for her, and...." There is nothing more for him to say.

Herr Mayer is no longer listening. Peritonitis. He knows all about peritonitis. His own mother succumbed to it when he was just a boy. He will never forget how horribly she suffered before she died.

Doctor Graff touches his arm. "You will not be shocked when you see her," he says. "She is resting comfortably." Herr Mayer moves robot-like, to the door of his wife's hospital room. He turns the handle and opens the door. He is immediately assaulted by the smell, an odor that is all too familiar to him, an odor that he will never forget as long as he lives. An odor that he will always associate with disaster and death. He is barely able to control the acid rising at the back of his throat as a wave of nausea sweeps over him. He swallows hard and forces himself to approach the bed. The room is dimly lit by one small overhead bulb, the curtains on the window drawn against the winter darkness. In the gloom he detects the form of his wife. She is lying on her back, eyes closed, and if one did not know better, and one did not see or hear or smell the liquid draining from somewhere in her body through a tube into a receptacle beneath the bed, one might think she was sleeping peacefully, so smooth and serene does her face appear despite its unnatural pallor. Her head is covered by a white nightcap, her hair tucked neatly beneath it. The narrow tube issuing from her nose is barely discernible. She is breathing evenly, her mouth slightly open.

A uniformed woman stands up at his approach. Ah, yes, the private nurse. He lifts his wife's hand lying limply on top of the counterpane. Was it only yesterday morning that he lifted her hand in similar fashion in their bedroom? "Marga", he hears himself saying, "*da bin Ich*, Gustav. Can you hear me?" There is no reply, not that he really expected one. There is no sound except for the whirring of machinery. He feels a hand on his shoulder. "Gustav," says the doctor, "she cannot hear you. She is receiving morphine. She is not in pain."

Herr Mayer turns at the sound of the doctor's voice. A shadow detaches itself from the darkness at the periphery of his vision and distracts him. The shadow is his son, Fritz, rising from a chair in a corner of the room. The boy hesitates, unsure whether to approach. Herr Mayer opens his arms in an uncharacteristic gesture, enveloping his son as he emerges from the gloom. He does not remember holding him like this since Fritz was a toddler, learning how to walk. Fritz collapses on his father's shoulder, letting out one tortured 'Mutti!' and then begins to sob silently, his whole body shaking uncontrollably. For once Herr Mayer is not even tempted to tell his son to stop crying, to act like a man; in fact, he has trouble controlling his own emotions. He wishes he could allow himself the luxury of weeping. Not just for his ill wife, but for his whole world that is crumbling around him.

Regaining his composure, he gently pushes his son away. He takes out his handkerchief, the one overlooked by the young Nazi who patted him down the day before, and hands it to Fritz.

"*Wo ist deine Schwester?*" he asks. Fritz looks around the room in bewilderment, as if seeing it for the first time, and as if the answer to his father's question lies somewhere in the gloom.

"I d-don't know," he stammers. "I th-think Henrietta was supposed to be here, but perhaps she's with Tante Bertha."

"*Nicht wichtig,*" says Herr Mayer. "It's not important. Come, we will go home and I will telephone your aunt. And then we'll see what Inge has left us for supper."

Chapter 12

❦

The Borneplatz *Synagoge* on the Judengasse is a massive brick structure, with lofty arched windows and a high, rounded cupola that sits on the corner of the roof like a cantor's gigantic yarmulke. Architecturally, the exterior of the building cannot be considered extraordinary. To the contrary, even at the time of its opening in 1860 it was thought that other synagogues in Germany, like those in Hanover and Berlin, for instance, were considerably more *eindrucksvoll*. The interior of the Borneplatz *shul*, however, is quite another story, and even today in 1935, it is often the target of discussion and a cause of contention and different opinions among its congregants, sometimes causing outright friction. Luminous green pillars support the women's section, and various arches are scattered around the interior. An inverted cupola lined in a dazzling azure blue, hangs high and protectively over the *Ner Tamid*, the eternal flame, which, in turn, hangs over the *Bimah* and the *Aron*, which holds the Torah scrolls. These unusual splashes of color are in sharp contrast to the rows of Spartan benches that line the sides and center of the main floor of the *shul* in military formation. It is not clear if the revolutionary interior design was the work of the general architect, Siegfried Kusnitzky, or whether the design was approved by the old-time *Yekkes* or, as is more likely, by their more progressive children. What is clear, however, is that it is not to everyone's taste; many of the older members feel the bright colors are garish and display a lack of modesty that stands totally against the upright, disciplined and restrained German temperament of the synagogue's *Yekke* founders.

It is Friday night, almost three full days and two nights since Frau Mayer was taken to hospital. The evening service is about to begin. Outside, a biting, gusty north wind has forced the temperature down to well below freezing. The ground is dotted with patches of ice, making walking hazardous despite the salt sprinkled on the streets and pavements near the *shul* and in front of nearby apartment buildings. There have been recent incidents of vandalism: swastikas and '*Juden raus*' and '*Schweine*' signs scrawled on the brickwork, and two of the *shul's* windows have been broken. The insults have been scrubbed clean but the windows are still boarded up. Several security guards now patrol the area and the various entrances to the building around the clock, not just on the Sabbath. The guards are all Jewish; it is difficult to find trustworthy non-Jews to guard the building, and it is rumored that soon it will, at any rate, be *verboten* to hire gentiles. It is also forbidden for Jews to carry firearms, but rumor has it that some of the guards hide revolvers under their clothing, most likely souvenirs from their days in the Kaiser's army. What they would do if accosted or attacked by Brownshirts is unclear, but so far, since the guards began their patrols, there have been no further incidents.

As is usual on Friday nights, the women's gallery is empty except for the 'regulars', a handful of intrepid and devout female worshippers, silent wraiths, almost invisible in their dark clothing. Tomorrow morning, the gallery will be packed with women of all ages, the older women costumed in muted, under-stated colors and styles, the younger ones fashionable in the latest Parisian fin-ery and feathered hats. This evening, because of the inadequacy of the radiators heating the cavernous chamber, most of the male worshippers have kept their overcoats on for warmth. Even the choir members have coats on under their robes. The male worshippers, normally hushed and dignified while waiting for the rabbi to arrive, are abuzz with gossip. Herr Forschheimer, the top-hatted *gabbai*, bangs his palm repeatedly on the lectern, asking for *Stille*, to no avail. *Haben Sie gehört?* Have you heard? Frau Mayer is in a coma. She has tubes coming out of every part of her body. She is dying. She is all alone. Herr Mayer has left town. He was not even with her during her operation. Nobody knows where the children are.

Samuel Gutman and his two older boys, Izaak and Joshua, arrive at *shul* early. Both boys are members of the choir. Izaak celebrated his Bar Mitzvah just over a year ago, an occasion that coincided with a change in his voice. As a result, he can no longer sing the soprano solos, and ten-year-old Joshua has now taken over his role. The boys disappear into the robing room at the front of the building, and Samuel retreats to his usual seat at the rear, partially hidden by one of the pillars. Samuel is grateful for this camouflage; he wishes he were completely invisible. He has already been barraged by questions from the curious men around him, who know that the Gutmans and Mayers are next-door neighbors. "*Entschuldigung.* Please excuse me," he has said repeatedly in answer to their questions. "I know as little as you do." The whispered and not-so-whispered rumors continue to fly back and forth among the waiting men with undisguised and uncharacteristic relish. Apparently Herr Mayer is not a favorite, despite his wealth and position of prominence in the *shul.* Or, perhaps, because of them.

Just at the moment when the gossipmongers' stories are really beginning to roil, – stories that are becoming more and more fantastic by the minute, a hush descends, a silence which all the *klapping* by the *gabbai* has been unable to achieve. All eyes turn to the main entrance. The rabbi enters, followed by Herr Mayer himself; trailing the twosome is Herr Doktor Graff. Herr Mayer is outfitted in his usual immaculate fashion: gleaming shoes and spectacles, a dark cashmere *Mantel* and scarf worn over a custom-made suit with sharply creased trousers, woven from the finest materials. His hands are encased in the softest leather. The impressive image is topped off by his special black Sabbath homburg. Herr Doktor Graff is similarly attired and is only slightly less *eindrucksvoll.* Rabbi Gutfreund's black pastoral robe is unable to hide the bulky overcoat beneath, nor his very visible paunch, but his black top hat compensates by contributing to his height and giving him an air of elegance.

All eyes are on Herr Mayer as the three men make their way down the length of the synagogue, shaking proffered hands on each side as they pass, and offering and returning Sabbath greetings, as is the custom among this congregation of male worshippers. Herr Mayer's outward demeanor shows nothing of his experiences over the last three days. A discerning eye might note that, if possible, Herr Mayer's bearing is even more austere and dignified than usual, his face perhaps a little more pale and gaunt, his smile a little more forced, his eyes behind the thick gleaming spectacles somewhat bloodshot and cloudy, lacking their usual keenness. He and the doctor take their adjacent seats in the front row near the prestigious eastern wall. Some of the men have the good grace to avert their eyes. Those in Herr Mayer's immediate vicinity stand to wish him and the doctor a *gut Shabbos*, with more handshaking, sometimes accompanied by almost imperceptible Teutonic bows and clicking of heels, a habit retained by many German Jewish men, along with their revolvers, from their past military service. German reserve and good manners prevent the curious from uttering a word more than the Sabbath greeting.

Rabbi Gutfreund ascends the steps to the lectern in front of the *Aron* and faces the congregation. He makes his usual Friday night announcements, as if nothing out of the ordinary has occurred. He nods to the cantor, who stands before the choir, baton raised. *"Anfangen, bitte."* he commands. The evening service begins.

Chapter 13

⟩✦⟨

This Friday night is ten-year-old Joshua's debut. At the end of the service, he is to sing the solo from Psalm 92. *Tzaddik katomer yifrach*. The righteous shall flourish like the date palm. Of all Lewandowski's compositions, this is Samuel's favorite, but he is nervous for his son. Josh has been practicing for weeks, and each time Samuel hears his sweet voice soaring and capturing those high notes with bulls-eye precision, his eyes tear up with emotion and pride. And not a little nostalgia. For he cannot help recalling how, at the same age his son is now, he sang those very same words to the very same tune, in this very same *shul*. Here in Borneplatz. How proud his father had been! Even now he can see his father's bearded face before his eyes and can almost feel him squeezing his shoulders in encouragement. Just as he, Samuel, had squeezed Josh's shoulders just a few minutes ago. Will he never stop missing his father, Samuel wonders. Oh, how his father would have loved to be here at this moment to hear his grandson performing his favorite *niggun*.

The boy does not disappoint. With great difficulty does Samuel manage to control his emotions as the pure soprano voice unfurls ribbon-like to the rafters of the *shul*, and it is only when the men around him slap his back and offer their hands in congratulation that he realizes he has been holding his breath. With the last bars still ringing in his ears, Samuel waits for his boys to emerge from the choir room. They and other fathers and sons are among the last to leave the synagogue amidst a small crowd of Sabbath well-wishers. The group disperses quickly. It is too cold to linger, and since the new regime and the 'incidents' it is no longer considered safe to congregate outside the *shul*. The '*gut Shabbos*' greetings that used to be passed back and forth from one Jew to another with firm handshakes, robust conviviality, and exchanges of the latest *Nachtrichten*, news of births and weddings and less fortunate events, are now imparted hurriedly and in muted voices, with eyes darting furtively over shoulders. Or not imparted at all.

Samuel and the boys are dressed warmly against the frigid temperature, which is dropping by the minute. The wind has died down; in fact nothing stirs in the naked branches of the trees along their route as they begin the short walk home, but the air is heavy with the threat of more snow, and with every exhaled breath plumes of smoke shoot up into the night air.

"Come *mein Schatzies*," Samuel urges, taking each of his sons by the arm, "let's hurry home. I don't know about you, but I can really do with a bowl of Oma's hot chicken *Suppe* tonight."

Each week, Izaak and Josh look forward to the Friday night walk home from *shul* with their father. This is a precious time, a rare few minutes when they have him all to themselves without the distraction of the twins. It is their time to tell him about their week at school, what they have learned, the marks they have earned; it is their time to confide any difficulties they have encountered, perhaps a teacher who was unfair, a classmate who was unexpectedly cruel. Sometimes, Samuel regales the boys with stories of his own school days; they love to hear about the pranks their father got up to. Sometimes, he tells them stories of *his* father, the grandfather they never knew.

Izaak, the elder by four years and the more spiritual of the two boys, is so enthused about this week's Torah portion, that he can barely contain himself, can't wait until they are seated at the dining room table for the Sabbath meal to reveal all he has learned. As soon as they leave the *shul* Izaak becomes impatient to discuss with his always willing father the commentaries of Rashi and Rambam. In private, Samuel and Hannah refer to him fondly as their *kleine*

Rabbiner. Our little rabbi. Josh, on the other hand, is more of an athlete than a student, and longs to regale his father with the latest achievement of his class's *Fussball* team.

"So, Izaak," Samuel finally says automatically and somewhat distractedly, after they have exchanged hurried Sabbath greetings with another family. "What can you tell me about this week's *Sedrah*."

The words spill out of Izaak's mouth and he almost trips over them in his excitement. "Isn't it *erstaunlich*, Papa, absolutely amazing, how the Torah emphasizes that we must never forget what Amalek did to us. You know, when the Israelites were crossing the desert and Amalek's army attacked them from the rear. In fact," and here the boy grabs his father's arm, making him and his brother stop in their tracks, as he lowers his voice to a dramatic whisper and his eyes grow wide and solemn, "Rabbi Breuer hinted that it is possible to compare Amalek to the new German regime. And not only that, Papa, wait till you hear the best part. Did you know that in the third chapter of the Torah, in *Bereishit*, there is a hint about the evil, wicked Haman of the Purim story? What d'you think of that, Papa? Isn't it astounding?" Izaak looks up at his father with wide-eyed expectation, waiting for his usual enthusiastic reaction. "Yes, that's *grossartig*, totally amazing," says Samuel. "I seem to remember learning about it a long time ago. Let me see, I think what you are referring to is a play on the Hebrew word *haman* in *Bereishit*. The word means 'plenty' or 'an abundance', something like that, *nicht wahr*?"

"Yes, yes" says Izaak excitedly, "that's it, Papa. I just don't remember exactly how Rabbi Breuer explained it."

"Well," says Samuel, "from what I recall, the commentaries compare Adam in the Garden of Eden to wicked Haman of the Purim story. Both men possessed an abundance of blessings, but were not satisfied with what they had. Adam was given a magical life in the Garden of Eden but was forbidden to eat from the Tree of Knowledge, which became the one thing he desired above all else, while Haman, whose riches and position in Persia were second only to the king himself, couldn't get Mordecai the Jew to bow to him, which became the one thing he wanted above all else. In both cases, the need of both men to possess the one thing they couldn't have was their downfall."

"Yes, Papa, now I remember. That's exactly what Rabbi Breuer told us. And then he said we must pray that Hitler's downfall will follow the same pattern as Haman's. Don't you agree, Papa?"

"Yes, yes, *mein Schatz*, I agree absolutely. It is also a lesson for us to always be satisfied with what we have, *nicht wahr?* But let's discuss this in more detail later, *mein Schatzens*, around the dinner table. It's too cold for conversation on the street, and besides, I can't think too clearly right now."

Izaak tries to hide his disappointment. He is a sensitive boy and something tells him that his father is preoccupied. Certainly, Samuel is not his usual talkative, joking self. Izaak has heard some of the whispered rumors in the *shul* and suspects his father is concerned about their neighbor, Frau Mayer. After that first routine question and brief discussion about the Torah portion, Samuel continues walking, his mouth pressed in a determined line, his eyes staring straight ahead at nothing in particular, his mind clearly elsewhere. Josh starts to say something, but receives an eye signal from Izaak and swallows his words; both boys continue walking in silence next to their father.

Young Izaak's instincts are correct. Samuel's head is preoccupied with the whole Mayer *Geschichte;* he can't seem to shake the matter from his mind. Poor Frau Mayer, he thinks, to be so ill, and with such a husband at such a time. A group of male worshippers from the *shul* overtake the Gutman trio, but Samuel doesn't even register their Sabbath greetings until, belatedly, he turns as if in a daze. By then the group has disappeared into a side street, and their greetings echo hollowly in the cold, still air. As he and the boys plod along silently through the night, Samuel goes over and over in his mind the unusual events of that afternoon...

➶✦

He had just come home from the shop, was just getting ready to bathe and shave in readiness for the Sabbath, when Hannah said, "Samuel, with Frau Mayer in hospital, don't you think it would be a *mitzvah* to invite Herr Mayer and his children to join us for dinner tonight?" Samuel groaned inwardly, but had to concede that Hannah was right and, not for the first time, he was awed by her. "You know," she reminded him. "Herr Sulzbacher and the Pragers are coming too, so you won't have to talk to him too much. Why don't you just go next door and invite him in person."

And so, despite his deep inclination against such a distasteful errand, Samuel found himself knocking on the Mayers' door. He expected the maid to open the door but, to his surprise, Herr Mayer himself appeared.

Samuel was taken aback. Who was this gaunt, haggard man standing before him, unshaven, unkempt, barely recognizable? The thick glasses were unable to hide Herr Mayer's bloodshot eyes. It took Samuel several moments to remember the purpose of his errand. Who would have thought the man would take his wife's illness so hard?

"Please forgive this *Störung*," he finally managed. "I don't mean to disturb you, Herr Mayer. But, you see, my wife is naturally concerned, er, that is, we are both concerned about Frau Mayer and are wondering whether…"

It was as if Herr Mayer was trying to place him, as if he couldn't remember Samuel, the neighbor to whom he had complained so many times about the noisy children. Who was this person on his doorstep and where on earth had he seen him before?

"We were wondering whether," Samuel plodded on haltingly, "with Frau Mayer in, er that is, with Frau Mayer away, you and your children might, er, might like to join us for Shabbat dinner tonight." There, what a relief. He had got it out. But all the while he was speaking he felt as if he were spitting pebbles with every word.

Herr Mayer was still staring at him, clearly puzzled. Suddenly, the man collected himself and appeared to focus. "*Danke schön*," he said stiffly, in a voice that sought to mask the obvious stress he was under. His eyes continued to tell a different story. "Please convey my thanks to Frau Gutman," he said, "but my children are with their aunt and uncle for the Sabbath, and I am well taken care of." With a curt bow, and the usual almost imperceptible clicking of heels, he closed the door in Samuel's face...

><

So engrossed is Samuel in his thoughts that only belatedly does he realize that the street is unusually dark, that the streetlights are not functioning. He slows his pace, then brings the boys to a halt. He feels Josh's shoulder tremble beneath his grip. Samuel and Hannah thought the boy had outgrown his fear of the dark; they were so pleased when, a little more than a year ago, Josh announced that he no longer needed a nightlight in his room. But then the 'incidents' began, and with them Josh's fears of 'monsters' returned. And so had the nightlight.

A break in the clouds allows the moon to illuminate the three young men congregated up ahead under one of the broken streetlights. Even at a distance of several yards, it is obvious by their stance and clothing that they are not Jewish; certainly not congregants on their way home from *shul*. Suddenly alert, Samuel instinctively pulls the boys into the center of the street. He wishes for the headlights of a car to materialize, but there is no vehicle in sight.

"Papa," says Josh, his voice unsteady, "I'm frightened."

"Sh, *mein Schatz*," Samuel whispers. "Not so loud. Don't be frightened. Come boys," he says, tightening his arms around his sons' shoulders. "Let's turn around and go the long way home. Try to walk normally, don't run."

Beneath his arm, Samuel feels Josh's shoulder quivering. The boy has always been too ashamed to tell Samuel that sometimes, walking to and from *shul* on these dark Friday nights in the winter, he feels shadows pursuing him, just waiting for the right moment to pounce and snatch him away from his father's side; that he sees the bare branches of the trees as long, spindly tentacles, just waiting to grab him around the neck and choke the life out of him.

Hannah and Samuel have tried to shield the children as much as possible from the 'incidents'. Even the twins have asked questions about the '*keine Juden*' slogans they heard a small crowd shouting outside the park. Recently, '*keine Juden*' signs have appeared on benches inside the park. Other scrawled messages have appeared, not only on benches but on the walls surrounding the park, messages complaining of the 'dirty, stinking Jew pigs, the money-grubbers'. The twins are too young to read the signs or to understand what they mean, too young to understand why Liesl is no longer allowed to take them to the park, why they can no longer swing on their favorite swings, why they can no longer try, with gales of giggles, to dislodge each other from their favorite seesaw.

The three retrace their steps at a normal pace, with Samuel restraining the boys' urge to run. They pass the Borneplatz *shul* once more, then turn into a side street leading down to the river. Here the street lights are working, but the street is deserted of cars and pedestrians. Samuel feels rather than hears the boys' sighs of relief as they near the corner where the street meets the Ober Main Anlage overlooking the river. Suddenly, without warning, the thugs are upon them. "*Weglaufen, Schatzies. Schnell.* Run boys, run on home. You know the way. Run as quickly as you can," Samuel manages to shout, before he feels the first blow on his head and the world turns black.

＊＊

When he comes to, he is lying on the cold ground. He tries to open his eyes and perceives, as if through a thick vapor, the face of Herr Mayer hovering above him. Surely he must be dreaming? He tries to move but then lets out a groan as pain cuts through his head. He thinks he hears Herr Mayer's voice. What a strange dream he is having. But then he feels the cold, hard surface of the ground beneath him, and memory returns. "My boys," he groans, trying to rise. Waves of nausea and dizziness force him to lie down again, and he has to close his eyes once more. "My boys. Where are my boys?" Even as the words force themselves with great effort past his lips, he wonders if that is really Herr Mayer bending over him. What on earth can that man be doing here?

"They are all right, Herr Gutman. Do not concern yourself. My man has taken them home. That is, he drove alongside them as they ran home. He will be back at any moment to help you also. Don't make any sudden moves, but let's see if you are able to sit up. *Langsam, langsam.* Slowly now."

Despite the pain, Samuel can't help but be amazed at the change in Herr Mayer. He is a different man. It is as if a metamorphosis has taken place. Through the fog in his brain, Samuel recalls a book he read recently, a German translation of a novel by an Englishman about two characters, a Doktor Jekyll and a Herr Hyde, who, in reality, are one and the same man. Gone is the stiff, forbidding neighbor. The concern in Herr Mayer's voice is palpable. With his assistance, Samuel manages to sit up slowly; the nausea and dizziness begin to subside.

"*Was ist passiert?* What happened? We were walking home from *shul*, the boys and I, and then…"

"You were accosted by three of Hitler's finest *Jugend*," says Herr Mayer dryly. "Luckily, I was delayed in *shul* for a few minutes, and my driver, who drives alongside me in the car when I walk home on Friday nights, saw what was happening. He jumped out and chased those *Schlagers* away."

Samuel puts his hand to his head. "Now I remember," he groans. "We saw them standing under the broken street light, and turned around to avoid them."

"They must have broken the light on purpose," says Herr Mayer, "intent on just this kind of mischief. Fortunately, your hat cushioned the blows, Herr Gutman, and Hans's arrival prevented any further damage. But you should have a doctor look at you. By the way, here is your hat. We found it in the gutter."

"Thank you, Herr Mayer. It's lucky for us that you and your man were passing. Who knows what might have happened if you hadn't come along." Samuel fingers the back of his head gingerly; a lump is beginning to form. Despite Herr Mayer's protests, he struggles to his feet. "I'm feeling much better, Herr Mayer. Thanks to you and your driver. But my wife and my mother-in-law must be frantic, especially when the boys tell them what happened. I need to get home."

"Ah, here *kommt* Hans," says Herr Mayer, just as the Daimler's headlights swing around the corner. "He will drive behind us to make sure we get home safely." With Herr Mayer holding his arm for support, Samuel is able to walk the short distance to their apartment building.

"Herr Mayer," he says, "I cannot thank you enough. And I would like to thank your man also. He may have saved my life. If there is anything I can do for you…"

Herr Mayer doesn't let him finish. "Hans will drive off as soon as he sees us enter the building, so your thanks to him will have to wait until after the Sabbath. But," he continues, "there *is* something you can do for me, Herr Gutman. If it is not too late to change my mind, may I accept your kind invitation for dinner tonight. That is, if you think you are up to it. But perhaps you should go straight to bed."

"Not at all, not at all, Herr Mayer. We will be honored. We are expecting other guests from the building, the Pragers and Frau Sulzbacher, and Hannah will be so pleased that you can join us after all. And I'm feeling stronger by the minute. See," he shakes off Herr Mayer's supporting hand. "I'm perfectly capable of walking on my own." Which he demonstrates by almost running the last few steps to the entrance of the apartment building.

"It will just be me, Herr Gutman," Herr Mayer says. "As I told you earlier, my children are spending the Sabbath with their uncle and aunt.

Chapter 14

"*Willkomen*, Henrietta. *Willkomen*, my boy!" exclaims Onkel Heinz heartily, at the same time giving his niece a bear hug and his nephew an avuncular slap on the shoulders. "We're so happy your father allowed you to spend the Sabbath with us. Of course," he adds more somberly, "it goes without saying that we're not happy about the reason for your visit, but I'm sure your dear Mutti will make a complete recovery. In the meantime, we hope you will accompany Tanta Bertha and me after dinner to the Friday night service at the *Neue Synagoge*. It will not be anything like the service you are used to, but we will all pray together for your mother's recovery. After all," he adds with a chuckle, "we all pray to the *selben Gott, nicht wahr?*"

Tanta Bertha emerges from an inner room in the spacious apartment, and envelopes Henrietta in her arms. Fritz stands by awkwardly, head down. He feels wretched. He desperately does not want to be here; he would like to be with his Mutti, in her hospital room, but Herr Mayer had objected strenuously. "That is no place for you, Fritz. Especially on Shabbat. Mutti has not yet regained consciousness, she cannot hear you or see you. She wouldn't know that you are there. So there is just no point to it. Besides," he adds, "she has the best nurses around the clock, and they know how to reach me in case of emergency, *Gott behüte*."

This is the children's first visit on a Shabbat to Onkel Heinz and Tante Bertha's new apartment and, for Henrietta, there is nowhere else she would rather be, except on the ice rink with Otto. The furnishings alone make the visit worthwhile; the apartment is covered from end to end with mysterious Chinese screens, lanterns, bamboo chairs, black enameled chests, sideboards made of Japanese wood and adorned with intricate brass hardware. In addition, there is an assortment of foreign accessories, accumulated on various holidays abroad, strewn seemingly haphazardly on tables and mantels.

For Henrietta, this Friday night at Tanta Bertha and Onkel Heinz's is an exciting experience, a thrilling *Offenbarung*. A revelation. Here, there is no strict Sabbath observance. Even though Tanta Bertha lights Sabbath candles, she performs the ritual in a very perfunctory manner, without covering her eyes or waving her hands three times around the flames. She doesn't even mumble a blessing. The hand-washing before *Kiddush* has none of the cere-mony and strict adherence to ritual that Henrietta and Fritz are used to; in fact, there is a lot of laughing and talking going on and a casual splashing in the kitchen sink that passes for the ritual washing. Onkel Heinz makes hasty blessings over the wine and braided challah loaves, then excuses himself to answer the telephone. There is no singing of *Shalom Aleichem* or reciting of any of the passages they are used to hearing at their parents' Sabbath table, where Friday night dinners are somber occasions. At home, Henrietta and Fritz are each expected to give a short recital about something they have learned at school regarding that week's Torah portion. Fritz actually enjoys giving a weekly exposition on the week's *Sedrah*, despite the faces Henrietta makes at him during his halting recitations and the kicks she delivers under the table. Henrietta is never able to recite anything because she's never learned anything; she daydreams in class instead of listening to the teacher. For her the Friday night dinners at home are a weekly torment.

Onkel Heinz and Tanta Bertha have no reservation about switching lights on and off, or speaking on the telephone, actions that are forbidden on the Sabbath. In the children's home, only Inge is allowed to turn the lights on and off. For dinner, instead of the customary menu of fish, followed by *Nudel Suppe* and roast chicken, Tante Bertha serves a most un-Sabbatical *Sauerbraten* together with all kinds of unusual side dishes that are incredibly tasty but totally foreign to Henrietta and Fritz, such as *Apfel* dumplings, and sausages stuffed with something delicious but unidentifiable. There is an exotic air to the food and everything around them. Onkel Heinz urges them to drink a glass of the Riesling which, he says, he has been keeping for a special occasion. "And tonight, with you, our dear niece and nephew here in our new home for the Sabbath, this is indeed a special occasion, *nicht wahr?*"

The first glass is followed by a second, and then a third. Everything is elegantly casual, with Tante Bertha talking and laughing and making Henrietta laugh throughout the meal. Even Fritz is charmed, and every now and then he even manages to forget why he is here and not at the hospital with his Mutti. For a short time he even forgets that tonight is the holy Sabbath. But then, when they have finished eating, instead of reciting the prescribed *Grace after Meals*, Onkel Heinz walks across the room and selects a cigar from the silver humidor on the *Anrichte*. Then he leans his big bulk over the table, reaches for the candelabra and lights the cigar from one of the flames, puffing away as if this were just any ordinary day of the week. Tante Bertha brings in a plate containing sliced apples and a slab of cheese. Fritz cannot hide his shock. Onkel Heinz winks at him conspiratorially, and says: "My dear boy, don't look so shocked. With everything that is going on in the world, surely the Almighty has better things to do than worry about whether I eat a piece of cheese right after meat. And, by the way, take it from me, there is nothing better than the taste of a Pippin apple combined with a good chunk of aged Camembert, not to mention a post-prandial cigar to round off a *fantastische Mahlzeit* such as we have just eaten, thanks to your Tante Bertha." He leans back in his chair, puffing contentedly. "Incidentally, my boy, the cheese is kosher, as was everything else we have eaten. However," he adds dryly, "I'd just as soon you didn't say anything to my dear brother about any of this, he might not approve."

Tante Bertha finds this hilariously funny, and emits a gust of laughter. "You can certainly say that again, Heinzschen!" she says, throwing her head back and holding her stomach with one hand, while her other hand tries unsuccessfully to contain the snorts of amusement spilling from her mouth.

Onkel Heinz joins in the laughter, rests his cigar on his plate, and rises from his seat to saunter around the table and stand behind Tanta Bertha's chair. He puts his arms around his wife from behind, and she leans her head back against his body, her eyes closed, the trace of a smile still on her lips. Her husband bends his huge frame over her and gently begins to plant little kisses up and down her face. "Has *mein Liebling* perhaps drunk a little too much wine?" he asks fondly as he continues kissing her face and stroking her arms. "Of course, my little *Puppe* deserves it, after such a fantastic *Mahltzeit*. Don't you agree, children?" He gently lands little kisses on Tanta Bertha's closed eyes, and she raises her arms, pulls her husband's head down until it is parallel with her own, and returns his kisses with some of her own.

Fritz looks away in embarrassment, but Henrietta's eyes are transfixed. There is something positively hypnotic about the scene. Something so *erotisch*, a word whose meaning Henrietta has only recently learned. It was from Otto's lips that she first heard the word. "Your hair," Otto told her, threading his fingers through her blonde curls, "is so *erotisch*. It drives me mad." She was embarrassed to tell him that she didn't know what he was talking about. Later, in the privacy of her room, she looked the word up in the dictionary, and blushed. Just the idea of her hair being an instrument of eroticism made her heart beat faster.

Tanta Bertha is wearing an *elegantes Kleid* of rich oriental silk brocade embossed with a pattern of dragons and Chinese symbols in a profusion of muted color. The floor-length hostess gown complements her lithe figure and dark, glistening hair that is pulled up in an intricate, sophisticated French knot. Onkel Heinz continues slowly stroking his wife's arms with his thick but surprisingly gentle hands. Up and down, up and down they travel and the silk fabric of Tanta Bertha's sleeves rustles in rhythm with the journey of Onkel Heinz's hands.

The children have never before witnessed anything like this. They have never seen any display of affection between their parents, much less an overt one such as this. Onkel Heinz's apparent approval of Tante Bertha's tipsy state is a revelation in itself, a departure from everything they have been taught. Henrietta herself is beginning to feel a little light-headed. At home, she is never allowed more than a few sips of sweet *Kiddush* wine, and the thought of her mother ever being tipsy is even more outrageous than imagining her father under the influence of alcohol.

Henrietta can understand now why, when her aunt and uncle lived in the apartment next door, her father never allowed her and Fritz to visit them on the Sabbath, and even forbade them to eat in their house. "I don't believe they are strictly kosher," Herr Mayer said, "certainly not to our standards, and if I find out that you have been eating there I will forbid you to set foot in their apartment ever again." She realizes that were it not for the present emergency situation with their mother, she and Fritz would never have been allowed to spend the Sabbath here. For Fritz, who is punctilious in his prayers and devotion to ritual, this Friday night presents a painful dilemma. Only his shyness and innate good manners prevent him from complaining about the lack of strict Sabbath observance that he is used to.

After dinner, they walk together to the *Neue Synagoge* for the Friday night service. The neighborhood is more upscale than the one where the children live. The apartment buildings are grander, the pedestrians more fashionably dressed, the vehicles of the latest vintage. To be sure, there are swastika flags and anti-Semitic signs hanging from balconies and shop fronts, but the walk is without incident.

Soft strains of organ music fill the air as they approach. The brick exterior of the building is not overpowering, certainly nothing impressive. But the interior is quite the opposite, making the children gasp as they enter the sanctuary. There are rows upon rows of upholstered seats that go on and on forever, curving gently out to both sides of the chamber without the interruption of a *Bimah* in the center; everywhere they look there are dramatic splashes of yellow in the décor. The *Bimah* is situated at the front, just before the curtained *Aron*; to the right of the *Bimah*, partially hidden, sits a man manipulating the multi keyboards of a gigantic organ.

Attending prayer services after dinner is a departure from Fritz's usual routine. At Borneplatz, prayer services are held *before* dinner. Who ever heard of services *after* dinner? And what a service it is! Men and women sitting together, without a partition to separate them. A mixed choir of men and women singing to the accompaniment of the organist. How can this be allowed? Surely it is forbidden to play a musical instrument on the Sabbath? Surely this is more like a church than a synagogue? The men, including the rabbi, are bare-headed; there is not a hat or yarmulke in sight, no head coverings at all except for a fashionable array of feathered creations on the heads of the women. Onkel Heinz has removed his hat and signaled to Fritz to remove the cap he always wears when outdoors. Fritz knows he should get up and leave, but he is turned to stone, unable to move. He cannot offend his aunt and uncle and, besides, where would he go? It is much too far to return to his parents' apartment or to the hospital where his Mutti lies ill. He would not even know how to get there. He sits through the service with his bare head bowed, nervously crumpling his cap between his fingers. He is tempted to pick at his face but knows Tanta Bertha will immediately stop him as she did earlier, back at the apartment. He is miserable. He wonders if his father is aware of what goes on in this so called *shul*; would he have allowed them to spend Shabbat with Tanta Bertha and Onkel Heinz if he knew? Surely not.

Chapter 15

Friday night at the Gutmans. Two heavy, multi-branched silver candelabra blaze side by side on the *Anrichte* against one wall of the dining room. Hannah and Naomi are setting the table with the best Rosenthal china, and the silver *Besteck* and Swedish crystal that Hannah and Samuel received almost twenty years ago as wedding gifts. After lighting the candles in one of the candelabra, Hannah's mother, Frau Fleissig, retires to her room to rest, something she has been doing quite often recently with the excuse that she is *ermudend* as a result of not having slept well the previous night. Hannah is sure that her mother's arthritic hip has been bothering her; her limp has become more pronounced, and sometimes, when Hannah passes the closed door of her bedroom, she hears her moaning. When Hannah questions her, Frau Fleissig tells her there is nothing wrong, that Hannah is imaging things, that she must stop fussing over her. The doctors insist there is nothing they can do for her. Hannah also suspects that her mother, who remembers all too well the anti-Semitism that prompted her family to flee Poland when Hannah was a little girl, has become depressed and worried ever since the new Chancellor was elected in 1933. With each 'incident' she has become more and more agitated, her nights robbed of sleep.

Liesl is in the twins' room at the far end of the apartment, with muffled sounds of the nightly tug-of-war emanating from that direction as she does battle to get them dressed for dinner after their bath.

When lighting her seven-pronged candelabra, Hannah invokes a special prayer for Frau Mayer. After her marriage, she began lighting the customary two candles on Friday nights. Then, with the birth of each of the five children, another candle was added, so that now there are a total of seven. She closes her eyes and encircles the flames three times with her hands, then utters the prescribed blessing. "Almighty God," she adds, "I beseech you to have mercy on my dear friend Marga Mayer. Whatever You have in store for her, I beg of You not to let her suffer."

Hannah and Naomi have almost finished the task they enjoy doing together every Friday night; the table is gleaming, the crystal stemware sending off little shoots of blue lightening, resembling the glitter of diamonds. The whole apartment is suffused with the delicious aroma of chicken *Suppe mit Knödel*, one of Frau Fleissig's specialties, a dish that is a particular favorite with all the Gutmans. Naomi has just begun telling her mother how exciting the first class in Shakespeare was, when they hear a pounding at the door. Hannah is immediately alarmed; she knows it cannot be Samuel for he carries a key. She hurries to open the door, and Izaak and Josh tumble in with tearstained, terror-filled faces. Josh throws himself into his mother's arms, and bursts into sobs. She is unable to make head or tail of what they are saying; they are completely incoherent. All she can do is hold them both against her and try to keep her voice from shaking, as she asks, "Where is your father, boys, what has happened to him?" Josh is unable to stop crying and it is several more moments before Izaak is able to relate what has happened. "Herr Mayer was there," he is finally able to get out. "He and his driver were passing by and they rescued us."

"Herr Mayer…?" She continues clasping both her sons to her, though it is difficult to know who is holding on tighter, the boys or Hannah. Her mind is in a frenzy of fear and incomprehension. Her first instinct is to go out and find Samuel, but Josh is crushing her so firmly that even if she wanted to she cannot pry him loose. "Sh, sh," she says repeatedly."Sh, sh." By the greatest of will, she succeeds in suppressing the tremor in her voice; she knows she must not show the boys how terrified she is. She strokes Josh's head. "There,

there. As long as you are all safe, that's all that matters." Naomi emerges from the dining room to see what the commotion is all about, and precisely at the same moment, in waltzes Samuel through the still open door, looking as if nothing untoward has occurred; only the dirty smudges on his face, a rip in the front of his overcoat and the crooked angle of his now misshapen hat give any clue as to what has happened.

And right behind him is their impeccably clad neighbor, Herr Gustav Mayer.

Hannah's relief on seeing her husband is so great that she doesn't immediately register Herr Mayer's presence. As soon as they see their father, both boys uncoil their arms from around their mother and throw themselves onto him, almost throwing him off balance. Hannah is unable to speak; her legs have turned to jelly. She sits down heavily on a nearby chair and covers her mouth with her hands to cut off the sobs gathering in her throat. Samuel gently pushes the boys from him, wanting to go to his wife, but before he can reach her, Naomi jumps on him as if she hasn't seen her father for at least a year.

He kisses his daughter, whispers reassuring words in her ear, then puts her aside, so he can finally get to Hannah. "*Schatzilein*, please. Nothing happened. I'm fine. The boys are fine. *Ich bitte dich*. I beg you not to make a fuss." Tenderly, he removes Hannah's hands from her face. "Come, *mein Schatz*" he says, pulling her up into his arms. "I'm sure you don't want to make your mother more nervous than she is already, and we certainly don't want the little ones asking questions, *nicht wahr*? He turns around, keeping Hannah firmly at his side. "*Schatzie*," he says, "see, we have an unexpected but very welcome guest."

Hannah manages to compose herself and turns to Herr Mayer apologetically, proffering her hand. "Herr Mayer," she says, "please excuse my bad manners. Samuel and I are delighted and honored to have you join us for Shabbat dinner, but more than that, how can I ever thank you for what you have done, for saving my husband's..." She cannot go on. Herr Mayer gives his little Teutonic bow. "My dear Frau Gutman," he says in his usual wooden manner, but with unusual gentleness, "let us not exaggerate. It was purely a matter of

Glück, mere chance that my driver and I happened to be passing at that precise moment." He doesn't give Hannah the opportunity to protest further, and changes the subject. "On my part, I thank you for your kind invitation and for being such a, er, such a good friend to Frau Mayer." Herr Mayer's words are hesitant; he is obviously uncomfortable and unaccustomed to expressing such personal sentiments. "I understand you, er, visited Frau Mayer in the hospital yesterday morning and brought much needed nourishment for my poor children. So it is *I* who must be thanking *you*." Now Hannah understands Herr Mayer's change of heart, why he decided belatedly to accept their dinner invitation, why his whole manner has changed. "It was nothing," she says, "absolutely *nichts*, the least I could do. I just pray that Frau Mayer will make a complete recovery." Herr Mayer merely inclines his head and says no more. "*Bitte*," says Hannah, and leads Herr Mayer into the drawing room, not realizing how his face has tightened at that word, how she has unwittingly reminded him of his recent meeting in Berlin.

Izaak and Josh are now sitting on the couch, their sister Naomi between them. From the way the boys are slumped, with their heads down, it is clear that they have not yet recovered from their experience. Naomi has one arm protectively around each of her brothers. Upon seeing Herr Mayer enter the room she jumps up, and nudges her brothers to do the same. After giving the children his slight bow and a Shabbat greeting, Herr Mayer addresses Naomi: "I am sure Henrietta misses you and would have liked to be here tonight." He then turns to the boys, "I believe you boys know my son, Fritz. You go to the same school, *nicht wahr?*" Herr Mayer's awkward attempt at small talk with the children is one-sided. The boys are still shell-shocked, unable to speak. Herr Mayer continues with stilted comments about the weather, and compliments the boys on their singing in the *shul* choir.

Hannah's reaction mirrors Samuel's. She cannot believe this is the same man whom she has so disliked for all these months. The change is astonishing.

Frau Sulzbacher and the Pragers arrive together. These neighbors are often guests of the Gutmans for Shabbat meals. The Pragers always accompany Frau

Sulzbacher on these occasions so that she does not have to climb up and down the stairs alone. Samuel emerges from the bedroom in a fresh shirt and suit, smiling his usual good-natured smile. He shakes hands with the Pragers and Frau Sulzbacher. Turning to Naomi, he says, "Be so good as to tell your grandmother that Frau Sulzbacher has arrived." The two elderly widows have become good friends. When Frau Fleissig emerges from her room, the two women immediately retire to one of the couches to exchange the latest *Nachtrichten*, and give each other a detailed description of their aches and pains. Liesl brings the twins in. Their faces have been scrubbed and shine like the faces of two cherubs, their golden curls tamed and still slightly damp from the bath. They appear unusually shy, probably intimidated by Herr Mayer's presence. Hannah whispers to Naomi, bidding her to lay an extra setting at the table for Herr Mayer. "Place him to Papa's right," she tells her.

The Pragers live in the apartment directly beneath the Gutmans, (but have never complained of the Gutman children's unruliness, perhaps because they are both somewhat hard of hearing). They are a friendly couple, both retired. Frau Prager used to teach French at the Lyzeum, and enjoys speaking to Naomi about her studies; her husband, Herr Doktor Prager, a civil engineer, immediately attempts to engage Herr Mayer in conversation about the latest infrastructure developments, asking Herr Mayer if EmEm is supplying any materials to the building authorities. He seems impervious to Herr Mayer's reluctance to discuss 'business'. But, by the time they all troop into the dining room, everyone is in a *gemütlich* mood. Even Izaak and Josh have loosened up, and manage to wring out an occasional smile.

After the Kiddush and ritual washing, Samuel summons each of his children to him by turn, placing his hands on their heads as he recites the priestly blessing for the boys, and the special blessing for Naomi, asking the Almighty to allow her to grow to emulate her four biblical foremothers, Sarah, Rebecca, Rachel and Leah. The twins squirm beneath their father's hands, not able to stand still for a moment, but during the meal they behave unusually well, and by the time Hannah and Liesl bring in the soup, Samuel has begun to relax.

Helped also by a generous shot of *Schnapps*, he is even able to ignore the intermittent throbbing in the lump at the back of his head. He realizes that he need not have had reservations about Herr Mayer, though he continues to be astonished by the change in the man. It is impossible to fathom that this is the same man who stood stiffly on his doorstep so many times over the last few months complaining about the noise. To be sure, every now and then, he senses that Herr Mayer's mind is elsewhere, that he is not really listening to the conversations swirling around him, which is not surprising considering the man's wife lies unconscious in hospital. But all in all, though Samuel would not go as far as to say that Herr Mayer has acquired charm, the man is being unexpectedly amiable. Samuel coaxes the boys to lead the guests in one of the Sabbath *Lieder,* exalting the Almighty. Everyone has the good sense to avoid talking about tonight's 'incident'; only Herr Prager mutters something under his breath about the "*schändlich* times we are living in", but in the generally uplifting atmosphere of the evening, the remark goes unheard or ignored.

Chapter 16

⇒⋲⇐

Frau Mayer's funeral takes place at the Borneplatz Friedhof, the Jewish cemetery, on a blustery, rainy day in March. Her brother, Manfred Kahn, her only
close blood relative, is unable to attend; he and his family have been living in
America for years. Herr Mayer notified Herr Kahn as soon as Frau Mayer's
terminal condition was known, but it was impossible for him to undertake the
voyage in time. The poor woman lingered in a moribund vegetative state for
several days before slipping away as unobtrusively as she had lived, with only
a young night nurse to witness her last breath.

Herr Mayer stands at the freshly dug gravesite, with Henrietta and Fritz
flanking him. Fritz cannot stop sobbing despite the comfort of his father's
arm around his shoulders. Herr Mayer does nothing to discourage Fritz's
tears. Henrietta stares unblinkingly and dry-eyed into the distance, as if these
proceedings have nothing to do with her. Herr Mayer tries to put his other
arm around her shoulders, but she immediately and disdainfully shrugs it off.
Despite the inclement weather, there is a commanding outpouring of respect
from the members of the Borneplatz congregation. Many of Herr Mayer's
business colleagues and customers have also come to pay their respects,
swelling the crowd clustered around the gaping hole in the ground and the
mound of earth and shovel waiting beside it. The wind has made short order
of the sea of black umbrellas. Those seeking shelter from the rain have found

it an exercise in futility to try and open their umbrellas; the wind has a mind of its own and turns the umbrellas every which way before they can be completely opened, in some cases, snatching them from their owner's grasp.

Herr Mayer's chauffeur, Hans, has the same problem with the large *Schirm* with which he is attempting to shield his employer and the Mayer children. The wind keeps whipping the umbrella inside out, and Hans does battle just trying to hold on to the handle. Finally, Herr Mayer turns to him and indicates, with a touch of irritation, that there is just no point to it, that Hans is better off closing it.

One part of Herr Mayer's mind is numb; he is barely conscious of the reason for his presence here. He can barely grasp that it is his wife who is being buried, that it is his wife's funeral he is attending. Today is the Fast of Esther, the day before the festival of Purim. He is fasting, as is his custom on this day, but feels no desire for any nourishment. He cannot absorb the platitudes mouthed by Rabbi Gutfreund, most of which are, at any rate, carried away on the wind before anyone can hear them. "…a woman of valor…. above rubies… devoted *Frau*…mother…a tragedy…so *traurig*…" The rabbi's instructions to him before they entered the hearse have also not fully sunk in. "Even though it is Purim tomorrow," said the rabbi, "which, as you know, is normally an occasion for rejoicing, you are not absolved from the rituals of mourning, from sitting *shiva*. *Jedoch*, nevertheless, we do not encourage condolence visits on Purim." At least, that is what he thinks the rabbi said.

Herr Mayer is past grieving. His grieving started and ended at precisely the same moment, ten days ago, when Doktor Graff told him of his wife's fatal condition. In the interim, he has become accustomed to her absence in his daily life. Were he given to introspection, he might wonder and be bothered by how little he misses her. It is as if her departure has barely made a ripple, as if she wafted, ghostlike, into his life, and then quietly wafted out of it.

By contrast, a part of Herr Mayer's mind is sharply alert and conscious of every slight movement, both near him and at the periphery of his vision. In particular, he has noticed the two men, clearly not Jewish, clearly not belonging to the funeral, standing some distance away at the edge of the crowd. They are both wearing the ubiquitous, sinister *Hakenkreuz* armbands. Though his eyesight is far from perfect despite the corrective lenses, even at this distance the black and white symbol with its red border sends a chilling message; he believes them to be the same two men he noticed standing near the apartment building the night of the 'incident', when he escorted an injured Samuel Gutman home. They may also be the same two men who have recently taken up positions across from EmEm's offices. Of course, he cannot swear to it, and he might be mistaken; quite possibly he is imagining things, quite possibly he is now in a permanent state of paranoia after the events in Berlin. But he doesn't think so.

It is clear to Herr Mayer that he is being watched.

He has fulfilled the first order on the list. A small consignment consisting of several cases of the new rifle that is one of EmEm's staples. As instructed, once the order was shipped, he rang the local telephone number provided at the bottom of the list. An unrecognizable male voice answered and Herr Mayer merely uttered the one word he was permitted: *Vershifft*. Shipped. He suspects this was a trial order, to see if he will obey the instructions given to him. The address listed for the customer was in a remote corner of Austria. Weber, his shipping manager, who has been with EmEm for longer than Herr Mayer can remember, raised his eyebrows, and began to question the new hinterland destination. Herr Mayer curtly instructed the poor man, "Just see to it," before turning quickly away. He has been avoiding telephone calls and requests for a meeting from Hausmann, EmEm's comptroller; he knows he can't evade him forever, but has not yet formulated a rational response to the complaints and questions he expects to receive from that quarter.

As he watches the coffin containing his wife being lowered into the ground, Herr Mayer suddenly feels a sliver of light edging its way into his head. Over the last few days different thoughts and ideas have swirled and struggled in his mind, each of them turned over and examined from every angle before being discarded. But, now, here in this cemetery, in the most unlikely of places and on the most unusual of days, it comes to him. The something that he must do.

It is imperative, he realizes, that he takes someone into his confidence. Something his father, who fiercely guarded his privacy, always discouraged. *It is* sehr wichtig, *very important that you work through your problems on your own,* was his mantra. "Surely you remember," he recalls his poetry-loving father saying, "*He travels fastest who travels alone.*"

And yet.

If only there was someone he could talk to, someone with a cool head to give him sound advice, someone like his late father. Never has he felt the loss of his father as keenly as he does at this moment. A man for whom decision-making came easily, as a matter of course, a man who was upright and scrupulously honest in all his dealings, who saw things simply, in terms of black and white, right and wrong. But today's problems are not ones his father could have foreseen, extraordinary circumstances his father, thankfully, did not have to face, did not live to see. Of course, there were anti-Semitic incidents even in his father's day, but there were no Nazis, no Chancellor named Adolf Hitler making outrageous demands with menacing threats, forcing impossible decisions on him. What would his father have done in these times, faced with these events?

Instinctively, he is convinced that he must take someone into his confidence. But who? Whom can he trust? And, if all his movements are being watched, as he suspects, how can he confide in anyone without Hitler's henchmen finding out?

It is only natural for him to consider his brother, Heinz, the lawyer, but he dismisses the thought before it can take root. He believes he can trust his brother, that is not the question; it is his sister-in-law Bertha who is the *Fragenzeichen.* He is not sure what it is about her that has given him misgivings from the very first moment he set eyes on her, but there it is, an unknown *Etwas,* an unknown something he cannot put his finger on. A question mark.

Unbidden, he thinks with wry envy of his Catholic employees who attend church regularly and unburden themselves in the confessional, and for a few moments he actually considers taking Rabbi Gutfreund into his confidence, momentarily forgetting that he is not partial to the man. When speaking to Herr Mayer the rabbi assumes an effusive, ingratiating, almost simpering manner that only arouses Herr Mayer's contempt. It is as if, by flattering him, the rabbi will obtain a larger donation for the synagogue. Even in the rabbi's sermons, Herr Mayer senses a kind of unctuousness that he finds undignified. And the irony of it is that it was essentially because of Herr Mayer that the rabbi was engaged by Borneplatz.

Some of the younger members of the *shul* had wanted a different candidate, a young rabbi who had trained in a seminary in Switzerland and had some revolutionary ideas about Jewish ritual and observance. On top of that, the young rabbi was clean-shaven. Herr Mayer and some of the other long-time members had put their collective foot down. As Doktor Graff said, "A prestigious synagogue like Borneplatz cannot have a beardless rabbi at its helm. If he dispenses with a beard, who knows what else he will dispense with? Personally, I want my rabbi to be more stringent in observance than I am." To which another committee member added the famous old German adage: *The passengers may get drunk but the coachman must remain sober.*

Rabbi Gutfreund came to Herr Mayer's attention through a business acquaintance, a member of the rabbi's prior congregation in a small *shul* on the outskirts of Berlin. He and other members of that synagogue had praised him to the skies.

Since then, Herr Mayer has come to believe privately, with no small amount of cynicism, that those former congregants wanted nothing more than to be rid of their rabbi, and were only too happy to relocate him to Borneplatz.

No. Herr Mayer decides emphatically, he cannot possibly confide in Rabbi Gutfreund, and dismisses him out of hand.

He, Gustav Mayer, a man who makes both monumental and insignificant business decisions on a daily basis, as did his father before him, with barely a moment's vacillation, now finds his mind reeling with indecision. Most immediate is the question of how he will be able to get through the prescribed seven days of mourning without going to his office. The list calls for another shipment, a more substantial one than the first, to be assembled and shipped before the end of the week. He has telephoned Weber, has given instructions, instructions that must seem puzzling, if not outright nonsensical to his staff. He has again provided a shipping address, this time another unheard of destination in an even more remote area, a corner of Bavaria that he hadn't known existed and had to look up on a map. He can only hope his employees ascribe his strange behavior to his wife's death, that he has become temporarily unhinged as a result. He has to assume his instructions will be obeyed to the letter, and that the shipment will go out on time so that he can once again ring the telephone number on the list, and utter the prescribed word. But what of the consequences if the list's instructions are not scrupulously obeyed, if, for example, there is a delay in assembling the order or a delay in delivery, as sometimes happens to shipments en route, despite all good intentions? The consequences of unforeseen problems with any of the shipments is something he cannot bear to contemplate.

There are subsequent items on the list with which he is not familiar, items which EmEm has never manufactured before, but for which Herr Mayer knows he must be prepared. He has already spoken to Becker, his plant manager, and instructed him to order and assemble the necessary raw materials. The man's reaction over the telephone was difficult to gauge precisely, but it was impossible not to detect the uncertainty in his voice as he took down the details Herr Mayer gave him.

Standing there, in the wind and rain, at his wife's graveside, listening to the drone of the rabbi's voice fading in and out, it suddenly comes to him. That there is only one person he can trust. He doesn't know why he is so sure, but instinctively, he knows he is right.

Yet, the nagging question still remains: does he have the right, is it *moralisch* to involve someone else? Once again, he wonders what his father would have done. Even as he and Fritz intone the mourner's Kaddish at the conclusion of the funeral service, Herr Mayer continues to wonder. But his wondering leaves him no wiser.

Chapter 17

⤛⤜

Henrietta is in a foul mood. It is bad enough that yesterday, on the Fast of Esther, her father didn't allow her to put anything into her mouth, and even went so far as to lock the door of the food pantry so that she almost died of starvation, but even worse, today, on Purim, she is forced to sit on a low stool next to her father and idiot brother. Except for Inge, who is busy in the kitchen, the three of them are alone in the apartment. There is an enormous rip at the shoulder of Henrietta's green jumper. The jumper was one of her favorites and she hadn't anticipated that the rabbi, waving a large pair of scissors in her face, would butcher it at the cemetery; it all happened so quickly, it was over before she was aware it had happened. "This is ridiculous," she fumes, not for the first time. "Absolutely *lächerlich*. It's not as if anyone is going to visit us today. You heard what the rabbi said, it's Purim, and nobody makes *shiva* calls on Purim. For heaven's sake, why can't I go to my room?" She doesn't add: *And listen to my favorite record while I dream of Otto.*

Herr Mayer is losing patience. "Henrietta, this is the last time I'm going to say it. Your mother is dead. *Todt*, do you understand? And the least you can do is show her the kind of respect now she is gone that you didn't show her while she was alive. Besides," he adds, "Rabbi Gutfreund will be here at any moment to give us a private reading of *Megillat Esther*. This is an enormous honor and I insist you remain here for that."

Henrietta grimaces, gets up from her stool and stamps her feet in annoyance, but to Herr Mayer's relief, only rolls her eyes and doesn't answer back. Instead, she begins to stride up and down the length of the room much as she did in her mother's hospital room a few days earlier. She is fuming. If her father only knew what she had planned for today, how she had stashed away in the back of her wardrobe the Purim costume, her little joke, that she had secretly purchased with her *Taschengeld*. She had not needed to involve Naomi; Tante Bertha had helped her. Henrietta had told her aunt that she needed a costume for a Purim party at school, and her aunt had taken her to a little shop in her *westlich* neighborhood. Henrietta had planned to bring it with her to the rink and change there. To surprise Otto.

So many times has she gone over it in her imagination: She walks slowly out of the dressing room on the points of her skates, wearing the little white, shimmering skirt and tight-fitting top to match, and on her legs, above the white skates, the sheer white stockings with black seams that make her legs look so ... so long and shapely, almost as shapely as the legs of that film actress Otto admires so much, Marlena something or other. And when he notices the glittering tiara buried in her hair, the hair that he says drives him so crazy... Oh, the expression that comes over his face, the way his eyes widen when he sees her. Just thinking of it makes her heart beat faster and her knees turn to rubber.

All her plans have been thwarted by her mother's death. She knows she should be sad, and of course she *is* sad; she certainly didn't wish for Mutti to die. She has tried to cry, but the tears refuse to come. She has tried to picture her mother, both when she was alive and healthy, and then recently, how she looked when she lay in the metal hospital bed, attached to a web of tubes. She has stared and stared at the photograph that Herr Mayer has placed prominently on the mantel. In it her mother is young and attractive and smiling into the camera. She has told herself that if she concentrates hard on this image she will be able to cry. But it is no use. Inevitably, her mind wanders elsewhere, to another place and another image that she cannot, and has no wish to dispel.

The mirrors in this room and the rest of the apartment have been covered with sheets, as is customary in a Jewish house of mourning. Fritz has barely moved from his stool except once to visit the washroom. He sits absolutely still, head down, not even scratching at his pimples; it is as if he has forgotten their existence. Or perhaps he is listening to an inner voice, the echo of his Mutti's voice, telling him tenderly to leave his face alone. Every now and then he fingers the jagged tear the rabbi made in the lapel of his jacket, slowly stroking it up and down as if drawing some measure of comfort from the act of mutilation, from the act of *keryah*, the tearing of garments worn by the bereaved.

Inge enters the room bearing a tray of food which she deposits silently on a table near the three stools. She is a bosomy, hefty woman, of German peasant stock, somewhere in her late forties. Her devotion to Marga Mayer was so complete, that she feels the loss as acutely as any member of the Mayer family. The minute she walks into the room, the tears that have all morning been springing up in her eyes, begin to flow down her ample cheeks. After setting her tray down she rushes back into the kitchen, throwing her apron over her face to smother the tears and sounds forming in her throat.

Henrietta immediately turns in mid-stride and races for the food. She is the only one of the three who has any appetite. "Come, my boy," says Herr Mayer to Fritz. "You must eat something. You fasted yesterday, but today is Purim, and it's a *mitzvah* to eat on Purim, *nicht wahr?* Come, I know Mutti would not want you to starve yourself." Fritz bestirs himself slowly, as if coming out of a trance, and walks over to the table. "How about you, Vati? What can I get for you?" Herr Mayer turns away; something in him cannot bear for Fritz to see how much he is affected by his offer. He, who has always considered Fritz's gentleness to be a maudlin manifestation of effeminacy, now, belatedly, realizes that he has misjudged his son. What he has criticized as a *Waschlappen* tendency in the boy is actually nothing less than a kind, considerate nature. Frau Mayer was right. Fritz is a sensitive boy. Without a doubt, he is his mother's son.

He accepts the plate of food from Fritz without looking at it, and gets up from his stool to walk over to the window. The wind of the night before has died down and the sun is struggling through the clouds, a harbinger of spring. The heavy drapes are tied back, and through the white lace curtains that cover the panes, he has an unobstructed view of the road and the river beyond it. In past years, on the Purim holiday, the streets below were filled with Jewish parents leading Jewish children dressed in an array of colorful costumes: little Mordecais and Hamans and Esthers wearing tricornered hats and gauzy pastel skirts and glittering paper crowns, carrying baskets of treats to exchange with neighbors and deliver to the poor. But since the horrific book burnings three years ago, the streets below have been empty of color on this holiday, empty of Jewish children.

For the first time since her death, the image of his wife infiltrates Herr Mayer's mind suddenly and easily, without any effort on his part. She is in the kitchen with Inge; the two of them are baking *Hamentaschen*, little triangular pastries filled with marmalade and other confections that will be sent together with an assortment of delicacies to their friends and neighbors to fulfill one of the obligations of the Purim holiday. A protective scarf envelops Frau Mayer's hair; she is rolling out dough with a *Teigrolle*, her face flushed from exertion and the heat of the oven, her nose flecked with flour. *Ach*, he thinks with surprise, how lovely, how *schön* she looks…

His musings are interrupted by the sight of the two men across the road, leaning against a parapet of the river's embankment. It is impossible for Herr Mayer not to notice them. Their features are indistinct at this distance, but there is no mistaking the armbands. They appear to be the same two men who attended the funeral, perhaps the same two men who daily take up positions across from his office. What would Frau Mayer have made of all this, he wonders for the first time. Would he have been able to talk to her about it? No, he decides, *sicher nicht*. Definitely not. From the beginning of their marriage, he had followed his father's advice and example. He can still hear his father's words: *A man's domain is his business; his wife's domain is the house and the children. And the two must never intersect.*

So deep is he in thought, that he fails to hear the door bell. Inge puts her head around the door to announce the arrival of the *Herr Rabbiner*.

"Henrietta. Fritz. Put your plates away *sofort*, and sit down," he says, ignoring Henrietta's look of disgust. "Rabbi Gutfreund is here to read *Megillat Esther* for us."

Chapter 18

In the Borneplatz synagogue, the atmosphere is subdued. The doors and windows have been securely locked and sealed; when the name 'Haman' leaves the cantor's lips, it is muffled from the ears of passersby. Wicked Haman, who plotted to exterminate the Jews of Persia, has become the personification of every evil that has befallen the Jews over the millennia of their existence, and never more so than in today's Germany. The racket created by the whirling *graggers*, the noisemakers, combined with the stomping of hundreds of feet and shouts of derision at each invocation of Haman's name can easily be misinterpreted by outsiders as being directed at the new Chancellor who has, from the start, and in his infamous book *Mein Kampf*, never hidden his feelings about *das Judische Volk*. And indeed, it would not be surprising if some members of the congregation, *sotto voce*, substitute the name of Adolf Hitler for that of Haman.

The annual Purim *Spiel*, which traditionally lampooned the Borneplatz clergy and prominent members of the community, has not been staged for several years. A general air of caution pervades, particularly in the Orthodox community, where the children's usual boisterousness on this annual holiday has to be restrained with constant warnings and shushing, and fingers held to parents' lips.

And where the grownups wait, with bated breath, for the next shoe to drop.

Chapter 19

⇒⇐

The Gutman apartment is pleasantly quiet; the children are either asleep, or at least as in the case of Naomi, reading in bed. Oma Fleissig excused herself early in the evening to lie down. Her hip is acting up, and the death of Frau Mayer has affected her deeply and unexpectedly. Hannah and Samuel are in their bedroom, preparing for bed.

Samuel is sitting on one of the beds in the act of removing his shoes. "*Schatzie,*" he says, "we need to talk." Hannah wrenches the scarf from her head, letting an abundance of blonde waves tumble down around her shoulders.

"How beautiful you are, *mein Schatz,*" says Samuel, taking her hand and pulling her down next to him. "You don't look a day older than the day I met you. In fact, to me you are even more beautiful today than you were on our wedding day. Though it doesn't seem possible."

"Oh you, you're such a flatterer," laughs Hannah, placing her head on his shoulder. "What is it you wanted to talk about?"

The Gutman bedroom contains two beds divided by a nightstand, just as the Mayers' bedroom does. But there the similarity ends. Where the Mayers' bedroom is filled with gloomy, heavy furniture and draperies, here there is all light and color, cheerful chintzy fabrics covered with a profusion of flowers and greenery. And though there are two beds, as is usual in an Orthodox Jewish marriage, most nights finds their owners sleeping together in one bed, entangled in each other's arms.

"I've hesitated to tell you, because I didn't want to upset you. But I feel I must." Hannah draws back in alarm. "What is it, what has happened? Are you ill? Is it one of the children?"

"No, no. *Gott sei dank Schatzie*, it has nothing to do with the children. And I am quite well." He reaches for her hand once more. "Today, for the second time, they threw bricks through the front windows of the shop. It's all boarded up now. I didn't think there was any point in replacing the glass again and again."

Hannah doesn't have to ask who 'they' are. She knows only too well. " B-but, this is terrible. Isn't there a night watchman, I thought…"

"Yes, there was. There was also someone guarding the entrance to the shop during the day. But they were useless. Less than useless. There were just too many of… of them. Two nights ago, they beat the watchman almost to death; the poor man is in a coma in hospital and the doctors don't know if he will recover. And today, the day guard had the good sense to run away when he saw them coming. Imagine, in broad daylight."

"Samuel," she says, clutching his hand, "I had no idea things are that bad. You say this is the second time, but you never said a word."

"I was hoping things would get better, that there would be no need to worry you, especially when I know how concerned you are about your mother."

"Oh, Samuel, you are always trying to protect me, and I know you mean well, but I'm not a child, and we promised long ago that we wouldn't have secrets from each other."

"I know, I know, *Schatzie*, I'm sorry. My mistake. Please forgive me."

"Of course I forgive you, but there must be something you can do. What about the *Politzei*? Surely you notified the *Politzei*."

"Ah, yes, the *Politzei*," says Samuel bitterly, "Frankfurt's finest. Don't you understand, *Schatzie*, the police look the other way. They may even be in league with the Brownshirts. That's why the hooligans can get away with what they're doing *ungestraft*, with impunity. At the very least the police are so afraid of their own necks that they've become impotent."

"Oh, Samuel. What can be done? This is just *furchtbar.*"

For a minute or two husband and wife sit on the edge of the bed, hand in hand, not speaking, each deep in thought, each brow furrowed with worry.

"Listen *Schatzie.* Do you remember I told you a couple of years ago that Herr Schiller from the bank made me an offer to purchase *Chez Gutman*?"

"Yes, of course I do, and I remember how we laughed about it because it was so ridiculous. And how you said you could never sell your father's creation, his 'third child'."

"Well," says Samuel, "things are a lot different today than they were then. This is not easy for me to say, *Schatzie*, but I've decided it's time to sell *Chez Gutman* after all."

"Oh Samuel! How terrible! I know how much the shop means to you. Surely this ...this situation can't go on..."

Samuel interrupts her. "Gerhardt Schiller has renewed his offer. In fact he's been after me for months, and of course now he's offering much less than he did originally, but I feel I have to accept. That I have no choice. I don't think Adolf Hitler is going away, *Schatzie*. Nor are his Brownshirts. In fact, I think things will get worse before they get better. I wouldn't be surprised," he adds, "if Schiller might not be behind the vandalism, even if indirectly, to force my hand. Of course, I can't prove it, but I've always suspected him of being a rabid anti-Semite, and the last time I visited his office he was wearing a swastika armband, which means he is now officially a Nazi party member and doesn't even try to hide it."

"Oh Samuel," Hannah says again. "I don't know what to say. I'm so, so sorry."

"I know *Schatzie*. Nobody is more sorry than I am. *Chez Gutman* meant so much to my father, but I know he would understand. After all, he left Odessa for much less reason, gave up a flourishing grain business to start all over again here in Frankfurt. Where he thought we would all be safe. How shocked he would be by this state of affairs. Yet, I know deep in my heart, without any doubt at all, that he would understand and support my decision. But, *Schatzie*, there's more." Samuel tightens his grip on her hand. "I don't really know how to say this and I know you won't want to hear it. But I think it's time we moved."

"Move? From this apartment? B-but Samuel, we just moved in. We haven't even lived here for one year. I don't feel we are even properly settled yet..."

"No. Not just from this apartment, *Schatzie*." Samuel's voice is so low, almost a whisper; Hannah can barely hear him. He cannot bear to look her in the face. "From Frankfurt," he says. "From Germany."

Hannah looks at him askance. "Samuel! You can't be serious! From Germany? Where would we go?" She jumps up in agitation, snatching her hand from his. "No, no. I don't believe you! You're overreacting. These incidents are very upsetting. I know. But they can't go on forever. They're going to stop eventually, they have to, everyone knows that." She strides to the other side of the room, turns and looks back at Samuel, who remains sitting on the edge of the bed, unmoving, his head bowed in an attitude of utter misery.

Hannah is alarmed. She has never seen her husband like this. So serious. So wretched. So dejected. Her Samuel, who is always cheerful and optimistic, always making jokes. She walks back and sits beside him once more, putting her arm around his neck and laying her head on his shoulder. "Samuel, I can't bear to see you like this. That Friday night incident a few weeks ago, and now the shop. It's affected you more than I realized."

Samuel raises his head and turns to Hannah, taking her in his arms and stroking her hair. "*Schatzie*. I don't want to alarm you, but at the same time I am keeping my promise to share everything with you. Much as I would like to shield you from all this...*Ärger*...from all this unpleasantness, I think it's time I tell you some of things that are going on. These are not things you will hear on the wireless or read in the paper.

"Judith telephoned me at the shop this morning. It was just after we had finished boarding up the broken display window; they were still sweeping up the broken glass and debris when she called. She sounded totally distraught. Bruno has been taken away."

"'Taken away'? What do you mean, 'taken away'? Who... Where ...?"

"The SS. They came during the night. They barely gave him time to throw on some clothes."

"But this is awful! How can they do that? What has he done? Where have they taken him?"

"Judith was afraid to say too much over the telephone. She thinks they took him to this new so called 'camp' for 'political prisoners'. It's called Dachau, just outside Munich."

"Political prisoners? That's ridiculous! What is he supposed to have done? He's no more political than you or I. He merely deals in antiques..."

"Judith wouldn't say any more, except that she's retained a lawyer to try and get him released. But *Schatzie*, they don't need a reason. From what I've heard they're grabbing people right and left off the streets, especially in large cities like Berlin and Hamburg. And, of course, Hitler's favorite town, Munich. Seemingly at random. Sometimes just for not giving the Heil Hitler salute. The other day, the Brownshirts beat up an American tourist in Berlin, near the Tiergarten; supposedly for not showing the proper respect when a group of them marched by. He wasn't even Jewish."

Hannah looks at him in disbelief. "But this can't be true. It's *unmöglich*. Totally impossible. How on earth do you know these things? Whoever told you must surely be exaggerating. It all sounds completely preposterous... but Bruno, poor Bruno, and poor Judith..."

Again Hannah springs to her feet in agitation, waving her hands as if swatting away a pesky fly. "I can't even begin to absorb any of this. It's just too shocking. Even after that Friday night when you were attacked, I kept thinking it was just an isolated incident. Just some young hooligans bent on mischief. Especially as things have been quiet ever since. But now you're telling me about the shop, and about Bruno, and everything else... I just don't know what to think anymore."

Samuel captures her hand again as she walks across the room, and pulls her down to sit next to him on the bed. "*Schatzie*", he says, "there is one more thing I haven't yet told you. Perhaps the most painful of all." He pauses. He has never had so much difficulty putting words together. "There are rumors, only unsubstantiated rumors mind you, but apparently…" He has trouble continuing. "There are rumors that they are rounding up the mentally impaired, the physically handicapped…" he cannot go on.

Hannah stares at him in horror. She tries once again to pull her hand away, but this time he has it firmly in his grasp and won't let her go. She claps her other hand over her mouth. "No, no, that can't be true. What do you mean 'rounding them up'? Why, what are they doing to them?"

Samuel is staring at the floor, as if the answers to Hannah's questions can be found at his feet, in the intricate design of the Persian carpet. He doesn't know if he is able to get the words past his lips. Finally, he gathers his strength to say what he knows he must say. "The rumor is that they are being…euthanized."

Hannah continues to look at him in horror and disbelief. "Naomi," she whispers, "Naomi." Tears begin to stream down her cheeks. "Naomi", she whispers again, her voice strangled with pain. "My Naomi."

It takes Samuel a full moment to find his voice again, and when he speaks, it is in a tone of utter despair. "That is why, *Schatzilein*, I believe we must seriously consider leaving and why I intend to check and make sure that our papers are all in order. Do you remember, *Schatzie*, I told you my father purchased some land in Palestine. I'm thinking we should pick ourselves up and move to Palestine. At least we know we'll be safe there. All we'll have to worry about," he says in an attempt to lighten the mood, "is a few Arabs on camels."

"Oh, Samuel. You're dreaming. How can we travel all that way with my mother? You know it's not that easy. And I would never leave without her. She can't possibly travel in her physical condition. I don't think she would be able to make it to another city in Germany, let alone to another country so far away.

It would kill her. On the other hand, if the rumors are true, we must think of Naomi…" She can't finish.

Samuel continues his examination of the carpet, and keeps Hannah's hand in a tight grip. With his free hand he holds his head in despair. "*Ich weiss*." he says. "*Ich weiss*. I know."

"Oh, *mein lieber Gott*," says Hannah. "What kind of monsters are these people?

Chapter 20

>❧

It is the eve of the Passover festival. The atmosphere in the Borneplatz *shul*, far from being festive, is even more subdued than it was a few weeks ago. In addition, there are undertones of nervous expectation. There have been no major incidents since the Friday night when Samuel Gutman and his two boys were attacked, but the Jewish community has every reason to be on the alert. Even before the advent of the Nazi regime, the Passover holiday has, historically, been a time for infamous accusations of 'blood libel' leveled by generally anti-Semitic gentile communities against their Jewish neighbors; accusations made as a matter of course and without the slightest provocation, on the ridiculous pretext that the Jews needed the blood of a gentile child to bake their unleavened bread.

Extra guards have been placed around the synagogue, and Rabbi Gutfreund has exhorted the congregation not to gather or dally or, as he put it, *trödeln*, outside the building after services but to go directly home to celebrate the Seder. At the same time, he tries to calm the atmosphere by an announcement from the pulpit. "I have," he says, "met with a Herr Schwimmer at the local Schutzstaffel headquarters." There is a collective murmur from his audience. The rabbi continues: "When Herr Schwimmer summoned me to his office, I admit I was somewhat apprehensive. But when I met him, I was pleasantly surprised. He was extremely warm and cordial to me. He is also obviously a well-educated and cultured man, and I left him feeling much more secure than I have felt for months. He specifically asked me to tell the Borneplatz congregation that we have nothing to fear from the new regime, that no Jew in Frankfurt need feel unsafe." Chortles of derisive laughter greet the rabbi's announcement, but he continues speaking as if he has not heard them. "Herr Schwimmer admitted that there are some hooligans wandering the streets, but he assured me that the authorities are doing whatever they can to rein them in, and that we are in no danger. I must say, he sounded very reasonable. And so, I think everyone should *sich beruhigen*. We need to calm down and not do anything rash." A low mumbling begins to build among the worshippers, some of whom look at each other in disbelief.

Herr Mayer is thankful that his innate ability at self-control enables him to sit and listen to the rabbi's nonsense without showing any reaction, when every instinct urges him to jump onto the lectern and throttle the man. *What a pompous jackass*, he thinks, *can he really believe what he is saying?* But the rabbi doesn't give the murmurs a chance to take hold. He hurriedly wishes the congregation the traditional *Yekke* greeting of *bau gut*, 'build well', a reference to the last song in the Haggadah that yearns for the rebuilding of the Holy Temple in Jerusalem. Then he quickly departs.

Apparently, the SS man, Herr Schwimmer, and his assurances are not enough for the rabbi to dispense with the special guard, who trails after him.

Samuel Gutman and his boys now walk home after *shul* services together with Herr Mayer, with Hans driving the Daimler at a snail's pace nearby. Tonight, Fritz is also with them, and the three boys walk behind the men. The Gutman boys and Fritz have become friendly as a result of the ride they share every morning to school, and though there is not a torrent of conversation between them, whatever words they do exchange are words that flow naturally without awkwardness. As soon as Herr Mayer learned of the arrangement made by his late wife, he expressed no objection to Fritz riding to school with the Gutman boys, but he insisted on paying his share. The Gutmans invited Herr Mayer and his family to celebrate the Seder with them, but he regretfully declined. Because of the recent death of his wife, he says, he will be conducting a quiet Seder with his two children in their apartment; it is possible, he adds, that his brother and sister-in-law will join them.

⇒⋐

The Gutmans' Seder seems as joyous as ever. Samuel and Hannah are determined that nothing will cloud the occasion, that the children and Oma Fleissig must be shielded as much as possible from outside events. For weeks now, ever since the feast of Purim, Liesl has been cleaning and scrubbing every corner of the apartment, washing curtains and windows, pounding clouds of dust out of the rugs; it is imperative that not one bread crumb, no hint of leaven remain when the Passover holiday begins. For the last few days, the apartment has been redolent with delicious aromas from the kitchen, where Hannah and Frau Fleissig have been cooking all sorts of savory, mouth-watering dishes, flour-free cakes and biscuits, and Oma Fleissig's special unbaked chocolate cake made with thick layers of chocolate cream spread between sheets of matzo, then chilled and cut into delectable squares.

Naomi asks if Tante Judith and Onkel Bruno and the Ehrlich cousins are coming to Frankfurt this year as they did in previous years, and Samuel is able to answer truthfully that they have all gone to Paris to spend the festival with Bruno's family. What Samuel doesn't reveal is that Judith only managed to get Bruno released from Dachau after paying an enormous fine and on condition they leave Germany within forty-eight hours. They have moved to Paris permanently. Samuel and Hannah still have no idea what Bruno was accused of by the Gestapo, what crime he is supposed to have committed.

The table is replete with the special Passover dishes and silverware that are stored, unused, during the rest of the year. In the center of the table resides the Seder plate, fashioned of two round tiers of heavy silver. The lower tier holds the requisite three matzot, and the top tier contains six circular indentations containing the symbolic foods of the Seder: the shank bone

Thin Ice • 129

and hardboiled egg in its charred shell, representing the burnt offering made by the Israelites when they left Egypt; the *marror*, the horseradish root, a reminder of the bitter lives led by the Jews when they were slaves in Egypt; the *charoset*, a mixture of chopped apples, nuts, cinnamon and red wine to mimic the consistency of the mortar used by the Jewish slaves to build the pyramids. The highlight of the Gutman Seder is the recitation of the *Ma Neshtana* by the twins, who suddenly are both overcome with a fit of shyness and have to be bribed and coaxed before finally, in unison, they begin with their enchanting lisp: "Why ith thith night different from all other *Nächte* of the year?" and then continue with the four questions. Everyone praises them excessively and their father rewards them with sweets.

"This is the bread of affliction," Samuel intones pointing to the *matzot*, "that our forefathers ate when we were slaves in Egypt..." As the Haggadah unfolds, the older children take turns to add different explanations and commentaries they have learned in school. Josh enumerates the three traits that distinguished the Israelites from their Egyptian taskmasters. "For one, they spoke a different language from the Egyptians," he says. "In addition, they dressed differently, and lastly, they refused to give their children Egyptian names, but gave them Hebrew names." Then it is Izaak's turn. The *kleiner Rabbiner* is in his element. He reads expressively, slowly: "In every generation, evil men rise up to destroy us. But the Holy One, Blessed be He, delivers us from their hands."

Samuel gazes around the table at his children, at his dear, dear Hannah, at his mother-in-law, at all his *Schatzies*, and he coughs to mask the sob which catches in his throat. The twins are sitting in his lap now, one on each knee, munching enthusiastically on their rewards. He looks at his daughter through blurred eyes. Is she really seventeen already? He remembers so clearly, as if yesterday, how, as a small girl, perhaps five or six, her little hand snugly enfolded inside his large one, she limped along beside him when he took her on outings to the park, or to another kindergartner's home; she was so proud to be walking with her Papa, so proud of her new shiny black shoes with the ankle straps, of the white ribbon bouncing up and down in her hair with every step she took. He cannot bear to think what might befall her if... He refuses to finish the thought. And his boys, Izaak and Joshua. How tall they've grown, how handsome and well-mannered and kind. He wishes his arms were long enough and strong enough to embrace them all, to grip them tight, to hold them close, to keep them safe. In his mind, Izaak's last recitation echoes over and over again. *Indeed, an evil man has arisen in our generation to try and destroy us. But surely, lieber Gott, surely You will not allow it. Surely You will save us once again?*

He suppresses the tears welling behind his eyes, gazes at his Hannah sitting opposite him at the other end of the dining table, and catches her eye. They exchange an identical, silent message: *I have never felt prouder of our children, nor cherished them as much as I do this night.*

Chapter 21

⇒✦⇐

The offices and chief manufacturing plant of EmEm are located in a sprawling cluster of low-lying buildings in an industrial section of Frankfurt, not far from the main railroad. There is a rail spur on EmEm's premises linking up to a main line, making shipping of its products very convenient. When it is not possible to ship by rail, shipments are hauled either by long distance lorries, or by *Lastkähne*, barges sailing along the River Main.

It is a balmy, summer's morning. Herr Mayer arrives at his office before any of his employees. After attending an early morning service at Borneplatz, he dispenses with breakfast and has Hans drop him off before sending him off on an errand. Lately, he has little appetite and, more often than not eats nothing until the end of the day. As early as Herr Mayer arrives, the two men with the swastika armbands – although he cannot be sure they are always the same two – have arrived before him on their motorcycle and are already at their station across from the EmEm buildings, leaning against a fence. By now, Herr Mayer is so used to seeing them, their presence barely registers. He notes, though, that Schultz is not at his post. He assumes that upon the arrival of the two men, the night guard felt his presence to be superfluous.

Herr Mayer doesn't turn on any lights as he makes his way down the corridor to his office, nor does he raise the blinds. Later, he will wonder at this. But now, as so often happens, Herr Mayer finds himself standing in the semi-darkness before the picture of his father. The morning light leaking through the slats of the blinds is bright enough for Herr Mayer to see his father quite clearly. He gazes intently at his father's image, willing him to give him some kind of message, some kind of direction that has so far escaped him. Anything. *Why can't you tell me what to do,* he asks, though no sound escapes his lips. *The school year is ending in a few weeks, and I don't know what to do with Henrietta. She refuses to come with me and Fritz to the lake house, and I can't force her. She says she will stay with Heinz and Bertha. That, I cannot allow. Not after what I heard went on that Shabbat when Marga was in hospital. She says she wants to practice her skating every day. I can't find anything wrong with that, Vater, and so we will all stay in Frankfurt for the summer.* He stares and stares at his uniformed father: perhaps if he stares long enough he will force him to reply, force a message out of him, force him to drop some kernel of advice, perhaps even one of his famous bon mots. He restrains himself from physically removing the photograph from the wall and shaking it. Without realizing it, he is beginning to speak audibly, albeit quietly. *And, on top of everything else, lieber Vater, the next shipment is due. A shipment of dynamite whose purpose I can only guess at. And, furthermore, Vater, what am I supposed to tell Weber and Hausmann? As it is, they already think I've lost my mind. And perhaps I have. When I instruct them to fill the next order they will be convinced.*

But his soldier father remains at attention, still stares silently into the distance, is still permanently fixed to the wall, unmoving, and is definitely not divulging one iota of advice to his son.

Herr Mayer walks back over to the window. He is about to raise the blinds, when he detects a movement outside, at the periphery of his vision. Through a chink in the slats he notices that the two Germans are still there, still leaning nonchalantly against the fence, one of them munching on a sandwich. Then he spots Hausmann entering the frame; he is riding his bicycle through the gate. He dismounts, locks the machine to the bicycle rack, then gives the Heil Hitler salute to the two men lounging across the way. There is something *verstohlen,* positively furtive about the way Hausmann raises his arm and looks over his shoulder before giving the salute, as if afraid someone might be watching.

Herr Mayer moves away from the blinds without raising them and walks back to his desk where he sits for a few moments, deep in thought, then swivels his chair around to look up at his father. *Also, lieber Vater,* he whispers, *was sagst du dazu??* What do you make of that?

He swings his chair again, so that he is once more sitting upright at his desk, his back to his silent, unforthcoming father. For a few moments more, he sits without moving, just thinking about what he has just seen. Why did Hausmann act so furtively? With the blinds still drawn and no lights on, he could not have known that Herr Mayer was already in the building. But why should he, Gustav Mayer, be surprised if some of his employees are sympathetic to the new regime? Nothing should shock or surprise him anymore. Not after the events in Berlin. Perhaps, though, he can allow himself a little disappointment; after all, Hausmann has been with EmEm since before Gustav Mayer joined the firm. He wonders if Hausmann is a true Nazi ideologue. Is it possible the man is merely trying to ingratiate himself with the Nazis to protect his family? Herr Mayer knows he will now have to be more vigilant, that he can no longer trust any employee. What does he really know about any of them? What, for instance, does he know about Hausmann, or for that matter about Weber, the long-time head of the shipping department who fought alongside Herr Mayer's father in the Prussian war? And what about his driver, Hans Bauer, who didn't return a Nazi salute when they were in Berlin together? Can he attach any meaning to Hans's omission?

No, he cannot afford the luxury of attaching any meaning to anything anymore.

Has Hans, have any of them, been ordered to watch him, to keep an eye on his movements?

Or is he being paranoid again?

At least, thinks Herr Mayer, *I can be sure that, whoever may be watching me, I have given them no reason to suspect that I am doing anything other than obeying orders.*

Or, on the other hand, that I have lost my mind.

There is only one employee on whose loyalty Herr Mayer can rely, and that is his faithful secretary, Gertrud Schneider, whom he inherited from his father along with so many of EmEm's employees. There is one big difference: Fraulein Schneider is Jewish. Very Jewish. And her loyalty to EmEm has always been absolute and unquestioning. However, he believes she will not be with him much longer. She is a spinster, not much older than himself, who has been with EmEm since she was a girl right out of secretarial school. She has told him that she is thinking of leaving Germany and moving to England where she has relatives. "To tell the truth," she said recently, "I'm frightened. I have trouble sleeping and am afraid to walk even to the grocery shop by myself. What kind of life is that? Besides," she added, "I know very well that I am the only Jew at EmEm, except, of course, for yourself, Herr Mayer. Nobody says anything to me outright but sometimes I feel they're avoiding me, and I find that very *unbequem*. Very uncomfortable."

Fraulein Schneider expressed her sorrow at the prospect of deserting him and EmEm, and although she hasn't actually given notice yet, he senses that her days at EmEm are numbered. He knows he will miss her terribly, but at the same time how can he blame her for wanting to get out of Germany, out of the lunatic asylum that the country is turning into?

He has still not taken steps to confide in the one person he feels he can trust. He has been constrained by his conscience, that part of him that asks over and over again if it is fair to involve someone else, to put a totally innocent person in danger. But now he knows he cannot wait much longer, that time may be running out.

Chapter 22

꒰ ꒱

School is over. The Nazi presence in Frankfurt is increasing and becoming more visible. Acts of vandalism against Jewish property are daily occurrences. Random physical attacks on Jews, such as the one perpetrated a few months earlier on Samuel Gutman, are also occurring with more frequency. More and more signs proclaiming '*keine Juden*' or '*Juden und Hunde Verboten*' are making their appearance, not only in public places like parks, libraries and museums, but on the windows and doors of private establishments owned by gentiles. More and more Jewish shops have either closed down and been abandoned or, like *Chez Gutman*, have been sold by their owners at obscenely low prices. Frankfurt's police are powerless to interfere, even if they wished to, which is doubtful. Some of the Gutmans' Jewish neighbors have moved away; some, like the Pragers, to relatives in Holland, some to France or England. Some have managed, despite the quotas, to obtain entry certificates from the British Mandate in Palestine; they are now waiting for transportation. Every now and then chilling reports circulate of young Jewish men, whom the Nazis suspect of Zionist or communist activities, being snatched from their beds in the middle of the night, leaving frantic families, whose inquiries to the authorities are met with callous indifference. The men have disappeared, not to be heard from again.

The head of the local SS, the Herr Schwimmer about whom the rabbi spoke so glowingly, has placed one of his men in the Borneplatz *shul* during services to monitor the rabbi's sermons, to make sure nothing subversive is being said about the Chancellor or the government. The man is in mufti, so as not to stand out among the worshippers; he even wears a hat. But, of course, everybody knows who he is and why he is there. The rabbi is quickly losing his innocence about the regime and has become adept at sprinkling his sermons with euphemisms. His congregants now understand that when he speaks obliquely of the hardships experienced by the Jews in Egypt and the pharaoh who enslaved them, he is actually referring to Germany and its new Führer.

Samuel has not dared broach the idea of moving again, but both he and Hannah feel the subject hanging over them, its heavy presence felt in the apartment like an unwelcome *Gast* who refuses to leave. They carefully avoid eye contact between them, and looks that used to be lovingly exchanged are now often averted. Hannah's usually joyful disposition has been replaced by a forced cheerfulness assumed for the sake of the children and her mother, a pretense that all is well, when clearly it is not. For the first time Samuel notices with dismay the faint lines that have appeared, seemingly overnight, near his *Schatzie's* eyes and around her mouth. He notices, too, that she prays more than usual, her prayer book lying open and neglected in her lap as she gazes sadly into the distance, unaware that her husband is observing her.

Like the Mayers, the Gutmans remain in Frankfurt for the summer. In years past, they used to pack up the children and Frau Fleissig and travel to a choice of vacation spots, sometimes joining the Ehrlich cousins on the French Riviera or at one of several kosher resorts on Lake Lugano or in the Swiss Alps. Frau Fleissig's hip has become so painful of late, that she rarely leaves her bed. She has begged Hannah and Samuel to take the children away without her. "Don't worry about me," she says. "Liesl will look after me. And believe me, I will enjoy the peace and *Ruhe* in the apartment without the twins." But Hannah will not hear of going on holiday without her mother.

It is no longer considered safe for the children to be out on the street unless accompanied by an adult, either a parent or Liesl. No longer can they walk alone to their friends' apartments; no longer can they be sent down on errands. No longer are they able to attend the Zionist youth groups that used to meet on Shabbat afternoons; the groups have been disbanded. "All of this is just a precaution, mind you, *Schatzies*," Samuel tells the three older children, not wishing to frighten them unduly. "We will still be able to have our Sunday outings and picnics in the countryside as we have always done, and of course on Shabbat morning we will all attend Borneplatz together."

Somehow, the summer passes without any picnics materializing. But none of the children complain about being restricted to the apartment. They overhear conversations about incidents of vandalism and physical assaults, and are relieved not to have to face their swastika-plastered neighborhood and the Brownshirts who roam the streets.

⇥⇤

"Mutti," says Naomi, "Why can't the doctors do anything about Oma's hip? It seems to me she's not getting any better."

Hannah and Naomi are in the kitchen, companionably mixing dough for the *Kuchen* and braided *challah* loaves they are preparing for the Sabbath. Now that Oma Fleissig is bedridden, Hannah has assumed the baking and cooking, with Naomi as her willing assistant. Liesl has taken the twins to a neighbor's apartment to spend the afternoon with one of their little friends. Izaak and Josh are in their room playing chess. Samuel has gone to the bank to meet with Herr Schiller and go over the final details of the sale of *Chez Gutman*.

Hannah is at a loss how to reply. Worried as she is about her mother, she also knows that Naomi has been her Oma's special love from the moment she was born. Hannah will never forget how her mother reacted when Naomi's handicap first came to light; how she took the child on her lap, held her close to her bosom, and then began jostling her up and down to the rhyming words of *hoppa, hoppa Reiter,* over and over again, sending the little girl into paroxysms of laughter. That scene plays over and over in Hannah's memory. As Naomi grew older, she and her grandmother developed an especially close relationship, often just sitting together hand-in-hand on the sofa without talking, or sometimes talking and laughing in undertones or whispering in each other's ear. Hannah and Samuel have never been privy to these exchanges between Naomi and her grandmother. In the past, Hannah has even experienced tiny pangs of jealousy in the realization she and her mother never had that special closeness that Naomi and Oma Fleissig share.

Now, hearing the tears in her daughter's voice, Hannah speaks carefully even though she knows that Naomi will not find her answer satisfactory. "Doctor Schwartz says that Oma has very bad arthritis in her hip, and that is causing the pain."

"But why can't the doctors do anything? Can't they operate?"

"According to Doctor Schwartz there doesn't seem to be much they can do, especially for a woman her age."

"Oh Mutti. I can't bear to hear her moaning like that. You know Oma doesn't like to complain. She must be suffering so much." Now Naomi cannot control her tears, which are sprinkling the egg whites she continues to whisk furiously for the meringues the little boys love. "Can't they at least give Oma something that will take away the pain? Maybe then she will be able to get out of bed and walk around again? Yesterday, when I went into her room to visit, she asked me to leave. She's never done that before." Naomi's voice chokes and Hannah has trouble controlling her own tears. She puts down the sack of flour she was about to replace in the bin, walks over to her daughter, puts her arm around her shoulders and says the only thing she can think of saying: "We must try to stay cheerful for Oma's sake, Naomi. We don't want Oma to see we are worried about her, *nicht wahr?* It will only make her more worried herself. Let's try, what do you say? I know it isn't easy, but let's try."

Naomi stops whipping the eggs. She raises her head, blinking back her tears. "You're right, Mutti. I'll try," she says, swallowing hard. "I'll really try."

Mother and daughter continue for a few moments in silence, measuring and pouring and mixing. Once more it is Naomi who breaks the silence.

"Mutti, why are those two men outside our building every day? They frighten me."

"I don't know," says Hannah. "I must admit they make me a bit uneasy, too. Perhaps they are guarding the building against hoodlums such as those who attacked Papa a few months ago. Let's hope they're here for our safety."

"But Mutti, that can't be. I think they're the same two men who came to Frau Mayer's funeral. I saw them quite clearly. They were standing in the rain at the back of the crowd. What were they doing there?"

Hannah sighs. She knows her Naomi is no fool, but the girl has taken her by surprise. "I don't know what those men are doing down there, but if you saw them at Frau Mayer's funeral, we have to assume they must have something to do with Herr Mayer."

"But what could it be, Mutti? What has Herr Mayer done? And how can we be certain they're not here because of us, or because of someone else in our building?"

"You're right, Naomi, we can't be certain. Have you asked Henrietta? What does she say? Come to think of it, we haven't seen much of Henrietta since her mother died. Is she all right?"

"I haven't had a chance to discuss it with Henrietta. The last time I spoke to her she told me she's going to be busy every day this summer with her skating schedule," says Naomi. Her head is turned away from Hannah, as she continues automatically whisking the egg whites which have already formed stiff peaks. "Except Shabbat, of course. She's training really hard. She wants to be on the *Deutshe* Olympics team this winter. Did you know that, Mutti?"

"But how *wunderbar*! That's quite an ambition to have. She must be a very good skater. I wonder how her father feels about it."

"I..I'm not sure how he feels, but Henrietta told me her mother used to be very encouraging. She said her mother was a very good skater when she was young, but gave it up when she married Herr Mayer."

Instinctively, Hannah feels there is something Naomi is not telling her. There is a false, bright note in Naomi's unusually talkative recital about Henrietta's skating plans, but Hannah is relieved that the subject of the two Nazis across the street has been deflected.

"Well," she says, "Perhaps you will be able to see her on Shabbat, at least, *nicht wahr?*"

Naomi doesn't reply, but continues furiously whipping the egg whites with undivided concentration.

And with that the subject of Henrietta is also dropped.

><

Naomi is conscientious about her piano practice in the same way that she is conscientious about her studies, but her favorite pastime is reading everything she can get her hands on. This summer, her particular enthusiasm is for poetry. Except for when she is called upon to help Hannah in the kitchen, and after she has finished piano practice, she devotes hours and hours each day devouring volume after volume. First she exhausts the books on her parents' shelves, then, because Frankfurt's main public library is now closed to Jews, she sends Liesl, armed with a request list and the task of persuading the librarian that the Goethe and Rilke and Heine books of poetry she is borrowing are for herself (a girl who can barely read!) Liesl returns staggering under her load. Naomi has always loved the poems of Rainer Maria Rilke, and even before Fraulein Schloss, her literature teacher, announced that they would be studying some of Rilke's poems in the coming term, she has familiarized herself with many of his works. At the moment, she is absorbed by his *Sonnets to Orpheus*. His words echo over and over again in her brain: *Wissen wir, Freunde, wissen wir nicht? Do we know it, friends, or do we not?* She has no idea what the poet is referring to, but for some inexplicable reason these words resonate within her; she is impatient to discuss the context and meaning with Fraulein Schloss when school starts again.

Apart from this absorbing interest, an unexpected friendship has prevented Naomi from being lonely this summer. At first, she is hurt and disappointed by Henrietta, with whom she had expected to spend a lot of time during the school vacation. During the week, Henrietta is at the ice rink from early morning until quite late. On two occasions, Naomi has knocked on the Mayers' door in the evening, only to be told by Inge that Henrietta is too tired to see her. The same excuse is given to Naomi on Shabbat afternoon. Henrietta has not attended *shul* once all summer.

On the other hand, Henrietta's brother Fritz has begun to visit Naomi's brothers. He plays chess with them, and helps them with their science homework. One afternoon, after a game of chess, instead of leaving through the front door to return to his own apartment, Fritz wanders into the Gutman kitchen, where Naomi is sitting at the table waiting for the kettle to boil. Naturally, she has a book open on the table in front of her.

It may never be known why Fritz Mayer wandered into the Gutman kitchen that summer afternoon. Perhaps he took a wrong turn on his way to the front door. Perhaps it was fate. Or just plain serendipity. Or, perhaps, it was deliberate, perhaps he was seeking Naomi out. What is known is that a friendship begins that afternoon between a nearly sixteen-year-old boy who, incidentally, stopped picking at his face after his mother's death, and a seventeen-year-old girl with a limp and a penchant for poetry. A friendship that will have long-lasting and far reaching consequences for both families.

That night, lying in bed, the lines from Rilke's sonnet unexpectedly saunter into Naomi's head. *Do we know it friends, or do we not?* Just as she is dropping off, an apparition floats into her semi-consciousness: the image of a boy's earnest, pockmarked face. *How strange*, she thinks, as she falls asleep, a smile on her lips, *how very strange*.

Chapter 23

ꭗ⬥

Samuel is lying in bed, trying in vain to fall asleep. He wanted to join Hannah in her bed, but as she has done on most nights these past few weeks, she has pleaded fatigue. He knows she is exhausted ministering to her mother, not to mention the extra kitchen chores she has had to undertake due to Frau Fleissig's infirmity. But he suspects the real reason for her rejection of him for the first time in their marriage is a result of their last conversation: she is worried sick not only about her mother, but about Naomi. If he had known the effect the subject would have on his *Schatzie*, he would never have brought it up. But, did he really have a choice? With all the unrest and rumors swirling around them he is more and more certain that it is no longer safe for them, for any Jew, to stay in Frankfurt. Or anywhere else in Germany. His late father's example is always before him. He can't allow himself to pretend that all is well, that their lives are unchanged. Nor can he allow Hannah to do so.

He is about to say "*Schatzie*, please, can't we talk about this", when he realizes that she is breathing steadily, that she has fallen asleep. He lies there, eyes closed, envying Hannah her ability to sleep. Samuel's sleeping habits, on the other hand, have become irregular ever since the sale of *Chez Gutman*; his dreams, when he does manage to sleep, are filled with chaotic, frightening images that wake him to a feeling of exhaustion such as he has never felt before, not even after a long day at the shop.

Perhaps some hot chocolate, he thinks, will help him to sleep. Just as he begins to get out of bed, he hears a scraping sound outside in the corridor, followed by a soft knocking on the front door. He eases himself from the bed, shrugs on his robe and quietly, so as not to wake Hannah, opens the bedroom door and slips out, closing it softly behind him. Again he hears the knocking, more persistent this time, and he hurries to open the front door.

He is astonished to find their neighbor on the doorstep. Herr Mayer is wearing a rich velvet smoking jacket in a dark shade of maroon that looks almost black in the dim light of the corridor. Herr Mayer holds a finger to his lips indicating the need for silence, looks furtively over his shoulder before shutting the door quietly behind him. Samuel reaches for the light switch, but Herr Mayer blocks his arm with an urgent whisper: *"Ich bitte Sie. Kein Licht"*

"Is something wrong, Herr Mayer, are you ill, is it the children...?"

"Nein, nein. We are all well, thank you, Herr Gutman, *Gott sei dank.* But there is something of a very delicate nature I must discuss with you."

They have been speaking in whispers, and can barely see each other's faces in the gloom of the vestibule. Samuel leads Herr Mayer by the arm into the kitchen at the other end of the apartment, away from the bedrooms, where there will be less chance of disturbing his sleeping family. He closes the kitchen door behind them as an extra precaution. Outside, the night is clear and balmy, under a full moon and a star-filled sky. The kitchen is awash with moonlight, the beams piercing the curtains and transforming Manet's lemons into two enormous bright yellow, shimmering flames.

"Bitte," Samuel whispers, indicating a chair for his visitor. "May I offer you a *Kaffee,* or perhaps a cup of hot chocolate?"

"No, no, thank you, perhaps just a glass of water, but please do not bother yourself on my account." Herr Mayer sounds distracted. "I will not keep you long." He does not sit immediately, but moves over to the window where he stands to the side of the curtains and peers out. "I am sure, Herr Gutman, you have noticed the two Nazis standing across from our apartment building day and night?" He doesn't wait for Samuel to reply. "See, they are still there. Perhaps not the same two who were there this morning, not that it makes any difference. There are always two of them. All the time. That is why I cannot allow you to turn on the light. They must not suspect that I am talking to you. Can I have your assurance that you will not reveal to anyone, not even to Frau Gutman, what I am about to relate. If you cannot give me that assurance I will leave immediately and nothing more need ever be said about my visit here tonight. It will be as if it never happened."

"Herr Mayer, my boys and I owe our very lives to you. You may be assured of my complete discretion. That is the very least I can do. I only wish I could repay you in a more substantial way."

Herr Mayer acknowledges Samuel's assurance with a barely discernible nod of his head. He takes a sip from the glass of water Samuel has placed before him. "I must apologize," he says, "for disturbing you so late at night. I wanted to wait until I felt sure all your children were asleep. I'm afraid you were probably also asleep and that my knocking woke you up."

"There's no need to apologize, Herr Mayer. I was not asleep. In fact I have been having trouble sleeping lately and was just thinking about getting up and perhaps making myself a cup of hot chocolate when I heard your knock."

"*Ja*," says Herr Mayer. "I have a feeling there are many Jews in Frankfurt this minute who are having difficulty sleeping. Probably all over Germany. But, please, don't let me stop you from preparing your hot chocolate."

Samuel fills the kettle and places it on the stove to boil. He sits down and waits for Herr Mayer to continue.

"I must be perfectly honest, Herr Gutman, and tell you that by relating these events to you, by confiding in you, not only am I putting my own life in danger, but by possessing the knowledge I am about to impart to you your life may also be at risk. That is why it has taken me so long to come to the conclusion that I must confide in you. Once again I emphasize, if you wish me to stop now, I will leave and not bother you again with my problems. Just one word from you, and that will be the end of the matter."

"Herr Mayer, we Jews are all living in strange times. Just as you came to my aid when I was in trouble, I will do everything and anything in my power to assist you. Whether or not I can do so is an *andere Sache*, quite another matter. But I am willing to try."

"Very well, Herr Gutman. I thank you. I just wanted to make it quite clear that you understand I am putting you at risk." Herr Mayer pauses again, sighs, examines his clasped hands resting on the table in front of him. Finally, he begins. "What I am about to tell you will undoubtedly sound like sheer fabrication. So completely far-fetched that you may even begin to think I am hallucinating, that I have lost my mind. That perhaps my wife's death has pushed me over the edge. That is quite understandable. Believe me, if you were to relate to me what I am about to reveal to you, I would think that, without a doubt, you were crazy. *Jedoch*, nothing could be further from the truth. You must believe me when I tell you I am as sane as I have ever been, and what I am about to tell you is the absolute truth.

"It all began this past winter. I was in my office one morning when I received a telephone call from the new Chancellor's office, summoning me, no, *ordering* me, to a meeting in Berlin that very week…"

With that beginning, Herr Mayer relates to Samuel Gutman the details of his meeting in Berlin with Göring and von Ribbentrop, and with Adolf Hitler himself. He continues: "The meeting was ordered for the very day Frau Mayer was taken ill. But how could I dare not show up? I had no way of canceling the appointment, at any rate. The party at the other end of the line hung up before I was able to utter one word; as a result, I had no idea who had called me, nor how to reach him. Now you will understand why I was unable to accompany my wife to the hospital. Which I know must have set many tongues wagging, but…" he spreads his hands and says, bitterly, "what could I do? I had no choice. Incidentally, Herr Gutman, in case you are wondering where the meeting took place, let me tell you I myself have wondered about it many times. As I told you, I was blindfolded, but the distance the car traveled from the corner where I was picked up could not have been more than a few meters; it certainly lasted no longer than one minute, if that. What I believe is that I was taken to the temporary Reichstag offices. I'm sure you remember the *Reichstagbrand* that took place about two years ago. The fire destroyed a good part of the Reichstag building. Since then, I understand, it has been completely repaired and restored but I believe the Nazis must have held on to the temporary quarters for precisely this kind of secret meeting, one that Herr Hitler might not wish to take place in the Reichstag proper, which would put an official stamp on it. After all, it was a meeting that never took place, *nicht wahr*? A meeting that was not a meeting." Herr Mayer's voice drips with sarcasm.

"So far, I have delivered two shipments consisting of various munitions. I followed the requirements of the list to the letter. The items ordered so far are, for the most part, quite commonplace, not much more than the kind used by the average farmer to keep the foxes out of the henhouse, or for the shooting and hunting parties the German hoi polloi still engage in. I tend to assume that the first orders were given to me as a test, to see if I obey, to see if I will try in some way to sabotage the shipments. By the way, I am not sure how much longer I can keep making these deliveries without going bankrupt. But that is not the point of my recitation. The financial aspect is a side issue entirely." Herr Mayer pauses, looks directly at Samuel. "Before I go any further, I must ask you, Herr Gutman, do you believe me?"

"I believe every word, Herr Mayer. Am I shocked? Of course I am. Who wouldn't be? But I know the truth when I hear it, and as fantastic as the events you've related sound, I believe you with all my heart. This is not something anyone could fabricate."

"Thank you Herr Gutman. And now let me get to the point. I take you to be an intelligent and informed man. It cannot have escaped you, just as it has not escaped me, what Hitler is doing. He is rearming Germany. As you know, that is in direct violation of the 1919 Treaty of Versailles. It did not take me long to reach that conclusion. I asked myself why he was not ordering some of the materiel on the list from foreign countries, such as France, for instance, which has some fine munitions factories. Could it be, I asked myself, that with

EmEm Hitler is able to dictate a ridiculous price which he could not demand from any other company? And why is he apparently not approaching German conglomerates such as Krupp and Mauser both of which have much larger facilities than EmEm and much greater production capacities? I realized almost immediately that it was not a matter of price – that Hitler simply enjoyed browbeating me because I am a Jew. I also rēalized almost immediately that he was approaching EmEm and EmEm alone. Were he to approach a foreign concern, he would almost certainly be tipping his hand. And as far as Krupp and Mauser are concerned, he is much less likely to be able to intimidate them with threats." Herr Mayer pauses. He takes a few sips of water.

"Let me interject here, Herr Gutman, that I have no illusions about the Krupps. I have been acquainted with Gustav and Bertha Krupp for years. I know the Krupps to be virulent anti-Semites. We have met many times at business conventions and unavoidable social events, and while their behavior to me has always been correct, I might say even cordial, it is not difficult to detect that undertone, that intangible *Etwas* by which every anti-Semite gives himself away. Apart from that, it is public knowledge that the Krupps have been ignoring the Versailles Treaty for years, that they manufacture and ship all kinds of munitions and arms, even tanks, to countries like Denmark and Turkey and Sweden. I assume they have had to do so in order to stay in business. After all, that is their livelihood." Herr Mayer takes several more sips, clears his throat, wipes his mouth with the serviette Samuel placed next to the glass of water, before continuing.

"What the Krupps feel about Hitler is anyone's guess. *Jedoch*, I did once overhear Frau Krupp say something dismissive about him right after he was elected Chancellor. The woman is an upper class snob and she made it clear that to her Hitler is nothing more than an Austrian *Hochstapler*, a confidence trickster and a common upstart who doesn't know his place. Hitler cannot be unaware of the Krupps' sentiments. Can he afford to risk the Krupps or the Mausers reporting his activities? Can he be certain that their loyalty to the *Vaterland* would seal their lips? Can he be sure that their eagerness for profit would keep them silent? No, I don't think so. Incidentally, there are rumors circulating that Hitler has been receiving munitions shipments from the Czechs, specifically Czepel which, ironically, is also owned by Jews."

Herr Mayer pauses. He removes his glasses with one hand and presses the bridge of his nose with the other. He is obviously tired and under tremendous stress. He replaces his glasses, stands up and begins pacing the kitchen, being careful to stay clear of the window. "As you can see, Herr Gutman, I am being watched. The same two men as those down there, or their identical twins – they all look alike to me – also stand guard outside my office all day. They were even present at Frau Mayer's funeral. Perhaps they think I will flee, that I'll leave the country. Even if I wanted to, I cannot leave. The first thing they did was confiscate my passport. If I need to leave the country on business, I must obtain permission from von Ribbentrop. What is more likely, those two Nazis are keeping an eye on who my visitors are, to make sure I don't inform on Herr Hitler's activities. Precisely what I am doing now in relating these events to you. By the way, I did not dare use the telephone because I believe they may have installed an eavesdropping device in all my instruments, both in my home and in my office. When I make a call, I sometimes hear a clicking sound and other strange noises."

Herr Mayer sits down once more, facing Samuel Gutman and says, "Germany is my home, Herr Gutman. I have always loved this country and I care deeply about it. Germany has been very good to my family for many generations. But now, to witness what is happening to the country I love… it is not easy to bear, not easy to accept." There is a wrenching, palpable sadness in Herr Mayer's voice. "On the one hand," he continues, "I can't help feeling it will have to stop soon. That the German *Volk* will rise up and rebel against Hitler and his henchmen. After all, this is the most civilized country in the world, *nicht wahr*? The country that produced Goethe and Wagner. But, on the other hand, what if it doesn't stop? What if Hitler and his hooligans stay in power? What if he wants another war to avenge the German defeat in the last one? *Schlisslich*, if Hitler were interested in keeping the armistice, if he were interested in living in peace, why would he need all these rifles and ammunition, and all the other materiel on the list?"

Herr Mayer rests his elbows on the kitchen table and holds his head in both hands, sending his glasses askew. By the light of the moon, Samuel is able to observe the man's ravaged face clearly. He thinks he can even detect, under Herr Mayer's yarmulke, that his already sparse hair has thinned even more, and that what little remains has become almost white. The kettle has begun to whistle, indicating that the water is boiling. He gets up and turns off the flame, without pouring himself the hot chocolate he had wanted earlier. After Herr Mayer's astonishing recital, the idea of hot chocolate seems an unwonted indulgence. He sits down again at the table, opposite his visitor.

"If you really wished to leave the country, Herr Mayer, I'm sure there are ways of crossing borders without a passport."

"I will never leave Germany Herr Gutman," Herr Mayer raises his head, adjusts his glasses, and though he remains seated his posture becomes militarily erect as his voice regains strength. "I am a German through and through. My ancestors have served this country for generations, with honor, and are all buried here in Frankfurt. And now my wife, too, is buried here. No, I will not think of leaving even though, between you and me, I do have ample wherewithal if I wished to leave. My late father had the prescience to open more than one Swiss bank account. Not that he could have foreseen any of these events. But no. Even though Germany may be turning its back on me, I have no intention of leaving.

"And that, Herr Gutman, brings me to the reason for my recitation. My first impulse, when I realized what Hitler was doing, was to run as fast as my legs could carry me to the nearest French or British Embassy and sound the alarm, to let them know that Hitler is rearming. But almost immediately, I realized I was being naïve, that there is absolutely no possibility that France and Britain are ignorant of Hitler's activities, that they don't know what he's up to. It is inconceivable to me that after Versailles they didn't plant spies in this country, at the very least to monitor troop movements and armament shipments, and the like. No, that is not what concerns me. What concerns me is…" Herr Mayer's voice becomes hoarse, and he takes a sip of water before continuing in firmer tones. "You may wonder why I did not refuse the orders they gave me or why I am not sabotaging the deliveries; indeed, why I am being so docile and obedient. But you see, Herr Gutman, what concerns me is my children. With the knowledge I possess my life is probably not worth very much. If it were just me alone, perhaps I would be able to be defiant – that is, if I could find the courage. But who knows what they might do to my children, or to my brother if I were to resist them? Of course, I know that once I have fulfilled the requirements on the list, once everything has been delivered in accordance with their specifications, I will be *entbehrlich*, completely expendable. In the meantime, the minimum that I dare to do in this *Spiel* is to try and slow things down a bit. I have already decided to risk delaying the next shipment, Herr Gutman. I intend to tell them it can't be helped. Which, believe it or not, is actually the truth. The items they have requested are some airplane parts that EmEm has never manufactured before and which necessitate the building of special molds and other equipment, perhaps even the erecting of another facility entirely. I won't bore you with the details. I don't even want to try and guess why Herr Hitler needs airplane parts. But, Hermann Göring is the head of the Luftwaffe, so…."

Herr Mayer reaches across the table and grasps Samuel's hand. "It is because of my children that I felt I had to involve someone. Unfortunately for you, Herr Gutman, I decided you were the most likely candidate. I would like to send my children out of the country, if possible, perhaps to America where Frau Mayer's brother lives. She once broached the possibility to me but I wouldn't hear of it. Of course, that was long before any of this happened." He releases Samuel's hand, stands up and begins pacing again. "I realize now that Frau Mayer was a lot wiser than I. About a lot of things. What worries me is what will happen to the children if I am unable to get them out of the country in time. This is where you come in, Herr Gutman. I know it is a lot to ask of anyone, but I feel I have no choice. If anything happens to me, may I count on you, Herr Gutman, to look after my children, to make sure they are safe?"

Before Samuel can reply, Herr Mayer continues. "Of course, you are probably wondering, Herr Gutman, why I have not approached my brother; after all, he is my children's uncle, *nicht wahr*? It is logical that I should think of him first. Perhaps I'm being paranoid, but I believe it is more than likely that Heinz is also under surveillance, precisely because he is my brother. Although it is entirely possible that they may be keeping an eye on him on his own account. It would not be surprising if his prominent international clients and connections are making the Nazis a bit nervous. I have deliberately not visited him or telephoned him for quite a while, and I was relieved to learn that he and his wife are out of the country for the summer. I have other reasons for not involving my brother, but they are not important to mention." He stops pacing and sits down at the table once more. "I don't have to tell you again, Herr Gutman, regardless of what your answer is, to be extremely *umsichtig* about this matter with your family. And of course," he points in the direction of the window, "with those thugs down there. They mustn't suspect a thing."

"Herr Mayer, as I have said before, please be assured of my complete discretion. Hopefully, it will never come to it, but if the necessity arises, I promise to do everything I can to protect your children. As a matter of fact, I have tried to persuade Hannah that it's time for us to leave Germany. But she won't hear of it. Not without her mother, who, as you may know, is in no physical condition to travel."

"Well, Herr Gutman, if and when you do decide to leave, I hope you will consider taking Henrietta and Fritz with you. But, even if you stay in Frankfurt, if something happens to me before I can get them out, I trust you will find a way to send them out of the country. It doesn't much matter where – just as long as they are safe."

Samuel doesn't hesitate. "Once more, Herr Mayer, you may rest assured that I will do everything in my power to keep your children safe. You have my solemn word."

The two men shake hands. Agreement has been reached. There is no need for further discussion.

They walk softly and silently to the front door of the apartment, and Herr Mayer, after carefully inspecting the corridor up and down, and after giving his automatic and almost imperceptible little bow and military clicking of heels, soundlessly slips away.

Samuel closes and locks the front door and slowly makes his way back to the bedroom. He is in a state of shock; it will take him time to absorb what he has just heard. He is wide awake and knows he will not be able to sleep. He is relieved to find that Hannah is still sleeping soundly. For a moment he just stands and observes the outline of her body, partially visible thanks to the single narrow spear of moonlight that has thrust its way through a chink in the drawn curtains and landed on her bed. He resists the temptation to lie down alongside her, to draw her close to him, to whisper in her ear how much he loves her, how he will protect her with his life. But he knows how exhausted she has been, how much she needs her sleep, and so, reluctantly, he lies down on his own bed, his head awhirl with Herr Mayer's revelations. It is *unerträglich*, he thinks, for one man to have to shoulder so much. Completely and utterly unbearable. Poor Herr Mayer, first to lose his wife so suddenly, and then for this to happen. And now, on top of everything else, to have to worry about the safety of his children. Automatically, he is reminded of the biblical story of Job.

With these thoughts and others stumbling around inside his head, before he knows it, he sinks, unexpectedly and surprisingly, into a deep, deep dreamless slumber.

Chapter 24

꒰⊱꒱

September brings with it an *Altweibersommer*, or, as the Americans like to call it, an Indian summer. The river has never looked more tranquil and inviting, the water positively glowing from the sun's rays. Except for the swastika flags fluttering everywhere, Frankfurt has never looked so alluring. The three Gutman children and the two Mayer children will now be ferried regularly to school by Hans. Herr Mayer has decreed this new arrangement; he says he prefers Hans driving the children in the Daimler rather than the different drivers previously sent by the car service to drive the boys to and from school. He feels it will be safer, and Samuel agrees. Each school day morning, Hans is to drive the three boys to their school first, then return to pick up the two girls, reversing the order in the afternoon when the school day is over. In the intervening hours, Hans will be at Herr Mayer's disposal, as usual. The arrangement takes into account the different schedules of the two schools.

The first day of the new school term falls on Monday, September 2nd. With the possible exception of Fritz, no-one has looked forward to this day more than Naomi. She calls for Henrietta and, together the two girls walk down the three flights to wait for Hans in the foyer of the building, as they have been instructed. Naomi is, as usual, weighed down by a heavy satchel bulging with books, while Henrietta's satchel is, also as usual, almost empty. Henrietta barely responds to Naomi's greeting. She seems listless and morose, certainly not her usual talkative self. Naomi doesn't know what to think. She can't help feeling hurt. Tentatively, she tests the water. "Henrietta, I'm so happy to see you. It..it's been a while."

Henrietta merely grunts in reply. She doesn't even look at Naomi.

"Is something the matter, Henrietta? Are you feeling all right?"

"Oh, *lass mich in Ruhe*, Naomi, just leave me alone, can't you!"

Naomi is too shocked and hurt to say anything more. Luckily, just at that moment the Daimler draws up outside the building. By the time the girls emerge, Hans is already holding the rear door of the car open for them. Naomi greets him formally with "*Guten Morgen*, Herr Bauer," and Hans smiles, tips his cap, and returns Fraulein Gutman's greeting. Henrietta remains silent, ignores Hans and the hand he extends to help her into the car, and sullenly flops herself onto the seat.

The short ride to the girls' *Gymnasium* is made in total silence. Naomi makes no further attempt to engage Henrietta, who, at any rate, has her head turned away from Naomi and is staring moodily out the window. Naomi tries to banish Henrietta and her foul temper from her mind and uses the time to recite silently over and over again Rilke's sonnet; she wants to be word perfect for Fraulein Schloss. Every now and then Hans inspects the girls through his rearview mirror, with the same speculative gaze that gave Herr Mayer some speculations of his own during their memorable drive back from Berlin. But, unlike Herr Mayer, the girls are not aware of Hans' attention, each girl being occupied with her own thoughts.

The day passes in a flurry of attendance-taking, the usual first-day-of-school class adjustments and assignments, and the distribution of text books. For Naomi the day is not nearly long enough. Her satchel is not roomy enough for all the extra books she has accumulated during the day, but she decides they are too precious to be left in her desk at school; she will carry them home. Laden down with the bulging satchel on her back and the additional burden of books in her arms, she waits for Henrietta at the designated spot just inside the school's doors.

When Henrietta joins her a few minutes later, it is evident that her mood of earlier in the day has not lifted. If anything, she seems even more grumpy and morose than she was in the morning. She doesn't bother to greet Naomi, and throws her almost empty satchel to the floor. The crowd of girls leaving school thins out until just the two of them, and one or two stragglers, remain inside the building. Henrietta stamps her foot in anger. "That Hans. Why can't he be on time, *um Gottes willen!*" She rants in this fashion for a few minutes. Hans has obviously been detained, and Herr Mayer has given Henrietta strict instructions that should there be a delay, the girls are to wait inside the school until Hans arrives.

Henrietta heaves her satchel from the floor and puts her arms through the straps. "Come Naomi," she says. "I don't know about you but I don't intend to wait any longer. We don't have far to go. It's a beautiful day and I feel like walking anyway." She opens the door, not waiting to see if Naomi is following.

"I..I don't think we should just leave, Henrietta," Naomi calls after her haltingly. "Hans will come and not find us and then…"

Henrietta doesn't let her finish. "Oh stop being such a *Schwächling*, Naomi. Are you coming or not?"

Naomi cannot bear to see Henrietta behave like this. She follows unwillingly, unhappily, dragging her foot more than usual under the weight of her satchel and all the extra books in her arms. She trudges along awkwardly. Henrietta has already turned the corner, out of Naomi's field of vision, when the music reaches them. Naomi follows, clumsily trying to catch up to Henrietta, and almost collides with her back. Henrietta has stopped on the pavement and is watching the group of Hitler *Jugend* marching down the middle of the road. They are singing the Horst Wessel song. The group is made up of almost identical teenage boys, about ten or twelve of them, all blonde and blue-eyed, in the desired Aryan mold, and all singing at the top of their voices: *Die Fahne hoch! The flag held high!. The ranks tightly closed.* And, indeed, the leader proudly carries an enormous swastika flag, waving it back and forth as he marches. A few pedestrians have also stopped to watch, some clap their hands in encouragement.

"Come," says Henrietta, "If you just follow me and don't look at them, we'll be fine."

"H..Henrietta," says Naomi, "P..perhaps we should go back to school and wait for Hans."

"Don't be silly, Naomi. Just follow me and stay close to the wall."

Reluctantly, Naomi obeys, limping clumsily behind Henrietta, staying close to the wall as she has been instructed, trying to make herself invisible. Suddenly, there is a shout: "*Eine Krüppel, a cripple!*" The word is taken up by the whole group. They have stopped singing and are now shouting in unison *Krüppel, Krüppel, Krüppel.* Neither girl realizes for a few moments that they are looking at Naomi, that the shouts are directed at her. At that very moment, Naomi stumbles and her books fly in all directions. As if from a great distance, as if in slow motion, she observes herself with almost disinterested curiosity, falling, falling. Then there is a thud as her body hits the ground. There is a ringing in her ears and she feels suspended in mid-air. Can this be what it is like to die, she wonders. Am I in heaven? Then the ringing in her ears turns into laughter. Hitler's young recruits are bursting with good cheer, having a good time. "Look at the *Krüppel*, she can't even walk properly, she must have been drinking." The leader approaches Naomi as she lies sprawled on the ground. "You must be *betrunken*," he says sneeringly, "perhaps a *Jüdische Trinker*. A Jewish drunk." He pokes at her leg with the swastika flag pole. Naomi is determined not to cry. She remains on the ground, immobile, her head turned to the wall. Henrietta, who has been watching in frozen horror, suddenly springs to life. She spreads her arms protectively in front of Naomi's prostrate body. "How dare you attack my friend," she screams. "What is your name, you...you, *Tier*? You animal, you. I will report you to my friends at SS headquarters!" The youth laughs in Henrietta's face, but backs slowly away, unsure who this angry blonde Valkyrie is. She seems to be too Aryan to be Jewish. He cannot take a chance. He beckons to the group, "*Weiter gehen, meine Kameraden.* Let's go, they're not worth bothering with."

Naomi is still on the ground, her shoulders heaving, as she begins to sob. Henrietta stoops down. "Come, Naomi," she says gently. "It is safe to get up now. The hooligans have gone. They won't bother us anymore." Naomi makes no move to stand. Henrietta tries again, more firmly, more like her usual self. "Naomi, let's go. You can't lie here all day." She lifts Naomi's hand, pulls her to her feet. Naomi's body is limp and unresponsive. Her arms dangle at her sides. Her face is smudged with dirt, her skirt is torn, and there is a big hole in her stocking where the flagpole did its damage. Later, a sizeable bruise will appear. Not one pedestrian has come to the girls' aid. It is as if they are all watching a staged performance or a spectator sport, and are not sure whether to applaud or not. "What are you all looking at?" Henrietta yells out. "You've had your fun, you can go home now!" Some in the crowd have the good grace to slink away in shame, while others remain nearby, mumbling about *die Juden* and the trouble they are causing. Naomi stands, motionless. She is no longer crying but stares into the distance at nothing in particular, letting Henrietta gather the strewn books. "Come, Naomi," Henrietta urges again. "We are almost home." She pulls the satchel from Naomi's back, holds it in one hand and carries Naomi's books in the other. Naomi limps along in a daze, and the two girls make their way home.

The two Nazi guards outside the apartment building observe the girls with indifference as they enter, as if they are used to seeing the girls enter every day in this manner, one wearing torn clothes and limping, and the other weighed down by two satchels and an armload of books. Naomi has difficulty negotiating the three flights of stairs; whether from pain or from shock, she is incapable of moving any faster. When Hannah opens the door she is almost knocked down by her daughter who collapses into her mother's arms. It is a scene too painful for Henrietta to watch, and she averts her eyes. Her feelings of guilt are fast dissipating, but this is an intimacy too private to witness. It is a scene that Henrietta will never forget, but will play over and over in her mind for the rest of her life; it is so unlike anything that could ever have taken place between herself and her mother. And the loss and realization of what might have been pummels her heart with such force that she feels almost as if it was she, not Naomi, who was assaulted.

"Frau Gutman," she says hesitantly. "It's my fault. It was my idea to walk home." With uncharacteristic contrition, she says, "Please forgive me, Frau Gutman."

Hannah holds out her hand to Henrietta, and leads the reluctant messenger into the apartment. "Henrietta, I'm sure it's not your fault," says Hannah gently. "But I don't quite understand why you were walking home to begin with. Did not Hans come to pick you up? Please tell me exactly what happened."

By now, Naomi has calmed down a little, and is even able to tell her mother how Henrietta courageously frightened the ruffians away. Hannah leads the girls into the kitchen, where she inspects the gash on Naomi's leg, controlling her instinct to gasp with horror at what she sees. Carefully, she cleans the wound with peroxide. "It's not nearly as bad as I thought when I first saw it," she says as matter-of-factly as she can. "In fact, it is really more of a flesh wound, nothing serious, but we'll have Doctor Schwartz look at it, just to make sure." While she administers first aid Henrietta relates the story of the 'incident'; her naturally defiant nature gradually takes over as she airily dismisses the danger she and Naomi faced. "They were just young, teenage *Kerle*, Frau Gutman, barely out of kindergarten." she says. "As soon as I stood up to them they ran like frightened rabbits. Isn't that right, Naomi?" She looks to Naomi for confirmation, and Naomi, always the peace-seeker and by now more relaxed as a result of her mother's ministrations, obligingly nods her head in agreement.

But, before leaving, Henrietta says, "Please Frau Gutman, can I ask you not to say anything to my father about this? I am in so much hot water with him as it is…"

Hannah says. "Don't worry, Henrietta. Naomi and I won't say a word to your father, nor will my husband. Please rest assured."

Chapter 25

But, of course, Herr Mayer already knows the first half of the story and cannot be kept in ignorance of the rest of it for long. It is just Henrietta's bad luck that heavy traffic prevented Hans from dropping Herr Mayer off at the EmEm offices. As a result, her father himself happens to be sitting in the Daimler when Hans arrives at the *Gymnasium*, albeit late, to pick the girls up. When Herr Mayer discovers that the girls left the school on foot, he knows immediately that his daughter must be behind this infraction of the rules; he is sure Naomi Gutman would never be so disobedient. "Hans", he says, addressing his chauffeur with unusual candor, "I am at my wits' end. What am I going to do with this girl? I just hope they arrived home safely." Hans clucks his tongue in sympathy and offers to drive after the girls, perhaps catch up with them, but Herr Mayer is already late for a meeting and, at any rate, it will soon be time for Hans to pick up the boys from their school. Herr Mayer instructs Hans to drive him straight to his office. Which is fortunate for Henrietta as it gives her father's anger a chance to cool.

Herr Mayer's secretary Gertrud has already left for the day, but Herr Mayer's customer is waiting for him, pacing up and down with impatience; thus Herr Mayer doesn't even have an opportunity to call his home to ascertain if Henrietta has arrived. He reasons that Inge would telephone him if there was a problem.

Herr Mayer's meeting lasts late into the evening. His customer, a loyal old-timer from the days of Herr Mayer's father, is irate at EmEm's delay in fulfilling recent orders. Herr Mayer has a difficult time placating him. EmEm has always prided itself on punctual deliveries made with Germanic precision, and this has never happened before. It is impossible for Herr Mayer to confess the real reasons for the delay: that shipments ordered by the new regime have had to take priority. He fabricates an unexpected snag in the manufacturing process. At long last, the client departs, seemingly mollified, and fortified by a generous glass of *Schnapps*.

Herr Mayer arrives home late. He would have liked to stop off at Borne-platz for the evening service, to recite the Kaddish prayer for Frau Mayer, as he has been doing intermittently since her death, but when Hans drives past the *shul* it is already locked up for the night. Fritz, too, is saying Kaddish for his mother whenever possible, but it is too dangerous for the boy to attend services on his own.

Herr Mayer enters a silent apartment, hangs up his hat on the stand near the front door, replaces it with the black velvet yarmulke that awaits him, then proceeds to the bedroom to change into his smoking jacket. He gazes for a moment at the bed once occupied by his wife, and slowly shakes his head, as if in disbelief, then turns off the light and makes his way to the kitchen. Exhaustion floods him in waves, in a way he does not remember ever experiencing before. Despite not having eaten very much during the day, he has little appetite. Earlier in the day, Inge's prepared box lunch would have gone to waste had he not thrust it into the astonished hands of one of the Nazis standing guard outside EmEm. He smiles wryly to himself at the memory of the man's shocked expression. But the anger that later suffused him because of Henrietta, then the *Ärger* with his customer - both have robbed him of all desire to eat. The children have had their supper and Inge has left for the day. Herr Mayer assumes that Henrietta and Fritz are both in their rooms. His stomach knots at the thought of confronting his daughter. He knows such a confrontation will only further drain his energy and cannot possibly end well.

He removes the plate of *Sauerbraten* that Inge left for him in the warming drawer beneath the stove. He makes the requisite blessing over the food, and then just sits and stares at it for a few moments before lifting his fork and knife. With a sigh, he begins to stab at the meat without enthusiasm. Then, with another sigh, he lays the fork and knife down on the plate and pushes it away from him. He notices with detachment that the gravy has begun to congeal. Suddenly, it dawns on him that there really is no reason for him to confront Henrietta. No reason at all for him to bring up the subject of her most recent infraction. She is, at any rate, immune to his reprimands and punishments; confronting her will only be an exercise in futility. No, he decides, let her wonder at his silence. His relief at arriving at this decision is so great, that his appetite is miraculously resurrected; he retrieves his plate, attacking the food, if not with actual relish, with something almost resembling enjoyment. He even begins to think of Henrietta with begrudging sympathy. Could it be, he wonders, that her rebelliousness, which has seemingly become more pronounced of late, as has her moodiness, is a form of belated grief over her mother's death? And then there is the added matter of her skating schedule having been disrupted because of the start of the new school term. He knows how she loves the ice.

These musings, which in the past have been so foreign to his nature, afford him a measure of relief, and he begins to slowly relax.

Yes, he ruminates, it has been a difficult day all around, *ohne Frage*. Without question. Apart from Henrietta and the upsetting meeting with his customer, Herr Mayer was finally cornered by Hausmann and Weber and had to respond to a barrage of questions about costs and other logistics involving the latest shipment on the list. He managed to stave off his employees' questions by vaguely referring to the mysterious shipments as an inducement to a new customer for future, more profitable business. He is not sure if Hausmann and Weber were placated, whether they even believed him.

He sighs once more, and looks around at the empty kitchen that was once Frau Mayer's domain, and such a great source of pride for her. He had made sure to install the latest equipment: the *Kuhlschrank*, a Frigidaire imported from America, from the hinterland of the state of Indiana, and the latest in automatic toasters. At the time of her death he was looking into purchasing a machine for washing dishes; he had heard that such a device had been invented by an Englishman. He remembers vividly Frau Mayer's delight and surprise the first time he demonstrated the new toaster's 'pop-up' feature. How she had thrown back her head and laughed, revealing her white, even teeth; how animated she became. He remembers that it was her laugh that had first attracted him to Marga Kahn after the first formal introductions were made. He remembers how she had teased him after accepting his proposal. "My married name will be Marga Mayer," she had said, laughing, "and my initials will be the same as your business, EmEm. I do hope you won't get confused!" It occurs to him now how seldom he had heard his wife laugh in recent years. And the realization creates in him a feeling he has never known before: a sense of deep and irremediable regret.

He finds it strange how, with the passage of time, he seems to miss his wife a little more each day. How, immediately after her death, he had seemed to adjust admirably to her absence, had barely noticed she was gone. Now he is abashed by his callousness.

How his life has changed, how his thinking has changed, *seit* Berlin.

'*Vor* Berlin' and '*seit* Berlin'. Before Berlin and since Berlin. That is how Herr Mayer now marks time and events.

He listens for sounds from the children's rooms. That Fritz is doing his homework is a certainty. That Henrietta is not doing her homework is equally certain. He had expected to hear music coming from Henrietta's gramophone, but there is total silence. He finishes his meal, puts the dirty plate and cutlery into the sink for Inge to find in the morning, and pours himself a cup of tea. The hot liquid soothes and adds to the relief that swept over him after making the decision not to confront his daughter. As he sits there, finally relaxing, he hears the opening strains of a violin piece drifting through the apartment. It takes him a few moments to realize that the music is not coming from Henrietta's phonograph but from Fritz's room. The boy has been taking violin lessons for years and practices conscientiously every day. To think that he, Gustav Mayer, had once considered Fritz's desire to learn the violin just another manifestation of the boy's lack of masculinity, that Frau Mayer, in a rare instance of revolt had gone against his wishes, now makes him cringe and want to bury his head in his hands. He finds himself doing something that, not so long ago, he would have scoffed at the very idea, something he has done more than once in recent weeks. "Marga," he whispers into the empty kitchen, "*Ich bitte dich.* Please, I beg you. Forgive me. Can you ever forgive me?"

As he walks back toward the bedroom, he passes Henrietta's door. He hears a sound, and pauses. What is that sound? It is a sound he does not recall ever hearing before. Can it be that Henrietta is crying? Can it be that he was right in his thinking earlier? That she is finally mourning her mother? Or, can it be that she feels contrite over her behavior today, that she is weeping with remorse?

He raises his hand to knock, then immediately drops it. No, it will not do for him to intrude on her grief. If, indeed, that is what this is. It may, after all, be good for Henrietta to finally shed some tears.

Besides, he fears he will not be welcome.

Chapter 26

>‹€

Samuel's old friend, Doktor Moishe Schwartz, the son of Zalman Schwartz of Odessa, drops by later that evening to examine Naomi's wound and dress it professionally. "You're a very lucky young lady," he says. "There doesn't seem to be an infection and no stitches are required."

Doktor Schwartz had persuaded his father to allow him to study medicine in Germany. After receiving his medical degree, instead of returning to Odessa, he opened a practice in Frankfurt, married a local girl, and settled his family in an apartment not too far from the Gutmans. He prescribes a mild sleeping draught for Naomi, and she is now sleeping peacefully after her ordeal. The boys, too, are all in bed, and Frau Fleissig is in her room, where she spends most of her days now.

It is quite late before Hannah and Samuel are finally able to retire to their bedroom. Samuel is seething with anger over the girls' *'kleine Abenteuer'*, their 'little adventure' as Naomi has been kind enough to call it in a show of loyalty to Henrietta. But he sees how upset Hannah is, and so remains silent. It is Hannah who brings it up.

"Samuel," she says, "you were right and I was wrong. I'm sorry." With one arm, he draws her tenderly to him, while his other hand gently removes her head scarf, releasing her blonde hair which comes tumbling down in a cascade of waves and curls. For the first time in weeks, she doesn't resist or make an excuse to turn from him, but puts her head on his shoulder in the old way, and begins to sob.

"*Schatzie, Ich bitte dich*, please, you mustn't blame yourself, it wasn't…."

She interrupts him. "When I think of what could have happened to Naomi today…"

It is Samuel's turn to interrupt. He is angry. "I could kill that Henrietta Mayer. What could she have been thinking? To be so *unverantwortlich!*"

"I agree it was irresponsible, but don't be too hard on Henrietta, Samuel. She is going through a difficult time, what with her mother dying like that and her father being so, well you know, so… so Herr Mayerisch. At any rate, it was Henrietta who protected Naomi from those hooligans."

"Yes, I understand, but if she had only obeyed instructions in the first place…"

"Naomi is also to blame Samuel. She didn't have to go along with Henrietta. She knows the rules as well as Henrietta, that they are supposed to wait for Herr Mayer's driver."

"*Schatzie*, You know how Naomi is. She's loyal to a fault and doesn't want to cause trouble."

"Well, what's done is done. And maybe what happened is for the best because it showed me that you're right, Samuel." She raises her head from his shoulder and looks him in the eye as she makes her pronouncement. "It is time for us to leave Germany."

He pulls her closer into his embrace. "Oh, *Schatzie*. I wish it weren't so. We have been so happy here in Frankfurt, God has been so good to us, and with His help…"

It is as if Hannah has not been listening. "Samuel, you must take the children and leave as soon as possible. Go to Palestine, go anywhere, but take them away from here. There is no future for them in Germany, especially not for Naomi. With her disability…" Her voice breaks; she cannot continue.

"What are you saying, *Schatzie?* That's out of the question! Do you think for a moment I would leave you, go without you? *Nein, nein, das kommt nicht in Frage.*" He is shocked that she could even suggest such a thing. "Either we all go together, or we all remain here. Together."

"Listen to me, Samuel. Listen carefully. I have given this a lot of thought. Even before today, the realization has been gradually coming over me. Slowly, to be sure, but I finally came to the conclusion that you are right." He is about to interrupt, but she puts her index finger against his lips. "Shush, Samuel. You must go ahead. You must take the children. I will stay with my mother and she and I together will follow you when we can. If we all go together she will only hinder our progress. Perhaps Moishe Schwartz will be able to medicate her so that we can travel in easy stages. Perhaps first to Holland or France. You will map it out for us. But after today I feel a sense of urgency that I didn't feel before. You must get Naomi away from this… this madness. And as long as you are taking her, the other children must accompany you too. It will give me peace of mind knowing that you are all safe."

Samuel is rendered silent, not just because of the speech his *Schatzie* has just delivered, but because of the strength of will she has just shown – a strength that he now suspects must have lain dormant for all the years of their marriage when it wasn't needed. Until now, when circumstances have forced it to the surface. He feels his eyes blurring with tears. How can he possibly leave his beloved *Schatzie* here with her ill mother? Here, in this madness, as Hannah called it, in this growing bedlam?

All he can say is, "Let's not make any hasty decisions now, *Schatzilein*. We are both too upset and tired to decide anything right now, certainly not 'on one foot', as the saying goes. In the morning, after a good night's sleep, we will be able to think more calmly and clearly. What do you say?"

For the first time in weeks, one bed in the Gutman bedroom remains undisturbed; in the second bed its two occupants sleep, as one.

Chapter 27

> ✳

Naomi and Fritz have taken to practicing together almost every evening, –
that is, when homework assignments allow. Fritz comes over carrying his violin
case in one hand and his music stand in the other; the latter he sets up next to
the Gutmans' Reisbach baby grand piano. At first, it is feared that the twins,
if they are not yet asleep for the night, will disrupt their playing despite the
warnings they have received not to utter a sound. But surprisingly, the two little boys sit cherub-like, a select audience of two, their faces turned up to the
musicians and their instruments, in rapt adoration, mesmerized by the per-
formers and the music.

Naomi's passion for the poetry of Rainer Maria Rilke, while by no means
forgotten, has taken a back seat to this new-found joy in her life. It was Fritz
Mayer's idea. One day he heard piano music seeping through the walls that
separate the Mayer and Gutman apartments. At first, he assumed the music
to be coming from the Gutmans' wireless, so professional did it sound. It
was only when the pianist faltered and re-played a passage that he realized
he was listening to Naomi Gutman. He used the pretext of a chess session
with Izaak and Josh to shyly approach her. Haltingly, afraid of being rejected,
he said, "Er, I wonder if you'd be interested, that is, I hope you won't think
me *frech*, if I ask if p..perhaps you might want to try and accompany me in a
piece for piano and violin. I think it might be f..fun, don't you?" He hastened

to add, "I'm not very good myself, incidentally, b..but, I would like to try if you're willing."

Naomi was overwhelmed; to Fritz's relief she shyly accepted his suggestion. Except for her parents, who hardly count, of course, nobody has ever shown her this kind of admiration and attention.

And so the rehearsals begin.

Chapter 28

⋙⋘

It is the evening of Sunday, September 15th. A calamitous day that will be known by historians and future Jewish generations as one of many grim milestones in German perfidy.

For Herr Mayer, it is an evening that will be engraved forever on his mental calendar for the personal and catastrophic tragedy he must always associate with it.

The Gutman and Mayer children have been back in school for two weeks; the new term is in full swing. Naomi is blissful in her studies, her 'little adventure' all but forgotten.

She and Fritz are rehearsing, albeit somewhat ambitiously, Beethoven's *Frühlingssonate*. They are having a little trouble with the third movement, the *Scherzo*, but they hope to be proficient enough to play the piece at a *soirée musicale* Samuel Gutman is planning in honor of Hannah's fortieth birthday celebration in a few weeks.

Thus occupied, Naomi and Fritz are unaware that every German who is not in person attending the Nazi Party Rally in Nuremberg is at home, glued to a wireless set; that every Jew, every Jew who has the good sense not to venture outside this evening, has his radio set *ebenso*, tuned to the hypnotic voice of Chancellor Hitler declaring the new laws that will permanently alter the status, and indeed, the life of every German Jew.

Naomi and Fritz are oblivious to everything, except the music and each other.

Hannah and Samuel are in the kitchen, listening to Hitler's speech over their short wave wireless. Even Frau Fleissig has managed to leave her room on this occasion to join them. The Chancellor's didactic, stentorian voice and words come through all too clearly. Even after his speech is over, even after the cheering of the crowds has faded away and the wireless has been muted, Hannah and Samuel and Frau Fleissig continue to sit in their chairs, paralyzed with disbelief. Not one of them utters a sound; what they have just heard has rendered each of them speechless. Then Frau Fleissig throws her head back against the chair and begins to make low moaning sounds; whether from physical pain or as a reaction to the announcements, is impossible to know. It is in this paralytic state that Izaak and Josh find their parents and grandmother when they enter the kitchen.

≫≪

Herr Mayer has taken the opportunity of an empty office to catch up on some paper work. The Nazi guards have not returned to their posts. It is late by the time Herr Mayer closes up, once again too late to participate in the evening prayers at Borneplatz. He is in his car, trying to relax to the grainy but welcome sound of Mozart's Jupiter, when suddenly the music is interrupted by Herr Hitler's voice – a voice he instantly recognizes. Immediately, Herr Mayer's chest tightens and his breathing becomes constricted. Beneath the brim of his hat, he feels droplets of sweat beginning to form as he tries to suppress the nausea rising in his throat. He senses, rather than sees Hans staring at him in the rearview mirror. It is that same gaze Herr Mayer has become accustomed to, except now there is an added intensity in the man's eyes, as if willing Herr Mayer to say something. He sees Hans's broad shoulders stiffen and grow taut as Hitler's diatribe continues, and in that small gesture, that almost imperceptible movement, all doubts Herr Mayer has had about the man are swept away. In that moment, though he will never completely understand why, he becomes convinced, *ohne Frage*, where Hans Bauer's loyalties lie. There is no longer any question.

Another voice replaces Hitler's, a voice Herr Mayer also recognizes all too well, that of Reichsmarshall Göring. The new laws are announced. At first the news doesn't seem too toxic: the Nazis have passed the Reich Flag Law, making the swastika symbol the official flag of the country. Herr Mayer begins to breathe more easily, and Hans flexes and loosens his shoulders. After all, hasn't the swastika been blanketing the country for years now? Surely by this time the whole populace is inured to its ubiquitous presence? Surely, all the Nazis are doing by this new law is making it official, *nicht wahr*?

But then Göring enumerates the new 'blood' laws. Herr Mayer's nausea returns and intensifies; he feels physically ill. He knows that if he listens to one more word he will vomit. He commands Hans peremptorily, with unusual severity and without his usual polite '*bitte*': "Turn off the radio. *Sofort.*"

It has started to drizzle; a fine curtain of moisture descends on the Daimler's windshield forming a design of fine Belgian lace. The streets are almost deserted of pedestrians, and they encounter few automobiles. It is as if the whole German *Volk*, indeed the whole of Germany, Jew and gentile alike, are behind closed doors, listening to their wireless sets. The red and black swastika flags seem to have multiplied and reproduced themselves, hanging and fluttering in every conceivable size from every window and door, so numerous that they appear dense and thick as quilts. As Herr Mayer gazes out the car window, it appears to him as if the whole of Frankfurt is wrapped in one gigantic swastika. He watches the rain gently dimpling the puddles forming in the roadside gutters, and wonders how Frau Mayer's grave is holding up; a visit from him is overdue.

They drive the remaining distance to the apartment in grim silence, broken only by the repetitive click-clicking of the efficient Bosch wiper blades. Herr Mayer is momentarily hypnotized and lulled by their movement, like a metronome in their tedious predictability.

With his usual respectful "*Gute Nacht*, Herr Mayer," Hans leaves him at the main door of the apartment building and drives off. Herr Mayer cannot fail to notice that here also, the Nazi guards are no longer at their usual post. They, too, he thinks wryly, must be indoors somewhere listening to the Führer's words. Wearily, like an old man, he holds on to the banister and heaves himself up the three flights to his apartment. He hopes Fritz has returned home after his practice session with the Gutman girl. He takes unexpected pleasure in the thought. He looks forward to seeing the children, looks forward to shedding his clothes, which, during the ride from his office have begun to feel confining. He has no appetite for the supper he knows awaits him; he wants nothing more than to burrow under his *Daunendecke*, and sleep, sleep, sleep, to forget about the list, to never leave his bed again. He wonders if the children have heard the news; he doubts it. As far as he knows, neither of them is in the habit of listening to the wireless and, despite the recent 'incident' involving Henrietta and the Gutman girl, neither of his children has shown the slightest interest in the current political situation.

Alas. The day is far from over for Herr Mayer. He has hardly turned the key in the lock when he becomes aware of the presence of a visitor. It is the cigar smoke that gives away the visitor's identity and, sure enough, coming toward him, with his unmistakable rolling gait, from the direction of the *Wohnzimmer* is his brother Heinz, with Henrietta and Fritz hovering behind him.

The two brothers have not seen or spoken to each other for weeks. Herr Mayer was unaware that his brother is back from his travels. He is dismayed by Heinz's unannounced and ill-timed visit. Suppressing his displeasure and pushing aside all thought of sleep, he reluctantly forces himself to hold out his hand in greeting. "Heinz," he says, "how good to see you. I didn't realize you had returned, when....?"

He is not given the opportunity to say more. Instead of taking his hand, Heinz falls heavily onto his older brother's shorter frame, sending his spectacles askew and almost toppling him over. A stunned Herr Mayer realizes that his brother is weeping.

"She is gone, Gustav. Just like that. One minute she was there and the next minute she was gone. She has left me." His voice chokes. Herr Mayer uses every remaining ounce of strength to pry his brother's arms from around his neck; the man has attached himself with leech-like determination.

"*Um Gottes willen*, Heinz," Herr Mayer says, straightening his spectacles. "For God's sake. Pull yourself together, my man. Come into the kitchen. I'll pour you a stiff drink and then you can tell me *was ist passiert*." He turns and, as if for the first time, notices Henrietta and Fritz standing by, watching helplessly. Henrietta's face is drained of all color. He wonders if she is ill, if she has been affected by her uncle's story. Although he has always disapproved of it, he knows that Henrietta and Bertha have long had a close relationship. Or, can her stricken appearance have anything to do with the sounds he heard coming from her room a few nights ago?

By the light of the kitchen, Herr Mayer can now better see his brother: haggard, unkempt, tie askew. Heinz's disheveled hair resembles a tangled skein of graying yarn, especially as he plows his fingers through it in a gesture of despair. It reminds Herr Mayer that a visit to the ersatz Luigi is overdue. Fritz brings whiskey glasses, and Herr Mayer pours a generous amount for his brother who, in one quick movement, gulps it greedily, then holds out the glass for another dose.

"Henrietta," says Herr Mayer. "Please see what Inge has left in the way of supper. Your uncle should eat something."

Henrietta is unusually quiet and submissive. She obediently opens the Frigidaire and sets out a plate with slices of bread, a slab of cheese, an apple, while Fritz assembles *Besteck*: a fork and knife. But Heinz pushes the plate of food away and begins to pace the kitchen. The agony on his twisted face is painful to behold; his stained, crooked teeth have never looked more repulsive to his brother.

The alcohol has obviously not yet done its work. "Calm yourself Heinz, sit down and tell me exactly what happened," says Herr Mayer with as much patience as he can muster. He has never seen Heinz so agitated. Heinz, who charms clients with words and manners and a raucous sense of humor. Heinz, who, despite rebelling against their father's wishes that he join EmEm, was for many years the favored child. Until it became clear that Heinz's love for German law had usurped Mosaic law and the Judaism practiced by generations of Mayers. It was then that their father's approval of the younger son was withdrawn and his affection cooled. It was only then that Gustav's worth was fully acknowledged and his father's affection transferred fully to the elder son. Yes, Herr Mayer reflects: Heinz was not only Vati's favorite, but Mutti's, too, until her early demise. It was not until after his father's death that he was finally able to acknowledge it without bitterness. He remembers how, as children, the younger Heinz was always the leader, the daredevil in their games and pranks, while he, Gustav, was always the cautious, cowardly son, not daring to climb the trees or scale the fences around the Mayer summer home in the foothills of Bavaria. Yet, it was also he, Gustav, who bore the blame and reprimands when Heinz came home with bleeding knees and elbows or, once, a broken arm as a result of his misadventures. It was Gustav who was responsible for his younger brother; who should have known better than to *betreten* into Herr Schussheim's garden and steal walnuts from his tree. Oh, the unfairness of it, how it rankled.

Aber doch.

And yet. Heinz will always remain his younger brother.

The story is quite ugly, but far from surprising.

"We came home just a few days ago from London. That was the last stop on our tour. As you know, Gustav, or perhaps you don't, we have been away most of the summer. It was not all business, although I did see several of my clients. I thought Bertha was having a lovely time. No, no, I *know* she was. It was so romantic, like our *Hochzeitreise* all over again." Heinz's eyes mist over, as he remembers his honeymoon. Or, perhaps, the alcohol is finally taking effect. "And then, a few hours ago, just as I was looking forward to a quiet evening at home, just the two of us, I came home from a meeting, and there she was, standing in the middle of the foyer surrounded by suitcases. She said she was waiting for me because she didn't think it was right to just leave me a note. She wanted to tell me face to face, in person." His voice becomes sarcastic, bitter. "She's no coward, my Bertha. No, no. She wanted to stick the knife in personally!"

Heinz holds out the whiskey glass for a refill, and downs it eagerly. "Perhaps you didn't know. Although you must have suspected. Even I used to hear the rumors. Marga knew; didn't she tell you? No, no, of course, not. Marga wouldn't say a word. She was never one to cause trouble. Bertha is not Jewish." Herr Mayer is about to say something, but Heinz holds up his hand. "Let me finish my tale of woe. There's not much more to tell, at any rate As you must have heard this evening, the Reichstag has adopted the new 'blood' laws: not only are we Jews stripped of full German citizenship, but it is now *verboten* for a German gentile to marry or cohabit with a Jew. And that's just about the heart of the whole *Geschichte*. Bertha is not willing to suffer the consequences of being married to a Jew. She's entitled to an immediate annulment. Incidentally, in case you ever wondered, that's also the reason she refused to become pregnant. I desperately wanted a child, but she didn't want to give birth to a 'Jew bastard', as she once put it." Heinz sits down heavily, folding himself into the chair. "Oh, she still loves me. Or so she said. 'I will always love you, Heinzschen, but love has nothing to do with it. I have to survive.' You will not believe what her last words were. She told me she was also doing this for my own good, that I would be imprisoned if it was discovered I was co-habiting with an Aryan under the new Law for the Protection of German Blood and Honor. Then she picked up her valises and left without so much as a backward glance."

Heinz is running out of steam. He throws back his head, and lowers his voice so that he is almost whispering, barely moving his lips. "I was too shocked to move. I was frozen, paralyzed. I just stood there like an idiot, with my mouth hanging open, in a state of complete *Unglaubigkeit*. Imagine," he says, "me, the big *Rechtsanwalt*, who talks for a living, who is never at a loss for words, who pleads before judges almost daily. I was rendered speechless."

Herr Mayer bites the "Good riddance" that almost escapes his lips. He feels no satisfaction to discover that the suspicions he has harbored all these years about Bertha have proved to be correct; there is no joy in the vindication. Yet, he cannot find words of comfort for his brother, and refrains from uttering platitudes.

"Come, Heinz," he says finally, "why don't you sleep here tonight? You are in no condition to drive home." Heinz's large frame is slumped in the chair; he is already fast asleep, head back, mouth slightly open, displaying his unfortunate dentures. He has begun to snore convincingly.

"Henrietta," says Herr Mayer, "*Sei so gut*, please make up the bed in the spare room. I assume you know where Inge keeps the linens and blankets. Fritz, you and I together will have to get your uncle into bed."

Herr Mayer's last thought as he and Fritz make Heinz comfortable is one of enormous relief. *Danken Gott*, he thinks, *that I didn't confide in Heinz about my meeting in Berlin.*

⇒⊱

Herr Mayer finally retreats to his bedroom. Without bothering to turn on any lights, he sits down heavily on the edge of his late wife's bed, the one nearest the door. He removes his glasses and massages the bridge of his nose. He is too sapped of strength to remove his clothes, but force of habit makes him kick off his shoes. It would not do to lie on top of the *Bettzeug* with his shoes on. He rests his head on the soft down pillow where once his wife's head had lain. Thankfully, he closes his eyes, as sleep overtakes him. "Marga," he whispers, as he begins to drift. "Marga…"

A knock on the door breaks through his semi-consciousness. "Vati", he hears, as if through a fog. "Can I come in. *Bitte*." The voice is unusually timid and beseeching, and it takes him a moment to realize to whom it belongs. It has been so long since she called him 'Vati'.

"*Hereinkommen*, Henrietta," he mumbles, forcing himself awake again. "Of course. Come in."

Chapter 29

⇒⊱⊰⇐

In the Gutman apartment, havoc reigns. The twins are racing in and out of the rooms, partially clad, completely unchecked and unrestrained. Naomi and Fritz's rehearsal is over and the twins' boundless energy, no longer tethered by the music, has found a renewed and uninterrupted outlet. It has taken but a few minutes after the radio broadcast ended for Hannah and Samuel to discover that they are immediate casualties of the new laws. Liesl struts into the kitchen without any hint of servility or respect in her manner, and informs her stunned employers that since she is not above forty-five years of age, is in fact barely twenty, she is no longer allowed to work for Jews. "*Es tut mir sehr Leit,*" she says, "I will miss the children, but I have no choice. The law is the law." She is gone before they can even register her departure, gone without even saying goodbye to her little charges, belying her expressions of regret.

Ever since Frau Fleissig took to her bed, the grumbling by Liesl began. About the extra work load, about the difficulty in handling the twins on her own, about the long hours. Sometimes, her outbursts bordered on insolence, but Hannah chose to ignore them. Now, Hannah is not so sure that it was the extra work that Liesl was objecting to; now she suspects that Liesl was merely expressing the anti-Semitic mood that has engulfed the whole country. And, how Liesl managed to learn of the new laws so quickly, how it was that she had her belongings already packed and waiting in her room, will always remain a mystery. But there it is; before they know it, the Gutmans are suddenly without any domestic help. So complete is their shock, that neither parent is fully conscious of the rambunctiousness of the little ones. Fortunately, their neighbor, Herr Mayer, has either become accustomed to the noise, or is not at home. There is also the deepening friendship and trust that has sprung up between Herr Mayer and the Gutmans over the last few months. At any rate, it is a long time since Herr Mayer last complained about the noise.

As she always does after their music session ends, Naomi accompanies Fritz and his violin to the door. She feels alive with happiness, unaware of the devastation that has overtaken her parents' world, and will soon affect her own, unaware that their lives are crashing down around them. She watches Fritz as he walks down the corridor. It has become a ritual between them: when he reaches the door of the Mayer apartment, he always turns and waves to her with the bow of his violin. She waves back, and he watches until she is safely back inside the Gutman apartment and he has heard the door close. Only then does he open his own door.

Slowly, and humming a passage from the just-rehearsed Spring Sonata, she joins her family in the kitchen. Her face lights up when she sees her grandmother sitting at the table with her parents and brothers. She limps over to embrace her. "Oma," she starts to say, "how *wunderbar*...." And then she sees their faces, one more somber than the other: Josh's eyes, filled with dread; her mother's lips closed tightly in a straight line, as if willing herself not to cry; her father's head bowed low over his clenched hands; her grandmother, leaning back in her chair, mumbling incoherently, her eyes half closed, her face contorted with pain; and Izaak looking from one adult to the other in questioning bewilderment.

They appear like actors in a grotesque tableau.

Or, as if someone has died.

Upon Naomi's entrance, Samuel raises his head. "Naomi, mein *Schatz*," he says, "be a good girl and fetch the twins before they hurt themselves and destroy the whole place in the process." She has never heard her father speak with such heavy resignation, as if every word he utters is an unbearable effort.

It does not take long for everyone to learn of Liesl's departure. The twins are soon ensconced comfortably on Samuel's lap, having spent all their energy; one of them is already fast asleep on his father's shoulder, and judging by his fluttering eyelids, the other one is about ready to join him. One of the twins stirs in his sleep, digging his head into his father's neck, drooling slightly onto Samuel's shirt. Samuel tightens his grip on both his little *Schatzies*, and makes a silent vow: *I will never let them go.* Aloud, he says, "You children are old enough to understand what is going on. Herr Hitler and the Nazis have today announced a whole series of new laws directed at us Jews. One of the laws forbids German gentiles under the age of forty-five to work for Jews. That is why Liesl has left us. She is not allowed to work for us anymore. If I hadn't sold *Chez Gutman* when I did, we would now have had to let our gentile employees go, and probably just close down. Another law strips all Jews of full German citizenship. We are not yet sure of all the ramifications, what it all means." He pauses to clear his throat. Hannah pours him a glass of water, but his hands are occupied with the twins and he is unable to drink.

"Papa," says Izaak. "You see, Rabbi Breuer was right. Hitler must be the new Haman. Just like in the Purim story."

"It certainly looks that way, *mein Schatz*, but God will not allow Hitler to destroy us, just as He did not allow Haman to destroy the Jews of Persia, *nicht wahr?* So, let me tell you what Mutti and I have planned. We have been talking about this for some time." He looks from one to the other. "We have decided that we can no longer stay here. It is time for us to leave Germany."

At first the children just stare at Samuel, as if they don't understand, as if he is speaking in tongues. Frau Fleissig shakes her head back and forth, mumbling. *"Es war unvermeidlich.* Inevitable. Predictable. Just a matter of time."

"Mama, *bitte*," Hannah pleads. "There is no point to that kind of talk. You are not helping and you are just upsetting the children."

It is as if the old woman has not heard. *"Ja, ja.* That is how it was in Poland. First the pogroms, then the laws *gegen* the Jews, then pack up and run in the middle of the *Nacht* like frightened animals. How does it go, that French saying? The more things change, the more they stay the same?" She falls into the Yiddish vernacular. *"Immer die selbe Sache. Die selbe Sache."*

Naomi is the first of the children to react. "Papa, Mutti. I don't understand. Is this because of what happened to me and Henrietta? I told you, we were in no real danger, and I promised you it would never happen again." Her eyes fill with tears. "I can't believe you're serious. Where do you want to go? I can't bear the thought of it, the thought of leaving here. No, no, you can't mean it." She looks for support to her grandmother. "Oma, tell them we can't leave. You can't possibly travel…" But Frau Fleissig's eyes are closed. She turns to her brothers, but Izaak and Josh refuse to meet her gaze.

"*Schatzie*, whatever we do and wherever we go, it is not because we want to leave. It is because the *Umstände*, the circumstances force us to leave." Samuel can't bear to look at his daughter. He knows how much she loves her school, her teachers, her studies; how secure she has become, despite her disability, in these familiar surroundings where she has grown up, the surroundings which are all she really knows despite the occasional trips abroad. And now there is, in addition, her budding friendship with young Fritz Mayer, which Samuel has not failed to notice; and which he has, in fact, been following with fond bemusement. He groans inwardly, but says, "As long as we are all together, *Schatzie*, that is the most important thing. *nicht wahr*?" Even to himself, his words sound hollow and unconvincing.

Naomi turns on her heel and flounces from the room in an unusual display of pique. This is so unlike her, that Hannah makes to go after her; but Samuel signals her to stay where she is. "Let her be, *Schatzie*," he says. "It will take time, but she will have to get used to the idea, just as we all must."

Josh is the first one to express any enthusiasm. "I think it's *grossartig*. A great idea," he says. "I would love to get away from all these horrible Nazis. They frighten me."

Izaak, too, begins to warm to the idea. "Where will we go, Papa? Can we go to Paris and stay with the Ehrlichs? We haven't seen them for ages."

"That's a possibility, of course, but we haven't decided yet where to go, *Schatzie*, or when, for that matter. There's a lot to be arranged and worked out before we can leave."

Hannah sits next to Frau Fleissig, holding her mother's hand. Earlier, when Hannah told her mother what she and Samuel were planning, that she would stay in Frankfurt with Frau Fleissig while Samuel would go ahead with the children, she practically leaped from her bed. "What do you mean? You think I am too ill to travel? I will show you, I am perfectly capable." Her weathered face became suffused with anger, wisps of grey hair flying in all directions around her head. "That will never happen, *niemals, nie,* do you hear me?" she almost screamed. "I am perfectly able to travel with you. You will see." With that, Frau Fleissig dismissed Hannah's hand with a wave, and insisted on walking to the kitchen unaided except for her wooden *Spatzierstock*.

Now, Frau Fleissig is rocking to and fro, mumbling incomprehensible Yiddish words under her breath. Hannah takes her mother's arm and gently pulls her to her feet. "*Komm*, Mama," she says. "Let me help you to your room." Samuel, too, stands up, still holding the sleeping twins, one on each shoulder. "Come, *meine Schatzies*," he says to Izaak and Josh. "I'm going to put the little ones to bed now, and it's time you boys were also asleep. We will discuss everything in more detail tomorrow."

Chapter 30

Monday morning, September 16th, finds Herr Mayer in his office at EmEm, once again arriving early, before any of his employees. He is expecting a shipment of wolfram this morning from one of EmEm's Swedish suppliers. The shipment is earmarked for the manufacture of grenades and other explosives on the list. Herr Mayer intends to personally inspect the manifest when the shipment arrives, to make sure that all is in order. The two Nazi watchdogs are not at their post, and he realizes that he has, in fact, not seen them for several days.

He swivels his desk chair so that he can begin the day by communing with his father. He hasn't addressed him for a while, and has just decided to tell him about Henrietta, when he hears a commotion outside. Suddenly, the door to his office crashes open to reveal the uniformed figure of Herr Göring taking up the whole doorway and almost blocking from view the two blonde Brownshirts behind him. Herr Mayer is unable to conceal his shock at this unexpected visitor. Unlike the occasion of their first meeting when Göring wore a Luftwaffe uniform, the Reichsmarshall is now encased in black from head to toe, in the uniform of the dreaded Schutzstaffel. In the split second of recognition, Herr Mayer's feeling of déjà vu is so overpowering, that he experiences again the fear he felt during that fateful visit to Berlin, feels once more the hot and cold flashes, is barely able to control the trembling of his limbs. The Reichsmarshall, on the other hand, is all smiles and bonhomie as he waddles in.

"I was not sure of finding you in so early, Herr Mayer," he says. "But I was prepared to wait for your arrival." Herr Mayer manages to collect himself, walks toward the Reichsmarshall and extends his hand, which is contemptuously ignored. Instead, Göring conveys his girth, which seems to have increased by several inches since their last meeting, over to Herr Mayer's desk chair. "*Ach so*, Herr Mayer," he says, dropping down into the chair with a sigh of relief. "We meet again. But this time the mountain has come to Muhammad, as the saying goes, *nicht wahr*?" He gives his belly a few affectionate pats to make sure Herr Mayer understands his little joke, and his hefty frame begins to wobble in all directions. Herr Mayer tries to conceal his alarm; he doesn't know what is expected of him, what the reason for this visit can be, what, if anything, he should read into the SS uniform. Is it a veiled threat or a warning of some kind? He has heard that Göring is the founder and head of the SS, has heard rumors that the man has a fondness for morphine, that his addiction makes him unpredictable, unstable. To cover his shock and confusion, he says, "May I offer the Reichsmarshall some refreshments? Perhaps a cup of coffee, or a glass of water?"

Göring ignores the offer, just as he ignored Herr Mayer's outstretched hand. He swivels Herr Mayer's chair around in the same way Herr Mayer did just a few minutes ago, and inspects the images lining the wall behind Herr Mayer's desk. "*Ach so*," he says. "The Mayer rogues gallery, I presume. Certainly well represented, I see." His eyes come to rest on the photograph of Herr Mayer's father. "What a momentous occasion that must have been," he sneers. "The Kaiser, no less. Well, thanks to the Führer we have rid ourselves of all that *Unsinn*, that nonsense." Göring stands, puts his face right up to the photograph, peers at it intently, then flicks his fingers at the protective glass. For a moment Herr Mayer is positive that Göring will tear the precious photograph from the wall, fling it to the ground, and stomp it to smithereens. But then Göring unexpectedly sits again and swivels the chair back to its original position. "Herr Mayer," he says, "the Führer insisted that we give you the honor of a personal visit from yours truly. Frankly, that is the only reason I have come. As far as I am concerned, a telephone call would have been more than sufficient, but that's the Führer for you, always thinking of others. Even Jews. *Also*, I am here to inform you that the Third Reich is no longer in need of your services. We have found much better and more important sources of supply. You will complete the current consignment, and then you will destroy the list and forget it ever existed."

Herr Mayer's immediate feeling of relief is short-lived. "Of course, we expect EmEm to continue functioning," Göring says. "However, without you at its helm." Herr Mayer is not sure he has heard correctly, but Göring has not finished. In fact, he is just warming up. "Because of events yesterday in Nuremberg, of which you cannot be unaware, we can no longer allow you to have Aryans in your employ. In addition, our government now considers you a heavy security risk. *Deshalb*. therefore, Mayer Metallgesellschaft will, as of today, be taken over by the Third Reich." Göring stands up and begins to stride toward the door with as much dispatch as his girth allows. Before reaching it, he turns. "Do not concern yourself about the outstanding account. It will be settled in due course. Let it not be said that the Führer does not honor his commitments." He makes a rasping noise at the back of his throat, brings up a great glob of phlegm, which he deposits expertly on the floor, before adding, "Even to Jews." He opens the door and barks "Heil Hitler" to an unseen presence. A voice Herr Mayer immediately recognizes answers the salute, and Hausmann, EmEm's comptroller marches into the office, his spine stiffened with military bearing, his arm encircled by a bright new swastika band. "As of this moment, Herr Hausmann will oversee the activities of Mayer Metallgesellschaft on behalf of the Third Reich. We expect you, Herr Mayer, to cooperate with him in every way. Do I make myself clear?" He doesn't wait for an answer. "And make sure that those offensive portraits on the wall behind your desk are immediately removed. If I hear that they are still there at the end of the day I will order them destroyed."

Herr Mayer's step is robot-like as he automatically follows the Reichsmarshall to his black Mercedes convertible, his whole body numb with shock.

Later, he will wonder how his legs were able to convey him, how they were able to move at all, how he managed to place one foot in front of the other, how he managed not to collapse. Hausmann follows closely behind him. Before entering his car, Göring turns once more. "By the way, Hausmann," he says. "it is obviously *unangebracht* for you to continue to ride to work on a bicycle. Not appropriate at all. Therefore, as of the first of October, I am requisitioning Herr Mayer's car and driver for your use. I'm sure Herr Mayer won't mind. He certainly won't be needing them anymore."

And what if he did mind? Unaccountably, Herr Mayer feels laughter rising in the back of his throat, and before he is even aware of it a little cough erupts from his mouth. Göring has been speaking as if Herr Mayer is invisible; he gives no indication that he is aware of Herr Mayer's presence beside the car. Hausmann has the good grace to look embarrassed, turning away, unable to look Herr Mayer in the eye. The Mercedes is driven off by one of the Brownshirts, with the Reichsmarshall, resembling a very stout, black-robed Buddha, taking up the whole of the rear seat.

Herr Mayer continues standing in the same spot for several moments, staring after the car long after it has turned the corner, long after he can no longer see the swastika flags on each side of its hood fluttering wildly in the autumn breeze. He is in no hurry to follow Hausmann back into his office. To the office that is no longer his, but now belongs to Hausmann. He is in no hurry to face Hausmann, his former employee. He is in no hurry, for that matter, to face any of his former staff. Certainly he is no hurry to remove the precious photographs and paintings of his ancestors from the wall. He concedes now how prescient his secretary Gertrud was. It is now two weeks since she left. She just packed up her things and departed without fuss or fanfare, without giving official notice. At the time, Herr Mayer was upset, even though she had been warning him for months about her plans to move to England. He had put a good face to it, even helped her with the paperwork, had given her a glowing reference. Yet he had still felt abandoned by her, his only Jewish employee, the only person at EmEm he had always been able to trust without question. Now he is relieved she is gone, glad that she had the good sense to leave before the Nuremberg laws came into effect, glad that she is safe somewhere in England.

Glad that she is not here to witness his humiliation.

So, he had not been wrong about Hausmann; he had not been paranoid; he had had every reason to suspect him.

But the realization brings him no satisfaction.

Chapter 31

֍

The first day of Rosh Hashanah, the Jewish New Year falls on September 28th, almost two weeks after the Nuremberg announcements. The Borneplatz *shul* is packed to the rafters, the men's section and the women's gallery filled to capacity. Since that terrible day, the Jews of Germany have lived in a state of limbo. The optimists are certain that things must blow over, that it is impossible for Hitler to remain in power; after all, this is Germany, *our* Germany, surely the voices of reason will prevail. The pessimists, on the other hand, consisting mostly of *Ost-Juden*, are more realistic, and unfortunately more experienced in such matters, cynically pointing out the simple but glaring truth that, generally, history has not tended to favor the Jews. In the meantime, both groups, optimists and pessimists alike, seem paralyzed by inaction, everyone waiting for the Rosh Hashanah and Yom Kippur holy days to pass before making any major decisions. Perhaps the prayers offered up on these holiest of days will result in a reprieve from Hitler's new draconian laws?

Today, the atmosphere in the synagogue is best described as 'charged'. There is an added and resounding fervor to the 'amens', a nervousness to the congregational responses. Even the choir members, usually poised and sedate, are somewhat unfocused; there is a lot of shifting of feet and clearing of throats. But then, as the service progresses, the somberness of the day takes hold. The cantor, uttering the heart-wrenching words, *Today it is written who will live and who will die, who by fire and who by water, who in his allotted time, and who before his allotted time,* breaks down in the middle of the sentence and cannot continue for several minutes. And later, when the choir sings the Lewandowski *niggun, You followed Me into the desert, to an uncultivated wasteland... Oh how precious is My son Efraim to Me,* the sobbing from both the men in the main sanctuary and the women up above in the gallery, threatens to drown out the voices of the cantor and the choir. When the final Kaddish is recited, the mourners' voices spiral all the way up to the *shul's* cupola, filling the cavernous chamber with echoes of despair and supplication.

This year, the first day of Rosh Hashanah coincides with the Sabbath, and so the sound of the *shofar* is not heard. The blowing of the ram's horn, normally the most important and awe-inspiring ritual of the day is, in the Orthodox tradition, forbidden on the Sabbath, as is the playing of all musical instruments.

At the close of the service, with the last notes of the choir's rendition of *Adon Olam* still suspended in the air, Rabbi Gutfreund slowly ascends the podium. He drags his feet with each step. Then he merely gazes out at the worshippers without uttering a word. For what seems like an eternity, he stares and stares at his congregants in silence. Then he closes his eyes, as if he can no longer bear to look at them.

Gone is his usual air of confidence. Gone is the pomposity, gone is every vestige of the sanctimonious manner that has always set Herr Mayer's teeth on edge.

"*Meine liebe Bruder und Schwester,*" the Rabbi begins hesitantly, adjusting his slipping *talith* around his shoulders. "My dear brothers and sisters." With apparent disregard for the SS man in the congregation's midst, he continues: "It is needless for me to point out that we are living in, er, uncertain times. Our new year, Rosh Hashanah, is a time of renewal, of change. Today begins the period known as the Ten Days of Atonement, which culminates with the holy fast day of Yom Kippur. Let us continue to pray, and with the help of *der Almächtige*, we will get through this, er, this difficult period just as our ancestors did in times past; with His help the situation must change for the better."

He clears his throat. "When you go home today and partake of your apple and honey, I pray that you will all taste the sweetness and renewal of the coming year, the year 5696 in our calendar. Now, may I ask you to please turn to Psalm 130 and recite the verses with me responsively."

There is a rustle of pages as the psalm is located in the prayer books. His voice shaking with emotion, Rabbi Gutfreund intones the Hebrew: *Out of the depths I cry to you, Oh Lord*. And the worshippers repeat the verse, the voices of hundreds of men and women, rising as one. Each succeeding verse is recited in the same manner, the sound bouncing off the walls and pillars of the huge chamber and encompassing the congregation. Then Rabbi Gutfreund slowly reads the final verse of the psalm, pausing dramatically between each word: *And... He... Will ... Redeem ... His...People*.

There is complete silence for several beats and then the whole congregation repeats these last words, with the same cadence and emphasis.

The Rabbi raises his head and for a long moment stares up at the women's gallery from where the sound of weeping can clearly be heard. Then he slowly lowers his head once more to gaze out at the congregation of male worshippers. For several moments, he says nothing, just stares at each of the men sitting immediately in front of him as if trying to imprint each man's features into his memory. Then he clears his throat, and says, "As you all know, it is our custom on Rosh Hashanah to perform *Taschlich*, when we ritualistically rid ourselves of sin by throwing pieces of bread into a flowing body of water. In the past, those of you who have wanted to practice this ritual, have gathered at a certain spot overlooking the river to do so. *Jedoch*, this year, it is with great sadness and reluctance that I urge you to refrain from the ritual. I have been warned that a crowd of Jews gathering in this way on one of our holiest days may present an invitation to violence on the part of some unruly young, er, men who are not of our faith."

It is believed, and later confirmed by eye witnesses, that it was at this point that the SS observer slipped out of the *shul* through a side door.

But the rabbi has not finished. He extends his arms as if to embrace the whole congregation, and in a voice unsteady and choked with feeling, exhorts,

"My fellow *Juden*," he pauses for a moment, then repeats, "My fellow *Juden*. My dear brothers and sisters." Again he pauses. Then, his voice breaking and filled with utter despair, cries out, "*Rettet euch!* I beg you, save yourselves!" He seems about to add something else, then changes his mind and slowly descends the steps of the podium, his head bowed, his beard quivering.

The reaction to Rabbi Gutfreund's directive is electric. There is an immediate and audible collective intake of breath. Then complete silence. It is as if a shockwave has ploughed through the *shul*, and in its wake left the congregants in a dumbfounded stupor, too stunned to react, too paralyzed to move or make any sound.

The Rabbi removes his *talith* and passes it to the waiting *gabbai*, then departs with his bodyguard in tow, his head still lowered, his eyes averted. He doesn't address another word to anyone, shakes no hands, doesn't even acknowledge the Rosh Hashanah greetings that some congregants, having recovered from their stupor, offer him as he passes.

Samuel is one of the first to bestir himself. Sitting as he does behind a pillar near the exit, he is usually one of the first to leave the building. His immediate reaction to the Rabbi's extraordinary *Diktat* is one of relief and vindication. Ever since the Rabbi, before the whole Borneplatz congregation, expressed his confidence in Herr Schwimmer, the local SS chief, Samuel has been uneasy, has felt the Rabbi was guilty of burying his head in the sand. But if Samuel has had any qualms about the decision he and Hannah have made to leave Germany, today's announcement by the Rabbi has erased all doubt.

He waits near the main door for his family. They will walk home together with Herr Mayer and Fritz. He wonders idly if Henrietta attended *shul* today. The Gutmans have not seen her recently; according to Naomi, Henrietta has been absent from school for the last few days, and Herr Mayer's driver has been taking Naomi to school without her. In answer to Naomi's inquiries, the Mayers' housekeeper has been evasive. Samuel and Hannah are too weighed down with their own problems to give much more than cursory attention to

Henrietta's absence; their plans to leave Germany are just beginning to coalesce, and there is the extra work thrust on them by Liesl's abrupt departure.

Samuel knows he must speak to Herr Mayer soon, that he has promised to include Henrietta and Fritz in the Gutman traveling plans. Somehow, the opportunity has not presented itself. In fact, today, Rosh Hashanah, is the first day he has seen Herr Mayer all week. It dawns on him that Herr Mayer has not even attended the daily morning services during the past week. A feeling of remorse fills him. He blames himself for being remiss and too much absorbed by his own family's affairs; he should have called on Herr Mayer days ago to make sure nothing was amiss. He cannot even recall if Naomi and Fritz rehearsed together this past week, and he must remember to ask Izaak and Josh if Fritz has been attending school or if he, like Henrietta, has been absent.

It is just past one o'clock, and Samuel is beginning to feel hunger pangs. It has been a long service, and he is looking forward to spending today's special meal, a combined Sabbath and Rosh Hashanah luncheon, surrounded by his family. He can almost taste the braided challah loaf dipped in honey, the special honey cake and other traditional sweet dishes Hannah has prepared to usher in a sweet new year. He is looking forward to listening to his boys expound on what they have learned about Rosh Hashanah and Yom Kippur and the Ten Days of Atonement. He hopes his mother-in-law will feel well enough to join them at the table. Lately, she has been valiantly trying to ignore the pain, leaving her bed as much as possible, as if training her body into shape for the journey that lies ahead.

It is a radiant early autumn day, the rain shower of the previous evening completely forgotten. Even the hosts of black and red swastika flags, tumbling friskily in the breeze, seem to have lost some of their menace.

Herr Mayer and Fritz emerge from the *shul* together; Izaak and Josh, who sang in the choir, are not far behind. The crowds pouring out of the front doors of the building are unusually hushed, as if still under the spell of the Rabbi's shocking exhortation. Hands are hurriedly shaken and pressed, eyes averted, as if wanting to mask the irony contained in the subdued wishes for a good year, a sweet year, a healthy year. Now the women, who take longer to come down from the balcony, are beginning to appear. Hannah and Naomi, arms linked, each holding one of the twins by the hand, join the men. Henrietta is nowhere to be seen. The crowd disperses in all directions with exceptional haste. Herr Mayer's Daimler appears a few yards away, inching slowly so as not to outpace them.

To Samuel's surprise, Herr Mayer beckons him aside. "Herr Gutman, "he says, his voice so low that he cannot be overheard by any curious bystander, and so low that Samuel, too, can barely hear him. "I trust your wife will forgive me if I ask you to take a little *Spatzier* with me along the river before going home. I hope you are not too hungry, but I have something of urgency to discuss with you and am still concerned that my apartment may not be safe for such a discussion. Hans will follow your family and Fritz to see that they arrive home safely. I promise not to keep you long."

Only now does Samuel notice Herr Mayer's bloodshot eyes behind his spectacles. If possible, the man looks even worse than he did a few months ago at Frau Mayer's funeral, as if he is once again not sleeping well. Samuel has no choice. His desire to walk home with his family has been thwarted. But, perhaps, he thinks, this has been ordained; he will use this opportunity to reveal to Herr Mayer the tentative plans he and Hannah have made to leave the country.

The two amble slowly along the embankment. To the casual observer they appear to be two well-dressed gentlemen taking a companionable midday airing. After several minutes of silence, Herr Mayer stops suddenly, and with uncharacteristic disregard for the sleeves of his immaculate black suit, leans his arms on the dusty parapet, and stares down at the water. Samuel stands next to him, waiting. Though he has developed a deep compassion for Herr Mayer and his problems, he hopes it will not take him too long to come to the point. Behind them pedestrians pass in each direction, some strolling at an unhurried pace, others with more purpose. Never has the River Main looked more peaceful and inviting, never have the sun's rays glittered more brilliantly on its surface. Samuel is reminded of the popular German anti-Semitic saying, *When the Jews celebrate their holy days, the weather is always perfect.* Herr Mayer inspects with riveted concentration a white and black-striped butterfly that has landed on his sleeve; the exquisite little creature flutters there for a moment before taking flight again. Today, there are various craft on the river: rowboats and sailboats and, plowing slowly through the center of the water. a covered barge with a sailor at the helm. The only jarring notes in this scene of bucolic normalcy, are the swastika flags fluttering atop the barge and the prominent swastika armband worn by the sailor steering the vessel. Surely, thinks Samuel, any sane German, enveloped by such perfect serenity, must believe that what is happening to his country is just a horrible nightmare from which he must soon awaken.

Herr Mayer is silent for so long, that Samuel begins to think the man has not only forgotten what it was he wanted to speak to him about, but that he has, *insgesamt*, forgotten Samuel's presence entirely. Tentatively, Samuel says, "Herr Mayer...", at the very same moment that Herr Mayer turns to him and says "Herr Gutman..." Herr Mayer gives that little cough of his just as Samuel, bowing slightly, holds out his arm, inviting Herr Mayer to proceed first. "*Bitte,* Herr Mayer," he says.

"Herr Gutman, I hardly know where to begin," says Herr Mayer, at the same time removing his arms from the parapet and dusting off the sleeves of his jacket with his hands. He turns away from the river and begins to stroll again; Samuel falls in beside him, adjusting his pace to the other man's. "First, you must have noticed that the Nazi guards are no longer at their post outside our apartment building. In fact, they have been gone for several days – I believe since the 15th when, as you know, our lives changed forever. The two watchdogs outside EmEm's offices are also gone. I can't say I miss them," he continues dryly, with another little cough. "I have come to the conclusion that their removal is connected with the fact that my role, or rather EmEm's role, as armaments supplier to the Third Reich has been abruptly terminated."

Samuel says, "Well, that *is* good news, isn't it, Herr Mayer?"

"Not exactly," says Herr Mayer. "Because of the new blood laws, the Nazis have taken over my company. This, despite the assurances I received in Berlin earlier this year to the contrary. Apparently, I am now considered to be a security risk. I am merely to stay on in an advisory capacity." He adds, "You are fortunate, indeed, Herr Gutman, to have sold your business. If you hadn't sold, you may be sure the Nazis would have found an excuse to confiscate it by now."

"You may be right, Herr Mayer. But this is preposterous. Absolutely outrageous. Isn't there anything you can do? Have you consulted your lawyers, your bankers, anyone?"

"What would be the point? I understand the Nazis are seizing Jewish businesses left and right. All that I would achieve by protesting their actions would be to hasten whatever fate is still in store for me. As a matter of fact, just the other day, I heard that a colleague of mine in Hamburg, who protested the seizure of his business, was immediately arrested and shipped to Dachau. Nobody has heard from him since. Who knows if he's still alive.

"Incidentally, Herr Gutman, they are taking possession of my car and driver also. *Anforderung* they call it. Requisitioning. So, as of next week, we will have to send the children to school by hired vehicles, as you used to do." The two men walk on for several paces in silence. Samuel is too shocked to comment. Herr Mayer finally speaks again. "My guess is that the whole world must know by now that Germany is rearming, and that Herr Hitler no longer cares what the world thinks, which is why he doesn't need to be secretive anymore, why he has terminated my services, why he can order whatever he needs from whichever source he wishes. After all, have you heard any protestations from any foreign government after the announcements of the 15th? I certainly haven't." Samuel has to admit that he hasn't heard or read of any objections to the Nuremberg Laws from any foreign source. "But, of course," Samuel says, "it is more than likely that objections have been raised through diplomatic channels, which have not been released to the German public; as we all know, our press is heavily censored, *nicht wahr?*"

"That is a possibility, of course. *Jedoch*, Herr Gutman, we cannot assume anything, can we? Nor can we rely on anything or anyone. After all, when was the last time you heard of any country running to the aid of the Jews? As for me personally, I cannot assume that after seizing my business they will merely forget about me. If you remember, I told you weeks ago, didn't I, when I first confided to you the whole *Sache*, that after my role is over, I will be expendable. Why would they want me around? I know too much. Not to mention," he adds bitterly, "that I have suddenly become a security risk. A 'heavy' one."

"In that case, Herr Mayer," says Samuel, "let me urge you once again to reconsider and get out of Germany while you still can."

"That is not possible anymore, even should I wish to," says Herr Mayer, shaking his head. "And I do not wish to." Samuel has never before heard such utter desolation in the man's voice. "I am glad, though, that the rabbi said what he did, that he finally seems to be facing reality; I begin to have hopes for him. I would never have suspected him capable of doing what he did today. He showed enormous courage." Herr Mayer turns his head away from Samuel, and lowers his voice so that Samuel has to strain to hear him. He says, "I am forced to bring up another subject entirely, Herr Gutman, one that is causing me more *Arger* than I felt even after the death of Frau Mayer." Herr Mayer pauses, clears his throat, and now his voice has become almost a whisper, "It concerns my daughter."

"Henrietta?" says Samuel, immediately alarmed. "Is she ill, I know we haven't seen her for some days, what...?"

"No, Herr Gutman. Henrietta is not ill. If only she were. Illness is something I know how to deal with, *nicht wahr*? No, she is not ill. It pains me to tell you that Henrietta has forsaken all the religious principles by which she was raised, everything that she has been taught, everything that Frau Mayer and I tried to instill in her. She has forgotten all decency and morality..." Herr Mayer bites his lip, unable for a moment to continue. Then, and it is as if he has difficulty enunciating the words, he says, "Herr Gutman, Henrietta...is with child. *Sie schwangert*."

Samuel stops in his tracks, too shaken to speak. Herr Mayer has moved ahead, and Samuel hastens to catch up to him. When he finds his voice, he says, "Surely you must be mistaken, Herr Mayer, Henrietta would never..."

"There is no mistake, Herr Gutman. I wish there were. I forced Henrietta to tell me who the fa… the other party is. It is her skating instructor, a young man I personally engaged to teach her. He came with excellent references and made a good *Eindruck* when I interviewed him. According to Henrietta, he has become a member of the Nazi party, has joined the SS, no less. Even if that were not the case, what would be the point of involving him? In the present atmosphere, it would be too dangerous to approach him at all. And even were these the best of times, the *Kerl* is better out of the picture. One less complication. After all, he is not Jewish."

The two men walk on in silence, Samuel trying to assimilate the shocking news. Herr Mayer continues. "I thought of taking the rabbi into my confidence, but then decided against it. He would probably tell me to consider her dead, that I should sit *shiva* again. That I refuse to do. *Jedoch*, I will not have her living under my roof. She has disgraced me, disgraced the memory of her mother, betrayed everything we stand for. At first, I considered placing her in the Jewish home for unwed mothers, that Pappenheim home. You may have heard of it, Herr Gutman. Ironically, Frau Mayer sat on the board. But I rejected the idea almost immediately. I feel that today no Jewish institution can be considered safe. However, my chauffeur, Hans, whom you have met, has a brother who owns a farm in a small village to the north of the city, near Bad Vibel. I have learned to trust the Bauers. They are good people, anti-Nazi, and have been loyal to my family for generations. They have agreed to say that Henrietta is a relative of Inge's from Dresden. Fortunately, with her light coloring, Henrietta can easily pass as a gentile. She will live on the farm, help with chores, and when her time comes…" Herr Mayer's last words trail off.

"You may well disapprove, Herr Gutman, but I have no wish to set eyes on Henrietta again. I have disowned her. Although I will not sit *shiva*, I can no longer consider her my daughter. I don't know if you can understand that, but there it is. Despite that, however, I have made sure that she is physically safe; on the Bauers' farm I feel confident she will be protected. After the events of the last few days, I cannot predict what will happen next. I am waiting for another shoe, or several shoes, to drop. These people are capable of anything. They have seized my business and my car; it may be just a matter of time, perhaps days, before they seize my bank accounts, my apartment, who knows what else? Fortunately, as I told you, my father established more than one Swiss account which I do not believe the Nazis can touch, even should they become aware of their existence. However, as a precaution, I have deposited a generous sum in the Bauers' bank account, to cover the expense of caring for Henrietta for the foreseeable future."

The two men continue walking, not speaking, one too shocked to say a word and the other lost in his bitter thoughts. Finally, Herr Mayer says, "Herr Gutman, you must be wondering why I am once again confiding in you in this fashion. Let me just say that I feel someone other than the Bauers should know where Henrietta is in the event anything happens to me. She has, of course, been given a new identity and a new name. The Bauers felt it would be easier for her to remember her new identity if she kept her first name. She is now Henrietta Meissner, orphaned daughter of Inge Bauer's brother, Hermann Meissner of Dresden, recently deceased.

"Now there will be one less person for you to take with you when you leave Germany, Herr Gutman. One less burden to encumber you. There is only Fritz."

Herr Mayer turns, and Samuel turns with him. The two men retrace their steps, with Herr Mayer picking up the pace. He has accomplished what he set out to accomplish, said what he had to say. No further words are necessary. Samuel's mind is awhirl with Herr Mayer's latest revelations. He finally manages to collect his thoughts before the two men part ways, enough to say, "Herr Mayer, please forgive me for saying this, which I'm sure you have already considered: regardless of the circumstances of its birth, the child will be Jewish." Herr Mayer nods his head. "Yes, Jewish," he echoes bitterly, and gives his little cough. The pain in his voice is palpable.

Just as they reach the apartment building Samuel says, "Let me take this opportunity to inform you, Herr Mayer, that my family and I are planning to leave Frankfurt before the end of the year. We will be more than pleased to take Fritz with us. I assume his travelling papers are all in order. I will let you know when our plans are completely finalized." Herr Mayer nods, and merely says, "*Danke.*" They climb the three flights of stairs in silence. When they reach the top floor, Samuel holds out his hand. He wants to wish Herr Mayer a sweet and healthy new year, the customary greeting, but he cannot bring the words out. Even to his own ears that greeting would now sound like a hollow mockery of itself.

Herr Mayer is also silent.. He has exhausted everything he intended to say. He takes Samuel's proffered hand, shakes it, gives his little bow with the almost imperceptible clicking of heels, and the two men part ways, each proceeding in the direction of his own apartment. Samuel watches as Herr Mayer, his back rigidly straight as always, strides slowly but with immense dignity down the corridor to his door. Unbidden, a picture of Herr Mayer and Fritz sitting by themselves at their Rosh Hashanah table leaps into Samuel's mind, and he is tempted to call after him, to invite them to join his family.

He will never understand why he resisted giving voice to the temptation, why he remained silent. In later years, whenever Samuel thinks back to this day, as he often does, the memory of his omission never fails to fill him with shame and deep, deep remorse.

Lieber Gott, Samuel says to himself as he watches Herr Mayer disappear into his apartment, *how much more can one man bear without going completely mad?*

Chapter 32

Henrietta cannot stop crying. Nor can she stop the almost incessant nausea. Even when she finally stops vomiting and weeping and manages to fall into a restless sleep, the tears well up behind her eyelids. When she wakes up, the pillow feels as if it has been drenched, the nausea again rises in her throat and she barely manages to reach the commode in time. She is having troubled dreams, filled with frightening images: huge swastika flags and groups of faceless blonde *Jugend* wearing black boots, singing and laughing and marching with exaggerated goose steps, always marching, marching, their legs reaching higher and higher into the air with each step they take.

Strangely enough, the one person she never dreams about is Otto. It is during her waking hours that she thinks of him. How will she ever be able to banish his image from her mind? How will she ever be able to erase the memory of their last meeting at the *Eisbahn*? Will she ever be able to forget how he looked, dressed in black from his peaked cap down to his new black leather skates, and the two new SS insignia sparkling in each lapel of his collar? For the first time, she is frightened of him, frightened to approach him. For the first time, he doesn't hold out his arms to her in welcome. To the contrary, for the first time, he looks at her coldly, as if at an unwelcome intruder, as if at a stranger.

It takes all of her courage, but she has to tell him, doesn't she? Will she ever be able to forget his reaction when, with her eyes down, she haltingly whispers her suspicions? His face, which for so long has filled her dreams, both waking and sleeping, the face which she can barely wait to see again every time they part, the face for which she has willingly done anything he asked – his face becomes contorted and ugly, his blue eyes almost closed into two angry fissures. She can barely recognize him. "What?" he sneers. "Do you think I could ever father a Jewish bastard? *Unmöglich*! Out of the question! Who knows how many other *Kerls* you've seduced with your Jewish wiles! I know your kind. You're nothing but another cheap, lying Jewish whore. Don't think I don't know the tricks you *Huren* play, trying to entrap decent German men like me." He waves his arm in dismissal. "Get out of my sight, and don't you ever let me see your face here again! Do you hear? If you ever dare show yourself here again I swear you'll be sorry!"

She will live forever with the memory of how he had sharply turned his back to her, how he had skated smoothly away, how he had proudly adjusted his brand new swastika armband.

And then, as she is leaving, she notices for the first time the *Juden Verboten* sign posted outside the rink.

Oh, how could she have been so stupid?

And what made her think her father might actually be sympathetic to her plight? At first, she curses him. How could he be so cruel? Especially now, with her mother no longer there to protect her? But day by day, her feelings toward her father have undergone a gradual change. Even though, through her tears, she cannot yet bring herself to think kindly of him, at the same time, she cannot really blame him anymore. Knowing his unbending nature, what choice did he have, what else could he have done but throw her out? If only her mother were still alive. For the first time since her death Henrietta has started to think of her mother, trying to pull her image into focus, remembering her tender ways, remembering how steadfastly patient and forgiving she was in the face of Henrietta's teenage rebellious outbursts. She remembers now with shame how she stood at her mother's gravesite, completely numb, only wishing for the funeral to be over so that she could rush back to Otto.

If only she now had a photograph of her mother, something tangible to jolt her memory; if only she had something to remind her of how her mother looked before she became ill. The only image of her mother that she recalls clearly is the one from the hospital room, when she lay unconscious and motionless in a metal bed, with a tangle of tubes snaking out of her body.

How she wishes she could now seek comfort in her mother's arms. "Mutti," she whispers, unwittingly echoing Herr Mayer's words. "Please forgive me."

When she thinks back to the last few months, as she cannot help doing over and over again, she feels she must have been hypnotized. Or under some kind of evil spell. There can be no other explanation for her actions.

꒰꒱

It is Rudi, the family Doberman, who nudges Henrietta out of her misery. The dog may once, in his heyday, have been a ferocious guard dog; today, however, no longer young, he has forgotten that he is supposed to be feral. Certainly, he no longer possesses one ounce of aggressiveness. As if feeling Henrietta's wretchedness and wanting to comfort her, he shyly sidles up against her during one of her bouts of weeping, and gently prods his reddish snout into her hip. Caught in the throes of a sob, Henrietta's gaze is drawn to the sleek black body and the head from which droopy, sympathetic eyes gaze at her with yearning. Automatically, her hand reaches down to stroke the animal, and the old dog's tail begins to wave from side to side with joy.

Hans's brother, Franz Bauer, his wife Gretchen and their sons Bernd and Gunther raise pigs. Henrietta has been given the attic room on the top floor of the farmhouse, right under the eaves. For the first few days, the stench from the pigsties is so pervasive that it fills her nostrils day and night, making sleep almost impossible even when there is a lull in her weeping and nausea. Over time, she becomes accustomed to it, and barely notices it anymore except when she has to actually enter the sties and feed the pigs their slop.

Her new surname, Meissner, is not so different-sounding from Mayer, not too difficult to remember. And she is relieved that she is able to keep her first name. Her initials, too, are unchanged. It is her new family history that is giving her trouble. Inge keeps impressing on her how vital it is that she not give away her true identity, that the Bauers must be convinced that she is Inge's pregnant niece, the daughter of her recently deceased brother, the poor little niece whose young, irresponsible husband, unable to face fatherhood, ran off and deserted her when he heard she was with child. Is it any wonder that she weeps? Is it any wonder that she vomits?

Henrietta is convinced that this new life is her punishment, a punishment that she must accept without complaint. Not that she has a choice in the matter. *If only I could speak to Tante Bertha*, she thinks. She remembers with painful nostalgia the times she spent with Tante Bertha. How they listened to music together. How they sang together. How they laughed together. *I know Tante Bertha would not judge me too harshly. That she would insist on being with me when*.... Her thoughts refuse to travel to that future date, a date so amorphous in her mind that she cannot imagine it ever arriving; it simply doesn't exist.

But she has been forbidden to contact anyone from her former life. Besides, Tante Bertha is no longer her aunt, and who knows where she is now, anyway? Didn't she hear Onkel Heinz's story with her own ears? And what of her brother Fritz, and her friend Naomi Gutman? It has slowly begun to dawn on her how for years she behaved with callous contempt toward her brother, how she bullied him, how she looked down on him as if on an insect not deserving her attention. And how for the last few months she had been inexcusably *gemein* to Naomi. The memory of Naomi lying in the dirt and that despicable Hitler *Jugend* poking at her with his swastika flagpole, makes her cringe with shame. It was all her fault.

Everything is her fault.

Now, the knowledge that she is forbidden to contact either of them, that she may never see Fritz or Naomi again, fills her with deep and agonizing grief. Never did she imagine herself capable of such excruciating remorse. She thinks now of Fritz with a fondness that astonishes her. She wonders if his pimples have cleared up, if he is still practicing his violin. She wonders if he will achieve his dream of becoming a physician or research scientist. If only she could send him a little note, if only she could tell him she is sorry she was so cruel to him, that she misses him. If only she could send a note to Naomi.

Of course, she would not blame either of them if they wanted nothing more to do with her.

Next time Inge comes to visit she will ask her to convey a message. She already suspects what the answer will be. But, surely Inge can't refuse to pass on a simple message, to let them know that Henrietta is all right, that she hopes they do not think too badly of her. Surely that is not too much to ask?

And what of her father? How she has always hated him! How could she have treated him with such lack of respect, with such disdain? How churlishly she behaved when all he wanted was for her to accompany him to a concert. Now, even toward him her feelings are beginning to soften. After all, despite banishing her, surely it was concern for her safety that made him find her this home with the Bauers? Surely it is out of concern for her safety that he has allowed her to pose as a gentile, to abandon the Jewish life he holds so dear, even accepting that she eat non-kosher food? How painful this must be for him! How much *Arger* she has given him!

In his heart he must always have loved her, despite all the grief and shame she has caused him. Must still love her.

How blind she has been!

⬥

She is amazed at herself, at how quickly she manages to adjust to the new routine and the farm chores. Physical work is a relief, easier than hated school subjects, easier than grappling with homework each evening. By the time the cold weather arrives, her belly has grown and her weeping has lessened. The disappearance of her nausea contributes to her growing sense of well-being.

She is even beginning to believe the lie that has been created for her: that the baby she is expecting has been fathered by a n'er-do-well profligate husband who deserted her in her time of need, that he may have come to a bad end, may in fact be dead. Gazing at the simple gold wedding ring on her finger helps her to believe the story. The fiction is less painful than the truth.

Franz Bauer is a taciturn man who transmits his instructions and opinions with grunts and hand signals. Physically, he is even heftier than his brother Hans, the perfect picture of a German *Bauer*. Gretchen, his wife, is the complete opposite. Petite, and annoyingly voluble, when standing next to her husband she is all but swallowed up. But she is a compassionate woman who has willingly taken Henrietta under her wing, teaching her to feed the animals, training her in the kitchen, to peel potatoes, chop vegetables, wash dishes, and never questioning Henrietta's inexperience in these domestic chores. Henrietta has even learned to milk the goat. Gretchen Bauer doesn't get upset when Henrietta sometimes oversleeps. When her husband grunts his disapproval, she tells him, "*Lass sie in Ruhe*. Leave her be. She's doing her best. Can't you see how she suffers? Just be patient, she will learn."

The two Bauer sons are grown men. Bernd, the older brother, is quiet like his father but there the similarity ends. Physically, he resembles his mother, dark hair, slight of build, of average height. Well-mannered but shy, he usually ignores Henrietta, but once, finding her weeping in a corner of the kitchen, he takes pity and stammers an offer to brew a cup of coffee. He is a bookworm, resents farm work, and would like nothing more than to spend all day reading books on anthropology. This he confides to Henrietta over coffee one rainy afternoon when both, once again, find themselves alone in the farm kitchen. The kitchen is the coziest and most lived-in room, its floor made up of rough wooden planks partially covered by a large, round sisal mat. A coal fire crackles in the grate, though it is rumored coal will soon be in short supply. In the future, they may have to chop down trees from the surrounding woods, and burn logs.

"I'd love to travel," Bernd tells Henrietta, "perhaps to Egypt, and dig for the remains of ancient pharaohs. I can't imagine spending the rest of my days shoveling *Scheisse* on the farm." He realizes what he has said, blushes and apologizes. "Excuse my language please." He tells her he wishes he could afford to go off and study in Heidelberg, or at a university abroad.

The younger brother, Gunther, is a tall, handsome, charming flirt, in the mold of Otto. With his blonde Aryan good looks, piercing blue eyes, and an engaging dimple in his chin, he is nothing at all like his darker, polite older brother. Once, he tries nuzzling up to Henrietta while they are both tossing hay in the barn; and once he gropes her when her hands are full with a little piglet she is carrying back to its mother. When she protests he pretends it is all a huge joke. So far, she has managed to fend him off. Henrietta wonders what would happen if she were to complain to the Bauers. She is afraid her life on the farm might become unendurable, even untenable. Worse, they might not believe her. After all, Gunther is their son, and seems to be his mother's favorite.

A few days later, both Bauer boys receive call-up notices. Henrietta breathes a sigh of relief. Bernd is to go into the navy, Gunther into the Wehrmacht.

Chapter 33

꒰꒱

The last day of November finds the Gutmans still in Frankfurt. It has been decided that they will travel first to Paris, where the Ehrlichs have taken up residence in an apartment at the rim of the Bois du Boulogne in the 16th arrondissement, an old apartment that was purchased long ago by Samuel's father, Izaak Gutman of Odessa. They will stay with the Ehrlichs for a few weeks. This will give them, and especially Frau Fleissig, an opportunity to rest and enjoy the Paris sights; then they will travel by train to Marseilles to board the ship that will take them to Palestine.

Because of the property in Palestine inherited by Samuel from his father, and as a result of connections Samuel has in the Zionist movement - not to mention a generous greasing of palms - the local authorities for the British Mandate in Palestine have granted certificates of entry to the Gutmans. Samuel has even managed to procure a certificate for Fritz Mayer. Just when everything seems in perfect order, a snag occurs.

A calamitous one.

In the process of authenticating the papers allowing the Gutmans to leave Germany, it is discovered that Frau Fleissig is not considered to be a German citizen. Never, in all the years the Gutmans and Frau Fleissig have traveled together to other European countries have they ever encountered any difficulties. But now, because of the new Nuremberg laws, the Nazi regime has labeled Frau Fleissig *staatsloss*, stateless. Even her prior Polish nationality is now in question. She has mislaid her birth certificate, cannot prove she was born in Poland. Fortunately, Hannah, though also Polish by birth, is a German citizen by virtue of her marriage to Samuel.

The government travel bureau is heavily guarded inside and out by Gestapo watchdogs. It is useless to protest. Useless and dangerous.

Frau Fleissig is ordered extradited to Poland. She is given forty-eight hours to leave Germany.

For the first time since his marriage, Samuel is angry with his mother-in-law. What on earth possessed her not to apply for German citizenship years ago? How could she have been so careless as to lose her birth certificate?

But, what is worse, Hannah insists on accompanying her mother back to Poland.

"Samuel," she says, "Mama cannot possibly make the *Reise* on her own. You know that as well as I do. Once we are in Poland, she and I will be able to travel freely. The first thing we will do is get her papers sorted out. After we rest up for a few days in Krakow, after we visit our relatives there, we will join you in Paris. You and the children must leave for France as we planned. I know it will not be easy for you to travel alone with all the children, especially the twins, but Naomi will help you, and Fritz Mayer will be a big help also. You know how the little ones look up to him."

"*Schatzie…*" he begins. But what is there to say? He has never felt so wretched, so helpless. His heart is drowning in despair and a premonition of disaster. He has never been filled with so much love and admiration for his wife, this splendid woman, whose strength he has only recently begun to discover. He knows she will not change her mind, that she is right. His mother-in-law cannot possibly undertake the journey to Poland by herself. And who else but her daughter should accompany Frau Fleissig? As to the rest of them, it is imperative that they leave, also. Life is becoming more and more difficult and dangerous, with daily incidents, and rumors swirling about arrests, incarcerations, and worse.

"Just remember," he says lamely, not knowing what else to say, "the new laws will not permit any of us to return to Germany once we leave."

Hannah looks at him as if he has lost his mind. "Return?" she says. "Return? As if anyone would want to return to this madhouse!"

They spend the hours before Hannah and Frau Fleissig's departure in a flurry of activity, packing valises, sorting and discarding items of clothing, shipping household goods in boxes and trunks to France and Palestine. Hannah packs the very minimum for her mother and herself. After all, they will not be spending much time in Poland, and it will be easier for them if they travel 'light'. She knows Samuel is sick with worry over their enforced separation. As she herself is. Because she feels his anguish, she tries to mask her own. Tries to hide how worried she is about her mother. How on earth is the old woman going to survive such an arduous journey in her physical condition? They are to change trains twice, once in Leipzig and a second time after they cross the border into Poland. The journey will take a minimum of twelve hours, depending on connections and unscheduled delays along the route, which they have been warned to expect. Samuel has instructed her to wire him as soon as they arrive safely at their hotel in Krakow. He and the children will stay on in Frankfurt for another week, leaving plenty of time to receive word from Hannah before they depart for Paris. They have no way of knowing if cables are going through these days. If necessary, he will write to her in care of *poste restante* in Krakow. She has marked down the Ehrlichs' Paris address in her little notebook.

As she folds and packs and chooses the items she and her mother will need, Hannah continues to hide her feelings from Samuel and the children, and more importantly, from her mother. She forces herself to hum a tune, as if she hasn't a care in the world. She doesn't know why the song that pops into her head is a Hebrew one she learned long ago in her Zionist youth group, *Artza Alinu. We are going up to our land.* How strange, she thinks, for this particular song to come to her at this particular moment. She cannot account for it.

"Mama," she says to Frau Fleissig with forced lightness in her voice, "I think you will need to take your fur coat and boots. You can wear them on the train. I hear the winters are even colder in Krakow than here in Frankfurt. And we mustn't forget our fur-lined gloves."

Naomi, too, feels the strain of parting from her mother and beloved grandmother, but, warned in advance by Hannah, tries to hold back her tears. Her distress at leaving Germany has all but vanished. Once she learned that Fritz is to accompany them, all her objections fell by the wayside and she began to welcome the impending journey. The twins, too young to understand what is going on, but sensing the tension in the air, chase each other up and down the apartment, more unruly and *ausgelassen* than ever. Izaak and Josh stay out of the way in their room, playing chess.

>€

In the Mayer apartment, the atmosphere is one of stoicism, all emotion suppressed with Teutonic restraint. Herr Mayer's manner is grim, but nevertheless he hovers with uncharacteristic attention as Fritz packs his trunk, giving him suggestions about what to take and what to leave behind. Fritz insists on taking his violin and some of his sheet music, especially the music for the Spring Sonata he and Naomi have been practicing. But there will be no room for the music stand; reluctantly, he must abandon it.

Unspoken between father and son is the name of the most recent missing family member. Herr Mayer has been forthright with Fritz, up to a point. It was not easy for him to explain the circumstances of Henrietta's disappearance from their lives. Tersely and awkwardly, he has told Fritz about Henrietta's situation, omitting the name of the party responsible for her condition; nor does he reveal where she is living. Fritz senses that Inge is somehow involved but, never very voluble to begin with, the housekeeper goes about her work in the apartment, close-mouthed as always.

Fritz is not sure how he should feel about Henrietta, and what she has done. Certainly, he is shocked. On the other hand, he doesn't miss the almost daily cruelty he experienced at her hands. Yet there is an ambivalence in his feelings that surprises him. How weird, he thinks, how weird that he sometimes finds himself listening for her saucy voice, listening for strains of music coming from her room, listening for her jaunty step as she enters the apartment after coming home from her ice skating lessons. He wanders into her room, a room that he was always forbidden to enter. He will take something of hers as an *Andenken*, something which will always remind him of her. He makes room in his trunk, taking out some of his precious books to fit it in.

He is excited to be leaving Frankfurt, to no longer have to face the bullies in his school, to no longer have to worry about the dangers lurking in the streets. He has only one regret, only one reason that makes him sad to leave: he will no longer be able to visit his Mutti's grave, no longer be able to place a stone of remembrance on the corner of the marble slab that bears her name, no longer be able to bend down and whisper how much he loves her, how much he misses her.

But just the thought of being able to see and talk to Naomi Gutman every day fills him with a quiet happiness, lifts his spirits, and makes every other thought or worry disappear.

Chapter 34

❧❧

The leave-taking at the *Hauptbahnhof* is wrenching. Hannah and Frau Fleissig have said their good-byes to the children in the apartment. Hannah and Samuel considered it best that the children not accompany them to the station. A porter assists Frau Fleissig into their first class compartment. Samuel has developed a steady, physical ache in the left side of his chest. He cannot bear to part from his precious *Schatzie*. Except for the birth of the children, they have never spent one night apart since their marriage almost twenty years ago. Until the last minute, even as Hannah ascends the steps into the train carriage, he is still begging her to reconsider, even though he knows it is useless, that she has no choice but to accompany her mother. As the train begins to move and gather speed, even as the tears stream down both their faces, he runs alongside, holding her hand through the window, begging, begging, begging. Until he is forced to let go. The train enters a tunnel and she vanishes from sight.

Can mere words do justice to the parting? Are there not scenes that words cannot adequately describe?

How can we explain how Samuel makes his way back to the apartment, when he himself does not remember how he arrives there?

These agonizing memories must be firmly stowed away.

Never to see daylight again.

Chapter 35

⇒⟫⟨⇐

They come for Herr Gustav Mayer on a Saturday night, after the end of the Sabbath. It is March 7, 1936. The date coincides with the Purim holiday. Earlier on that same day, Hitler's armies marched into the industrial Rhineland. The annexation is accomplished without a shot being fired. And, on this selfsame day, Herr Mayer's housekeeper Inge, flouting his orders never to utter his daughter's name in his presence, informs him that he has become a grandfather.

The news, though not unexpected, affects him unexpectedly. It is a girl. Henrietta has named her Marga.

Herr Mayer's health is deteriorating. He has had no appetite for a long time; in fact, his appetite began to languish long before his business was seized. His eyesight has worsened. He needs new, stronger eyeglasses but cannot rouse himself enough to visit the optician. One of his molars is loose but he is uninterested in making an appointment with his dentist. Most of his remaining hair has fallen out and he is almost bald. He thinks sometimes wistfully of his barber, Luigi, and what he would say were he to see him now. It is months since he visited the barbershop.

He rarely leaves the apartment anymore, except to walk over to pray at the Borneplatz *shul*.

Herr Mayer's services as consultant to EmEm have dwindled; Hausmann rarely calls on him anymore. He is surprised that he still receives a monthly remuneration. Herr Mayer knows that cannot go on forever. He believes it is Hausmann's doing, that this may be Hausmann's way of atoning, of letting Herr Mayer know that what has happened is not his fault, that he is acting out of self-preservation, that he is not a Nazi. Herr Mayer cannot bring himself to blame the man.

Were it not for Inge's care, Herr Mayer's wardrobe would no longer be so immaculate. As it is, he has lost so much weight that his clothes hang on him as they would on a scarecrow. Herr Doktor Graff visits him regularly, urging him to eat more, to take better care of his health, to get his eyesight checked, shaking his head helplessly as he departs after each visit.

This evening, he finds himself wandering into his daughter's empty room. He doesn't know why. This is the first time he has been in Henrietta's room since he sent her away. He notices a record on the turntable of the gramophone, the gramophone he gave her for one of her birthdays. He realizes immediately that the record must have been the last music Henrietta listened to. He cranks up the machine, lowers the arm, and the needle catches in the groove. He sits down in the nearby rocking chair to listen. With the first notes, he recognizes the opening bars of *Die Zauberflöte*, the overture. He recalls now that Henrietta had developed a love of opera. As for himself, he no longer plays the music of his favorite composer, that is to say, his *ersterer* favorite composer. Once he learned that Wagner is Hitler's favorite composer, and that he was an ardent anti-Semite, he lost all desire to play his compositions; in fact, when Wagner's music is played on the wireless, which seems to be almost non-stop these days, he immediately turns it off.

The Gutman apartment remains empty. Herr Mayer misses them, even misses the noise of those rambunctious little devils, but he is happy to hear that they have reached the safety of Paris, that they will soon be on their way to Palestine, relieved above all else that Fritz is safe. What a shame that Frau Gutman is still stranded in Poland with her mother. He has heard from Herr Gutman. Frau Fleissig fell and broke her hip shortly after their arrival in Krakow. Apparently, there are medical complications, making it impossible for the old woman to travel.

He has also recently heard from his brother Heinz, a letter bearing a Dutch postmark. Not only is his brother safely ensconced in Amsterdam where he has clients, but he writes that he has a new lady friend; not surprisingly, again a gentile. Heinz writes as he speaks. *What can I do? They can't keep their hands off me.* Just the thought of it brings a trace of a smile to Herr Mayer's lips. Heinz is still the same incorrigible *Kerl* he remembers from their youth; he will never change.

Herr Mayer has just returned from the Borneplatz *shul* where he attended the reading of the *Megillah*. It was a somber service. There are now several Gestapo agents scattered among the congregation, monitoring what is said and done in the synagogue. They sit quite openly in their full Gestapo regalia. The sound of the traditional noise-makers, the *graggers*, was lifeless this evening, totally lacking in enthusiasm. The assistant rabbi, who has taken over for Rabbi Gutfreund, is careful when conducting the services, very circumspect in his sermons. Herr Mayer thinks back to the previous Purim when he was sitting *shiva* for Frau Mayer. What a difference one year has made; so much has happened since then. Just as he nears the apartment building, large white flakes begin to drift down from the sky. It has been overcast all day, the air heavy with the warning of snow. It has been a long, harsh winter, and is by no means over yet.

Rabbi Gutfreund has disappeared. Some say he managed to leave the country, but nobody has heard from him. Others say he was seized immediately after he made his extraordinary exhortation at the last Rosh Hashanah service. Rumor has it that he is interned in Sachsenhausen, the new camp for 'political prisoners'. Another rumor places him in Dachau. Herr Mayer hopes the first rumor is the true one, that the poor man has been able to leave the country, that he has been rewarded for his courage, that he is safe somewhere, perhaps in South America; anywhere but here in Germany. He thinks back with wry amusement to their last conversation, when the rabbi had the temerity to suggest that Herr Mayer consider re-marrying. He even had someone in mind, one of the many unfortunate widows in the *shul*. As if he would ever have considered it.

Yesterday, he ordered a taxi and rode to the *Friedhof* for his monthly visit. He was disturbed to find evidence of vandalism; gravestones toppled over, swastikas defacing the slabs. He is glad that he insisted on a simple stone for Frau Mayer, set flush into the ground, making it a less tempting target. He has paid the cemetery in advance for 'eternal' care of the grave. Whatever that means.

As he always does at the end of each visit, he recites the mourner's Kaddish over her grave.

They come for him under cover of darkness, after Inge has left and he is alone in the apartment. There are two of them, in Gestapo uniforms. Or perhaps they are SS. It is impossible to tell the difference, not that it matters. He is not at all surprised to see them; has, in fact, been wondering for many months what was taking them so long. Their black uniforms are dusted with snow; it must really be coming down now. They are polite, suggesting he pack some warm clothing, enough to fit into a small valise. One of them sits patiently in the *Wohnzimmer*, admiring the furnishings, while the other accompanies Herr Mayer into the bedroom to oversee the packing. Perhaps they are concerned that if left alone he will harm himself, or harm them, that perhaps he possesses an old Luger in his bedside *Schrank*. So foolish of them. If he had wanted to harm himself he has had ample time and opportunity. He lifts the photograph of his father from the *Schrank*, where it has resided ever since he was ordered to remove it from his office. He stares for a moment at the ever silent image, then carefully tucks it into the folds of his clothing. He hesitates over his *tefillin*, then slips them, too, into the valise.

Herr Mayer leaves his apartment for the last time. He raises his hand to the small, unobtrusive *mezuzah* affixed to the doorpost of the front door, lets his fingers linger for a moment, then brings them to his lips. The Mozart is still playing, and trails after him down the corridor, but the recording is running down, dissonant and piercing to his ears, like the screeching of a cat. They escort him down the three flights, then into the waiting black Mercedes with the ubiquitous swastika flags on the hood. The snow has begun to settle on the roof of the car. The pavement, too, is speckled white. He turns to take one last look at the apartment building. The snow is blurring his vision, but through the darkness and the whirling flakes he notices chinks of light escaping from some of the windows. He lifts his head to look up at the familiar top floor where the Mayer and Gutman apartments sit side by side, but there is nothing to see. Both apartments are shrouded in blackness.

He is placed in the back seat between the two Gestapo agents; a third uniform is at the wheel.

The car begins to move.

Chapter 36

※

"*Komm mein kleines Kaninchen*. Come out of there, my little funny bunny rabbit, before you get hurt." Henrietta gently scolds her daughter who has disappeared under the kitchen sink. Henrietta plucks the baby up into her arms and covers the little begrimed face with kisses, at the same time tickling her tummy, causing her to squirm and squeal with delight. Little Marga is almost three years old; in fact, it will be her birthday in just a few days. Henrietta is filled with wonder every time she looks at her. She has almost forgotten the genesis of her daughter's birth; has sometimes even trouble remembering the name of the *Schlager* whose very touch she had once so wildly and foolishly craved. She shudders at the thought. This child belongs to *her*, and to her alone. The little face is a replica of her own, sparkling blue eyes, thick strawberry blonde curls that halo the little head like a warm woolen cap; much like the curls that once were Henrietta's, the golden locks that she was once told were *erotisch*, the locks that she long ago lopped off.

During the months of her pregnancy – a period that seemed as if it would never end – Henrietta felt only resentment toward the fetus growing inside her, resentment that she had been forced to abandon the life she knew, that she had been forced to assume a new identity, to live in secrecy and constant fear of being discovered. Strangely, she no longer feels any bitterness toward the other actor in the *Geschichte*; she has long ago accepted responsibility for her role. Of all the things she misses, it is her music she misses most. She thinks with longing of her gramophone, the last birthday present she received from her father, and is now filled with shame when she recalls how churlishly she accepted it from him. Even the Friday night rituals that she used to scorn now fill her with nostalgia. Sometimes, on Friday nights, lying in her narrow cot, she tries to recall the words of the Shabbat liturgy and the songs her parents and Fritz, (usually without Henrietta's participation), sang at the dinner table. Sadly, the words and melodies have slipped from her memory.

The little attic room under the farmhouse roof has become Henrietta's sanctuary. Even though it is unbearably hot in summer, and frigidly cold in winter, it is only in the privacy of her room that she can let her guard down. The farmhouse has only recently acquired electricity, but the wiring doesn't reach up to the attic, where Henrietta uses a paraffin lamp and wax candles for illumination. Sometimes she lights two candles, and pantomimes the way she remembers her Mutti embracing the air over the flames, waving her hands three times over them, then covering her eyes with her hands. She wishes she could recall the blessing, but the words elude her. Every now and then, usually when she is not thinking about it, a Hebrew word unexpectedly skips into her head, giving her hope that she has not forgotten everything entirely.

The farm is in an isolated area, several kilometers from the nearest village. Henrietta has never had occasion to venture outside its boundaries. She has no need to. When the Bauer boys were still on the farm, once a month they and their father would hitch up the horse and wagon, load the pigs and other livestock for sale at the market, and go off for several hours. Now, Franz Bauer drives off on his own. When he returns, Henrietta and Gretchen help him unload supplies and replenish the shelves in the kitchen and cellar.

The baby arrives. Without fanfare, a short labor, not too much pain, and a normal delivery that takes place in the attic, where Henrietta is attended by Inge and Gretchen. Never could she have anticipated the emotions that flood through her from the minute they place the helpless little bundle in her arms. When she beholds the miniature face for the first time, peeking out from the swaddling blanket, clean and smooth as a china doll's, she is suffused with feelings that are completely foreign to her. Never did she suspect that she had it in her to feel this kind of passion, this kind of tenderness. So different from anything she has ever felt before. A feeling that has grown in intensity every day and sometimes overwhelms her with frightening force.

⁂

Henrietta is relieved that the Bauers don't insist that she attend church. Every Sunday, dressed in their Sabbath finery, they trundle off in the horse-drawn wagon to the village church. Nobody in the household seems to expect Henrietta to join them. First it was her pregnancy and the nausea that prevented it, now it is the baby who cannot be left alone. Once or twice, there was casual talk about a church christening for her daughter, but so far Henrietta has managed to evade the issue, and it is has been some time since the subject was last brought up. When Inge and Hans visit, they are always circumspect, careful not to risk being overheard. It is not unreasonable for 'Aunt' Inge to follow Henrietta outside to chat, perhaps to hold her little 'great-niece', thus freeing Henrietta's hands to feed the pigs and chickens. Only then does Henrietta hear news of her family.

It is from Inge that she learns that her father's company, EmEm, has been taken over by the Nazis, that her brother Fritz and the Gutmans have left Frankfurt and are in Paris, that Frau Gutman is in Poland with her mother.

And, later, that her father was taken away by the Gestapo. Destination unknown.

Over time, Henrietta has heard snatches of broadcasts on the Bauers' wireless, has heard political talk at the kitchen table, discussions in which she is always careful not to participate. She cannot assume that Franz and Gretchen have the same political leanings as Hans and Inge, she cannot assume that they are anti-Nazi. She has learned not to show any reaction, to remain silent, to avoid risk. Once, about a year ago, when Hans and Inge were visiting, there was a heated discussion among the four Bauers about Hitler's recent *Anschluss* of Austria. Franz, as usual, merely grunted, saying hardly a word, and Hans and Inge, always careful, contributed little. It was Gretchen who said, "We should be proud that Germany is becoming strong again, that we no longer need to feel humiliated as we did after the war, *nicht wahr?*" Not receiving the expected support from Inge or the men, she turned to Henrietta, who was at the sink, washing dishes, and asked, "Henrietta, don't you think I'm right? Don't you agree?"

"*Enschuldigung, bitte*", Henrietta said, continuing her task, her back turned. "Excuse me, please. I'm afraid I wasn't listening," and the subject was dropped.

Inge has been clothing little Marga from the boxes of baby clothes put away years ago by Frau Mayer when Henrietta and Fritz were little, and which she removed from the Mayer apartment at Herr Mayer's bidding. These old clothes she supplements every now and then from the allowance deposited by Herr Mayer. Henrietta receives no wages for her chores on the farm. She works for her board and keep. Inge brings her the few toiletries and sundry items she needs. Henrietta doesn't know what she would do without Inge. She no longer takes Inge's devotion for granted. She recognizes the sacrifices Inge and Hans are making, the risks they are taking by their loyalty to the Mayer family.

After EmEm was taken over by the Nazis, and after Herr Mayer's Daimler was confiscated, Hans continued to drive for Hausmann. But after a few months, his services were terminated. No explanation was given. Unemployed, unable to find another position, he gratefully accepted Franz's offer to work on the farm. Franz, too, is grateful to have another pair of hands to help out, now that Bernd and Gunther have been called up. And so, to Henrietta's delight, Hans and Inge now live on the Bauer farm.

❦

During the three years that Henrietta has been on the farm, Inge has told her about the 'incidents' that have been occurring with more and more frequency and brutality against the Jews of Frankfurt. As they stroll through the fields with little Marga skipping ahead alongside her canine friend, Inge tries to describe to Henrietta the events of a terrible November night, a night that has been labeled *Kristallnacht*, night of broken glass; the night that saw the burning and destruction of thousands of synagogues all over Germany.

Including the Borneplatz Synagogue in Frankfurt.

Henrietta listens in horror. "What are you saying?" she says. She cannot begin to grasp it. That indestructible old building destroyed? Reduced to a heap of smoldering rubble? How is it possible? She cannot begin to imagine it. The Borneplatz *shul* is a historic Jewish landmark that has been there forever. It is part of her childhood landscape. No, it cannot be. Impossible. "What are you saying?" she repeats. "Are you sure?" Inge merely hangs her head, her eyes downcast.. "That is not the only Jewish building destroyed," Inge says finally. "Many Jewish businesses were attacked and broken into that night, many burnt down. The streets were filled with broken glass and bricks and piles of rubble, and fires everywhere. And not just in Frankfurt. All across the country. Even in Austria. The next day, the Jews themselves were forced to clean up the debris, to scrub the streets. To add insult to injury, they were forced to pay for the damage to their own property. Do you remember Herr Doktor Graff? He was one of the Jews scrubbing the streets. The Herr Doktor himself. Later, I heard he suffered a heart attack."

Henrietta cannot bring the image into focus. The elegant, erect, dignified Herr Doktor Graff scrubbing the street on his knees? She stands there, staring at Inge, numb with shock. She has not yet even begun to absorb the seizure of EmEm, the business that has been in the Mayer family for generations, the pain it must have caused her father. She still cannot grasp that her father was arrested, that he has disappeared. She is unable to imagine what might have happened to him. And what of the apartment? She cannot bear to think of it inhabited by strangers. Even worse, what if a strange girl is now living in her room, using her possessions, sleeping in her bed, listening to her beloved records on her phonograph?

And now, broken glass, Jews scrubbing the streets.

It is too much.

"Henrietta," says Inge, interrupting Henrietta's agonizing thoughts and images. "Do you remember your neighbors the Gutmans? It's a good thing they left Frankfurt when they did. Mr. Gutman's shop would certainly have been destroyed if he still owned it. It is no longer safe for Jews to live in Frankfurt. Whoever can leave is leaving. The situation is getting worse by the day, by the hour. Hans and I are ashamed of our countrymen, we're ashamed to be German. Believe me, Henrietta, if there was a way for us to leave Germany, even though we are not Jewish, we would." Henrietta has never heard Inge speak at such length and with such passion; the woman has never been so loquacious.

"And so, Henrietta," continues Inge, "I don't know how much longer you will be safe here on the farm. I don't know how much longer your identity will go undiscovered. I am worried for you, but I am even more worried for little Marga. We must think of sending her away to safety." Henrietta's face crumbles in horror, but Inge rushes on. "Many Jewish parents are trying to send their children to England, where there are families who have arranged to take care of them until it is safe for them to be reunited with their parents. There are several groups organizing these *Kindertransports* as they are called. Our dear Führer," she adds sarcastically, "is allowing very few Jewish adults to leave the country anymore, but children may still leave. I have a friend in the Quaker Society who has become active in sending Jewish children out of the country. If you want me to…" Inge gets no further.

Henrietta runs ahead with her hands clapped over her ears. She whirls around, her face distorted, furious. She stamps her foot. "Are you out of your mind, Inge? Have you gone completely mad? How could you even think I would send my three-year-old baby away? *Nein! Nein!* Never. I would chop off my arms before I would do that! That child is all I have. She is more precious to me than life itself." She waves her arms in anguish and turns away, unable to hold back the sobs. "I don't want to hear anything more about this, and please don't dare bring up the subject again."

Gunther is home on leave. He comes home every few months, staying for a few days each time. Henrietta dreads his visits. He is no longer in the Wehrmacht. He now wears the uniform of the Waffen SS. Henrietta has to force herself not to cringe with fear, but to look him in the eyes. Even his parents seem uncomfortable with his new allegiance. Henrietta sees how they avert their eyes when he comes down each morning, striding like a peacock into the kitchen in his sparkling black uniform. They say nothing. She supposes they are glad to see him.

Unfortunately, his furloughs rarely coincide with those of his brother. When Bernd is home Gunther is less likely to bother Henrietta. Today, he follows her out into the yard. She has taken Marga with her to feed the chickens and collect the eggs. Rudi, the Doberman, now a slow old hound, tags along faithfully behind them. He follows Henrietta wherever she goes. He automatically included baby Marga in his devotion and is fiercely protective of her, as well. He patiently, and without complaint, allows the child to pull his tail.

The child's ceramic cheeks are flushed from the cold. To Henrietta she has never looked so pretty, so precious, so like a little *Puppe*. She is bundled up in a hooded, fur-lined jacket that Inge says Henrietta used to wear when she was little. Faithful Inge has cut out the labels from Henrietta's old clothes, hoping to hide their superior quality. The ground is thick with mud from the recent thaw, and both mother and child are trudging through it in their rubber wellingtons. Henrietta holds Marga's mittened hand tightly in her own, and in her free hand carries the bowl of chickenfeed. The child delights in splashing and squelching up and down in the mud amid squeals of laughter as the wet dirt goes flying in all directions, sometimes landing on Rudi, who good-naturedly doesn't seem to mind at all.

Gunther comes up behind them outside the chicken coop, just as Henrietta holds the bowl out for Marga; the child loves throwing the chickens their food, and makes little chirping noises all the while, enticing them to come to her.

Gunther places a hand on Henrietta's shoulder. She stays absolutely still, paralyzed by his touch. Rudi emits a little growl. "*Also*," Gunther says sarcastically. "*Die schöne* Henrietta Meissner. *Und die kleine* Marga Meissner." Henrietta doesn't dare turn her head, tries not to move. "It's so *komisch*," he says, "really strange. My unit was stationed in Dresden for a couple of days, and I thought to myself, wouldn't it be a good idea to look up Henrietta's relatives, to give them Henrietta's regards. I thought, wouldn't that make our Henrietta happy." She hopes he cannot sense how her knees have turned to jelly at his words, that he cannot see how the blood has drained from her face. "And, can you guess what happened? I found several Meissners, but not one of them seemed to know a Henrietta. Not one of them had heard of you. Now, don't you find that funny?" He removes his hand and steps around her so that they are almost face to face, but Henrietta keeps her eyes averted, busying herself with little Marga and the chickenfeed. "Come to think of it," he continues, "I've been wondering for a long time how strange it is for a girl who's supposed to have grown up on a farm to be a vegetarian. What's even more strange is how you've never attended church since you've arrived here. I don't remember you going to church even once, at least not when I've been around, not even to christen your daughter. So, I ask myself, 'Gunther,' I ask, 'what might be the reason for such strange behavior?' And d'you know what I answer? I answer the only thing I can come up with which is, could it be that our Henrietta is actually not of our religious persuasion? Could it be," he lowers his voice to a dramatic whisper, "that she might actually be … Jewish?" His blue eyes have taken on the look of flint.

Henrietta feels her heart turning over. She tightens her grip on the little hand, and tries to control the trembling. She is frightened. Has always been frightened of Gunther. She knows he can be cruel, has seen his cruelty when once, believing himself unobserved, he kicked the aging Doberman out of his way with his boot. But now a spark of the old Henrietta, the Valkyrie who came to Naomi's defense so long ago, asserts itself. "What *Quatsch!*", she says, tossing her head in that certain way that once drove someone wild. Or so he said. "What utter nonsense! You don't know what you're talking about. How dare you make such disgusting accusations!"

She sees him falter, not sure anymore. Just as that young Hitler *Jugend* had backed away, unsure whom he was dealing with. He looks away, mumbles, "We'll see, we'll see, won't we?" Then aims his boot at the growling Rudi before retreating to the house.

Henrietta is sure she is going to collapse. What she has just done has drained her of every last ounce of strength. She cannot move her legs. She has become a statue, unable to pull her feet out of the mud. She stands perfectly still. Then forces herself to hold the bowl out for little Marga, then to bend her head and join in with her daughter's chirping noises. "Look, Mutti," the little girl says as the chickens gather in front of her, pecking at the food. "I think they like me."

"Of course they like you, my little bunny rabbit, they love you, but not nearly as much as Mutti loves you. Nobody loves you as much as your Mutti loves you, *nicht wahr?*"

The child leans her body into Henrietta's legs.

Henrietta stays outside in the farmyard for as long as she dares without arousing suspicion about her long absence from the house. Little Marga keeps kicking the mud with her boots and laughing delightedly when the sprays of dirt fly through the air and land on Rudi. Finally, with dusk rapidly approaching, and Henrietta's pulse almost back to normal, she and the child, trailed by a mud-speckled dog, return to the house. To Henrietta's relief, Gunther is nowhere to be seen.

At Marga's bedtime, Inge comes up for her nightly hug and kiss. Henrietta sits on one side of the bed, Inge on the other, each holding one of Marga's little hands. As always, Henrietta closes this nightly ritual with Brahms' lullaby. Her voice has retained its purity, but now has an added timbre to it, a depth of feeling, a painfully acquired maturity, the anguish of these past few years. She tries to keep her voice steady as she begins to sing,

Guten Abend, gute Nacht, mit Rosen bedacht...

But it is no use. Her voice breaks. She cannot go on

Little Marga's eyes are already closed. All that splashing outside in the cold and mud has exhausted her. Henrietta's eyes are filled with tears of pain and resignation. "Inge," she whispers urgently. We need to talk. *Sofort.* Immediately."

Part Two

❦

Cardiff, Wales. November, 1950

Chapter 37

≫€

"Come on, Meggy, pay attention will you, you're daydreaming again." With a start, Megan's eyes return to the book lying on the desk in front of her. Her best friend, Gwen Owen, is tutoring her for the O levels. "I'm so sorry Gwenny, I really am, I don't know what's come over me, but I seem to have trouble concentrating today. I think I should go home. I'm just wasting your time. You could be reading or doing a million other things you like to do. I'm really sorry."

"Don't you worry about me, Megan Rhys. It's you I'm worried about. You haven't been yourself for days. D'you want to tell me what's going on? If there's something bothering you, you know you can tell me, don't you?"

The girls have been in the same class ever since kindergarten, when Megan defended Gwen against the bullies in the playground. The two of them still laugh sometimes, remembering how Megan screamed in fury and launched herself at the boys who tugged the ribbons at the end of Gwen's plaits, or pulled her glasses off, or snatched her book to play monkey-in-the-middle with it. They'd call her horrible names, mocking the ungainly and myopic girl. Megan still bears a scar on her hand, evidence of the stitches she needed after one of her many confrontations with the bullies.

Gwen has rarely had to study, while Megan sits night after night in a state of bewilderment, trying to make sense of the homework assignments. When

Gwen was admitted to prestigious Cardiff High School, she turned it down so as not to be separated from Megan who was accepted by the lower ranked Canton High.

"There's nothing bothering me, I promise. I would tell you if there was. You know I tell you everything. I just didn't sleep well last night, is all, probably anxiety over the O levels. You know how I get before an exam, Gwenny. Just thinking about it gives me a stomachache or a headache, and sometimes both at the same time."

"You poor thing. Remember how sick you were once, and I had to hold your head over the sink in the school W.C." Megan laughs wryly at the recollection. "Yes, I remember it all too well. That was just before Mr. Davies' big history exam. I thought I'd really studied but all of a sudden everything just flew out of my head, and I couldn't remember a single date or battle or anything."

Megan closes the algebra text book and stands up. "It's no use, Gwen. I just can't seem to put my mind to these equations today. Please forgive me. You've been so sweet and patient with me, and I really appreciate it. Besides, it's getting dark and my parents will be waiting for me for tea." She gathers her things, puts on her coat and slips her arms through the straps of her satchel. "Will you be coming to church with us tomorrow as usual, Gwenny?"

"Of course I will. You know I wouldn't miss a Sunday morning with you and your Mum and Da for anything. By the way, have you told your parents yet, about you know what?"

"No, not yet. I'm intending to tell them today. During tea."

⊰⊱

It's a miserable, cold Saturday afternoon, with the days getting shorter and shorter and the damp seeping into everyone's bones with rheumatic intent. Dusk is beginning to roll in and Megan feels the first hint of drizzle as she starts to walk home from Gwen's house. As soon as she begins to cross the street to the other side of Llandaff Road, something makes her look up. It's the new sign. It would be impossible to miss it. She steps back onto the pavement, and just stares and stares up at the sign with disbelief and dismay, barely conscious of the moisture now running down her face. The sign takes up the whole space above the shop's display window, almost all the way up to the next storey, and extends sideways, over and past the two doors - the main door leading into the shop, and the second door leading to the upstairs living quarters - almost to the edge of the building. The letters are ablaze in a bright, dazzling shade of emerald green, superimposed on a white background. The letters are huge and blaring, impossible to ignore.

WILLIAM RHYS AND DAUGHTER
DRAPERS

So, this is the surprise her Da had told her to expect any day now. She'd done her best to wheedle it out of him, even putting her arms around his neck and planting kisses up and down his stubbly cheeks, the way she used to when she was little, but nothing had helped. She'd tried to enlist her Mum, who usually takes her part in everything, but to no avail. Mum had merely smiled her usual good-natured smile but kept out of it. Her Da had chuckled, lit up one of his Woodbines, patted Megan on the shoulder, and gone back to filling out his pool forms. "You'll never guess, sweet girl o' mine", he'd said. "So be patient. All in good time, all in good time."

She is mortified. She knows everyone, even Gwen, will tease her mercilessly when they see the sign. What could her Da have been thinking? What on earth made him believe this would make her happy? Just because she sometimes helps out in the shop when she's not in school? Of course, she loves being in the shop, selling the customers their buttons and zippers and hooks, measuring out the colorful ribbons and materials the way Da has trained her, chatting with the old ladies like Mrs. Evans and Mrs. Morgan, holding her hand over her mouth to suppress the laughter when Da winks at her behind their backs.

She knows she's going to have to put a good face to it, to pretend to be ever so pleased with the surprise. Why, he might be watching her reaction right this minute from behind the curtains in the flat above the shop. In case he is, she plasters a big smile across her face, tosses the blonde curls that are beginning to tighten into corkscrews because of the rain that is now coming down in earnest, and heads for the door.

⊸⊷

Megan is the only child of Glynis and William Rhys. The couple were childless for so long that they'd just about given up, when Megan miraculously appeared. They have poured every ounce of love they possess into the girl. Sometimes Megan wishes her Mum was young and pretty like Gwen's mother, who goes dancing with her husband at least once a week and knows all the popular songs, always singing along when they're played on the wireless. Megan can't imagine calling her Mum by her Christian name the way Gwen and Shaun do theirs. Mrs. Owen has more than once urged Megan to call her Cynthia, but Megan persists in calling her Mrs. Owen.

The Rhys's shop is in a good location on the busy thoroughfare, Llandaff Road. Because there is no other shop like it for miles around, the Rhys's are able to make a respectable living. They haven't always lived in this part of town. As newly-weds, Glynis and William started out, like many of their other friends, in one of the poorer areas of Cardiff, near Roath Park. William, tall and muscular, had been a dock worker in the Cardiff shipyards, and Glynis a typist in the shipyards' office, which is how they met. Both of them hated their jobs. But then, in a stroke of good luck (or, as Glynis likes to add, *and by the mercy of Jesus*), they'd heard about the shop on Llandaff Road that had living quarters above it. With their savings and a small inheritance from Glynis's parents, they'd scraped together enough for a down payment. Just as they were getting on their feet, the German armies invaded Poland and the war, the second world war of their lives, began.

William, at 37, was not going to wait to be called up. He'd been too young in the last war, had missed all the action against the Boche, so in 1940 he enlisted and eventually found himself on the front lines. He never talks about those harrowing months in the European theatre, nor how he received the wound that stiffened one of his arms, making it difficult for him to lift anything heavy. While he was away, Glynis somehow managed on her own. Both her parents were dead, and William's father, widowed when William was in his teens, had succumbed to cancer just before the war.

Megan was four years old when her Da left to join the army. It was a difficult time for the child, but Glynis, with patience, hard work and resourcefulness, valiantly got them through it until William was demobbed and safely home once more.

The Rhys's live in the flat above the shop and their needs are simple and few. In the summer they close the shop for a fortnight and rent a house in Weston-super-Mare. For as long as Megan can remember, her friend Gwen has come with them for the two weeks' summer holiday. When the sun is out, William and Glynis carry their deckchairs, umbrella and picnic basket down to the beach, and spend the days watching Megan and Gwen dig for seashells and buried treasure, build sandcastles, and splash in the ocean. Rainy days are spent indoors, playing Snakes and Ladders and Tiddlywinks, dominoes and draughts, listening to music programs on the wireless, and helping Glynis bake muffins and scones. The girls also invent their own secret games and language, accompanied by a lot of giggling and roving torches under the covers after Glynis calls 'lights out'.

Lately, William Rhys talks of selling up and retiring, but Megan doesn't believe a word of it. Her Da loves the shop too much, and what he would do if he retired is far from clear.

≫◄

"Is that you, Meggy love?"

Megan hears her Mum call as she runs up the stairs into the kitchen where, as she expected, her mother is soaking her swollen feet in a bowl of hot water and Epsom salts. Megan leans over to give her Mum a hug and kiss.

"Are the feet no better then, Mum?" she asks.

"Och, no. But no worse either, thank the Lord. To be sure, the damp weather doesn't help. Be a good girl, Meggy love, and put the kettle up for our tea. The table's laid and everything's ready but for the tea."

Glynis Rhys is a cheerful, unstylish woman in her upper forties, but looks older. Unmindful of the latest fashions and diet fads, her body is trending toward the upper limits of weight, and her face, which has never been called beautiful, except by her adoring husband, has in recent years become puffy, her cheeks overblown. It is her eyes that are her saving grace; an unusual shade of aquamarine, they sparkle with good humor, and can accurately be called the mirror to Glynis's soul. And after twenty-six years of marriage, William still calls her the love of his life.

Megan sheds her satchel in the corner, hangs up her duffle coat and scarf, and fills the kettle at the sink. "Where's me Da," she asks.

Her mother laughs. "Gone into hiding, I should think. Probably too embarrassed to come out. Not that I blame him. Be a love, Meggy, and hand me that towel before you go off in search of him."

Megan knows exactly where her father must be. Even though the shop is closed now, he loves nothing better than to go down to rummage around, to sort and rearrange the shelves. She knows this is his favorite time, when the place is silent and peaceful, with no customers to disturb him. Usually, he doesn't even switch on the overhead light, but tinkers in the gloom, or merely turns on the small table lamp at the side of the counter where the cash register stands, and where the ledgers are kept in a drawer. She goes down the back stairs off the scullery, creeping quietly, avoiding the third rung that creaks at the slightest provocation. She'll pretend to surprise him even though he must know she's home and won't be surprised at all. Sure enough, she finds him bent over a carton, his back to her in the semi-darkness. She tiptoes behind him throwing her arms around his neck and covering his eyes with her hands.

"Guess who," she says.

"Let's see," he says, straightening up without turning around, and going along with their age-old game. "Could it be that Mrs. Evans who's come to pay the five quid she owes?"

She giggles. "No, it's not Mrs. Evans."

"Well, let's see then. Could it be that nice Mrs. Morgan who's had her eye on me forever and a day?"

"No, it's definitely not Mrs. Morgan." She's trying to keep from laughing outright. That's the effect her Da always has on her.

"Then it must be…" and he snatches her hands from his eyes, whirls around and pulls her into a bear hug, "me very own daughter, Megan Rhys."

"Oh Da," she says, returning his embrace. "What a lovely surprise!"

"What d'you mean?"

"Oh, now don't pretend you don't know what I mean. The sign, Da. I couldn't believe it when I saw it. 'William Rhys and Daughter'. Thanks ever so, Da."

Her father looks embarrassed. "T'was something I've been wanting to do for some time," he mumbles. "No need to make a fuss about it, lass. Shall we go up and see what your Mum's got laid out for our tea?" Megan links her arm through his. Father and daughter, make their way up the stairs together.

Saturday high tea, which is really supper, is the most eagerly anticipated meal of the week in the Rhys household. It is the only meal when all three are able to eat together without interruption, without customers or visitors, not even Gwen. It is only during this precious time together that William and Glynis are able to talk and listen to their daughter when she vents her frustration over school work, to show sympathy and understanding for her teenage problems. After tea, and after the dishes are washed and dried and put away, Glynis picks up her knitting or darning, William lights up a cigarette, takes out his football pools, and Megan reluctantly opens her satchel and pulls out her homework. Then, one of them turns on the wireless to listen to the Saturday Promenade Concert. This week the program lists Beethoven's Sixth Symphony, the Pastoral, coming from London's Royal Albert Hall, Henry Wood conducting.

The Rhys's have made it a policy to close the shop by four o'clock on Saturdays, even though it's the busiest day of the week. As she always does, Megan helped her parents wait on customers all morning, then left at noon to study at Gwen's house.

It was during those few hours when Megan was absent from home, that William, with the help of a neighbor, put the sign up to surprise her.

⇒⇐

William sits down at the head of the table, reaches out to each side of him and clasps Glynis's and Megan's hands. They bow their heads and close their eyes as he recites grace. *For what we are about to receive may the Lord make us truly thankful, and may we always be mindful of the needs of others. For Jesus's sake.* In unison, all three intone *Amen.*

A coal fire crackles happily in the kitchen grate, and the room is warm and inviting, despite the heavy rain now battering the window panes with the intensity of a typical Welsh squall, and the wind howling down the chimney. For a few minutes they are busy passing the bread and butter, the sliced ham, tomatoes and cucumbers, the scones and cream, too occupied to speak. Glynis moves to get up, but Megan say, "I'll do it, Mums. You rest those feet of yours."

"Ta, love," says Glynis, and Megan goes over to the stove to fetch the kettle, then pours hot water over the waiting tea leaves in the teapot. While the tea is steeping, William shyly says, "So Meggy mine, you really like the sign then, do you?"

"It's lovely, Da. But why didn't you add Mum's name to it too? Glynis and William Rhys and Daughter."

"Indeed, there's a thought. But your Mum and I discussed it, didn't we, and she said she'd rather not see her name up there unless there's neon lights all around it like on the marquees at the flicks. Isn't that right, Glyn love?"

"Och, you're such a tease, Will. But your Da's right, Meggy, in that I didn't want my name up there, didn't think it would bring in any more customers. But 'William Rhys and Daughter', now that's different, that is, that has a ring to it, and will bring more people into the shop if only out of curiosity. Anyhow, we've barely seen you all week, Meggy, what with all the studying you've been doing, and us being so busy in the shop this morning before Christmas, with no chance to breathe let alone talk to each other. So let's hear how things are going for the O levels."

"Oh, Mums. You know what a dunce I am when it comes to studying. If it wasn't for Gwen, I'm sure I would've been put back a form long ago. Maybe two."

"Don't say things like that, my girl," her father says. "We know no such thing. You're a lot cleverer than you give yourself credit for. Look at the way you handle the customers. That Mrs. Griffith, for instance, I was ready to throw the bloody woman through the door, I was, but you had her eating out of your hand in one minute flat. That takes a lot more brains than book learning, that does."

"Thanks for the vote of confidence, Da, but you're not exactly impartial, are you?" She begins to pour the tea into their cups. "At any rate, I've been keeping a bit of surprise for you also."

"Have you now? Cough it up, girl, what is it?"

It is Megan's turn to look embarrassed. She tries to sound casual. "Well, on Friday, at assembly, the headmistress announced that your own Megan Rhys has been named the new assistant sports captain of Canton High School for Girls."

For a moment, both parents just stare at their daughter in open-mouthed astonishment. Of course, they've known for years that Megan has an affinity for sports and gymnastics, that she's on the lacrosse team, is the goalie on the ice hockey team, and plays on Canton High's tennis team. But this? Never could they have imagined anything like this. After all, Megan's young for such an appointment, not yet fifteen.

"Why, if that isn't absolutely the grandest, absolutely the most splendid news I've ever heard!" Her Mum is the first to react. Her father says, "I'm over the moon for you, Meggy, love. What an honor that is, indeed. But why didn't you tell us yesterday? Seems you've been harboring this news to yourself all weekend. And wasn't that Gwen Owen that popped in yesterday after school, or am I imagining it, and did she not utter a word about it either?"

"That's my fault, Da. I swore Gwenny to secrecy. The thing is, which is why I didn't tell you right away, the thing is, I'm not sure I should accept." She hastens to add, "I know it's a huge honor, and all, but…"

"But what? What do you mean, not accept? Why on earth not?"

"I'm so far behind with my studying. As it is, I don't know how I'll ever be able to pass the O levels. Being assistant sports captain is a big responsibility; it'll take up all my spare time. It's not just playing in matches, it means extra practice hours, and never being able to get out of playing like I sometimes do now if I don't feel like it. The girl who's the head sports captain won't hear of it."

"Och, Meggy," says her mother. "I know you. Somehow you'll manage."

"No Mum. I just don't see how I can do both. Besides," she looks miserable. "There's something else."

"What then?"

"I'm not sure if I should tell you this, how you'll take it."

"Let your Mum and me be the judge of that, me girl," says Will. "Spit it out. What's the something else?"

"Well, you see, much as I love the lacrosse and tennis and all, there's only one sport that I'm really, *really* mad for like no other." She puts down the teapot, reaches for the sugar, spoons some into her cup and begins stirring. "It's the ice skating, you see. I just love to be on the ice. Sometimes, after hockey practice, Laurie, our coach, shows me how to do figure eights and lutzes and all kinds of jumps. She says I'm a natural, the way I've taken to it. She tells me I should be getting professional instruction and maybe try out for the English Olympics team. She thinks with some serious training I might be ready for the 1952 winter games in Norway."

During this startling announcement Megan hasn't been able to look her parents in the eye. She just keeps stirring her tea mechanically, eyes downcast. They, in turn, both continue to stare at her in amazement. It is several moments before her father finally finds his tongue.

"Well, if this isn't a right to do. Indeed it is." His Welsh intonation becomes ever more pronounced in direct proportion to his consternation, with the end of his sentences taking on the upward lilt of a question.

"Well," he says again. "Well, well. Your mother and I will have to discuss this once we've managed to chew it over and swallow it. Isn't it, Glyn?"

"With all due respect, Will love, I don't think there's much to discuss. Our Meggy's always been an avid sports girl, but has never taken to school work and book learning. As you well know. All these years we've watched her trying and trying so hard, sometimes staying up till midnight and beyond over her books. And why? Because she's a good girl and wants to please us." Glynis looks across the table at her daughter, her eyes filled with love and understanding. She reaches over and takes Megan's hand, her voice almost a whisper. "Isn't that so, lovey? And now, if you've discovered something you really want to do, something that, as you say, you're mad for, I for one won't stand in your way." She adds, "I wish I'd found something when I was your age that I was mad for. Perhaps I wouldn't have landed up as a typist in the shipyards."

"Now, now, Glyn. Don't you be forgetting that in all likelihood you and I would never have met if you hadn't worked in the shipyards."

"No, indeed, I'm not forgetting, Will," Glynis says. "And I'm also not forgetting that you rescued me from that typewriter, praise be Jesus, just as I'm not forgetting what's most important: that he spared you during the war and brought you safely back to us. But let's also not be forgetting what it was we were talking about. I for one think our Meggy's fortunate to be having something at this young age that really excites her. And it's not as if there's anything harmful to skating; as far as I can see it's a very wholesome sport, isn't it? And our Meggy has the perfect body and build for it, too."

"Oh Mum." Megan begins to cry.

"Now, now. Don't cry, Meggy love. There's nothing to cry about. Your father and I just want you to be happy, isn't it, Will?"

"Darn right, Glyn, that we do. But I'm not thinking it's a good idea for Meggy to drop the school work entirely. Perhaps it can just be postponed until after the 1952 Olympics. Not that we know whether she'll be good enough to get into the Olympics in the first place, do we now? Indeed, we can't know what the future holds at all, can we? But one thing we do know is that it's good to have some form of education under the belt, be it the O levels or merely some knowledge of shorthand and typing with a little bookkeeping thrown in. Who knows if somewhere down the line our Meggy won't have to go to work and earn a living just as you once did, Glyn."

"Oh Da." Megan begins crying again.

"Now, now, Meggy. There's no need for that."

"But what am I going to tell Gwenny? She's held herself back all these years because of me. How can I just desert her like that?"

"Now you listen to me, Meggy," says her mother. "It'll no doubt come as a great relief to Gwen Owen not to have a millstone around her neck by the name of Megan Rhys. In a manner of speaking, that is. Now she'll be able to take off at her own speed. Gwen's been a good, loyal friend, an exceptional friend, I dare say, but it's not healthy what she's been doing, and some day she would no doubt come to resent you for keeping her back, just as you might come to resent her for being so possessive and keeping you from making other friends. Your father and I have discussed it more than once, but it wasn't for us to interfere. Isn't it, Will?"

"Indeed. Yes, yes, indeed we've discussed it many times," says William. "And I'm sure Gwen's parents have discussed it too and wouldn't be averse to seeing a change in the relationship." After a pause he says, "What do you say to me and your Mum going over to the school and speaking to that headmistress of yours about postponing your studies for a year or so while you go into training? Surely, they must have provisions for such a postponement? After all, what happens if a girl is seriously ill and has to drop out of school temporarily? And if you are good enough to be included in the Olympics team, it can only be good for the school's reputation, a feather in their cap I should think."

Their exchange has usurped the Beethoven; for the first time in many Saturdays the wireless remains silent.

When she undresses for bed that night, Megan's heart feels ready to burst with love for her Mum and Da; she resolves never again to wish for her Mum to be young and pretty and fashionable like Mrs. Owen. The relief she feels at the prospect of being able to forget about her studies is so overwhelming, that she even forgets that she still has to tell Gwen that she may be dropping out of school for a while. On the wall, over her bed, hangs the little wooden crucifix that she won as a Sunday school prize when she was ten. She kneels next to her bed, as she does every night, rests her arms on the counterpane, her palms pressed together, her fingers pointing skyward, and recites the Lord's Prayer. *Our Father who art in heaven, hallowed be Thy name…* When she's finished, she offers up another prayer, in her own words. *Dear Jesus,* she prays. *Make me worthy of the faith my Mum and Da have in me, and make sure I don't let them down. And please, please don't let Gwen be angry with me when I tell her. For thy name's sake. Amen.*

That night, Megan has the dream again.

Chapter 38

>⋲

To Megan, the Monday morning school assembly seems more tedious than ever. The girls stand in rows, in the order of their forms, with the first form at the front of the hall, near the stage, and the upper forms toward the back. All the girls wear the school uniform: navy tunics and ties, white shirts, navy felt hats with upturned brims encircled with a yellow and navy grosgrain ribbon bearing a miniature version of the school shield in the center; and a navy blazer, on the pocket of which is stitched a larger version of the school's shield and heraldry, and the school's motto: *Semper sersum.* Always upward.

First the prayers, then a hymn. Today it's *Rock of Ages.* After that, Miss Bryce, the headmistress, strides onto the stage and speaks into the microphone. "Would the teacher standing nearest the rear door please open it to admit the Jewish girls." All heads turn to watch as three girls of different ages enter and join their forms. The Jewish girls, either by choice or school policy, are excluded from the Christian prayers and hymns. By the way the three girls walk with their heads down, Megan can tell they're embarrassed to be the focus of everyone's attention. Megan hates this part of the assembly more than anything. She can't understand why Miss Bryce makes such a to-do about it. Why can't the Jewish girls just stay for the prayers and hymns with everyone else, but without having to join in? She feels sorry for them, especially the youngest girl who has to walk the length of the hall until she reaches the first form.

What torture it must be, Megan thinks, *to have to run this gauntlet every morning.* Gwen, who is standing next to her, nudges her in the waist with her thumb, and whispers in her ear, as she often does, hissing her annoyance at having to stand still all this time to wait for the three Jewish girls.

Miss Bryce makes the usual announcements, but Megan isn't listening. Her mind is occupied with something else entirely. Today her parents are coming to school to talk to the headmistress, and after that they're to meet with Laurie the skating coach. Her parents will be putting up the *Closed* sign in the shop's window to attend these meetings, an act so rare, that Megan cannot remember any precedent for it, except when they close the shop for the two weeks' summer holiday, or for Christmas. Her parents don't own a car and will have to take the bus and tram, the same way she and Gwen do to get to and from school each day. Megan's heart begins to race in nervous anticipation, and then races some more when she remembers that she still hasn't said a word to Gwen.

The day passes in a blur. Later, Megan will remember only vaguely that she was called into Miss Bryce's office to find her parents sitting in front of the headmistress' desk with big smiles on their faces. The meeting with Laurie Turnbull is equally hazy in her memory. Everything is settled so quickly that Megan has no time to think about it. She hopes her parents will wait for her so they can all ride home together, but Glynis and William say they must hurry back to the shop.

As is their habit, Megan and Gwen walk to the tram stop together after school.

"Meggy, what was all that about today? You were called out of class twice, and the second time you didn't even come back until school was nearly over. Have you done something wrong?"

"Oh Gwenny. I've been wanting to tell you all about it. But until I was sure there was something to tell there didn't seem to be any point."

The tram grinds to a screeching stop and they board and find their usual seats in the back. Gwen looks at Megan questioningly, her brown eyes large and expectant, magnified behind the thick lenses. She is not very tall, a stone or so overweight, probably because she loves food and hates to exercise, often expressing her disdain for anything athletic. The bond between the two girls seems unlikely on the surface but, as Gwen's mother Cynthia says, it just goes to prove the popular belief that opposites attract. Gwen is a voracious reader and is rarely seen without a book in her hands. Megan, on the other hand, reads only what is absolutely necessary for school, though sometimes she indulges in popular romances; she is willowy and slender, has the coordination of a natural athlete, and takes to all sports with the enthusiasm of a parched traveler to water.

Megan is nervous about breaking the news to Gwen. She doesn't know how she'll take it. Trying to sound off-hand, she says, "Laurie the hockey coach spoke to Miss Bryce about me. Seems she thinks I should go in for some training on the ice, maybe enter some competitions. Of course," she adds dismissively, "I know it's never going to happen, but still..." Gwen simply stares at her, without expression. Megan ploughs on, trying to sound casual and uncaring. "So, Miss Bryce says I can curtail my classes while I train for a few weeks to see...." Her voice trails off, and she turns away avoiding Gwen's gaze, to look out the window.

"Well, well." Gwen says finally, and for a few moments says nothing more. Then she says, brightly, "But that's fantastic Meggy. I'm happy for you. I truly am. Of course, we won't be able to spend much time together anymore, I understand that."

"Oh Gwenny. Don't say that. You're my best friend. You'll still come to church and dinner with us every Sunday, just as always, won't you?"

"I suppose so, but it won't be the same will it? How can it be if we won't be in class together, won't be studying together? But it'll be wonderful for you, and like I said, I'm happy for you." Then she adds slyly, "But there's someone who's not going to be so happy, can you guess who?" Seeing Megan's baffled look she says, "Don't look so innocent, Megan Rhys. My brother Shaun, of course. Don't tell me you haven't noticed he's sweet on you."

Megan blushes. "What nonsense! I don't believe that for a moment, Gwenny. But Shaun'll always be welcome to come over with you for Sunday dinner any time he wants to. That will never change. Let's make a solemn promise that that will never change."

"All right, I promise," says Gwen. They both clamber off the tram at the next stop to wait for the Llandaff Road bus. Gwen turns briefly and gives Megan a quick hug. "I feel like walking the rest of the way", she says. "Ta, ta. See you soon, baboon." Automatically, Megan replies, "Make it a habit, rabbit." But Gwen is already walking away and waves her hand without turning around. Megan watches as Gwen trudges along the pavement, her bulging satchel bouncing on her back. She is tempted to follow her, but something holds her back. For the first time, Gwen doesn't seem to want her company.

Megan rides the bus one stop past her usual one and hops off at the entrance to St. Mary's. It's almost five o'clock and already dark, but it's a clear evening, with the moon rising over the horizon and the sky full of stars. This stretch of Llandaff Road is so brightly lit by street lamps that the absence of daylight is barely missed. It is as if the town is still making up for the blackout years of the war. As she expected, the front door of the church is bolted. She goes round to the side door, which is rarely locked. She knows that in all probability Vicar Lowell will be either in the vestry or in his study.

Megan tiptoes through to the main chapel, the hushed, darkened atmosphere flooding over her in a familiar combination of awe and comfort. She often visits at this hour, when she's likely to have the place to herself, when she can concentrate and commune with the figure on the enormous cross above the altar. Only the muffled sounds of traffic remind her that there is another world outside this peaceful sanctuary.

She genuflects, crosses herself, then kneels and bows her head, praying silently. *Dear Jesus. How can I ever thank you? Even though I never prayed for this to happen you answered me as if I did.*

Behind her she hears footsteps and recognizes the uneven step of Vicar Lowell, and the thunk-thunk of his walking stick.

She stands, genuflects once more, before turning to greet him with a smile.

"I didn't mean to disturb your prayers, my child," says the vicar.

Megan assures him that she has finished praying. "In fact, I came to see you, Father, because I have some exciting news." She tells him what has happened, and the old man's wrinkled face creases into a smile of pleasure. He takes one of her hands in both of his. "How wonderful, my child, how blessed you are and how strange are the ways of our Lord. I wish you much success and look forward to hearing all about your triumphs in the skating world."

"Thank you, Father," Megan says, then adds, "There's something else, Father."

"Oh, and what might that be, my child?"

" I've been having strange dreams. Not dreams, actually. Just one dream. The same one every few weeks."

"Hmm. You have, have you? How peculiar. And does it frighten you?"

"No, Father. I can't say it frightens me, but I find it a bit disturbing."

The vicar sits down in the nearest pew, and holds out his arm, inviting Megan to sit beside him. Megan notices with dismay the tremor in the old man's outstretched hand, and her heart fills with sadness.

"Would you like to tell me about it, my child?"

She speaks slowly, haltingly, eyes closed in concentration, as she tries to recall every detail of the dream. "Well, I think I'm in a farmyard. Yes, that's it. It must be a farm of some kind, because I can clearly hear the grunting of pigs, even though I don't see them. I don't see myself either, but somehow I know I'm there. Oh, and there's this huge black dog and a beautiful lady with blonde hair. I never see the lady's face, but something tells me she must be beautiful. Just at the moment when she's about to turn and reveal herself, I always wake up." She opens her eyes and turns to the vicar. "What can be the meaning of it, Father? As far as I remember, I've never set foot on a farm, let alone been near a live pig, so isn't it strange how I know what that grunting sound is? I'm convinced the sound came from pigs even though I didn't actually see any in my dream."

"Hmm. Hmm," says the vicar again. "Hmm. How peculiar. I can't say I know what to make of it, my child. Unlike Joseph of the bible, I don't claim to be an interpreter of dreams. The pharaoh in ancient Egypt also dreamed about certain animals; in his case it was cows rather than pigs, fat cows and thin cows, and young Joseph had no problem finding a meaning to his dream. I don't know what Joseph would have made of your dream, my child. I certainly cannot make head or tail of it. As to the lady, while I will not go so far as to say she is the personification of our holy Virgin Mother, for whom this church is named, whoever she is it seems to me she may be protecting you in the same way."

Megan's face lights up. "Do you really think so, Father?" The vicar just pats her hand and smiles. "Yes, my child, that I do. Indeed I do." The old man accompanies Megan to the church door and watches her walk away. As if she knows that the vicar is still there, Megan turns after a few yards and waves to him. He waves back and continues to watch until he can no longer see her.

For many minutes more, the vicar remains in the doorway of the church, gazing into the night, deep in thought.

Chapter 39

William and Glynis continue sitting at the breakfast table long after Megan has left for school, and long after they should have gone downstairs to turn the *Closed* sign over to the *Open* side, and unlock the shop's front door in accordance with the posted hours. This is an unprecedented departure from their normal routine, but both are feeling too wretched to move.

"Well, Glyn, looks like we've painted ourselves into a corner, isn't it? We should have listened to Vicar Lowell years ago. And later, when we had to go down and fill out all those application forms for the school, we should have told the child then instead of asking the headmistress to keep it confidential. I'll never forget the look of disapproval on that woman's face. If looks could kill!"

"Och, Will. Indeed. If we'd only told her then, by now she would have long been used to the idea."

Glynis buries her head in her hands and groans. Then starts to sob quietly.

William takes a long drag of his cigarette, puts his arm around his wife, and says, "I know, I know. Don't I know it. But I wish you wouldn't take on like that, love."

For the last hour, the two of them have been drinking tea nonstop. Now William rouses himself to reach for the teapot and refresh their cups, even though the tea is now barely tepid. Then he lights a new Woodbine with the stub of the previous one. He's been chain-smoking since the early hours.

Through her tears, Glynis says, "D'you remember, Will, when we first laid eyes on her?"

"As if I need reminding! Indeed. It's like it happened yesterday, to my mind."

It was in those hectic, turbulent days of summer, the summer of 1939. Glynis had heard about a group of German children who had recently been brought to England by the Quaker Society. It was generally feared that war was inevitable, and the children were being placed in foster homes 'for the duration'.

Neither Glynis nor William had ever wished to adopt a child. William was especially adamant about wanting what he termed his own 'biological issue'; for years he was convinced it was going to happen, that it was just a matter of time. It was Glynis who persuaded him to accompany her to London to look the refugee children over. "Should there be war", she said, "as seems likely, this will be the least we can do to contribute to the war effort. And it won't be permanent. It won't be forever, just until the children's parents come to reclaim them."

Glynis and William were immediately drawn to a pretty, blonde three-year-old child. They were shown the child's birth certificate, a document headed with two German words: *Geburts Zeugnis*, on which was stamped, very prominently, a black swastika. The name of the mother was listed as Henrietta Meissner, and the child was listed as her *ehelich Töchter*, legitimate daughter. Date of birth: March 7, 1936. Name of father: (blank); Religion: Unknown.

Just the sight of the swastika on the child's birth certificate made them both shudder in horror.

Ironically, it was William whose heart was instantly and permanently stolen by the three-year-old Marga Meissner, the little girl with the blonde halo of curls, a name tag pinned to her fur-lined coat. The little girl with the bluest eyes he had ever seen, standing lost and forlorn, sobbing her little heart out.

Eventually, the child stopped crying, stopped having nightmares, stopped muttering to herself in an incomprehensible, guttural tongue about a Mutti and someone called Rudi. Day by day, the child forgot the little German she knew until, in no time at all, she was jabbering away in English like a native. With a Welsh inflection.

Not wishing to burden the child with a German name, they picked a popular Welsh name that also began with the letter 'M': Megan.

Almost immediately, Glynis and William noticed that little Megan was drawn to dogs wherever they went. Once, she fearlessly approached a large black, fierce looking hound that turned out to be surprisingly gentle when its owner allowed the child to pet him. They considered getting her a dog, but felt that their flat was too small. Instead, they rescued a little ginger kitten from a litter that was about to be drowned. Unimaginatively, they named it Kitty.

It was Kitty who helped the child adjust to her new life. Kitty it was who slept with her at night, curled up at the end of her bed, or sometimes next to her head on the pillow. Two years ago Kitty, old and blind by then, had to be put down. Megan refused to replace her.

Little Megan was affectionate from the start, crawling into their laps without being cajoled, and laying her head on their shoulders in a display of blind trust. It seemed as if the child knew instinctively that with Glynis and William Rhys she had found safe haven.

After the war, in an attempt to find the child's family, the Rhys's put out inquiries through the Quaker Society, through the Red Cross, through every known refugee organization, but all their inquiries met a brick wall. The Quaker offices on the Euston Road in London had been bombed during the Blitz, and many of their records destroyed. The Rhys's contacted every Meissner they could find in West Germany, a laborious and time-consuming process, but not one of them had ever heard of a Henrietta Meissner or a child named Marga Meissner. The limited access they had to the authorities in East Germany also led nowhere.

By the middle of 1947, when it was clear that all their detective work had led to the same dead end, the Rhys's formally applied, and were given permission to adopt Megan legally.

Of course, they fully intended to tell the eleven-year-old girl what they knew about her origins. Of course, they did. Of course they meant to tell the child that she was adopted. Of course they did. Even without the vicar's urging, they knew it was the right thing to do. Of course they did.

But somehow they kept finding one excuse after another to keep pushing it off.

They kept dallying and procrastinating. And now there will be all kinds of applications to fill out, a passport to be requested so that Megan can compete on the Continent. Now they no longer have a choice; Megan is almost fifteen and must be told the truth.

⊰⊱

Just as Glynis mechanically raises her cup to her lips to sip at the now stone cold tea, they hear a knocking on the downstairs side door. William goes down and comes back up accompanied by the black-clad, out-of-breath Vicar Lowell.

"Is there something wrong? Are you both well," he asks. "I was afraid to find someone ill, what with your shop not yet open. Highly unusual, isn't it?"

William pulls out a chair for the vicar, as Glynis says, "No, no, Father. Thank the Lord we're both well. But you are just the person we're wanting to see, and if you hadn't by some miracle materialized we would no doubt have soon been on our way to the church, isn't it, Will?"

"Indeed it is."

"Will you be joining us for some tea, Father? Perhaps a spot of breakfast? I'm just about to make a fresh pot."

"I assume this has to do with Megan, and that you've both finally come to your senses."

"Yes Father. That we have. At first we were thinking Christmas Day might be as good a time as any, when she'll have a rare day off from practicing. But then we realized that her name's been entered for the February Regionals in Swansea, so we're thinking to wait till she gets that behind her, not to upset her before…"

"So, there you go again, Glynis Rhys. More excuses. I don't blame you, but this state of affairs cannot continue. You owe it to the child to tell her. You wouldn't want her to find out from somebody else, would you now?"

Glynis becomes alarmed. "Why, has Megan said anything to you, Father? Does she suspect something?"

"No, no. Nothing of that nature. But I have felt for a long time that I must once and for all insist that she be told."

William says, "You're right, Father. Cowards we are, indeed. Which is why I'm wondering whether… well, that is, how would it be if you were to tell her? Would you consider it?" He has the grace to look embarrassed.

"No, no, William. Absolutely not. This must come from you, her parents. Not from me. Not from any third party. Both for the child's sake and for your own. However, if you think my support is needed, I will be glad to be present when you speak to her. But that's as far as I will go. I cannot and will not be the one to tell her."

Glynis and William both nod their heads slowly, with resignation. "Yes," says William. "I suppose you're right Father. It must come from us. But if you can see your way to being here, as you say, as our support, that would be most welcome and we would be very grateful. When Megan comes back from Swansea, though, not before."

"Very well," says the vicar. "And I'll be after you to make sure you don't change your minds again. I'll take that cup of tea now, Glynis, if I may, and one of those delicious looking crumpets with strawberry jam."

Chapter 40

∌€

Laurie Turnbull is a hard taskmaster. She insists that Megan's training begin immediately, even though it is only a few weeks before Christmas. "There's not a moment to lose," she says, "if we're going to get you ready in time for next winter's Olympics."

The first days pass in a frenzy of shopping: new skates, not just one pair, but three, new training outfits, new skating costumes. Before Laurie even allows Megan on the ice, she must spend many grueling days at the gym and on the track to improve her stamina and strength. The Rhys's happily participate, not only by paying for Megan's trainer and equipment, but also foregoing Megan's help in the shop during the annual Christmas rush. They've taken to waiting up for her every night when she comes home, utterly spent and exhausted, often collapsing in their arms, too tired to eat.

Gwen was right. Megan is no longer able to spend time with her. Even their Sunday routine is now a thing of the past. They no longer attend church together, or have dinner afterward. Megan trains on Sundays just as she does every other day of the week.

Megan has never felt so well, so strong, so alive. She is bursting with energy. And at night her sleep is sound and deep. And dreamless.

∌€

It is Christmas Eve, a night when the Rhys's attend the special midnight high mass at St. Mary's. Tomorrow, Christmas Day, Megan has been given the whole day off, the first in weeks. Laurie has warned her not to expect to 'laze around' on the day after Christmas; Boxing Day will be 'business as usual'.

This evening, Megan has barely time to bathe and dress before Gwen and Shaun arrive. Megan has not seen them in weeks. As they have always done in years past, Gwen and Shaun share in the turkey supper prepared by Glynis, and then accompany them to St. Mary's for the mass.

Because it's a festive occasion, they eat in the formal dining room. There's a coal fire blazing in the grate and above it, hanging from the mantel, are three Christmas stockings to be filled by Father Christmas when he slides down the chimney. The mantel is buried in an avalanche of Christmas cards, and in the corner of the room stands a sparkling Christmas tree, decorated with colorful balls and bells, tinsel and angels. Scattered beneath its branches are an assortment of gifts wrapped in colorful paper, of various sizes and shapes, not to be opened until the following morning. For the first time in years, Megan was not able to take part in decorating the tree because of her rigorous training schedule. To her surprise, William tells her that Shaun Owen phoned earlier in the week, volunteering his services, which her Da gratefully accepted.

"Indeed, I couldn't have done it on me own," William says. "Why, just getting up the ladder to attach the angel on the top might have been the death of me. So, ta again, Shaun lad."

Shaun is tall, polite, good-looking. He is studious like his sister, but there the resemblance ends. He blushes with embarrassment. "It was nothing, Mr. Rhys, and I enjoyed doing it. It's a lovely tradition and I miss it in our house. We've never had a tree." Megan becomes aware, for the first time, that though his remarks are addressed to her Da, he is looking at her. She wonders if there is any truth to what Gwen said to her on the tram. She has always liked Shaun, but surely only as a friend, as an extension of her friendship with his sister. She cannot imagine having any other feelings for him. She notices Gwen watching her and she turns away, but not in time to hide the blood rising in her cheeks, and not before she catches Gwen's knowing smile.

At supper, Gwen casually lets drop that she has passed all her O levels and is now concentrating on studying for the A levels. "You're such a brain, Gwenny," Megan tells her. "You'll no doubt be a doctor of something or other before you're twenty."

How wise my parents were, thinks Megan, and catches an *I told you so* smile from Glynis when she goes into the kitchen to stack the dirty plates.

After supper, the five of them make their way together to St. Mary's, with Glynis and William letting the three young people walk ahead. It will be a white and cold Christmas. As they walk, little puffs of smoke erupt from their mouths in miniature clouds. The snow on the ground is at least two inches deep, covered by a patina of glistening frost, and the sky is still sending down intermittent flurries. They pass doorways and windowsills from which icicles hang like gleaming spears. They stop for a few moments to listen to a group of carolers singing *Old King Wenceslas* and *Silent Night*. There are very few vehicles on the road, and the voices of the singers carry on the cold night air with a rare and pure clarity.

Gwen says, "I just noticed the new sign above your shop for the first time today, Meggy. What a lark that is, I must say. 'William Rhys and Daughter'. Blimey!" She laughs as if this is the biggest joke she's heard in ages.

Megan feels herself bristle. She had expected that Gwen might tease her about the sign but something in her friend's tone is unsettling. She drops Gwen's hand. They always walk hand-in-hand, sometimes swinging their linked hands as they walk. It is Shaun who comes to Megan's defense. "Knock it off, Gwen. This is her parents' way of thanking Megan for helping out in the shop so much. Nothing wrong with that. As far as I'm concerned, it's a huge compliment. Isn't that right, Megan?"

"Oh, sorry, Meggy. Of course, I didn't mean anything by it. Just got a big kick out of it, is all," says Gwen, and retrieves Megan's hand.

Megan has always loved the Christmas Eve midnight mass. She loves the pomp and circumstance of the rituals, the blazing candles on each side of the altar in their tall, embossed silver holders, the ornate alb and other vestments worn by Vicar Lowell and his attendants, the sweetly innocent *a cappella* chanting of the boys' choir, the smell of incense that pervades the air, the reading of the Lesson. She loves the manger scene reproduced at one side of the altar: the crèche with the holy baby inside, and the figures of the three wise men, each bearded and robed in different colored kaftans and headgear, each carrying myrrh and frankincense and gifts for the newborn king.

High above the worshippers, the lone figure on the cross watches, imperturbably.

Gwen kneels down next to Megan in the Rhys pew. "I've missed you, Meggy," she whispers in a conciliatory tone. "Me too," says Megan automatically. Then realizes that she's not being truthful, she hasn't missed Gwen at all. Indeed, she has had no time to miss Gwen or anyone else.

But she has no regrets. None whatsoever.

She does feel a tad guilty, though. She takes Gwen's hand and squeezes it. "It's my turn to be happy for you, Gwenny," she whispers. "You're going to be a huge success, I just know it."

Chapter 41

The weeks after Christmas fly by in a rush of training and practice. Every morning, Laurie picks Megan up in her little black Austin Minor and takes her to the practice rink on the other side of town, then drops her back home in the evening. Megan feels her body becoming ever stronger and firmer, her mind becoming more confident. Yet, she cannot allow herself to dream of Oslo. She doesn't even allow herself to mention it in her prayers. However exhausted she is at night, she never misses saying her prayers. In addition to the Lord's Prayer and the blessings she seeks for her Mum and Da, she says simply, *Thank you, sweet Jesus, for bringing me this far.*

She knows that if she is meant to compete in the Olympics, Jesus will bring it about.

Megan doesn't feel ready for the February Regionals. She's not confident about the double axel. "It's important that you get your feet wet," Laurie insists. "You've got to get used to competing, even if you lose. The first time is a hurdle you must get over. After that, trust me, it will become easier."

Megan and Laurie have become good friends, despite the difference in age. Laurie is single, in her early thirties, athletic and trim, serious and driven. The promise she sees in Megan has prompted her to take a leave of absence from her position as athletic coach at Canton High; she now devotes herself exclusively to Megan's training. Megan trusts Laurie. If Laurie believes her to be ready, then so be it, she must be ready.

Swansea is a triumph. Of sorts. Megan had expected to be nervous before the competition, but, instead, a strange calm overtakes her. Later, she wonders if it is because of the dream she had the previous night, the dream she has not had for weeks and that slid into her sleep for the first time since the start of training. This time, in addition to the grunting of pigs, she hears a cackling sound, a sort of chatter in the background. When she wakes up she wonders if the sound might have been the cheeping of chickens. Once again, the beautiful lady doesn't reveal her face. But, could it be that Vicar Lowell is right, that the lady in her dream is protecting her, as if she were the Virgin Mother herself?

She skates smoothly, executing a perfect double axel. But then, almost at the end of her routine, after the layback spin, she unaccountably stumbles. Laurie has trained her well. "If you make a mistake, just continue with the routine as if nothing were amiss. It's possible the other girls will make worse mistakes."

And that is exactly what happens. Megan places second, making her eligible for the Nationals to be held in London in May.

⇒⇐

March 7th is Megan's 15th birthday. It falls on a Friday and Laurie insists on the usual practice sessions. "We're getting too close to the Nationals, we can't let up now," she says. She relents on Sunday, giving Megan the afternoon off to celebrate. Glynis has ordered Megan's favorite chocolate cake from the bakery, with her name and a big *15* in a circle of pink icing and *Happy Returns* engraved on top; there are fifteen candles, and an extra one for good luck. Megan's friend Gwen is expected but cancels at the last minute. She has a big exam the next day, and must study. She has sent a birthday card, delivered in person by her brother, Shaun.

Shaun seems to have grown, not just in height but also in self assurance. He is nineteen now, in his first year at Cardiff University. He's expecting to transfer next year to London, to the LSE for courses in business and economics. He is wearing glasses with tortoiseshell frames; they make him seem more mature, and at the same time more vulnerable. For the first time, Megan feels a little shy in his presence.

Lately, whenever Megan comes home from training on Saturdays and Sundays, Shaun seems to be there, chatting away with her parents. And they always have a good reason for his being there. "Isn't it grand that Shaun's come to help your Da reorganize the top shelves? You know how hard it is for him to reach them, what with his gammy arm, and all."

That evening, Shaun approaches Megan without his usual diffidence. He congratulates her on her Swansea triumph, then mentions that there's a new American flick at the Odeon, *The African Queen* with Humphrey Bogart, would she like to see it? For a moment, she's very tempted, but turns him down with the excuse that she has to get up early the next day for her training session.

The naked disappointment on his face almost makes her change her mind. She hates to hurt him. *But I'm only just fifteen, I'm not ready for dates or boyfriends.* Besides, she knows she must be single-minded, focused only on her skating. And there's no point giving him ideas, is there? No point in leading him on. None at all.

⇒⊷⊱

After they've finished washing the dishes and tidied up the kitchen, and after Shaun has left, William says, "Meggy, me girl, your Mum and I have something to talk to you about. Something important to tell you. Something we should have told you years ago."

"What is it, Da? Is it to do with the skating? Is it costing too much, is that it?" She looks guiltily at her Mum. But Glynis is sitting at the table, examining her hands, not able to meet Megan's eye.

"No, no, lass. Nothing of the sort. Let's the three of us have a nice cup of tea, and get it done." He looks nervously at his wife for support, but Glynis seems paralyzed in her chair.

From a manila folder, he removes two items: the first is an official-looking document with a black swastika stamped on it, then something that looks to be a label of some sort, or a name tag. Both the document and the tag are faded and yellowed with age. The document has deep creases in it, where it has been folded and refolded, and the writing on the name tag has all but disappeared. Megan looks at the items, her brow furrowed in puzzlement. They seem to be mementos of the war, collected by her Da when he was overseas. But why…?

Her Da says, "Your Mum and I had hoped the vicar would join us, to make this easier for all of us, but the poor man is laid up with bronchitis. And we have put this off long enough. Indeed, we have put it off far too long and cannot put it off any longer."

By now, Megan is truly alarmed. "What is it, Da. Mum? Are you ill? What are those things? You're beginning to frighten me."

"No, no. Indeed, we are both well. As well as can be expected at our age, that is."

He pauses, and then begins to speak.

Chapter 42

꧁꧂

At the beginning of May, Megan and Laurie travel to London by train. They are to stay for two weeks at a Bed & Breakfast near the Streatham Ice Arena, where Megan is to practice and where the Nationals are to be held. This is the first time Megan has traveled such a distance without her parents. Glynis would have loved to go with them to see Megan perform. She has been to London only once before, and that was just before the war, when she and William went to meet and fall in love with the tiny three-year-old German refugee. During the war, with William away in the army, and what with the London Blitz, followed by the V1 and V2 rockets raining down on the capital, it was dangerous to venture to the city. At any rate, there was no point to such a buying trip, what with fabrics and other goods needed for the shop being in short supply.

Cardiff experienced its share of bombing too, especially near the ship-yards, but Glynis never for one moment considered sending Megan into the countryside with the flood of evacuee children streaming out of the city; she just didn't have the heart for it. After what the poor child had endured already at such a young age, how could Glynis send her away again? Better for Megan to stay with Glynis in the bomb shelter than go through another separation.

In the years since his return from the war, with supplies becoming more readily available from overseas, William now makes regular trips to London to replenish the shop's shelves. Glynis stays in Cardiff to keep the shop open and to take care of Megan. Now, though William urges her to go and see Megan perform, she feels physically unable. Her legs are just too swollen, she says, to undertake the journey.

"Anyway," Glynis says, "after what we've just told her, it's entirely possible she wouldn't be wanting me presence there at all."

And William cannot disagree.

※

The night before the competition, Megan has the dream again. On the following day, throughout her routines, a fragment of the dream hovers persistently at the periphery of her consciousness. Megan executes her routines perfectly, including a brilliant Biellmann spin and triple axel, prompting the spectators to applaud repeatedly. At the end of the competition she is in first place, her spot on the Olympics team assured. She is ecstatic, flushed with victory. She and Laurie hug each other in mutual triumph and congratulations, and Laurie insists on treating Megan to a gala high tea at Lyon's Corner House on Oxford Street.

She's glad she didn't confide in Laurie, relieved to be able to behave normally around her. Laurie doesn't seem to suspect a thing. At any rate, any strange behavior before the competition would, most certainly, have been attributed to nerves.

She's glad she hasn't told Gwen. Or Shaun. She wonders how they'll react.

Does she have to tell them? She's not sure.

※

Megan's first impulse is to run to the nearest telephone and ring her parents. But then she remembers.

She knows that she was able to get through her routines only because of the lady in her dream, that the lady was watching over her, guiding her.

She has tried not to think about what she learned on her birthday. *My birthday present*, she thinks. She has tried to push it to the back of her mind, tried to behave normally to her parents. Even though they're not really her parents. She doesn't know how she's supposed to feel, what she's supposed to think. All these years they'd kept it from her. Her Da, who had made that sign above the shop; her Mum who would know by now about her triumph. They would have heard the news on the wireless. She can picture the two of them reading all about it tomorrow in the sports pages of the *South Wales Echo*.

But who was her real mother? The mysterious Henrietta Meissner listed on her birth certificate? Her German birth certificate with that chilling insignia on it.

And Vicar Lowell? He, too, has known all along. Yet he said nothing. Not a word.

It is all too upsetting, too confusing...

⇒⇐

After William finishes talking, Megan just sits and stares at them in disbelief. For how long, she doesn't remember. At first she's convinced it must be a hoax, one that will end in hugs and laughter. But slowly, as she gazes from one face to the other, after she examines the two items laid out on the kitchen table, she begins to understand that this is not a joking matter. The power of speech has deserted her. She begins to feel ill, is sure she will bring up everything she's ever eaten. There is a steady ache in the region of her heart.

She doesn't know what propels her. Without uttering a sound, she stands up, pulls her coat off the hook near the door, and rushes out into the night.

Neither of them tries to stop her.

She walks and walks and walks, without direction, without a destination. The rain that fell during the day has stopped, and she sloshes through one puddle after another. Her legs and feet become soaked through to the skin, but she doesn't seem to notice.

How could they have kept it from her all these years?

Was everything a lie? All the kisses and hugs, all the teasing and joking? The laughter, the fun?

No, no. In the depths of her heart she is certain they really love her. That sign over the shop. *William Rhys and Daughter*. What more evidence does she need of their love? But why didn't they tell her the truth before? Why the secrecy? And were it not for the applications that now have to be filled out, would they ever have told her?

She walks aimlessly for almost an hour, her head churning with turmoil and confusion. Eventually, back on Llandaff Road, she slows her pace. They must have thought they were protecting her, they must have been acting from love. Perhaps they were right. Perhaps she wasn't mature enough when she was younger. Who knows how she might have reacted?

Glynis and William Rhys have always been there for her, from her earliest memory. They have nursed her through all her childhood illnesses, comforted and held her in a darkened room for days when she had measles. They have supported her through all her scholastic struggles at school. All of her life they have shored her up, given her confidence, encouraged her. How many times over the years did she come running home in tears after failing an exam, only to find comfort in her Mum's arms?

But her Mum's arms cannot console her now.

She feels unmoored. And, for the first time in her life, completely alone.

She wishes she could find out the meaning of the two words that appear on the English translation attached to her German birth certificate. The two words that keep repeating themselves like a mantra in her head, 'Religion: Unknown'.

And if Glynis and William are not her real parents, who are? And what has happened to them?

She finds herself at the gate of St. Mary's. The church is shrouded in darkness except for a small electric sconce illuminating the front door. She's about to go round to the side; she must talk to the vicar. Perhaps he can explain it all.

But then she remembers: he is ill.

She slinks back home, exhausted. Glynis and William have gone to bed, though there's a chink of light escaping from under their bedroom door, so she knows they're not asleep. They are waiting up until they know she's safely home.

As they always do.

She strips off her wet clothes, drops them in a pile on the floor in the center of her room. She crawls into bed, for the first time forgetting to say her prayers, and turns off the bedside lamp. She is drained, spent, but knows she will not be able to sleep. She cannot feel her feet, they are two lumps of ice. Her body begins to shake. From the first-aid course she took at school she knows she may be in shock. She forces herself to take a deep breath, then to exhale slowly. *A deep breath, then exhale slowly. A deep breath, then exhale slowly.* The trembling begins to subside and she turns on her side. There is a rustling sound, then the feel of paper beneath her cheek. She leans over and turns the light on again. There is a note on her pillow. In William's handwriting.

We love you, Meggy, come what may. We hope you can forgive us. Your Mum and Da.

Still in bed, she joins her hands in prayer mode. *Dear Jesus. Show me the way. Please show me the way.* And then bursts into tears.

She lies awake for a long time, not bothering to turn the light off again, the tears rolling down her cheeks. She stares up at the little crucifix hanging on the wall above her bed, willing the miniature figure on the cross to tell her what to do.

At three o'clock, she reaches a decision. She gets out of bed, goes over to her desk, sits down and writes: *Dear Mum and Da: I love you too.*

There is no longer a light on in their bedroom as she slips the note under the door.

She gets back into bed, and turns off the light. And falls into a deep, dreamless sleep.

Chapter 43

≫✦≪

Not long after Megan's departure for London and glory, the Rhys's receive the telephone call they have wished for and dreaded for years. The woman on the phone introduces herself in very careful and heavily accented English as Gertrud Schneider, formerly of Frankfurt-am-Main, a city now in the western part of the post-war divided Germany. She has had, she says, great difficulty in tracking them down. She wishes to come and see them in person. It is regarding their daughter.

She says she will be traveling by train from London, where she lives. They arrange for her to visit three days hence, on a Sunday, when the shop is closed. She will arrive in the early afternoon after Glynis and William return from church. This will also give Miss Schneider the opportunity to take the last train back to London after her visit.

Glynis and William wait for their visitor in a peculiar mixture of anxiety and relief. It is as if they can now finally exhale.

"Thank the good lord Jesus that Meggy's away," says Glynis. William merely grunts, and lights up another Woodbine. His ashtray is filled with cigarette stubs. Glynis empties the stubs into the kitchen dustbin and returns the ashtray to the table.

And now, Glynis and William sit at their kitchen table staring at the strange woman sitting across from them. She looks to be a woman in her sixties or early seventies; she is wearing a black cloche hat over short gray hair, a severe black suit, thick lisle stockings, low-heeled serviceable black shoes with laces. As if she were in mourning.

Glynis pours tea and puts out a plate of Cadbury's chocolate biscuits. William is chain-smoking, and the three of them sit staring at each other: the hosts waiting, not knowing what to expect, their visitor not sure how to begin.

Miss Schneider takes a sip of tea. "Thank you," she says, "you are very kind." The 'thank you' comes out as 'senk you'. She wipes her lips with the paper serviette, refolds it and tucks it neatly beneath the rim of the saucer. "It took me years to become accustomed to drinking tea with milk in the English manner, but now I am used to it. After all, I am now a naturalized British citizen and when in Rome…" She gives a little grimace that is perhaps meant to be a smile. Glynis smiles in return, an acknowledgment of the woman's attempt to lighten the mood, but more to encourage her to get on with it.

"As I told you on the telephone," says their visitor finally, "it has taken me a long time to track you down. It was not easy. In fact, I have been trying ever since the day the war in Europe ended. But, let me begin at the beginning."

All this time, Miss Schneider has kept her handbag on her lap, having resisted Glynis's attempt to relieve her of it when she took her coat. Now she opens the clasp, and removes some papers.

"Here is my old German passport, and a copy of my naturalization certificate," she says, laying them on the table. Neither Glynis nor William makes any attempt to look at them. "I was fortunate to leave Germany in 1935, just before the Nuremberg laws were passed." Seeing her listeners' looks of bewilderment, she elaborates in her careful, stilted English. "The Nuremberg laws of September 1935 were made to restrict the lives of all German Jews." Her pronunciation of the word 'Jews' comes out as 'Chews', and it takes both Glynis and William a split second to decipher it. "It was immediately *verboten*, that is, forbidden, for Jews to own businesses, to inter-marry, to hold positions of high office, to frequent parks and other public places. Travel was also restricted. The new laws stripped Jews of all rights, including full German citizenship." She clears her throat, takes another sip of tea, carefully dabs at her lips with the serviette. Once more, she delves into her handbag, this time taking out an opened pack of Player's, which she offers to her hosts. They decline, but she shakes out a cigarette from the pack and William reaches across the table to light it for her. Glynis scurries to find another ashtray, and comes back with a heavy amber glass souvenir imprinted with the words 'Weston-super-Mare'. Miss Schneider inhales deeply, then removes a speck of tobacco from her lip with her thumb and forefinger, as tendrils of smoke spiral from her nostrils. She rests the smoldering cigarette on the rim of the ashtray, before continuing.

"Even before the Nuremberg laws, we experienced all kinds of incidents targeting Jews. People were rounded up and sent away for no reason, never to be seen again. Jewish shops and businesses were attacked and covered with anti-Jewish slogans. If you remember, Adolf Hitler was elected Chancellor in 1933, but he had long before that made no secret of how he felt about the Jews.

"I was fortunate. I had a cousin who was living in London; she kept urging me to leave Germany. I knew she was right but I kept putting it off. Since my teens, I had been working for a company called Mayer Metallgesellschaft. It was owned by Jews. I came to EmEm, as we used to call it, straight from secretarial school. They manufactured all kinds of armaments, munitions, those kinds of things. I started off as a clerk in the shipping department; eventually I became private secretary to Julius Mayer, the owner. When he died, I stayed on as secretary to his son Gustav Mayer." Miss Schneider's eyes cloud over at the recollection, and her voice begins to tremble. She takes another sip of the now cooled tea, picks up the cigarette which has been burning down in the ashtray, taps off the accumulated ash, and takes another deep drag. The cup clatters against the saucer as she replaces it with an unsteady hand. But she quickly tightens her already erect posture, takes another pull at the cigarette, hitches up her chin and exhales the smoke into the air through her nose.

"I can see you are wondering where this will lead. Please rest assured, I will soon get to the point, but I must give you some background first. I was very sad to leave the employ of Gustav Mayer. He and his father were very good to me, very generous. But I had become frightened by all the anti-Jewish sentiment and the increasing violence. It was becoming dangerous just to go down to the grocery shop. I stopped sleeping at night.

"Herr Mayer, that is, Mr. Mayer was sorry to see me go, very sorry, but he understood and he himself urged me to leave while I was still able to. Of course," she adds drily, "little did Mr. Mayer know that the Nazis would pursue me and catch up with me in the London Blitz. I was living with my cousin in Bayswater at the time; there was a direct hit, and her flat, in fact the whole building, was destroyed. My cousin was at home that day with a bad cold and didn't go down to the shelter when the siren sounded; she was killed outright." Miss Schneider takes another drag at her cigarette. "I was at work."

For the last few minutes, a growing feeling of sympathy for the woman sitting across from her has come over Glynis. She and William have never experienced the kind of suffering that is spilling from this woman's mouth. Yes, it is true William has seen war, was in the front lines, while she, in his absence, was left with a small child to raise, was forced to manage a business on her own, to juggle ration coupons, to cope with the air raids. But Will had come home safely, more or less in one piece; they had both weathered the storm. After the war, like much of the general public, they had read and heard stories about Hitler's treatment of the Jews, about concentration camps and gas chambers. But, also like much of the general public, they were too busy trying to rebuild their lives to give much more than a moment's horrified attention to what the Nazis had done. And then promptly put it out of their minds.

They have never before met anyone who has experienced what this woman has experienced, seen what this woman has seen; they have never before heard the kind of personal account they are hearing now.

Glynis has the urge to offer the woman something to eat, something more substantial than the biscuits on the table, which so far have remained untouched, but she's reluctant to interrupt Miss Schneider's narrative.

"Yes. I was very fortunate to survive. I was also fortunate to find employment as an interpreter for the British army. I hope you will not blame me when

I tell you that it gave me a kind of perverse pleasure, a kind of *Schadenfreude*, as it is called in German, to interview German prisoners of war." Miss Schneider pauses, continues to regard her listeners earnestly and says, "But I have not come to talk to you about myself, have I?" She grinds out the stub of her cigarette in the ashtray, and Glynis notices for the first time that her fingers are badly stained from tobacco. She is obviously a heavy smoker. Suddenly, Miss Schneider stands up. "May I request the use of your…your facilities? It has been a long journey for me."

Glynis jumps up, embarrassed by her thoughtlessness in not offering their guest the use of the W.C. before. Flustered, she apologizes profusely as she leads the way down the corridor and opens the door to the lavatory, pointing to the guest towels and soap, wishing all the while that she could do something else for Miss Schneider, but not knowing what. "Please, help yourself, do, and if there's anything else you might be needing, just let me know."

"Senk you. You are very kind."

Glynis returns to the kitchen where William still sits at the table, in the same position as she left him; he doesn't seem to have moved a hair since she got up to take Miss Schneider to the loo. She puts a hand on his shoulder and he raises his head. They look at each other wordlessly for a moment, then he says simply, "Bloody hell. Indeed it is. Bloody hell," and lights up another Woodbine.

Glynis opens the bread bin and busies herself making cucumber and cheese sandwiches. The poor woman must be starved after her long journey from London. She castigates herself for not thinking about it earlier.

They hear the lavatory flush, then the running of water in the sink. When Miss Schneider emerges from the corridor, her handbag hooked over her arm, they see that she has removed her hat; she is holding it in her hand. She has brushed her short gray hair back neatly; she looks refreshed.

Glynis brings the plate of sandwiches and a fresh pot of tea to the table. But Miss Schneider is anxious to finish her story. "Senk you," she says again. "You are very kind. I took some food with me on the train, and I have eaten.

Perhaps I will partake later, but now it is important that I explain to you the purpose of my visit. After you have heard everything, you may wish to show me the door, rather than show me such hospitality," once again making an attempt at levity. "After I have finished, you will perhaps wish to see the back of me.

"Where was I. *Ach, Ja.* Gustav Mayer. My employer. His wife died not long before I left Frankfurt, and he was left with two teenage children. Henrietta and Fritz. I was already living in London when I received a letter from him. He must have known that his letters might be opened and censored by the Nazis, and indeed, big portions of his letter were blacked out, totally illegible. But from what was left, I gathered that Henrietta was in some kind of trouble. Also, that his son Fritz had left the country in the care of their neighbors, that he was in Paris, en route to Palestine. Mr. Mayer wrote that he had decided to retire from his business and was merely staying on at EmEm in a consulting capacity. When I read that, I realized immediately that he was being circumspect. I was sure that there was no possibility of Herr ... I mean Mr. Mayer, retiring. EmEm had been in the Mayer family for generations, for centuries. The company was his whole life. It was quite obvious to me that the business must have been seized by the Nazis.

"I never heard from Mr. Mayer again. I wrote to him but my letters went unanswered. The last letter was returned to me unopened with the words 'Not at this address, return to sender' on the envelope.

"In September 1939, as you well know, the war began, and normal correspondence between England and Germany was no longer possible. By that time, I had not heard from Gustav Mayer for over three years, and I feared the worst.

"After the war, in 1945, I tried many times to find out what had happened to him but my efforts were unsuccessful. Then I remembered that in the only letter I received from him he mentioned that his son Fritz was on his way to Palestine. I contacted the Jewish Agency, but for a long time they were unable to help me. What with all the concentration camp survivors and the flood of other refugees arriving in Palestine from Europe after the war, the Agency was swamped with more pressing matters. Then the State of Israel was announced and immediately the War of Independence commenced. Even so, I kept pestering the Agency until finally, just a few months ago, they sent me a report. They had found a Fritz Mayer living in Haifa, working as a research chemist at the Haifa Technion. They included a long list of other men by the name of Mayer who are residents of the new state. But there was only one whose first name was Fritz.

"*Jedoch*, …that is to say, nevertheless, I could not be certain this was the Fritz Mayer I was looking for, that he was Gustav Mayer's son. So, I immediately wrote to him."

It is obvious that Miss Schneider is getting tired, not only from the way she lapses into German every now and then, but from the way her voice has become weaker and her posture has crumbled almost into a slouch. Glynis once again offers her some sandwiches and a fresh cup of tea, but the woman has an urgent need to go on.

"Senk you," she says again, repeating the mantra. "You are very kind." She has long ago stubbed out her last cigarette. Now, she shakes another one from the pack and once again William reaches over and lights it for her. She takes a deep pull, then balances it on the edge of the ashtray. She removes a folded flower-embroidered handkerchief from her handbag, dabs at her eyes and nose, before refolding it carefully and replacing it. "There is not much more. I beg you to allow me to finish. Much as I appreciate your hospitality, that is not the purpose of my visit.

"I finally heard from Fritz Mayer. He is, indeed, the son of the late Gustav Mayer, my employer in Frankfurt. He wrote that his father was arrested in 1936 and interned in Dachau concentration camp. Perhaps you have heard of it, *ja?*" She doesn't wait for an answer. "Apparently, he died in the camp of 'natural causes' shortly after he arrived there." She adds bitterly, "As if one can believe that anyone died of natural causes in the camps.

"Fritz wrote that he fought in the War of Independence, that he was wounded - he did not say how - that he is married to Naomi Gutman, the daughter of the neighbor under whose protection he came to Palestine. They have one child, a girl. They live in Haifa, on Mount Carmel.

"Now I come to the important part of Fritz's letter. Important for you, that is, Mr. and Mrs. Rhys. It is about Fritz's sister Henrietta.

"In 1936, Henrietta Mayer gave birth to a child, a girl. Out of wedlock. The father was her skating instructor. He was not Jewish. In fact, he was a Nazi, a member of the Gestapo. As soon as Henrietta's father, Gustav Mayer, learned of her pregnancy, he turned her out of his house. However, despite his anger and disappointment he was concerned for her safety. He arranged for her to live on a farm, with relatives of the couple who worked for him as chauffeur and housekeeper. He obtained new identity papers for her. Her name was changed from Henrietta Mayer to Henrietta Meissner."

Glynis gives an involuntary gasp. Then smacks her hand over her mouth as she recognizes the name. William sits stonily, smoking, showing no reaction. As if he has known all along where Miss Schneider's story is leading. He is relieved that Glynis and Miss Schneider cannot read his mind, cannot know what he is thinking, cannot know how he is imagining Megan's laugh when he imitates and exaggerates Miss Schneider's accent, the 'senk you' and 'Chewish', just as he often imitates some of their customers' speech patterns and mannerisms, and sends his daughter into fits of laughter at his mimicry.

But, at the same time, he knows he will refrain. He has no desire to mimic this poor woman. Quite to the contrary, his heart is racked by her words; he cannot remember ever being so deeply affected.

Miss Schneider continues, more slowly, enunciating each word with care. "In 1939, through the efforts of the Quaker Society, Henrietta was able to send her three-year-old daughter to England. The child's official name was Marga Meissner. Her real name was, of course, Marga Mayer. She was named for Henrietta's late mother.

"I managed to trace the child to England, but then the trail was lost. However, with the help of Fritz Mayer and his father-in-law, I was able to contact Gustav Mayer's former housekeeper, Inge Bauer. Mrs. Bauer, as I mentioned before, was the wife of Mr. Mayer's chauffeur. Her husband died during the war. It took me a long time to find Frau... Mrs. Bauer, because she no longer lives in Frankfurt. After the death of her husband, she moved to Dresden where she has family. Dresden is now in communist East Germany. I won't bore you with all the details, but it was Mrs. Bauer who eventually led me to you."

Miss Schneider looks around the kitchen and, as if seeing it for the first time, notices the Welsh dresser that takes up almost one whole wall. Displayed on it, and intermingled with Glynis's best Wedgewood and Royal Albert pieces, are various framed photographs, all apparently of the same girl at different ages and stages, and in different poses. One of them shows her in a graceful pose on the ice, wearing ice skates and a fetching skating costume, her head thrown to the side, her arms outstretched, as if about to leap into the air.

Abruptly, Miss Schneider stands, clutching her handbag and cloche, and wanders over to the photographs. She peers at them intently for several moments, looking from one to another.

"Is this...?" She doesn't say more. She doesn't need to.

Glynis and William have remained at the table, frozen in place. Miss Schneider returns to her seat, once again opens her handbag and removes an envelope. From the envelope she slides out a photograph, much handled and yellowed with age. It is the image of a beautiful young girl, of perhaps fifteen or sixteen, with an abundance of flowing curls and an impish grin. The resemblance to the photographs on the Rhys's kitchen dresser is uncanny.

There can be no mistake.

Chapter 44

⇒✦⇐

Glynis and William are too agitated to sleep after their guest's departure. Miss Schneider had left the sandwiches untouched, had politely requested William to telephone for a taxi to take her to the railway station. "Senk you," she said again, in her careful, accented English. "You are very kind."

They assume she managed to catch the last train to London, as she had planned. It was raining when she left them, but she had waved away their offer of an umbrella. She has left them her address and telephone number. She has also left them Fritz Mayer's address in Haifa. He has no telephone at his home, there being a long waiting list for telephones in the new State of Israel. Miss Schneider told them that Fritz is very anxious to hear from his niece, that he longs 'to be united' with his sister's child. She also told them that Fritz, in his letter, reminded her that the late Mrs. Mayer had a brother by the name of Manfred Kahn who has been living in the United States since long before the war. He is Megan's great-uncle. Apparently, Fritz's father, Mr. Mayer, also had a brother, a Heinz Mayer who had been a well-known lawyer in Frankfurt. According to Miss Schneider, Heinz Mayer left Germany at the end of 1935 and settled in Holland, only to be captured by the Nazis when that country was invaded. He died of typhoid in Bergen Belsen concentration camp just before the camp was liberated by the Americans.

Before Miss Schneider left she also told them what they had been afraid to ask.

Henrietta had been captured by the Nazis and sent to Ravensbrück, the cruelest, most notorious women's concentration camp in Germany. A friend of Henrietta's in the camp, who survived, reported that Henrietta collapsed and died on the enforced death march from Ravensbrück in the spring of 1945, just as the Russians were approaching. Henrietta died in her friend's arms, delirious at the end, muttering over and over again about a little bunny rabbit. Miss Schneider added that Inge Bauer has always suspected that her nephew Gunther Bauer, a member of the SS, discovered Henrietta's true identity and reported her to the Nazis. Fortunately, by then she had sent her daughter away, and the child had already reached the safety of England.

Just before she left, almost as an afterthought, Miss Schneider told them that the self-same Gunther Bauer was later captured by the Americans, tried and found guilty of war crimes. He was considered to have been one of the most viscous and sadistic Nazi guards in the Mauthausen concentration camp in Austria. He was sentenced to hang. However, shortly before he was to be executed, he carried out the sentence himself: he was found hanged in his prison cell.

Miss Schneider imparted one last piece of information before climbing into the waiting taxi. Inge Bauer has in her possession a letter Henrietta wrote before she was deported to Ravensbrück. It is in a sealed envelope, addressed in German to *My daughter Marga*, followed by the words, *To be opened in the event of my death*. Mrs. Bauer is keeping the letter safe in the hope that she will one day be able to turn it over in person to Henrietta's daughter. She has left instructions with another nephew, Bernd Bauer, the infamous Gunther's brother, that should she die before she is able to fulfill this mission, the letter is to be sent to Fritz Mayer in Israel.

➤❦

"What a bloody state of affairs, isn't it, Glyn?" says William, as he kicks off his shoes and prepares for bed, knowing he will never be able to sleep a wink.

"That's the one thing we didn't tell Meggy, isn't it," says Glynis. "That she's Jewish, as we suspected. When she finds out, or more likely figures it out for herself, she'll hate us even more for not telling her."

William doesn't even try to mask his groan. "What do you say we both go over to St. Mary's after we close shop tomorrow, and speak to Vicar Lowell," he says. "Let's see how he thinks we should handle the matter. He and Megan are close, or used to be at any rate. If you remember, he offered to help us with this before, but was too ill at the time. Now he'll have another chance."

"Let's face it, Will, Megan's clever enough to work it out for herself, and then sure as I'm lying here in bed she'll blame us the more so for keeping it from her. Even though the birth certificate doesn't specify the child's religion, who but a Jewish mother in Germany could have parted with her child like that, who else would have been forced to send her three-year-old away? Just the thought of it is enough to send me round the bend. But we can't keep Miss Schneider's visit from her, Will. Indeed, the minute she comes home we'll have to tell her. I shudder to think how she'll take the news, coming right on the heels of learning she's adopted."

Both lie on their backs, side by side in the large bed they have shared since their marriage. They hold hands, as has become their habit before letting sleep overtake them. But at midnight, when they would normally be fast asleep, both are still wide awake.

"What d'you say to some piping hot chocolate, Glyn love?" says William. "With lots of hot milk. That should send us off. Things will look better in the morning, no doubt, in the bright light of day."

They both throw on dressing gowns and return to the kitchen where Glynis puts up a saucepan of milk to boil. "Did not the thought occur to you, Will, as it did to me that Megan's affinity for skating came from her ... her real parents? From both of them? Seems they were both skaters, he an instructor, no less."

"Aye, that it did," says William, "but let's get one thing straight, Glyn. You and I are Megan's parents, her *real* parents. We're the ones who've raised her. We're the ones who've taken care of her. We're the ones who love her to smithereens. Indeed, let there be no mistake on that score. None whatsoever, as far as I'm concerned. And as far as the skating instructor is concerned, let's not forget what Miss Schneider told us. He was a Nazi, one of the very worst kind. A member of the SS. If possible, the SS was even more brutal than the Gestapo, if I remember correctly."

"I don't think we have to tell Megan about him, what d'you think, Will? Surely, there's enough for her to take in without that? Our poor little Meggy. How I wish we could spare her all of this. Surely we can at least omit the details about the father?"

"I should think so, Glyn, but as far as I can see our greatest concern is not to let any of this interfere with her plans for the Olympics."

Glynis lets out a groan. "Oh, sweet Jesus. I wasn't even thinking of that, but you're right, Will. My heaven, you're right."

"I say we don't make any decisions until we've spoken to the Vicar, Glyn love. Also, let's see how Meggy is when she gets back before we give her any more news of her German family. Let's see if she's yet been able to digest the news we've already given her. That's enough of a shock for her to be going on with, isn't it? And let's see if she's even ready to talk to us."

"Och Will. I know you're right, love. I know we've got to be patient with her, give her time. But she's such a soft-hearted, compassionate child, has always been loving to us. I know she'll come round eventually. But it's bloody hard, is all I can say. Bloody hard it is."

Chapter 45

⟫⟪

It is two weeks since Megan's triumphant return from the Nationals. On the surface, everything seems normal in the Rhys household. Perhaps there is not quite the spontaneous display of affection that Megan used to show; perhaps there are some awkward pauses in their exchanges; perhaps there is an occasional averting of eyes; a tendency to tiptoe around each other with excessive politeness. Perhaps at the Saturday high tea, always so eagerly anticipated, the conversation doesn't flow with the usual easiness and laughter. Fortunately, there are the Saturday concerts to fill the silence.

Glynis and William have told Megan about Miss Schneider's visit, that Megan has family in Israel, that she was born Jewish. The news of her Jewishness did not appear to shock her. She said she had suspected as much. She gives no outward sign of being affected by the news. She attends church as usual.

This morning, she's at her desk in her room trying to write the letter Glynis has urged her to write. It is not going well, judging by the mountain of scrunched up efforts rapidly filling the wastebasket at her feet. The first one started *Dear Fritz*, (no, not respectful enough); then *Dear Uncle Fritz* (no, too intimate, she's never even met him); then *Dear Mr. Mayer*, (no, too cold and formal, and being he's a scientist, perhaps it should be *Dr. Mayer?*).

Oh dear, this is much more difficult than she anticipated. She groans and stands up in despair. Everything is too confusing.

Laurie is taking a holiday, thus Megan, by default, is on holiday too. The welcome she received when she came home from London was more than she expected. There were signs and colored streamers all over the front door and shop window; even the new sign above the window was so smothered with them, the letters were no longer visible. The mantels in the kitchen and dining room were covered with hundreds of congratulatory cards from customers and friends and a multitude of well-wishing strangers. Canton High School sent a giant billboard-sized card signed by the student body and teachers with the school motto *Semper Sersum!* emblazoned on the top in splashes of color. In the center of the kitchen table was an enormous basket of yellow daffodils, the national flower of Wales, sent by the City of Cardiff, together with a card signed by William Muston, the mayor himself, expressing the city's pride at this fantastic achievement by its 'native daughter'.

Megan is overwhelmed by all the unexpected fuss, and embarrassed, too. She doesn't feel she has done anything special to deserve it. She receives a card from Gwen, congratulating her. Gwen is in France on a student exchange program; she will be spending a whole year there with a family in Provence, to perfect her French. When she returns to England, Gwen writes, she will be applying to one of the Oxford colleges for early admission. With Gwen away, Megan has told her parents it will be too lonely to spend two weeks in Weston-super-Mare as they've done in past summers. Glynis and her swollen feet are only too happy to stay home. "You and your Da can take some day outings without me, Meggy love," she says, "I don't mind at all."

At the first opportunity, Megan walks over to St. Mary's and, in the privacy of the empty church, offers up her thanks to Jesus for her success. She finds Vicar

Lowell in his vestry, and receives from him his special, warm congratulations. Then they have a long, long talk.

Later, the vicar telephones the Rhys's, relieving them of some of their anxiety. "You have nothing to fear," he tells them, "Megan seems to be taking it all in stride. She told me she has no problem with her German mother being Jewish. It doesn't make any difference to her. She says it was through the Quakers and the mercy of Jesus that her life was saved, but" he adds, "she did say she has no objection to writing to her new relatives in Israel. However, as to meeting them, she is uncertain of her feelings. At any rate, I think that will have to wait."

There are two things the vicar doesn't tell Glynis and William. He does not tell them that Megan, upon being shown the photograph of Henrietta that Miss Schneider had given the Rhys's, is now convinced that Henrietta is the lady of her dream, that Henrietta is watching over her. Nor does he tell them that Megan has shown curiosity about the man who fathered her. That she has asked certain questions; questions the vicar has been unable to answer.

꧁꧂

Finally, the letter is written.

Dear Fritz Mayer, she writes.

My name is Megan Rhys. I am the adopted daughter of Glynis and William Rhys. As you can see from my address, we live in Cardiff, Wales. Your friend Miss Schneider visited my parents and told them that your sister Henrietta was my mother. I was very sorry to hear what happened to her. Miss Schneider said you would like to meet me. I would like to meet you, too. But at this time it is not possible because I am training for next winter's Olympics games to be held in February in Oslo, Norway.

She's not sure how to sign off. *Yours sincerely* sounds too formal. In the end, she simply writes *With best wishes, yours, Megan Rhys.*

Chapter 46

During the two weeks of this unexpected interruption in her training, it seems to Megan, that every time she turns around, Shaun Owen is there, his bicycle locked to the lamppost outside the shop. Sometimes, Megan finds him at the kitchen table enjoying breakfast with her Mum and Da when she comes down after indulging in the rare luxury of a sleep-in; often she finds him helping her parents out in the shop in the middle of the day. At other times he drops in for supper because he just 'happened to be passing by'.

One day, Shaun almost collides with the postman making his delivery. He offers to bring the letters up to the Rhys's flat. "Ta, lad," says the postman. "I'm late with me rounds as it is, and you'll save me a climb up them stairs." Idly, Shaun flips through the pile of letters. His attention is immediately drawn to an airmail letter with a foreign stamp. It's addressed to Megan. His curiosity gets the better of him. He turns the envelope over. The return address is 'Haifa, Israel'.

"Post delivery," he announces, coming into the kitchen, and holding out the pile to Glynis who is peeling potatoes at the sink. "No doubt all bills," she says, without looking up from her task. "Just throw them on the sideboard there, Shaun love." He points to the letter with the foreign stamp. "Now who on earth can be writing to Megan," he asks her. "from the holy land, of all places?"

Glynis turns around, wiping her hands on her pinafore before picking up the stack of letters. "It's curiosity that killed the cat, young man, I always say." Glynis smiles to take the sting out of her words. She prevaricates: "Our Megan has pen pals all over the world, don't you know, skating pals mostly."

Now that she's home and not training, Megan has no ready excuse when Shaun invites her to the flicks. And her Mum encourages it. "Go on with you now, lovey, and enjoy it while you can," urges Glynis. "Before you know it that taskmaster Laurie'll be back and you won't have time to breathe again."

One night they see *An American in Paris* at the Regent, which Megan loved, and the following week *A Place in the Sun* at the Odeon, which she found depressing. A few days later, on a warm, hazy summer's day, they pack up a picnic, take the bus and tram to Castle Road and wander through the grounds surrounding medieval Cardiff Castle. The castle itself is closed for renovations. Though Megan must have ridden past it a hundred times, she's never been inside. Later, they spread a blanket on the grass of nearby Bute Park, munch on ham and cheese sandwiches and sweet greenhouse straw-berries. Shaun, who has visited the castle many times, is enthusiastic and knowledgeable about its history. He lists battles and dates, warming to his subject when talking about the moat; he's excited that it's being repaired. "We'll have to come back once all the renovations are completed," he says. "I can't wait to see how they've restored it on the inside." Megan is too po-lite to tell him that she has no interest in this castle or any castles, for that matter. Besides, she can't understand some of the long words he's been using. If she remembers, she'll look up 'anachronistic' in the dictionary when she gets home.

Despite being a bit bored by his history lesson, she finds Shaun com-fortable to be with. He tells her about his studies at Cardiff University, re-minds her that he will be going off to live in London that autumn where he'll attend London University's School of Economics. Briefly, they talk about Gwen, and how seldom either of them hears from her. For the first time, he takes her hand.

Megan is tempted to confide in him the news of her adoption, to tell him about Miss Schneider's visit, but something holds her back. After all, what reason is there for Shaun to know?

"I'll miss you, Meggy, when I'm in London," he says. "Will you write to me?" She promises that she will.

><

The letter from Haifa is not the first Megan has received from Fritz Mayer. He is careful how he addresses her, always calling her *my dear niece Megan* and never forgetting to send *warm wishes to your parents*. She writes back, complimenting him on his English, which is surprisingly good, and he replies that he picked it up while serving in the Haganah, the Israeli army, during Israel's War of Independence. At the end of his most recent letter, his wife Naomi has added a few lines. Her English is not as fluent as Fritz's, and betrays a tendency to translate literally from her mother tongue. She writes, *I was the best friend of your mother. We have attended the same school. Henrietta, too, loved the skating. All the family are wishing you, dear Megan, large success in the Olympics and are cheering for you, and all are hoping before much longer to be meeting you.*

Megan finds herself looking forward to the letters with the foreign stamp and symbols, the foreign words printed in strange hieroglyphics. No longer hesitant about replying, she answers each letter almost immediately. Vicar Lowell has told her that in Israel they speak Hebrew, the language of the Old Testament, and that they write from right to left.

How strange, she thinks. *To speak Hebrew and write from right to left, yet to know how to write English as we do, from left to right. And German, too. They must all be geniuses.*

One evening, arriving home after a grueling day of training, Megan finds a large parcel waiting for her. The Israeli stamps show its origin, and the parcel is covered with an assortment of excise and customs stamps. It is addressed to Megan Rhys, and the franking date indicates that it has been en route for over a month. The contents are not listed on the customs declaration, which merely states: *Gift*. Megan picks the parcel up, it is quite heavy. She looks at her Mum questioningly, but Glynis is as puzzled as she is. She tries to shake it, but nothing shifts inside, nothing to give a clue as to its contents. Gingerly, Megan tears at the brown paper wrapping, then opens the carton beneath. She finds herself looking at a pair of skates.

There is a short note in Fritz Mayer's handwriting. *These are the skates worn by my sister. I took them with me when I left Germany. I thought you might like to have them.*

Megan doesn't notice how her Mum has silently turned away, disturbed by the contents of the parcel, by the note.

The skates are obviously old and worn, the once white leather stiff and cracked and yellowed with age. Hesitantly, Megan picks one of them up and reverently passes her hand over the rough leather surface, then over the dull blade in its weathered sheath. Her thoughts automatically go to the owner of the skates. *When did she last wear them? Where was she? Was she already pregnant with me?* And then, because she cannot help herself, she asks, *And was* **he** *there too when she last wore them?* She feels awed, as if she is holding a holy relic in her hands. How will she ever bring herself to try them on? No, no. It comes to her suddenly, with absolute certainty, that she cannot bear to wear them, cannot bear even to try them on, to place her feet into them. The skates are not meant to be worn.

She goes in search of a hook and hammer, then hangs the skates on the wall above her bed. Alongside the crucifix.

Chapter 47

Laurie is back from holiday, and training begins in earnest again, leaving little time for anything or anyone else. Shaun included.

The summer ends and the months fly by in a steady, grueling routine of practice, practice, and more practice. Each day seems to meld into the next, and into the one before it, sometimes leaving Megan unaware what day it is; as far as she is concerned. it might as soon be Monday as Friday. Before she realizes it, Christmas is upon them again, with the winter Olympics just a few weeks away. She has heard nothing from Gwen since the summer; nor has she herself had time to write to her old friend. Shaun is home from London for the Christmas holidays and tells Megan that Gwen has decided to stay in France for *Noël*. As he did last year, Shaun helps her Da decorate the tree, helps out for the Christmas rush in the shop.

After the ritual turkey supper, they walk together to midnight mass, as they did the previous Christmas. There are four of them this time instead of five, with Gwen's absence barely noted. Glynis has visited Dr. Hughes, the new panel doctor assigned to the Rhys's by the National Health Service. True, she had to wait in his surgery for hours, but the new medicine he gave her seems to be helping. The swelling in her feet has gone down, and walking is much easier. Dr. Hughes told her it might help if she lost a few pounds.

Now that she feels better, Glynis is determined to see Megan perform in the Oslo games. The Olympics are to start on Thursday, February 14th. The date is marked on Glynis's calendar, and etched into her brain. She has looked into purchasing her ticket for the day before, for the 13th. She tells William, "I'm not superstitious, as you know…" He interrupts, laughing. "I know no such thing, Glyn, love. Aren't you always reading the tea leaves? And, just the other day you sprinkled salt over your shoulder, I don't even remember why."

"Oh, that's just me having me bit of fun, that is," she says, adding, "but I just can't see being trapped up there in an airplane, miles above the earth on the 13th if I don't have to, that's all."

"Indeed, you're right, Glyn," he says, trying to keep a straight face. "Why take chances, love."

She has her ticket for Tuesday the 12th. Megan and Laurie will be leaving a full week before the games, to give Megan plenty of time to practice on the same rink where the figure-skating competitions will be held.

In contrast to the previous year, this Christmas is dry, with no hint of snow. Though seasonably cold, the air is clear and bracingly fresh.

"I've missed you, Megan," says Shaun as they approach St. Mary's. "I hope you've missed me too, even though you never answered any of my letters."

Megan is contrite. "I'm really sorry Shaun. Of course I missed you, but you can't imagine how busy I've been with the training. When I come home at night I'm just too knackered to write letters."

"What about your pen pals?" he says, a trace of bitterness creeping into his voice. "Don't tell me you've also not had time to write to them, especially the one in Israel."

Megan stops walking. She looks up at him. "What do you mean, my pen pals? And how d'you know about Israel?"

"Don't get yourself into a twist, Meg. One day when I was over at your place, I noticed a letter addressed to you, with a foreign stamp. It was from Israel. Your Mum said you've a pen pal there, and other pen pals all over the world. Came as quite a surprise to me, I can tell you."

Megan bursts out laughing. She almost says, *Comes as quite a surprise to me too.* Instead she says, "Yes, indeed, I've pen pals all over the world. Even in Timbuktu." She's still laughing, unable to control it. Once started, she can't stop. Shaun watches in bewilderment. She's doubled over, sputtering with mirth that turns into a cough. She leans against a wall, holding her stomach. "I…I'm sorry, Shaun," she says, wiping her eyes with her gloved hand. "It's just too funny, that's all." In a more serious tone she adds, "One day, perhaps I'll tell you all about it. But now's not the time."

Glynis and William have been walking ahead of them. They're already sitting in their pew by the time Megan and Shaun arrive. Megan slides in next to her Mum. "A pen pal is it that I have?" she whispers to Glynis, deliberately putting on the broadest Welsh inflection. "That's rich, that is. Indeed." Glynis merely smiles and elbows Megan in the arm. "Sh," she says, "there's the vicar, ready to begin."

⪼⪻

There are two subjects on which Glynis and William have a rare difference of opinion, and which are causing unusual dissention between them. One of them is Shaun. Glynis looks fondly on the budding friendship between Megan and Shaun, and encourages it. William, on the other hand, thinks fifteen-year-old girls are too young to be thinking seriously of boys. Glynis says, "I see no harm in it, Will, none at all. With Gwen away and Megan no longer at school min- gling with other girls, the only person she sees all day is Laurie, who's nowhere near her age and not a suitable friend for a fifteen-year-old girl. And what with being on the ice day after day, she needs a friend closer to her own age. Shaun is a good lad, a serious lad, and he seems smitten with her. Anyway, right at this moment it's a long distance friendship, being he's in school in London. So where's the harm?"

"You may be right Glyn, love," says Will, "but I've come to be very fond of the lad, and don't want to see him hurt. Our Meggy's too young to be thinking of a steady relationship; and, indeed, as far as I can see, she doesn't have deep feelings for Shaun at all. The only thing that seems to excite her is the skating."

"I'm not so sure about that," says Glyn. "But as you always like to say, Will, 'time will tell' won't it?"

The other subject that they can't agree on is the correspondence between Megan and Israel, an exchange of letters that is becoming more and more frequent.

Again, it is Glynis who takes the more favorable view. She and William are down in the shop after closing time, tidying up, replacing items on the shelves. Glynis says, "To my mind, our poor Meggy must be thinking about Henrietta, thinking how she died, what happened to her. Sure it is that she's too sensitive to bring it up in our presence. She seems to have found a receptive ear in the Vicar and I hope he's able to answer all her questions to her satisfaction. And sure it is also she must be wondering about the man who fathered her. It would only be natural, wouldn't it?" She looks up from the ledger into which she's been entering numbers. "What harm can it do, Will, for her to be in touch with her fam..., that is, her German mother's family, especially when they live at such a great distance from us?" Not receiving an immediate answer, she continues, "There's something else, Will, something that might not have occurred to you. Do you remember what that Miss Schneider said about war claims? What did she call them, something like 'restitution', wasn't it?" William says "Reparations, I think she called them. Reparations. What about it, Glyn?"

"Well, seems to me she was hinting strongly that Meggy might come into a sizeable inheritance if the Germans give back the business they seized from this Fritz Mayer's father – you know, the man who would have been Meggy's grandfather. How can we deprive her of that, Will?"

Will is emphatically opposed. "Indeed we can, Glynis. In my mind that's not a good enough reason to stay in touch with them. I can't stop her from writing to this Mayer chap, if she's so disposed, but I don't want her to be harboring any thoughts along those lines. As far as I'm concerned, our Megan'll be well enough fixed once we're gone, and I hope you're not putting any thoughts into her head. Indeed, those are thoughts she shouldn't be having."

Neither subject being settled to the satisfaction of either of them, both matters are dropped, and Glynis and William climb the stairs to their living quarters to eat supper and listen to the six o'clock BBC news.

Chapter 48

⇒﹣

Megan and Laurie take an SAS flight from London's Heathrow to Garder-moen, Oslo's main airport. The plane is filled with competing athletes from all over the U.K. After landing in Oslo, they all pile into a waiting bus to take them to their lodgings. The Olympics committee has named that cluster of housing 'The Olympics Village', the first of its kind. Practice begins the fol-lowing day on the Jorda Amfi outdoor rink where the compulsory figure skat-ing competitions will take place. The free-style routines will take place indoors at Bislett Stadion.

Glynis arrives, as planned, on the 12th. She takes a taxi to the small hotel near the indoor stadium, where she has reserved a room. She and Megan have arranged to meet at the stadium on the following day during Megan's morning practice session.

It is Wednesday, February 13th. Glynis has received instructions how to get from her hotel to Bislett Stadion. When she emerges from the hotel, she looks up at a sky that is battleship grey, thickly overcast; the temperature is frigid, several degrees below freezing. She is wearing her fleece-lined coat with hood and scarf, fur-lined boots and gloves. She resists the temptation to take a taxi; Dr. Hughes has emphasized that walking will do her good, and so she walks the short distance. By the time she reaches the stadium she can no longer feel her hands and feet. She sits in the front row of the almost empty stadium, stamping her numb feet on the ground and clapping her gloved hands together, trying to thaw out. At the same time, she looks for her daughter among the several skaters practicing on the rink. She spots Megan almost immediately. That golden halo of curls above the red warm-up jacket is impossible to miss. Megan has not yet noticed her mother. She is practicing her figure-eights, swirling this way and that, trying to skate repeatedly over the same grooves in the ice. To Glynis's untrained and by no means unbiased eyes Megan's execution could not be more perfect. How graceful her Meggy is, how readily her body bends so easily and naturally as she takes the curves. Surely there cannot be a more beautiful, more talented, more elegant skater in the whole competition.

It is as these happy thoughts are running through Glynis' head, that disaster strikes.

Later, Glynis will swear to William that the accident was no accident, that it was deliberate. After all, she was there, she saw it happen, saw how that Romanian girl, even though there was plenty of room for her to avoid Megan, pretended to trip, and bumped into Megan, making her fall onto the ice, with one leg bent at an awkward angle beneath her body. The Romanian girl didn't even stop, but had the gall to continue blithely gliding across the ice to the other end of the arena, as if she hadn't noticed a thing. Laurie is distraught, but not convinced that it was deliberate; just at the moment of collision, she was turned away, talking to one of the stadium officials. Nobody else seems to have seen a thing.

Even during the confusion of those first moments, Glynis remembers the date. It's the 13th, the date she had been so careful to avoid. How painfully ironic. What was it Will had said to her? Oh yes, *Why take chances.*

Megan is in considerable pain, but uncomplaining. She is taken by ambulance to Kristiansund hospital where it is determined there is a hairline fracture in her left leg. Fortunately, they say, it is a clean break. They put a cast on her leg, and then release her. She will be allowed to fly home on Friday the 15th.

The following day, Saturday the 16th, is the day Megan was to have competed in the first women's figure skating competition.

Chapter 49

Her parents and Laurie keep assuring and reassuring Megan that she will be able to try again in four years for the next winter Olympics. She will still be young enough, only twenty. Little do they know that she doesn't need their assurances. They are puzzled by her calm, philosophical acceptance of the accident. They cannot know that Megan is convinced there is a divine plan at work, that Jesus has sent the lady of her dream to guide and protect her. She cannot tell them, has not even told Vicar Lowell, that in all her practice sessions in Oslo, including that last one when the accident occurred, the face of her dream lady, the face of the lady whom she now knows to be Henrietta, her mother, was always spectrally in front of her eyes. She cannot tell them how the lady guided her every movement, guided every stroke of her skates. She cannot tell them what she believes: that if the lady allowed the accident to happen, there must be a good explanation, one that has not yet been revealed to her.

Thankfully, they cannot hear what she says to Jesus before she falls asleep. "Thank you, sweet Jesus," she says. "I know there must be a reason for my accident, why I was not meant to compete in the Olympics. I know that one day you will show me the reason."

They cannot know, and would be alarmed if they did know, the questions that race through her mind after she concludes her prayer. How she looks up at the wall above her pillow, her gaze shifting from the crucifix to the skates, and back again.

Who was I praying to? she asks herself. *Jesus or Henrietta?*

She is inundated with condolence cards, get-well cards, all manner of good wishes from fans in every corner of the city and every corner of Wales, from out-of-the-way mining communities in the Rhondda Valley, places she would never have suspected had ever heard of the Olympics, much less of Megan Rhys. She had no idea that the whole world seems to have been watching her, supporting her, focused on her success. Shaun writes to her almost every day. From Gwen she receives a short note of sympathy, signed off, for the first time in many months with their unique signal: *See you soon, baboon.*

A letter that she receives from Miss Schneider is in formal, stilted English. The letter puzzles her, and unaccountably makes her uneasy. *We have never met,* writes Miss Schneider, *but I feel as if I know you because I knew your mother in Germany when she was approximately the same age you are now. She was also a proficient skater. She would have been very proud of you, as would your dear grandfather, Mr. Gustav Mayer. I offer you my sincere sympathy and good wishes for your speedy recovery.*

An airmail letter arrives from Haifa, bearing those quaint stamps and Hebrew writing that have become familiar, and that she finds herself looking for with eager anticipation. *My dear niece Megan,* writes Fritz Mayer. *Naomi and I were so sorry to hear of your accident. We hope you are not too upset at not being able to compete in the Olympics. The important thing is for your leg to heal properly.*

It seems strange, even to herself, that she is not as upset as those around her, not as upset as they expect her to be. Her Da says little, but when he does he attempts to make a joke that always falls flat; he hugs her more frequently, and lights up his Woodbines more often than usual. Her Mum tries to present a cheerful front, but Megan detects a false note to her liveliness, a forced brightness in her voice. "Mum," Megan says, "don't worry about me, please. It's not the end of the world, really. And as soon as I can get this cast off, I'm going back to Canton High." William, overhearing, says, "There's me girl, Meggy," and comes over to give her one of his hugs.

Megan has made a decision. Even though she knows she's at the age when she can leave school legally and permanently, she's decided she wants to graduate. While she is recuperating, she begins to study again for the O levels, finding it much easier to concentrate now than when she was in school, feeling less pressured than when she was studying with Gwen. For the first time she realizes that she is not stupid. If she manages to squeak through the exams, she knows exactly what she would like to do.

The one thing she knows she definitely does *not* want to do, even though she has not yet told her parents or Laurie, is to train and compete in another winter Olympics. She is afraid they will not understand how, with the accident, the urge to compete seems to have left her. It is as if the accident has expelled from her body the passion she once had for skating, as if it has siphoned out all thought of competition from her brain.

She is no longer *mad* for the sport. It no longer excites her as it did just a few short weeks ago. But how can she expect them to understand when she herself doesn't understand it?

Chapter 50

≫❦❦

Winter 1955.

For the last three years, Megan has been the physical education instructor at Llandaff Secondary School for Girls. After her graduation from Canton High, she took a special course in gymnastics, at which she excelled. She was immediately awarded this position. She loves her job, which doesn't seem like a job at all. She loves her young students and they respond to her enthusiasm. They have so much fun together doing the exercise routines.

She has fulfilled the decision she made after Oslo, the first decision she ever made without consulting her parents or Vicar Lowell.

It was to be the first of many.

≫❦

Gwen is finally coming home for Christmas. She has been at Balliol for the past three years, and, until now, has spent all her summer and winter holidays in France. Shaun told Megan that Gwen will be coming down from Oxford early, with firsts in English and French literature. Megan isn't at all surprised; hasn't she always known that Gwen is brilliant? It is over three years since the girls last saw each other, and Megan is filled with excited anticipation.

Gwen and Shaun are expected to join the Rhys's for supper on Christmas Eve. After supper, they will all walk to St. Mary's together for midnight mass, just as they used to in years past. It is her Da, who surprisingly voices misgivings. "I hope you won't be disappointed, Meggy mine," he says. "You and Gwen haven't seen each other for ages. Your Mum and I were discussing it just last evening. You've each taken completely different paths. Indeed, I should think both of you are quite different people by now."

"Not to mention that we're both also grown up," Megan says, smiling. "Not to worry on my account, Da. I'm a big girl now and I've no unreasonable expectations from Gwen. At least, I don't think I have."

Gwen's appearance is a surprise, a pleasant one. She has slimmed down, has discarded her glasses for contact lenses, is dressed with casual French flair, and her auburn hair, which was always an unruly mess in the past, now sports a stylish short, blunt cut. She has even assumed a certain charm, something she never had before, has become understatedly sophisticated. She embraces and kisses Megan warmly, is equally generous in greeting Glynis and William, hugging them both. "My," she says, looking around the Rhys's kitchen. "Nothing's changed. It's good to be back."

Shaun is his usual easy self. He is now in a graduate program in economics at LSE. He has already been offered a position with a financial firm in the City; he is to start working after he earns his degree in a few months. His devotion to Megan is unflagging, and he's not shy about wearing his heart on his sleeve. Her feelings for him are not as easy to read.

Supper is a joyous meal of reunion. The conversation flows freely and naturally. Gwen has become quite a raconteur and regales everyone with tales of France and the *Frogs*, as she calls the French with derisive humor. Everyone is relaxed. There is a lot of laughter.

Then it happens. After supper. On the way to church.

Glynis and William walk on ahead, with the three young people following them at a leisurely pace. Everyone is bundled up against the cold. It was sleeting earlier in the day and though the downpour has ceased the air remains replete with moisture. The moon and stars are completely hidden by thick cloud cover; as a result the streets are darker than usual, somewhat eerie. The roads and pavements are icy and treacherous, and the few intrepid drivers maneuver their vehicles gingerly to avoid skidding. Megan and Gwen walk hand-in-hand, just as they used to in the old days, with Shaun loping along happily next to Megan. Gwen says, "So, Megan, what's this I hear from Shaun about a friend you have in Israel, of all places? You're not keeping secrets from me, are you?"

Now is the time to tell them. Megan has discussed it with her parents, and they have agreed that it's high time for Shaun to know. And as for Gwen, is she not Megan's best friend? And are they not all adults now? Surely there is no reason for secrecy.

Megan tries to sound offhand. "I've been writing to an uncle of mine in Haifa. You know, of course, that I'm adopted." Brother and sister stop in their tracks, bringing Megan to a halt, also. "I know no such thing," says Gwen slowly. "You must be joking." Shaun just stares at Megan, as if she is talking in tongues.

This is not a good beginning, thinks Megan, no longer sure if she should tell them. But now that she's started, she must finish. The three resume walking. "I wouldn't joke about something like that, Gwenny. My Mum and Da chose me from among a group of refugees from Germany, just before the war. I was three years old and don't remember a thing about it."

"But why…that is to say…" Megan has never known Gwen to stutter. "So, that means you were born in Germany. What about your real parents, what happened to them?" This is the question Megan has been dreading. She says, "My mother was killed by the Nazis."

"So your mother…, that is, your *real* mother… she must have been Jewish. And that means that you were born Jewish, does it not?"

"Yeees. I suppose so."

Gwen is silent for a moment. Once again, she stops walking, and Megan and Shaun stop too. Abruptly, Gwen drops Megan's hand, and steps away from her. "But I don't understand. You go to church, you pray to Jesus." Her face has become strangely contorted, almost ugly. She stares at her hand, the hand that has held Megan's, and begins to wave it back and forth through the air as if it has suffered a burn. Or as if she is ridding it of something vile. "At Canton High you should have been one of those girls who came in after prayers."

Shaun says, "Gwenny, what has all that got to do with anything? Megan can worship anyway she wants to."

"When I lived in France I became very au courant with the news and politics. Don't you know it was the Jews who drove the Arabs out of Palestine in 1948? And what about Jesus? It was the Jews who killed him. That's common knowledge."

Shaun puts his arm around Megan's shoulders. She is trembling. "What has any of that got to do with Meggy?"

"I've just lost my desire to go to St. Mary's with you. Excuse me." Gwen suddenly pivots on her heel and walks away, in the opposite direction.

Megan is crying, silently. She cannot begin to absorb Gwen's ugly accusations. Gwen has been her friend forever. How could she…? Shaun presses Megan to his chest as she sobs. Glynis and William have long disappeared.

"Megan, don't take on so. You mustn't listen to Gwen. She doesn't know what she's talking about. She's always had a 'thing' about Jews; I don't know where she picked it up. I would have thought she'd be more enlightened by now. She may be going to Oxford but she's nothing but an ignorant, stupid cow. As for me, it certainly comes as a surprise to hear you were adopted, and that you were born Jewish, but it doesn't make one ounce of difference to me. Why should it?"

⇒✦⇐

Megan will never know how she was able to sit through the service, the midnight mass she has always loved. Glynis looks at her questioningly as she slips into the pew, obviously puzzled by Gwen's absence. Megan barely registers the vicar's gestures, the rituals, is barely conscious of the sweet singing of the boys' choir. She automatically mouths the words of the hymns, does not remember kneeling and crossing herself, but she must have done or Glynis would have said something. She cannot remember what she said to her Mum about Gwen, perhaps she mumbled something about a headache. She wishes she could speak to Vicar Lowell, to hear his calming voice, to ask his wise counsel. But she cannot bother him now when his every minute is completely occupied with Christmas, with ministering and feeding the poor in the parish during this, the most important season of the year. She cannot bring herself to talk to her parents about Gwen. She doesn't wish to distress them.

She barely registers Shaun's departure. She hopes she said a tolerable goodbye to him, that he doesn't feel hurt; she would not want to hurt him.

Before climbing into bed that night, she kneels and says her prayers, as usual. She recites the Our Father, then looks up at the cross above her bed and the skates hanging from the hook next to it. "Dear Jesus," she begins. And cannot go on.

She lies in bed, her mind in a state of turmoil. Was her friendship with Gwen nothing but a hollow fraud? She remembers now Gwen's reaction whenever the Jewish girls filed into the assembly hall at Canton High; how Gwen used to nudge her, how she used to sneer and whisper, how she resented having to wait for the Jewish girls to take their places. How is it that she didn't notice it? Or was it that she chose not to notice it? She is filled with shame. Shame for herself and shame for Gwen. For Gwen, who was so often bullied as a child.

How wise, how insightful her Da was. Had he seen something in Gwen, something that had escaped her all these years? She remembers how, years ago, she had once asked Vicar Lowell, "Did the Jews kill Jesus?"

"No," he sighed. "That malicious canard has been spread by anti-Semites for centuries and, I'm ashamed to say, encouraged by the church. Tragically, it has led to centuries of persecution and Jewish suffering: the Crusades, the Spanish Inquisition, blood libels. Hitler took advantage of it in his 'Final So-lution'. But, no, it was the Romans who were responsible for Jesus's death."

How could brilliant, educated Gwen believe otherwise?

Surprisingly, Megan falls asleep almost immediately, emotionally exhausted. She has the dream again, for the first time in many months. Tonight she sees the face of the lady more clearly than ever. Tonight she hears the grunting of the pigs, the chatter of the chickens; everything is clearer and louder than ever before. Tonight a golden halo shimmers from the lady's head.

When Megan wakes up the next morning, Christmas Day, her heart no longer aches, and she is almost able to think of Gwen without pain.

She lies in bed, remembering the dream, imagining Henrietta wearing the skates that are now suspended from the wall above her bed, sees her twirling on the ice, a vision of grace.

Was Miss Schneider right? Had Megan lived with Henrietta on a farm? Were there pigs and chickens there? Was there a black dog, just like the one in her dream?

And what of the man who fathered her? What was he like? Megan cannot conjure up any picture of him, cannot imagine him at all.

Of course Henrietta loved him. Of course Megan was conceived in love.

Was his name Meissner? Why is his name not listed on her birth certificate as the father? Why didn't Henrietta marry him? Why does Megan's birth certificate list her mother's name as Meissner, not Mayer? And why was the birth listed as 'legitimate' when she was born out of wedlock? Could it have been to hide Henrietta's Jewish identity?

These questions now run unfettered through her head.

Megan throws back the blankets and leaps out of bed. Her room is unheated, but she doesn't feel the cold as she stands barefoot, staring for a long time at Henrietta's skates, deep in thought. She has completely forgotten that today is Christmas, that presents are waiting to be opened under the tree, that the stockings hanging from the mantel are waiting to be explored.

And, standing there in her bare feet in the cold room, she makes one of the most momentous decisions of her life.

Chapter 51

⇒⋘

In his letters to Megan, Fritz Mayer has often expressed his and Naomi's desire to meet her. If they were able to, he writes, they would love nothing better than to fly to Wales to see her, but it is impossible for him to leave in the middle of his important research at the Technion; difficult for Naomi to leave her students for any length of time – she teaches piano; difficult for them to travel with a small child. Their little Hadassah, who was named for his sister Henrietta, is five years old. Hadassah was Henrietta's Hebrew name. He adds that it was also one of the names of Queen Esther of the bible, who saved the Jews from the evil Haman in Persia.

If it is a matter of money, he writes, nothing would make him happier than to send her a ticket. For her to fly to Israel to visit them, for the family to meet her.

Megan has not told her parents about Fritz Mayer's offer. She knows they would be offended by it; her Da would certainly be horrified. She senses his discomfort when he sees one of those foreign aerograms in the post. She sees how he averts his eyes, the way he immediately lights up a cigarette. Megan herself is uneasy about accepting Fritz Mayer's offer. Despite his *My dear niece* salutations, is he not in reality a stranger to her? Certainly, she cannot bring herself to call him *Uncle*.

Living at home, she has been able to save her wages, and can afford to purchase her own ticket with her own money. She will wait until the end of the school year, until the summer holidays.

Glynis is not surprised. She has braced herself for this, has seen it coming for a long time; it has just been a matter of when. William, on the other hand, cannot bear it. Megan comes up behind him as he sits morosely at the kitchen table on the Sunday morning before her departure. He is drinking his first tea of the morning and puffing on his umpteenth Woodbine. Megan notices with dismay that his hand is unsteady, that some of the tea sloshes into the saucer before he can bring the cup to his lips. Glynis has left the breakfast table to get dressed for church. Megan coils her arms loosely around William's neck. "Oh, Da," she says, noticing for the first time that the hair sprouting from his unshaven cheeks is almost as white as the thinning, monkish tonsure on his head. He had once been so proud of his thick, dark thatch of hair, had often jokingly boasted how he would never become bald. No, not he, indeed. *I'm a Welshman born and bred, and Welshmen die with all their hair.* She rests her smooth cheek against his rough white stubble. "Oh, Da," she says again. "Don't take on so. It's only for a couple of weeks. I'll be back before you even notice I'm gone." By way of answer, he merely grunts, takes another sip of tea, another drag of his cigarette. She whispers in his ear. "Don't worry, Da. I'll always be your Meggy. I love you and Mum to pieces, don't you know? You two are all the family I need, all the family I want. But I wish you'd understand. I have to do this." He grunts again, but this time presses her arm against his neck and says gruffly, "I can't pretend it's not hard, because indeed it is. But I'm trying to understand, indeed I am." He sighs, stands up, letting her arms fall from his neck, and she notices, for the first time, that his back is no longer upright, that he is stooped and listing to one side. She is saddened by the re- alization that her Da is growing old. He says, "I'd better go shave and throw some clothes on, or you-know-who'll have me hide again." He attempts a laugh, and Megan laughs with him, relieved. He gives her a hug before disap- pearing down the hall.

Chapter 52

⇒❦⇐

After writing to Fritz Mayer, giving him the date of her arrival and the details of her flight, she receives one last letter from him before her departure. He is *elated* he says at the prospect of her visit, as is the whole family. Naomi adds an unusually long paragraph to Fritz's letter, in her carefully translated English:

I am joining Fritz in expressing to you my happiness at your forthcoming visit. We are all so anxious to meet with you. In advance, I wish to prepare you for meeting my dear mother, Hannah Gutman. When the war started in 1939, due to strange circumstances, my mother and grandmother were trapped in Poland. Both of them were forced by the Nazis into the Krakow ghetto where they lived with thousands of other Jews under sub-human conditions. My grandmother was unable to survive for long; she died almost immediately. In 1942 the ghetto was liquidated and my mother was sent to a slave labor camp. For the last year of the war, until liberation, she was a prisoner in Auschwitz concentration camp. Perhaps you have heard of Auschwitz? It is a miracle that she survived. You cannot imagine what we, especially my father, went through during the war years, not knowing if she was alive or dead. Of course, this was nothing compared to what she went through. After the war, we learned through the Red Cross that she was alive, that she was in a displaced persons camp in Germany. My father immediately traveled to Germany to bring her home. She was very ill when the camp was liberated, and the doctors thought she would not recover. My mother is not the same person she was before the war. We could not expect her to be, after what she went through. She cannot cry, and has trouble sleeping. My father and brothers take very good care of her. We have told her of your forthcoming visit, and she is largely anticipating it. In fact, she is taking lessons in English in preparation.

Shaun, who is still living in London, meets Megan's train at Paddington. From there, they take a taxi to Heathrow. In the taxi he takes her hand. "Megan," he says, "I can't pretend I'm thrilled about this trip of yours. I'm scared that you won't come back."

"Don't talk nonsense, Shaun," she says. "Of course I'm coming back. Don't be silly."

"You know how I feel about you, Meggy. I've loved you forever, for as long as I can remember. Soon I'll have a steady job and be able to afford to get married. Please tell me you'll marry me, that when you come back we can announce our engagement."

"Oh Shaun. I feel so honored. Truly honored. I wish I could give you an answer, but I'm so nervous about this trip, about meeting all these new relatives, it's all I can think of right now. Can we talk about it again when I get back?"

He is crestfallen. "You promise?"

"Yes, I promise."

Chapter 53

⇒⊱⇐

The BOAC flight to Tel Aviv is smooth and uneventful, with barely any turbulence. Megan had hoped to sleep on the plane, after not having slept very much the night before. But she is too excited, filled with a jumble of thoughts and feelings that she cannot begin to sort out. She had been dreading Shaun's proposal for a long time, and had been hoping to put it off. She is so fond of him; she supposes she must love him. She smiles wryly at the thought of being Gwen's sister-in-law, then pushes Shaun's marriage proposal to the back of her mind.

Thoughts of Fritz and Naomi, of their letters, fill her mind. Megan has heard of Auschwitz concentration camp, as a vague, shadowy, sinister place that people mention now and then to embrace and characterize, with one noun, all of the evil perpetrated by the Nazis. The knowledge that Naomi's mother has actually survived such a nightmare, suddenly makes Megan feel unworthy and apprehensive. And humbled. What can she possibly say to a woman who has suffered what Hannah Gutman has suffered?

The seat next to Megan is occupied by a black-garbed man with a gray beard and a black velvet *kippah* on his head. Megan knows what the word means from one of Fritz Mayer's letters. In his letter, Fritz explained that he wears a *kippah* on his head for religious reasons. He also said that he and his family eat only food that is kosher. Megan consulted a dictionary and visited the library, where she researched the history of Palestine and the 1948 war in which Fritz was wounded. She was particularly curious about Gwen's accusation that the Jews drove the Arabs out of their land. In one account of the war the writer asserted just the opposite, that the Jews asked their Arab neighbors to stay on in the new State of Israel, to not abandon their homes; that it was the Arab authorities who assured their people that once Israel was vanquished, they would all be able to return. Other accounts were conflicting, depending on the views of the writer. She doesn't want to arrive in Israel ignorant about the country and its customs. She is still not completely sure what eating kosher food entails. So far, she has discovered that it means not eating pork and shellfish, and that religiously observant Jews do not eat meat products together with milk products.

The man next to her spends the whole flight reading from a book filled with those Hebrew hieroglyphics that Megan now recognizes. At dinner time, the flight attendant brings him a special tray, tightly sealed in layers and layers of paper and foil wrapping. Megan can't help staring. The man, who has not said a word to her during the flight, now turns to her and says, simply, "This is a kosher meal." When he unwraps his tray, Megan is puzzled, because the chicken and potatoes don't look any different from the meal that she was served.

They land at Lydda airport. Through the window of the plane the tarmac appears in shimmering waves of heat. Megan has been warned that the heat in this part of the world is like nowhere else on earth. As soon as the plane lands, the man next to her closes his eyes and his lips begin to move. Megan assumes he is saying a prayer of thanks for their safe landing. She is tempted to offer a prayer of her own, wonders for a fleeting moment if it is appropriate to invoke Jesus in this land inhabited by Jews, then remembers seeing a group of nuns at the rear of the plane. She silently mouths her own few words of thanks, "Dear Jesus, thank you for bringing me safely to the holy land."

A bus ferries the passengers from the plane to the terminal. The hall is bursting with noise, with people jostling each other and yelling in a jumble of foreign languages; the air is redolent with stale sweat and cigarettes smoke and other odors that are unidentifiable. Suddenly, Megan spies a man holding up a sign with her name on it. *Megan Rhys*. She recognizes Fritz Mayer from the photograph he sent her. He is tall and thin and wears a short-sleeved shirt, open at the neck and tucked into khaki trousers; he has a shock of almost black hair in which is buried a barely discernible blue and white knitted *kippah*. When she gets closer she notices that his handsome face is slightly pock-marked; he is leaning on a cane.

The meeting is riddled with awkwardness and confusion. At the same time that Fritz Mayer shakes Megan's hand warmly and says "At long last. How we have been looking forward to this day," the dark-haired woman next to him, raises her hand to her lips, the blood draining from her face, as she whispers, over and over again, "Henrietta. Henrietta. This is Henrietta." Fritz Mayer turns to her and says gently, "Naomi, this is Megan, Henrietta's daughter, *nicht wahr?*"

"Forgive me, please," says Naomi. "Seeing you gave me a shock. You are resembling her so much. That is all." Megan finds herself enfolded in Naomi's arms. Releasing her, Naomi says, "And this is our Hadassah. She is not speaking English yet." Naomi's German accent is much more pronounced than Fritz's, and she speaks as carefully as she writes. "But she will be learning English in school, when she is older." Little Hadassah holds on to her mother's skirt and smiles shyly up at Megan. The child has dark curly hair and seems tall for her age; she resembles her father. Naomi takes hold of Megan's arm. "Come, we will find your luggage."

Megan notices that Naomi walks with a slight limp. But it is Fritz who has the greater difficulty walking. Casually, he remarks, "I lost my left leg in the 1948 war." And Naomi adds with a smile, "He was jealous of my limp for years, but I think he has overdone it, no?" They both laugh; apparently this is an old joke between them. Then, changing the subject, Fritz says, "I hope you are not too tired, Megan. The whole family is anxious to meet you and we promised to bring you directly to Jerusalem, rather than to our apartment in Haifa."

Megan assures him that she is not the least bit tired. She wonders who *the whole family* is, she is not aware of anyone else being related to her except for Fritz and Naomi and little Hadassah. There is a short wait until her suitcase comes off the carousel. They are surrounded by people who are also waiting for their luggage. Many of them are pushing and shoving each other, shouting in a cacophony of languages, waving their hands in emphasis. Megan thinks that some of the shouted messages do not sound complimentary, that they even sound like curses. Fritz, seeing her shocked expression, laughs and says, "Welcome to the Mediterranean, Megan. Here in Israel we have a melting pot of people from all over the world, and everyone yells to make themselves heard." Megan's suitcase is found, and Naomi, sensitive to the strangeness of the occasion, keeps the conversation flowing as they walk through the terminal to the car park. She asks Megan details about the flight, was it comfortable, did she have enough to eat, were her parents in good health when she left them?

Finally, they come out into the open, and the blistering July heat hits Megan so forcefully that she gasps in surprise. "It should be cooler in Jerusalem," says Fritz.

⇒◆⇐

In later years, Megan will always remember with forceful clarity, as if it had occurred only yesterday, that first ride into Jerusalem in Fritz Mayer's jeep. Little Hadassah sitting in the front passenger seat next to her father, Megan and Naomi in the back. Naomi pointing out the different milestones as they drive, the palpable love and pride in her voice for the country she is describing. The cluster of small adobe houses on the left, all painted blue. *That is an Arab village.* And, a little further, *See those rusting, burnt-out hulks at the side of the road, they are military vehicles, detritus of the 1948 war. Now we are going uphill into Jerusalem. Look at the hills, all of Jerusalem is surrounded by hills.*

She will never forget her first view of the Jerusalem hills, the evening shadows playing over the slopes in a variety of shifting shades, now grey, then green, no, blue, even black. They pass an Arab riding on a donkey, a woman, presumably his wife, walks behind him holding a bundle on her head. More houses. *Another Arab village.* So there are Arab villages in Israel? In spite of what she has read, in the back of her mind Megan still hears the echo of Gwen's voice. *The Jews drove the Arabs out.*

Then they are driving down the streets of Jerusalem itself. *There is the famous King David Hotel. And there, opposite, is the YMCA. One day during your visit we will climb the YMCA tower. From there we can see part of the Old City, part of the Wailing Wall. It is the only place from which we can see it. We are not allowed into the Old City. It is occupied by the Jordanians.* Megan has difficulty taking it all in. *In a few minutes we will arrive in the German colony, where my parents live.*

They turn off Emek Refa'im into a small, unpaved side street, passing a scattering of modest homes. Fritz stops before a low slung whitewashed house with a small adobe courtyard in the front; the wheels of the jeep send up a spray of gravel and dust as he brakes. Just as they get out of the car, a man and woman, walking arm-in-arm, emerge through the front gate. The man says in German-accented English, "We were looking out for you." Little Hadassah has already run ahead and thrown her arms around the woman's thighs. The woman puts her hand on the child's head and tousles her curls. "Let me introduce you to my parents, Hannah and Samuel Gutman," says Naomi, as she kisses each of them. "Mutti, Papa, this is Megan, Henrietta's daughter."

"Welcome, welcome, says Samuel", holding out his hand for Megan to shake. "We are so happy to be meeting you." He turns to his wife, repeating the introduction made by Naomi. "*Schatzie*, this is Megan, Henrietta's daughter." Hannah solemnly holds out her hand to Megan. "Yes," she says gravely, "you are looking exactly like her. But exactly." She turns to her husband, "*Aber genau. Nein?* But exactly, no?"

Hannah takes Megan's hand and leads her into the house, bringing her into the living room. "Come," she says gently, "you must be tired and hungry after your long journey and…" She is not allowed to finish. Before Megan knows what is happening, she is surrounded by a swarm of people, all talking at the same time in English, German, and what she assumes must be Hebrew. Far from being overwhelmed, she feels transported on the wings of their welcome, embraced and included in their blatant affection for each other. Her travel fatigue magically lifted, she feels charged with elation, and a slight touch of envy. *So this is what it feels like to have a large family*, she thinks, she who has always been an only, and sometimes lonely child. *How lucky they all are*. She sees how Hannah is the magnet for their attention, how they all, surreptitiously, hover over her like a brood of mother hens. *What a beauty she must have been*, she thinks, *her face is still beautiful, though grey and drawn and so, so sad. And that row of numbers tattooed on her arm. Are they what I think they are?"*

Samuel interrupts her musings. He tells her that since living in Israel, he and his children are all known by their Hebrew names. Thus, he is no longer Samuel but has become Shmuel. He explains that Naomi and Hannah's names sound almost the same in Hebrew as in German and English. "The children want me to change our surname also," he says. "They tell me 'Gutman' is too German. But I am not yet ready to do that."

Megan sees in Shmuel's face a slightly coarser and rugged version of Naomi's finer features. "Let me introduce you to everyone formally," he says, putting his arm around her shoulders and leading her around the room.

She meets Yitzchak, the rabbi. Laughingly Shmuel says, "Yitzchak was always known as our little rabbi. Now he is our big rabbi!" Yitzchak looks most unrabbinic, despite the truncated beard; like Fritz, he wears a short-sleeved, open-necked shirt, but instead of trousers, he wears khaki shorts. He, too, has a small knitted *kippah* on his head. "And this is Yitzchak's wife, Ofra, and their two boys, Ilan and Ari. She meets Joshua, known now as Yash, his wife Batya and their daughter, Michal. Megan knows she will never remember all their names, and prays she will not be put to the test. Yash works with his father. They own a ladies clothing store on Ben Yehuda Street called Chez Gutman II. It is astonishing to her how everyone speaks English, some better than others. Ofra and Batya tell Megan that they all learned to speak English in the army. "You were also in the army?" she asks, wide-eyed. They laugh. "Yes, here in Israel, the girls serve in the army just like the boys. Except one year less. We serve for only two years, the boys serve for three."

Megan meets the twins, Shimon and Binyamin. They are almost identical: both tall and slim, with curls that are a muted shade of blonde. They are stunningly handsome in their casual uniforms: khaki shirts, open-necked in the Israeli style, shorts, and sandals; only their epaulets give evidence of their rank. Shimon is a pilot in the air force, Binyamin a major in the army. Both are career soldiers. Shimon laughs at Megan's surprised reaction on hearing that girls serve in the army. "In Israel we have complete equality of the sexes," he says, in perfect, only slightly accented English. "The girls clean out the latrines just the same as the boys do." Megan joins in the laughter.

Binyamin is the quieter twin, his eyes taking everything in, but saying little. It is when he shakes her hand that she feels it, that something that she will never find the words to describe, that something that she has read about in the romance novels she consumed when she and Gwen rode the tram to school. She used to force Gwen to lift her head out of the latest Shakespeare play or poetry anthology, and breathlessly read aloud to her about that *electric charge* the heroine felt at first meeting the man of her dreams, how their eyes met, and in that moment they were both *lost* or *drowned* or *consumed* in a whirlpool of passion. How the two of them used to giggle!

Megan has often heard her Mum and Da talk about how it was love at first sight for them in the Cardiff shipyards, but she has never taken them seriously, has always rolled her eyes, has always taken it all with a gigantic grain of salt.

Until now.

She feels flustered. She is sure she is blushing.

She doesn't know where to look. She hopes he hasn't noticed, but his eyes are still on her, have not left her face from the moment he said "*Shalom* Megan."

Chapter 54

⇒◉⇐

They eat supper, sitting on benches, at two adjoining tables on the patio at the back of the house. The sun is rapidly slipping behind the Judean hills, and night rolls in suddenly, without warning. Paraffin lanterns dot the tables, attracting moths and other insects, and throwing off just enough illumination for everyone to see what they are eating. There are bowls and platters filled with different foods that Megan has never seen before, foods that are foreign and exotic to her palate, dishes with names like hummus and tahini, tabouli salad, deep fried felafel balls, pungent lamb stew, stuffed grape leaves, all flavored with mysterious savory spices. Before they sit, everyone washes at an outdoor sink. Shmuel explains to Megan that this is a Jewish ritual, that a blessing is said when washing the hands, and then another blessing when partaking of the pita bread. *Not so different from the grace my Da always says at the table,* Megan thinks, as she takes the tin cup and, imitating the others, pours water over each fisted hand. There is a lot of laughter and joking, especially around Shimon. Naomi and Ofra and Batya make sure that Megan always has food on her plate, that her glass is filled and refilled from the carafes of water and wine. Hannah and Shmuel sit next to each other at one end of the table, and Megan observes how Shmuel tenderly places food on his wife's plate, how he coaxes her to eat. Soon, Hannah excuses herself. She addresses Megan, "You will be excusing me, please." Shmuel puts his arm around her and leads her indoors. "My mother has a headache," explains Naomi, "she is suffering from the migraines."

Megan is relieved that Binyamin is sitting at the other end of the table. She tries to keep her eyes away from him, but they keep wandering in his direction, and every time she dares look at him he is staring directly at her. She makes up her mind not to look at him again, but then, toward the end of the meal, he gets up from his seat, walks around the table to stand directly behind her. "Megan," he says, bending down, his head almost touching hers. "Come, please, if you have finished eating. Allow me to show you my mother's garden."

She feels herself moving without volition, in slow motion, floating over the bench. He doesn't touch her, but she feels as if he had. It is a warm, humid night, but she shivers involuntarily. "Are you cold?" he asks. "Shall I get you a shawl?"

"No, no. Of course not. It's just…" She doesn't know what she is saying, her words vanish into the night. Perhaps she has drunk too much wine?

They walk side by side down a path and over a grass lawn. There is just enough light from the moon and the table lanterns for Megan to see the flowers he points out: the lush white tea rose bushes; the red and pink bougainvillea tumbling thickly over the garden wall; the yellow eyes of the elegant purple irises, staring at them brazenly through the blackness of the night. "My mother plants all the flowers herself. She works in the garden every day. Except on Shabbat, of course. This is her therapy. Without the garden, I don't know how she would survive. On the other side of that hedge is her vegetable garden. She grows tomatoes and cucumbers and radishes, and how do you call them, those purple vegetables? In Hebrew we call them *chatzilim.*"

Megan says, "Do you mean eggplant?"

"Yes, yes, that's it. Eggplant. I can never remember that word. We eat a lot of eggplants in Israel."

She says, "Please forgive me for asking. Is that number on your mother's arm from when she was in the concentration camp?"

"Yes. My mother was in Auschwitz."

"This is the first time I have seen... met someone who was in a concentration camp."

"There are many survivors of the camps in Israel. Some of them fought in the 1948 war. Many survived the Nazis only to die at the hands of the Arabs. My mother was one of the lucky ones. Certainly luckier than both my grandmothers, and luckier than my father's sister and her family. My aunt and uncle left Germany before we did, and settled in Paris. My father's mother joined them there. They thought they would be safe in France. Like my mother, they ended up in Auschwitz, but they didn't survive. After the war, survivors told my father that my grandmother and my aunt and the children were immediately sent to the gas chamber when they arrived in Auschwitz. My uncle lasted a bit longer; he either died of illness or starvation or was killed by the Nazis before the liberation." She hears him swallow hard, before he continues. "As I said, my mother was one of the lucky ones: she had a husband and family waiting for her. Most of the survivors arrived here after losing their whole families; they had no relatives here to help them. Many entered what was then Palestine, illegally, before 1948, when the British were in charge and there was a strict quota."

They walk for a few moments in silence as Megan tries to absorb what Binyamin has just related. It is a lot to take in at once.

But he has not finished. "Shimon and I were not quite five years old when our family was separated. When our mother came back nearly ten years later, she was a stranger to us. And we were strangers to her. We were teenagers by then. It was a very difficult adjustment for all of us."

"Your mother must have suffered so much. Yet she is still so beautiful."

"Yes, she is beautiful, isn't she, even though her hair is totally white. Naomi is the oldest so she remembers very well how she used to be. According to Naomi our mother used to cover her hair with a scarf, for religious reasons, but now she can't bear to have anything touching her head; she says it brings on the migraines."

They walk for a little while longer without exchanging a word. Far from being awkward, the silence has a calming effect. Megan feels as if she is walking with an old friend, not someone she just met for the first time only a few hours ago. She tilts her head up to the sky. It is a clear night, the moon still full but just beginning to wane, the stars hanging low, luminous and bright; she feels she can almost reach up and snatch one from the heavens. "Am I imagining it, or are the stars closer in this part of the world?" He laughs. "A lot of people say that. Remember, Israel is part of the mysterious Levant."

She begins talking about things she has never spoken about to anyone, except to Vicar Lowell. "I was three when my mother sent me away. I don't remember her at all."

He says, "Naomi has told me a little about your story. Your mother must have been very strong and must have loved you very much to part from you like that; she saved your life."

"Yes, you're right. It is only recently that I have begun to fully appreciate what she did, the sacrifice she made by sending me to England. I can't even imagine how painful that must have been." Then she adds,. "I wish I knew who my father was. Nobody seems to know anything about him. Do you think Naomi and Fritz know anything?"

"They never mentioned anything, as far as I can recall," he says. "It's possible they know something. But I think it's more likely that my father might know. He was a good friend of your grandfather. It seems we were neighbors in Frankfurt. Of course, I don't remember a thing about that time."

Binyamin stops walking, making her stop also. He turns to her. "Megan, you are Jewish, you know. In Judaism this is determined by the mother, the biological mother. And Henrietta Mayer, your mother, was Jewish. I don't remember her, by the way. But we all love her brother, Fritz, who is my brother-in-law. We've been trying to get him to change his German name to his Hebrew one, Efraim, but so far, he has refused.. 'Fritz' is so typically German, isn't it? But Naomi thinks it's his way of always keeping the memory of his mother alive. He was very attached to her and she always called him by his German name, Fritz. Perhaps it is just as well he kept his German name, otherwise we might not have found you. In her search, Miss Schneider might not have connected Efraim Mayer to Fritz Mayer."

Megan notices his use of *we*. *We might not have found you*. She says, "I know you're right, but I've never felt Jewish. I was adopted by a Christian family. I was raised to believe in Jesus. He is the one I always pray to. As a matter of fact, right after I learned I was adopted, I even considered becoming a nun."

"And now?" he asks.

"It's been a long time since I gave up that idea. I don't think I'm worthy to be a nun, I am not nun material. Besides that, my parents don't have any family and I think they have their hearts set on becoming grandparents." She feels herself blushing and hastens to add, "Of course, the Rhys's are my parents. I love them. They are the only parents I have ever known. They have always been very good to me. More than good." She is about to cry.

He is gentle in what he says next, as if he knows he must tread carefully. "Megan, it was your mother, your Jewish mother, who saved your life. And God, of course. We mustn't leave God out of the equation. What the Quakers did, what your new parents did was absolutely splendid, but don't you see, Megan, they were merely God's messengers?" He pauses, then says, "And don't get me wrong, I have nothing against Jesus, but we Jews don't pray to an intermediary. When we pray, we pray directly to God. Of course," he adds dryly, "God doesn't always hear us, or if He does, He often doesn't choose to reply."

The moment is fraught with emotion. Megan cannot begin to process Binyamin's words. She is overcome with feelings that are as disturbingly foreign to her as everything around her. She will need time to absorb it all.

Standing there, looking up into his face – he is almost a head taller than she is - she imprints his features into her memory. The crop of sandy-hued curls that he seems to have trouble taming, the straight nose with the almost imperceptible bump on the bridge, the white even teeth except for the slightly chipped incisor, the strong, determined chin, the face and arms bronzed by the Mediterranean sun. And above all, the eyes, hooded beneath long thick lashes, dark blue and unsettling, but steadfast and sincere. She has never met anyone with eyes like Binyamin's. At the supper table, she had surreptitiously examined his twin's eyes. Shimon's eyes are the same shade of blue, the lashes also long and lush, but lacking the disquieting effect of Binyamin's eyes.

They begin to saunter aimlessly again. The garden is not very large, and by now they have walked around its perimeter several times.

He says, "Megan, before we go in, I want to tell you that I hope today is as important for you as it is for me, and that you will always remember the date. Thursday, July 26, 1956. It is the date you arrived in Israel, but more important, it is the date on which we met for the first time, you and I. I felt it the minute I saw you." Her heart surges, but he gives her no chance to say anything. He says, "Unfortunately, today's date is important for another reason. Today is also the date that Gamal Abdel Nasser, the president of Egypt decided to close the Suez Canal to Israeli ships. This is the same Egypt mentioned in the bible, the same Egypt that enslaved our ancestors, the same Egypt that is still bothered by us. It seems we will always be a thorn in Egypt's side. So, Shimon and I have been called back to our units. We will be leaving tonight."

What can she say? Part of her is in agony at his last pronouncement. How can this be happening when they have only just met? And another part of her... Is there another part? Her head is reeling. She is unable to find her voice.

He says, "Just before this happened, I was appointed military attaché to our embassy in London, or, as you Brits call it, the Court of St. James. That will almost certainly be postponed now, perhaps cancelled altogether, depending on how long Mr. Nasser keeps it up. Our prime minister, David Ben Gurion, is hoping the French and British will get him to see the light, but I'm not holding my breath. We can't rule out another war." He adds cynically, "In Israel, there is always the possibility of another war just around the corner. Our scriptures tell us that in every generation there arise those who seek our destruction. Yesterday it was Adolf Hitler; today Nasser gets the prize. Tomorrow, who knows? Perhaps another of our Arab neighbors."

They begin to walk back to the house. As they near the open french doors at the rear they hear Shimon's voice calling, in Hebrew, "Benny, we have to leave. It's getting late."

He calls back, "Okay. *Tov. Be'seder.* I'm coming."

He stops, holds out his hand to Megan, and looks at her steadily. "Megan, in Israel we never say goodbye. We say, *lehitra'ot.* Which means 'until we meet again'." She gives him her hand, and he holds it between both of his. They stand there in this way for several moments, hands clasped, looking at each other, neither saying a word.

And then he is gone.

Chapter 55

⇒€

Megan remains standing outside in the garden; she cannot bring herself to go back into the house. She stands quite still, closes her eyes and imbibes the sounds of the night: the racket of the cicadas and crickets competing with each other, a squirrel scurrying up a tree, the muffled barking of a distant dog, the howl of a jackal up in the Judean hills. The night is warm and fragrant, filled with the thrumming of invisible insects. There is not a breath of air. She opens her eyes, but still cannot leave this spot, still feels the warmth of his hands on hers, still sees, or perhaps she imagines it, an indentation in the grass where he stood opposite her just moments ago, before he vanished.

From inside the house comes the sound of someone clattering in the kitchen. She forces her feet to move, to go inside. She wanders into the deserted living room, then into the kitchen where she finds Naomi, washing dishes, clearing away the debris of their meal. The older brothers, their wives and children have left. Megan lifts a dishtowel from a rack and begins to dry the draining plates. Naomi smiles her thanks, and says, in her formal English, "Fritz is putting Hadassah to bed. I am hoping it will be satisfactory for you to sleep in the room of the twins. I am hoping the beds are comfortable. I have provided you a towel."

"Thank you, Naomi. I'm so tired, I think I could sleep anywhere tonight."

"Benny told me that you know about the news, about Egypt. I am sorry to tell you that because of the situation the whole of Israel is on alert. My two married brothers are in the reserves and in case of war they will also be called back to their units. Unfortunately, we will be unable to tour the country with you as we planned. I am hoping you understand."

"Of course," says Megan. "The situation is very upsetting. Please don't concern yourself on my account. I am just happy to be here with all of you. That is enough for me."

"At least we will be able to show you parts of Jerusalem."

❧

The house is a sprawling one-storey structure with several internal corridors leading to various rooms. The street itself is relatively new, with just a scattering of completed houses, one several yards down from the Gutman house, and one across the street; two other houses are in various stages of construction, surrounded by scaffolding and building materials. The Gutman house is simply but functionally furnished with modern, diverse Scandinavian pieces. The floors are covered in white tiles, for coolness and easy washing, or *sponga* as Megan soon learns to call it. Here and there are scattered colorful rugs and mats and decorative cushions. Electric ceiling fans circulate the air in each room without making the temperature noticeably cooler. Naomi shows Megan the twins' room at the end of one of the corridors, and the bathroom next to it, then bids her, "*Laila tov*, goodnight. I hope you are sleeping well."

The room is unexpectedly neat. Megan wonders if it is because the boys are used to the Spartan orderliness of the military. Or because they usually live on base. She is curious about Binyamin's possessions, but resists the temptation to open drawers.

It is not difficult to guess which bed belongs to which twin. The beds are separated by a desk. On the wall above Shimon's bed is tacked an oversized colored poster of a jet fighter plane, with a very conspicuous blue and white Star of David on each wing, and Shimon, looking very dashing in his pilot's uniform, and goggles pushed up onto his forehead, smiling and waving merrily from the cockpit. The wall above the other bed also displays a large poster. It is a blown-up photograph of a bearded man, his face barely visible beneath a black and white striped fringed prayer shawl that is draped over his head and shoulders. He is holding something to his mouth, a horn of some kind that he seems to be blowing as if it were a musical instrument. Certainly, an unusual musical instrument, and not like any Megan has ever seen before. Studying the image more closely, she thinks the horn blower is Binyamin's brother, Yitzchak, the rabbi.

She finds her suitcase on the desk chair, probably placed there by Fritz or one of the brothers. Now she opens it to unpack: a nightgown and toiletries, her crumpled clothes, which she hangs in the corner wardrobe on a few empty hangers that are scattered between a man's beige sports jacket, some trousers, a white short-sleeved shirt. She puts her face up against the jacket, sniffs at it, willing it to give off a clue as to its provenance; she wonders if it is his. But if she expected the jacket to betray its owner, she is disappointed; the garment gives off no whiff of ownership.

It is a relief to finally shed the blouse and skirt and underwear she has been wearing since she got up that morning; she feels as if they have been glued to her ever since she got off the plane. Was it only this morning that she was in her room above the shop on Llandaff Road in Cardiff? She thinks of her Mum and Da; what are they doing at this moment? She can't remember what the time difference is between Wales and Israel. Three hours? Four?

And Shaun? She realizes with a guilty start that she hasn't thought of him at all.

Suddenly, a wave of overpowering fatigue washes over her. She cannot remember being so tired even when she was training for the Olympics. It becomes an enormous effort just to lift the folded towel, drape it over her arm, take the toothbrush and toothpaste from her wash bag and drag herself to the bathroom.

Finally, finally. She switches off the light and almost collapses on top of the bed, Binyamin's bed, not even bothering to remove the covers or get under the sheet. The bed, too, gives no clue as to its usual occupant, though she feels it must be his despite the antiseptic linens. The ceiling fan whirs and whirs, circulating the hot air around the room, rustling some papers on the desk and gently swaying the sheer curtains that are tied back from the open window. The repetitive rhythm is lulling her to sleep. A multitude of thoughts tumble around in her head, but she is too tired to sift through them. Too tired even to pray to Jesus. She feels herself drifting, drifting, the image of Binyamin's face taking up the space behind her closed eyes.

How long she sleeps, she doesn't know, but suddenly she is once again wide awake, her nightgown sticking to her body. She looks at the illuminated dial of her watch. It is just past midnight. She has slept barely an hour. Her mouth is dry. She needs to find something to drink.

She goes out into the corridor, trying to orient herself. For a moment she doesn't remember where the kitchen is.. Then she sees a light, and moves toward it.

Shmuel Gutman is sitting at the kitchen table, writing. He looks up at her and smiles. "Can't sleep?" he asks. "Come in and keep me company. You are probably not yet used to the time change and the heat."

Strangely, she feels no embarrassment to be sitting in her nightgown. It is as if it is her Da who is at the kitchen table opposite her, and she has come to keep him company. As she often does at home.

He is still dressed as he was at supper. Perhaps, like his wife, he also has trouble sleeping. She sees now that it is not only Naomi who resembles him, that Shmuel Gutman's features are also echoed in various degrees in the faces of his sons. He must have been very handsome in his youth, she thinks. He is still a good-looking man, even with his sparse, completely white hair, and his face textured with worry lines.

He offers Megan cold seltzer from the ice box. For the first time, she notices that there is no refrigerator in the kitchen, just an old-fashioned ice box, such as she has seen only in pictures. Shmuel registers her surprise. He says, "The ice man comes twice a week and delivers blocks of ice. I have been trying for the last few years to import an electric refrigerator, but the only country where I can get one right now, - that is, without going through a mountain of red tape, is from Germany. The Germans are sending them over by the shipload as part of war reparations. But Hannah refuses to have anything in the house that is made in Germany." He hastens to add, "Not that I blame her, of course. We should not be helping the German economy after what they did to us. Before we left Germany, we shipped perhaps a dozen crates of dishes and other household belongings from our apartment. But they remain unpacked - beautiful Rosenthal china that Hannah chose years ago, at the time of our marriage. She has always had excellent taste. But, now she cannot bear the sight of them."

He sees Megan continuing her inspection of the kitchen, notices her gaze alight on the painting of the two lemons that had once adorned their Frankfurt kitchen. "We were lucky to get the Manet out of Germany. After the war ended, we began to hear stories of Jewish art stolen and confiscated by the Nazis. But at the time we left Germany it seems the customs officials didn't recognize the painting's value. At any rate, they allowed us to ship it through."

Megan listens, sipping at her seltzer. She says, "Binyamin told me a little of your wife's wartime experiences." How it thrills her to say his name. How proud she is of the way she is able to pronounce it, the Hebrewness of it, how it slides so easily off her tongue. Bin-ya-min.

"I wish you could have known her before," he says wistfully, remembering. "She was full of joy and grace. Always happy, always laughing. Of course, as you saw, she is still beautiful but no-one can come out of that cauldron, - how do you say it in English - unscathed? She has not told anyone, not even me, everything she went through. Sometimes I wish she would cry. But she is unable to shed tears. She talks of her mother though; she is racked with guilt over her mother's death in the ghetto. I try over and over again to reason with her, to convince her that there is nothing she could have done to save her, but still she feels she did not do enough for her mother. She feels responsible for her death. I think that, more than anything, is what is causing her migraines."

They sit in companionable silence, she contemplating and absorbing what she has just heard; he wondering if it is appropriate to talk to her about her grandfather, Gustav Mayer.

Megan says, "It must have been so difficult for you, not knowing if your wife was alive or dead for all those years of the war."

He sighs. "When Hitler invaded Poland and it became clear that Hannah and her mother were stranded, I became hysterical. And when we stopped receiving letters from them, when our letters were returned with the words 'addressee unknown', I became completely unhinged. I did not know how I could go on living. Without Naomi and Fritz, I don't know what would have happened to the boys, especially the twins. I was incapable of taking care of them. For a long time I was a broken man, unable to function." His eyes have clouded over, his voice is hoarse with emotion. "The children had such a difficult time adjusting to the new country, the new language, new schools. But despite their own difficulties, they were all so patient with me. I will never get over how they pampered me, waited on me hand and foot, tried to get me to laugh. Fritz, who was still a teenager when we arrived in Palestine, became like another son to me, even before he and Naomi married. Slowly, slowly, I came out of my stupor. Apart from the care I received from the children, what helped me was opening the shop on Ben Yehuda Street. It kept me busy, kept my mind occupied during the day. Of course, the nights were another matter. It was during that period that I forgot how to sleep. I have not slept properly ever since those days.

"And then, of course, when we received the news that my wife was alive, that she had survived the horror…" His voice breaks. There is no need for him to say anything more. He gets up again, opens the ice box, retrieves the seltzer bottle and replenishes both their glasses.

They sit in this way, opposite each other at the kitchen table, for several minutes in complete silence, except for the sipping from their seltzer glasses. Finally, it is Megan who broaches the subject he had earlier wondered if he dare bring up.

"Mr. Gutman, Binyamin also told me that you were a good friend of my…that is…that you and he…" She is finding it difficult to say the word, so he says it for her.

"Your grandfather, you mean?"

"Yes. My… grandfather." There, she has said it. She had feared it would be disloyal to her Mum and Da to acknowledge this other relationship, but surprisingly she feels no sense of disloyalty. "What was he like? Can you tell me about him?"

"Of course. With pleasure." He sighs with relief at being able to move away from his personal journey. "We were next door neighbors in Frankfurt. He was the most upright, decent, most honorable man I have ever met. It is strange, really, how we became friends. At first, after we moved into the apartment next to the Mayers, your grandfather complained about the noise the children were making, especially Binyamin and Shimon." He smiles, reminiscing. "You can't imagine what little hooligans they were." Then he becomes serious again. "Ironically, I have to thank Adolf Hitler for bringing us together. The Nazis made certain business demands of your grandfather; they wanted him to manufacture and supply them with quantities of armaments, which he did reluctantly. Of course, he had no choice, he had to obey. Once they didn't need him anymore, that was as good as a death sentence. He knew it, we both knew it. I begged him to leave the country, but he refused. He wouldn't even think of it. He said he would never leave Germany where his ancestors had lived for so many centuries, where his father had fought for the Kaiser, where they were all buried. Including his wife, Fritz's mother, your grandmother. For whom you were named, incidentally."

Megan is mesmerized. She had no idea that the Mayer family had such a long, and illustrious German history. Shmuel stands up, goes back to the ice box, refills their glasses. When he sits down again, he utters the name that she has been afraid he might avoid, the name that she wasn't sure she should bring up. "Your grandfather was a very private man, but he needed to confide in someone. I was very honored to be chosen as his confidant. He made me promise that if anything happened to him, I would take care of his two children. Henrietta and Fritz. Of course, you know that Henrietta was your mother."

"Yes. I know. When Miss Schneider visited my parents in Cardiff some time ago, she said she had been my grandfather's secretary. She told them about my…about Henrietta."

"That's right. Now I remember. She traced you through Fritz and your grandfather's housekeeper, Inge Bauer. How devoted Fraulein Schneider was to your grandfather, to have persevered in her search the way she did!"

Megan says, "How fortunate for Fritz that you managed to bring him with you when you left Germany. And how wonderful that you were able to fulfill your promise to my… grandfather in that way. I don't remember my…mother at all. According to Miss Schneider I was born on a farm, and Hen…my mother had to hide her identity, and pretend she wasn't Jewish."

"Yes, that's right. I see you have learned some of the details. Inge Bauer suggested the farm for Henrietta. It belonged to her husband's brother."

"But, what I don't understand is why Henrietta had to go into hiding. Why couldn't she have left the country with you, just as Fritz did?"

"That's a very logical question, my dear Megan. But you have to remember that those were very turbulent, uncertain times. Your grandmother had died recently, and the Nazis had just placed numerous restrictions and prohibitions on the Jewish population. One law was the prohibition of a Jew and non-Jew to marry or even to co-habit. Henrietta told her father that she was pregnant and that the baby's father was not Jewish. Your grandfather was furious, but abortion was completely out of the question. Not only was it totally against his religious principles, but the procedure itself in those days was too dangerous to risk." He pauses, takes a sip of seltzer, clears his throat. "Perhaps your grandfather might have been persuaded to handle the situation differently if his wife, your grandmother, had lived. But he felt so ashamed; he could not allow Henrietta to continue living under his roof. At the time, I was not yet sure of our departure date from Germany. If it had been discovered before we left that Henrietta was carrying a child fathered by a German, a so-called Aryan, who knows what the Nazis might have done to her? Or to your grandfather, for that matter, for harboring her? Incidentally, there was a Jewish home for unwed mothers nearby, but with the Nazis in power, your grandfather did not think Henrietta would be safe there. That is why he arranged to change her identity and send her to the farm. So you see, no matter how angry he was, he loved his daughter and was very much concerned with keeping her safe."

He drains his glass, wipes his mouth.

Megan sits in silence for a few moments. Then she poses the question Shmuel has been dreading. Tentatively, she asks, "And what of my... father? Who was he? Do you know anything about him?"

She sees him weighing his answer carefully. He does not look at her directly as he says, "Your father was Henrietta's ice skating instructor. That is all I know."

Immediately, she senses that he knows more, but is not willing to say more. She asks, "Did he know that she was pregnant?" She is not sure how to phrase her next questions. And does she really want to know the answers? "What I mean is, did he offer to help? Or did he abandon her? Did he know that she was on the farm? Did he know me?"

"I'm sorry. I wish I could tell you more. The only reason your grandfather, who, as I said, was normally a very private man, the only reason he told me as much as he did was, as he put it, because he wanted someone other than the Bauers to know where Henrietta was hiding."

Megan is now so wide awake, she wonders if sleep will ever be possible again. She says, "Thank you for telling me what you did, Mr. Gutman. I'm very grateful. I do hope I have not been keeping you from your bed. I know it's very late."

"No, no, my dear. Indeed not. I never get to bed before one or two in the morning. As a matter of fact, when you came in I was writing a letter to Manfred Kahn in New York. Do you know who that is?"

"Er. I'm not sure. I know I recognize the name, but..."

"He is the brother of Marga Mayer, your grandmother. He is your great-uncle. We have been corresponding for some years. He, too, has expressed a desire to see you, Megan. Unfortunately, he is no longer young and not well enough to travel, but there are many cousins on that side of your family who are also anxious to meet you."

"This is all so overwhelming for me, Mr. Gutman."

"Yes, I'm sure it must be. From not having any family at all, to now be surrounded by so many... so many Jews!" He laughs, to let her know he is joking. "I'm sure it is very confusing. But eventually it will all sort itself out, you will see. Get a good night's sleep, if you can, my dear. Tomorrow is *Erev Shabbat*, the eve of our Sabbath. It is always a very busy day, when the house is made spic and span, and special meals are prepared to welcome the Sabbath Queen."

She goes back to bed. She is still wide awake, so many thoughts tripping over each other in her head. At some time during the night, the Jerusalem coolness promised by Fritz finally makes its appearance. She can feel the fresh cool air fanning her face and body. Her thoughts keep coming back to the skating instructor. She wonders about the love between Henrietta and ...him. He must have been several years older than Henrietta, probably a practiced flirt with his young female students; it was probably easy for a sheltered girl like Henrietta to succumb to his charm. On the other hand, he may have sincerely loved her. Thinking of her own reaction when she met Binyamin earlier that evening, she is beginning to understand how an innocent seventeen-year-old girl might easily have been seduced.

She senses that Mr. Gutman knows something he is not telling her. She wonders if it would be possible to discover the identity of her...of the skating instructor. How difficult could it be? Surely Frankfurt cannot have had more than one skating rink before the war? Even Cardiff, one of the largest cities in the U.K., has only one ice rink. If Mr. Gutman doesn't know the name of the Frankfurt ice rink, or for some reason refuses to tell her, surely there must be a way of finding out.

And if she finds out, what then?

She awakens to the sound of birdsong, to beams of daylight piercing her eyelids, and her nose assailed by the fragrance of something delicious cooking in the kitchen. Some time during the night she must have slipped under the covers, but she has no recollection of doing so. She remembers what Mr. Gutman told her, and has memorized the words. Today is *Erev Shabbat*, the eve of the Sabbath. He had called the Sabbath *the Queen*. It captures her imagination to hear the Sabbath referred to as a queen. How quaint. How wonderfully romantic!

She lies there for a moment, yawning and stretching, letting the sounds and smells wash over her. Eventually, she rouses herself. Through the window, she spots a solitary palm tree, its fronds swaying gently in the breeze. In the morning light she sees the Jerusalem hills, the shadows and shades of green and brown, blue and gold dancing over them. Turning back to the room, her eyes are drawn to a framed photograph on the desk, which she had overlooked the night before. It is a picture of the whole Gutman family, apparently taken before the war, when they were all still together in Frankfurt. Hannah and Shmuel stand behind an elderly seated woman, presumably Hannah's late mother. Megan recognizes Naomi, but if she hadn't known who the four boys are, she would not have recognized them. Yitzhak, young and beardless, and Yash, who must have been no more than ten years old at the time - both handsome and quite tall even then - and the little three- or four-year-old twins in identical sailor suits, posed on each side of Hannah's mother, looking angelic and innocent with their mops of golden curls. Even in this black and white image, she detects the unmistakable look of mischief in their eyes. Megan studies the photograph carefully, giving special attention to Hannah. Yes, she can see what Mr. Gutman meant. His wife was not only young and beautiful under the artistically tied head scarf, but the joy in her smile almost leaps from the picture. Megan can't help smiling, just looking at her. The mood is positively contagious.

It is impossible to tell which of the twins in the picture is Binyamin.

Showered, and dressed in a cool, light green cotton frock, Megan stands at the entrance to the door-less kitchen, without entering. She sees Hannah at the far counter, her back toward Megan; she has been chopping vegetables on a wooden board, but now is just standing there, unmoving, holding the chopping knife and gazing out the window. Megan suddenly feels shy and intrusive. But Hannah, having heard her, or merely sensing her presence, says, without turning around, "*Boker tov*, good morning, my child." Her voice is distant, as if her mind is elsewhere. But then she turns around, smiles her sad smile and points to the table in the corner on which stands a glass of freshly squeezed orange juice alongside a plate of finely chopped vegetables - cucumbers, tomatoes, celery - a bowl of yogurt, a basket of fresh rolls. She asks, "Have you been well sleeping, I hope? Come, partake please of the Israeli salad and *leben*, that I have prepared for you. I am hoping you will like them."

Megan is wide-eyed at the array of foods, so different from her usual breakfast of bacon and eggs, sometimes porridge, sometimes kippers on toast. Most of all, she feels overwhelmed by the solicitous attention. Just at that moment Naomi appears, also asking about Megan's welfare and if she slept well. "Will you be drinking coffee, or are you drinking only tea?"

"Thank you, Naomi. Please don't bother about me. Whichever is easier for you. I drink either one. But I'm curious, what is that tantalizing aroma? It's been driving me mad."

Naomi laughs and turns to Hannah who has once again busied herself at the other side of the kitchen. "Mutti," she says, "Megan is wanting to know what you are cooking that smells so delicious?"

"*Ach, ja*. That is the chicken *Suppe*. My mother's recipe. She was famous for her chicken *Suppe*. Even in this heat, we always eat the chicken *Suppe* on Shabbat."

"Well, I can't wait to taste it. And, please, do let me help. Mr. Gutman told me that this is a busy day, the *Erev Shabbat*."

Hannah says, "We are almost finished with the cooking, but it will make me very happy if you wish to assist me in the garden. But of course first finish your breakfast, please."

Chapter 56

≫≪

Megan follows Hannah out through the french doors into the garden, just as she had followed Binyamin, - was it only a few hours ago? She is nervous. She wonders if Hannah expects her to speak, and, more importantly, what is there for Megan to say to her, to this woman who has experienced such unspeakable horror in her life? Hannah hands her a trowel, and shows her how to root out the weeds in the flower beds that she says grow faster than she can keep up with them, while she, armed with a small pair of shears, begins to prune the rose bushes. Megan slips on the gardening gloves and floppy hat that Hannah has also given her. The sun, despite the early hour, is already high in the sky and beats down with an intensity that Megan has never before experienced.

They work in silence for several minutes. It is Hannah who, to Megan's relief, breaks the silence. "In a little while we will be watering the plants, *ja*? We cannot use too much water because we are having a serious shortage."

Megan says, "Is it always so hot?"

"Yes. And I am never getting used to it. But never. And then in the winter the rains come. Very heavy rains. I am never getting used to that also."

They work for another few minutes, and then Hannah straightens up, holding her back with one gloved hand, and says, "Your grandmother and I became very good friends. She used to visit me often and we used to drink coffee together, and talk. *Kaffeklatsch*, we used to call it. In that way, I got to know her. She was a wonderful, sensitive woman. Very courageous. Your grandfather, well, he was an upstanding, fine man, but not easy to live with. He had a tendency to be, how do you say, rigid in the manner of a lot of German men. But how your grandmother loved your mother and Fritz! And how she suffered at the end - it was all so sudden, and she was so brave." She removes one of the gardening gloves in order to knead her back more effectively with her hand. "Megan, I have never told anyone this before, but when I was in Auschwitz… no, in fact, already when I was in the train, in the crowded cattle car on the way to Auschwitz, it was the thought of Marga Mayer that helped me survive. All around me were men and women, groaning and vomiting, and dying, and the children, oh the children, crying and crying, the crying never stopped. I could not bear to look at them; they reminded me of my own children and … But then I remembered Marga Mayer, and it was from her that I received the courage to continue. I also prayed a lot, but that did not always sustain me. Needless to say, I constantly thought of my husband and my children, and my dear mother who was, like Marga Mayer, a strong woman, too. But thinking of them, especially thinking of my mother who died in my arms in the Krakow ghetto, often left me with a feeling of hopelessness and, how do you say, despair *ja*? not strength. Only by thinking of Marga Mayer was I able to retain a little strength and the will to live.

"And later, after the liberation, when I was recovering from the typhoid in the DP camp hospital in Germany, I often thought of Marga. And just thinking of her gave me strength." Hannah pauses, looks vacantly toward the distant hills, then turns in Megan's direction. "You know, Marga is the name Henrietta gave you when you were born. How proud your grandmother would have been of you! Let me tell you, even today, when sometimes I feel, how do you say, depressed, *ja*? I see her face in front of me and I recall her courage and…"

Hannah doesn't finish the sentence. Megan will never remember how it happened, but suddenly she has flown across the few feet separating them to Hannah's side, with her arms around the older woman; and Hannah is holding on to her and sobbing silently into her shoulder. How long they stand in this way, intertwined, Megan will also never remember, until Hannah throws back her head, her eyes still full of tears, then looks at Megan and begins to laugh and laugh and laugh, as if she will never stop. Megan becomes alarmed. Naomi too, hearing her mother's unusual laughter, comes running out of the house just as Hannah's laughter begins to subside. She wipes her eyes with the hand still wearing one of the gardening gloves, leaving streaks of dirt on her cheeks, and says, "*Ach*, how good that feels! It is as if I have been liberated once again. Naomi, you worry too much about me. I will be all right. And Megan, thank you, thank you. Thank you for coming to us. From my whole heart, I thank you. Your visit is the best medicine for me. Come," she links one arm through Megan's and the other through Naomi's. "Come girls, enough with this gardening." She walks with an eager spring in her step that was not there earlier. "Let us go inside. I am hoping Shmuel and Fritz are back from morning prayers. I have suddenly a large longing to see my husband."

Chapter 57

꩜

For Megan, each hour, each minute of the following days are filled with the wonder of new experiences. In later years, when she looks back and remembers, she has trouble picking out the moment that left the deepest, most lasting impression on her soul. But, of course, it has to be the Friday night with the welcoming of the Sabbath 'Queen'. She helps Naomi lay the table: the dazzling white table cloth, simple white dishes and glasses, a large arrangement of yellow roses in the center, nothing ornate except for the silver candelabra with seven branches blazing away on the sideboard. Fritz and Naomi, each holding one of Hadassah's hands, singing and harmonizing words and tunes that, though foreign and incomprehensible to Megan, arouse unknown emotions in her; Hannah and Shmuel gazing lovingly at their family, arms entwined, the sadness, at least temporarily, erased from Hannah's face. The special foods, the *Suppe*, the sweet noodle pudding they call *Yerushalmi kugel*, the rice-stuffed eggplant or *chatzilim*, (the English word for which Binyamin said he can never remember)...and on and on.

Shmuel explains that Yitzchak and Yash and their families would have loved to join them, but it is too far for them to walk from their homes. He says, "In observance of the Sabbath, we do not drive or ride in any vehicles." They all stand as he sings a blessing over a sacramental silver goblet filled with sweet red wine.

And then, just as the meal is almost over, and the final blessings are about to be recited, the door is flung open and in walks Binyamin, looking incredibly handsome in his formal light khaki army uniform. He has unexpectedly been given a few hours' leave for Shabbat, and has walked the three kilometers from his army base. Oh, the joy that leaps up in her throat! She wants never to forget how she felt at that moment. And then the shyness that rushes over her when he sits in the chair next to her and says, "*Shabbat shalom*, Megan", then whispers laughingly into her ear, "Did you miss me?"

He says he must return to his unit first thing in the morning, that Shimon and his fellow pilots are on full alert and have to stay with their squadron on the air base indefinitely, that he has heard that negotiations are ongoing at the highest levels of government, but that the Egyptians remain obdurate and have not yet given any indication of softening their position.

Some of this Megan picks up and assumes, rather than understands, because although they all try to include her by speaking English, when the conversation becomes political they automatically lapse into Hebrew, with some German words and phrases thrown in. Hannah, noting Megan's bewilderment, says, "Megan, you are not alone. I am also not understanding everything. My Hebrew is even worse than is my English."

After dinner, the two of them take a stroll on Emek Refa'im. All the restaurants are shut for the Sabbath, the streets empty of traffic except for an occasional vehicle, often a police car; the few pedestrians they encounter exchange greetings of *Shabbat shalom*. Binyamin takes Megan's hand. He says, "Is it my imagination, or was my mother's mood unusually happy and playful this evening?" She tells him what took place that morning in the garden, how Hannah had cried, really cried, then laughed, alarming her and Naomi. He says, "But this is a miracle! It must be all your doing. You have performed a miracle." He lifts her hand to his mouth and kisses the back of it in courtly European fashion. She laughs to hide the effect his kiss has on her, to hide the frisson, the tremor it has sent throughout her body. She feels... She is at a loss to describe, even to herself, what she feels. She wonders, *is this how Henrietta felt when she was with the skating instructor?*

She tells him about the conversation she had with his father about Henrietta's skating instructor in Frankfurt. "It's strange, even to me, how curious I've become about him. I never gave him much thought before, not even after Miss Schneider's visit." She turns to him. "Binyamin, please be honest with me. Would you think me crazy if I decided to travel to Frankfurt to investigate? I have this urgent need to know who he was, and what became of him."

"No-o. I wouldn't think you crazy, Megan, but perhaps a bit impulsive. You might be opening – how do you say in English - a can of worms? – a can which might be better left unopened. Not that I would blame you, of course. If I were in your shoes I would also want to know more."

She considers what he has said. Of course he is right. But still… She says, "I've never said this to anyone, but he may still be alive. After all, he wasn't Jewish."

He says, "That's true, and he might have been in the German army. He was probably the right age." He resists adding that it is possible he could have been a member of the Nazi party.

"Yes," she says quietly. "I have considered that. Or, that he may have been killed in the war. Wouldn't it be ironic if he actually fought against the British? If he fought on the same battlefield as my father, that is, against William Rhys, the man I consider my father. Regardless. Whether he's alive or dead, I would like to know. And," she adds quietly, to Binyamin's surprise, "I have also considered that he might even have been a Nazi. If he was, I would like to know that, too."

They walk on. Wisely, he changes the subject. He asks her if she has any regrets about giving up skating, and she tells him no, she has no regrets whatsoever, how she loves what she is doing now, how fulfilling it is to teach gymnastics to young girls.

As they walk back to the house, he tells her how much it pleases him to know that she is sleeping in his bed, and once again she feels that small pleasurable flutter in her stomach. Inside the house, they part, she to go to bed, to his bed in his room, he to sleep somewhere else in the house. He squeezes her hand. "*Laila tov*, Megan, good night and *Shabbat shalom*. I am leaving very early in the morning, probably long before you get up. I have a long walk back to the base. But I am so glad I had this chance to see you again."

"I am too, Binyamin. *Shabbat shalom.* Sleep well," she says, "and stay safe." *For me,* she says silently, *stay safe for me.*

Chapter 58

⋙ ⋘

Fritz has managed to take a few days off from the Technion in honor of Megan's visit. He and Naomi had planned to bring Megan back with them to Haifa and from there to tour the country, but because of the possibility of war at any moment, they remain in Jerusalem.

On Sunday, they deposit Hadassah into the care of her grandmother. Fritz explains that it is almost impossible to find a parking spot in Jerusalem, so they leave the jeep and take a bus to the YMCA on King David Street. As promised, they climb to the top of the tower. That is, Naomi and Megan climb and leave Fritz waiting for them at the bottom. The stairs are too difficult for him to negotiate with his prosthetic leg.

As they are walking up the stairs, Naomi says, "I have not had the opportunity to speak with you, Megan. I wish to tell you how grateful I am for what you did for my mother."

"Please, Naomi. I don't know what you're talking about. I did absolutely nothing. Your mother had a need to talk and I happened to be there, that's all."

Naomi laughs, takes Megan's arm. "Well, whatever happened, she is almost a different person since last Friday when you helped her in the garden. I have not seen her so, how do you say, so animated, since before the war. Even if she becomes depressed again, which is very likely, at least we know now that she is capable of being happy."

They reach the top level from where they are able to look out over the old city of Jerusalem. Naomi has brought along a pair of binoculars and hands them to Megan. "See that wall just ahead? That is the Wailing Wall. It is the western wall, one of the outer walls of our Holy Temple, the only remnant left standing. And over there is the Garden of Gethsemane where Jesus was said to pray and walk with his disciples, and over in that direction, is the Via Delarosa where, it is said, Jesus was made to carry the cross on which he was crucified." She points out different landmarks, churches of different denominations, Greek Orthodox, Armenian. Christian. "And over there is the Mount of Olives, on which is situated an ancient Jewish cemetery. In the distance, that great golden dome over there, that is the Temple Mount, the site of the Holy of Holies, the most sacred part of our Temple. As we told you when we drove into Jerusalem last Thursday, we are prohibited from visiting any of these places." Not hiding her bitterness, she adds, "Not only is the old city of Jerusalem closed to us, but the Arabs have desecrated most of our holy places."

Megan has not said a word. Now Naomi turns to her and, to her dismay, sees that from beneath the binoculars still fixed to Megan's eyes, tears are seeping down her face. Naomi puts her arm around Megan's shoulders. "Are you all right, Megan? Did I say something to upset you?"

"No, no. Of course not. It is just that…when you were speaking of Jesus, I pictured him so clearly, bent over as he walked with the heavy cross on his back, stumbling because of the weight of his burden, and knowing full well that the cross was for him, that he would soon be hanging on it. I couldn't bear it."

"Megan, Jesus was Jewish. Some say he was even a rabbi, a teacher, a scholar. He just did not, how do you say, see eye to eye with a lot of the other rabbis of that time. You see, we Jews are always questioning, always analyzing. Always discussing and debating. Our Talmud is a book of discussions and debates about Jewish law. Back and forth, back and forth. Sometimes, the discussions get a bit heated and end up in arguments, which is what we assume happened between Jesus and the other rabbis. But we are like one big family, where everyone can quarrel and disagree, but still love and respect each other."

Naomi is relieved to see Megan smiling, no longer in tears. Megan has removed the binoculars from her eyes. The tears on her cheeks have dried. "I am trying to understand," she says. "When I get back home, I would like to take a course in Jewish history. I also would love to learn to speak Hebrew."

"That would be wonderful, Megan. Here in Israel there are many new immigrants. They take a course called Ulpan, and learn to speak Hebrew very quickly. You will find the history of our people is very old and very complicated. Until the State of Israel was born it was one long story of anti-Semitism and persecution. And now Egypt...

"But I should not spoil our day with depressing talk. Megan, look through the binoculars once again before we go down. The King David Hotel is just below us, across the street. Aren't the grounds beautiful? Do you see the enormous swimming pool, and the outside restaurant on the terrace? The hotel was a favorite spot for the British during the Mandate, that is until Menachem Begin and his Irgun blew up the annex, which the British were using as their headquarters. Don't look so shocked, Megan. The British considered Begin and his people to be terrorists. But the Irgun never harmed civilians. To us they were heroes." She turns, takes Megan's arm, and says "Come, let us go back down, Fritz will be getting impatient. We can walk over to the King David for lunch. They have a wonderful dairy restaurant."

⇒⇐

It is Monday morning. At nine o'clock the air is still, not even a hint of breeze to stir the palm fronds, with the sun beating down with burning intensity. Fritz and Naomi have planned to take Megan to visit the Knesset building, perhaps even to sit in on the sessions about the Suez issue. Megan has been looking forward to the visit ever since Fritz told her, "Megan, I want to prepare you. You will be shocked at the behavior of some of the Knesset members. It is much less formal than your British parliament. I understand that in parliament, when one member wishes to insult another, he says very politely,

'The honorable member is an ass.' In the Knesset, there is no such delicacy. Often, there are shouting matches, with insults hurled back and forth faster than ping-pong balls."

They are almost ready to leave. Fritz has gone to load the jeep with refreshments. Hadassah is coming with them, and the little girl is jumping up and down with excitement at the prospect of an outing with her parents and her new foreign cousin. Just at that moment, a uniformed messenger arrives on a bicycle. He delivers a Western Union telegram addressed to Megan Rhys.

As soon as she sees it, her heart sinks. She cannot bear to open it. She knows the news cannot be good. But open it she must. She reads: *Father had stroke stop if possible please return immediately stop need your help stop Mum.*

Chapter 59

꘎

It all happens so quickly. Fritz calling the airline, changing her booking, finding one of the last seats available on that day's BOAC flight, ordering a special kosher meal for her. She stuffs her clothes into the suitcase; there are quick goodbyes, no, not goodbyes, *lehitra'ot Megan, until we meet again*, they all tell her, and a breathless jeep ride to Lydda airport. Fritz presses an envelope into her hand *to be opened and read when you are on the plane*. She checks in, passes through customs. And then she is airborne. As the plane takes off, she catches a glimpse of the burgeoning town of Tel Aviv, which she was not able to visit, the glistening Mediterranean, the sandy beach of Bat Yam, an arid expanse of desert in the distance. She was just beginning to inhale the country, has not even scratched the surface; there is so much she wants to see, to do. Will she ever come back? And if she does, will Binyamin be here, waiting for her?

Does he know yet that she left? She longs to know how it made him feel. When they parted Friday night he promised to write to her.

꘎

Before she knows it she is back in Cardiff, visiting her Da in Rookwood Hospital. He is propped up in a metal bed, eyes closed. Thus, she is able to observe him before he sees her. His large, muscular frame seems shrunken, the whole of his body somehow diminished. The hospital gown cannot hide the grey hair sprouting from his chest; the unshaven hair on his face, too, is completely white. Glynis had told her that the right side of his face is paralyzed, that he has lost the use of his right arm and leg, that speech is difficult. His face contorts into a grotesque smile when he sees her, and his eyes fill with moisture.

Glynis has warned her to be cheerful, not to wear a long face in her Da's presence. She almost throws herself onto him and he manages to put his left arm around her. She holds back her tears. "Oh, Da. I'm so happy to see you." Then, in a stab at humor and with the broadest Welsh inflection, she says, "I can't turn my back for a moment, is it, without you getting into trouble?" There is a rumble at the back of his throat; he is trying to laugh.

⊰⊱

Glynis is harried, what with managing the shop and at the same time running back and forth to the hospital. Before Megan's return, she had to close the shop for several hours each day in order to be with William at the hospital. Now she and Megan are able to take turns: some days Megan stays in the shop while Glynis is at the hospital; other days they change places.

The days fly by for Megan in a flurry of activity, fatigue, and worry about her Da. He should be coming home in a few days, will mostly be confined to a wheelchair, or to his bed. A physical therapist, sent by the NHS, will visit twice a week to try and get him to walk again; a speech therapist will teach him to talk again.

She is anxious to speak to the vicar, but there has been no opportunity to visit St. Mary's. Late one night, after waiting on customers in the shop all day, she feels an urgent need to soak in a hot bath. It is only when she finally sinks back into the hot, bubbly water that she is able to relax. Those few days in Israel no longer seem real to her, surely she must have dreamed them, must have dreamed meeting Fritz and Naomi and Hadassah, must have dreamed meeting the Gutman family. And Binyamin, was he also a dream? A phantom, a figment of her imagination?

In a sudden burst of memory, she recalls the envelope Fritz gave her just as she was leaving, with instructions not to open it until she was in the air. During the flight home she had forgotten all about it, had been too agitated over her Da, too upset over her abrupt departure to think of it. And then, since coming home there has not been a moment to breathe, and the envelope has remained forgotten.

She soaks a little longer, closes her eyes and lets her thoughts roam. Shaun was in regular touch with her Mum while Megan was in Israel. He knows about her Da, knows that she has returned home. This morning he rang from London; he will be coming home after his final exams and before he begins his job in the City. Slyly, he reminded her of her promise. What had she promised him? She has no recollection of making any promises.

She doesn't want to think about Shaun, but when she does think of him, his face always transforms into Binyamin's. She is impatient to hear from Binyamin. Each day, she races down to meet the postman before he can set foot on the stairs, quickly flips through the pile of bills and sundry items, looking in vain… for what? She has never seen his handwriting, has no way of recognizing it. But instinctively she feels she will know it. When she sees it, she will know it is his.

She dries herself off and slips into her nightgown. In her room, she gazes up at Henrietta's skates and at the hook where once the crucifix hung above her bed. It now resides in the drawer of her bedside table. She has not been praying to Jesus. It doesn't seem right to thank Jesus for bringing them together. She wants to pray to the same God that Binyamin prays to, to the same God that she hopes Binyamin is thanking for having met her. Just as she thanks Him, and begs Him to keep Binyamin safe. But she is not sure if she has been using the correct form of address. She will ask the vicar when she sees him.

Now, where did she put the envelope that Fritz gave her? She thinks for a moment, then remembers. She takes down her suitcase from the top of the wardrobe. Sure enough, there is the envelope, just where she had put it, tucked into one of the inside pockets. She fishes it out. A little note from Fritz is attached in a separate envelope:

This letter for you was delivered before you arrived in Israel. I did not want to give it to you during your stay in case it contained something that might make you sad. It was forwarded to me by Bernd Bauer, the nephew of Inge Bauer who was your grandfather's housekeeper. The nephew said in his note to me that his aunt had died recently. She had left instructions for him to send the enclosed letter to me in case of her death, and that I was to pass it on to you. She had hoped to deliver it to you in person. It is from my sister Henrietta. Naturally, I did not open the letter because it is addressed to you. I am sorry to say that it must be in German and you will have to get it translated.

Megan sits on the edge of her bed contemplating the strange handwriting and foreign words on the outside of the envelope. Taking great care not to tear it, she gently manages to unglue the envelope flap. She slides out a thin sheet of paper, bearing the same strange handwriting in a language that is completely foreign to her. The ink has begun to fade. She looks for a signature at the bottom of the page. *Mutti.*

Megan is now wide awake. Gingerly, she holds the letter in her hand as if it were holy. She is overcome with the same feeling she had when she unpacked Henrietta's skates from the parcel she received from Fritz. She is touching the same piece of paper that once Henrietta had touched, holding the same piece of paper that...her mother...had once held in her hands, the paper that must contain her mother's last words to her.

Her heart is beating frantically. How frustrating that she cannot understand what it says! The only person who will be able to translate it for her is Miss Schneider. Of course, Fritz and Naomi and all the Gutmans know German fluently, but they are too far away, and it would take too long. She knows she must not entrust the original letter to the post. She remembers that the local library has a mimeograph machine. She will get a copy made and send it to Miss Schneider.

But then she remembers that she neglected to answer the letter she received from Miss Schneider after her skating accident in Norway. She can no longer recall why she didn't answer. She hopes Miss Schneider has forgiven her rudeness and will be willing to translate Henrietta's letter for her.

Chapter 60

⇒✦⇐

William is brought home by ambulance. Glynis and Megan are both relieved to no longer have to run back and forth to the hospital. They make a big fuss of William's homecoming. "See the beautiful welcome sign our Meggy has made for you, Will love?", Glynis says, pointing to the colorful poster Megan has strung across the kitchen mantel. But Megan believes his eyes are still not able to focus fully, that he did not look at the welcome sign, although at Glynis's words she thinks she detected a slight twitching of his lips.

Glynis and Megan spend their days divided between tending to the shop and taking care of William. Glynis dresses him, assists him to the bathroom, helps him with his personal needs. Glynis tells Megan that the bedpan shames and depresses him. The therapists arrive on their scheduled visits. The speech therapist, a young woman who introduces herself as *Miss* Llewelyn without providing a Christian name, is not much older than Megan, and a recent graduate in her field. She is a quiet girl, not particularly attractive, but not ugly either. She seems a little unsure of herself; perhaps this is her first job since graduating from the speech therapy program. The physical therapist, Andrew, is also young, heftily built, a useful asset when it comes to lifting and moving a man the size of Megan's Da.

William begins to take a few unsteady steps with the aid of a walker. He is beginning to make sounds, at first unintelligible, but eventually some words are discernible. Water, light, tea. Apparently Miss Llewelyn knows her craft.

By this time, Glynis is worn out, but there is a limit to how much Megan can lighten her load. William becomes agitated if Megan attempts to dress him or do anything for him of an intimate nature. He only allows her to shave him, which he seems to enjoy. And she loves to do it, to whip up the lather in the bowl and slather his face with it before taking the razor and gently, ever so gently, scraping his cheeks and, oh so carefully, his neck. She tries to keep up a silly patter as she goes about the task, telling him what a labor of love this is, dabbing a glob of cream on his nose with the brush and holding the mirror to his face so he can see that he looks like a clown. As the days and weeks pass, his laughter becomes more recognizable, his face less contorted. She knows he will never be the same, but an echo of the Da she has always known is beginning to return.

As soon as she arrived home from Israel, Megan resigned from her job. It was a difficult but necessary decision. After all, isn't this why she cut her trip short? She will stay home indefinitely, for as long as she is needed.

Megan is relieved that her Mum has been too busy and exhausted to ask much about Israel. "You had a good time, did you, love?" was about the extent of it, her Mum not even waiting for Megan's answer, her attention already taken up with her patient.

Glynis has also been too preoccupied to notice that the crucifix is missing from Megan's wall. More than anything, Megan is relieved that her Mum has also been too distracted to notice that she no longer eats ham and bacon, that she has developed a distaste for prawns.

⇒⊱⊰⇐

Shaun arrives. Megan has been dreading his visit.

Shaun says, "I'm sorry about your father, Megan. You know how fond I am of him, and your Mum too, of course."

"Yes, I know, and they are fond of you too, Shaun." She cannot look at him.

"And you, Megan, what about you? Are you fond of me? As fond as I am of you? Remember, you promised to consider my proposal when you returned from Israel."

So that was it! Now she remembers her promise. But it has to be a clean break. She will not insult him with the excuse of her Da's illness. It would not be fair to him. She has searched her heart; she cannot marry Shaun.

"Shaun," she says, "Yes, indeed. I'm very, very fond of you. You have always been my dear friend. But I'm very sorry. I cannot marry you."

He just stares at her for a moment. Then says, "It's funny, you know. I had a feeling. Even before you left, I had a feeling. Just tell me, has it something to do with your relatives in Israel? With your finding out that you're Jewish? Because you know, I'm not Gwen. It makes no difference to me."

"No, Shaun," she says gently. "It has nothing to do with Israel or being Jewish. I just don't think it would work. In fact, I know it wouldn't."

She hates what she is doing, what she has to do. She can see he is devastated by her answer. She hates to hurt him.

She accompanies him to the door. She knows she will probably never see him again. He bends to kiss her cheek. A gentleman to the end.

Surely she should be feeling some regret? She is sad, but feels only an overpowering sense of relief.

Chapter 61

≫ ≪

August segues into September. She receives several Jewish new year's cards from Israel. One from Fritz and Naomi has a picture of a man holding the same kind of horn to his lips that she noticed on the poster above Binyamin's bed. The printed message on the card reads, *As we blow the shofar this Rosh Hashanah, let us usher in a year of peace.* Both Fritz and Naomi have added hand-written messages to the card. *We all miss you. We hope your father has recovered his health, and that you will come and see us again very soon.* The *all* is underlined. Megan looks up 'shofar' in her dictionary. A ram's horn. She remembers vaguely reading somewhere in the bible about a ram's horn. Wasn't it in con-nection with Abraham and the near-sacrifice of his son Isaac? It has been a long time since she opened a bible.

From Hannah and Shmuel comes a card with a loving message. Hannah writes, *The weather is turning cooler and the garden is looking very beautiful. It is waiting for your return, dear Megan, as are we.*

A few days later she receives the first missive from Binyamin. She feels her stomach churning when she picks up the envelope with his name *Binyamin Gutman* on the back flap. *Finally, finally.* Her hand trembles as she opens it. His handwriting is small and neat. *Shalom dearest Megan. This is my first oppor-tunity to write. We have been on maneuvers for weeks. I think of you constantly.* He signs off, *I send my love to you, Binyamin.*

Her heart soars. She had expected more, had expected to hear much sooner. But this is enough for now. More than enough. *Dearest Megan. Love.* He is still thinking of her. *Constantly.* He has written, that is all that matters. He has not given a return address. There is a postscript that she almost missed. *I will try to write again.* Instinctively, she doesn't think it would be a good idea to send a letter to him in care of his parents' address. She will have to wait until she hears from him again.

That night, she lies in bed and whispers, "Dear God, can You hear me? Thank You. Thank You." Even as she says it, then drifts into sleep, she cannot stop smiling.

※

She waits impatiently to hear from Miss Schneider. When Megan telephoned her a few weeks ago with her request, Miss Schneider was most gracious. Megan resists the temptation to ring her again. The woman is doing her a favor; she must be patient.

Finally, during the second week of October, Miss Schneider telephones from London and, in her formal, stilted English, says, "I have today posted to you the translation of your dear mother's letter. Please forgive me that I was unable to do it sooner. First Rosh Hashanah prevented me - that is the Jewish new year - then it was the fast of Yom Kippur followed by the Tabernacles holiday of Succoth, and I did not have an opportunity to give it my full attention until after the holidays were over. You should be receiving the letter tomorrow or the next day."

Megan waits for the post with trepidation. She hopes she has thanked Miss Schneider sufficiently. The letter arrives while Megan is in the shop, waiting on customers. It takes every ounce of self-control, every ounce of will power not to abandon them and run to her room and tear the envelope open. Yet, after the customers have left, after she has closed the shop at the end of the day and is finally able to go up to her room, she hesitates before opening it, afraid of what it might contain. Her hands are unsteady just as they were when she received Binyamin's letter; her heart is racing. Slowly, she removes Miss Schneider's English translation from the envelope, and begins to read.

My dearest little bunny rabbit,

 But, of course, when you read this you will no longer be little, no longer a bunny rabbit. And I will no longer be alive.

 When I was seventeen, I did something very foolish. I thought myself in love with someone who was not deserving of my love. He was not even Jewish. But, from that foolishness, came you, my sweet Marga, my dearest child, and because of you I can have no regrets.

 I hope that by sending you away your life has been saved, that you have found a wonderful family to take care of you. I know that by the time you read this you will have grown into a lovely young woman of whom I would surely be proud.

 Whichever path your life will lead you, I pray to the Almighty that you will find happiness and true love. I pray that regardless of the family who has sheltered you all these years, you will never forget your Mayer origins. Never forget that you are Jewish. I have named you after my dear mother, your grandmother, Marga. Secretly, in my heart, I also gave you her Hebrew name, Malka. It means queen in Hebrew. She was a queen of a woman.

 My dearest daughter, I have loved you more than life itself.

Mutti

⊰⊱

Through her tears, Megan reads the letter again, and again, and then once more, until her tears begin to smudge the words so faithfully translated by

Miss Schneider. She folds the letter carefully and slips it back into its envelope. She sits without moving for a long time, holding the envelope in her hand. Her heart is still galloping, her tears still flowing.

She has just read her mother's farewell.

Each word echoes.

Mutti.

Never forget that you are Jewish…

I also gave you her Hebrew name, Malka. It means queen…

Jerusalem. The Shabbat Queen.

She continues sitting for many more minutes, in silent contemplation. Until her heart steadies; her tears lessen.

She stands up, places the translated letter under her pillow. Next to her mother's original letter. Next to Binyamin's letter.

She is grateful for her Mum's lack of curiosity about her correspondence; her Mum is completely absorbed with her Da.

Every night, Megan reads both letters before falling asleep, until she can recite them both by heart.

Chapter 62

⇒❦⇐

Since her return from Israel, Megan has taken to reading the newspaper every morning at breakfast. She is trying to follow the news from Israel. In the evenings at supper, unless her Mum objects because she wants 'peace and quiet', she listens to the 6 o'clock news on the wireless. It is all too complicated and difficult for her to grasp completely. On October 29th the war begins. Israel attacks Egyptian positions in the Sinai peninsula. Israeli paratroopers are dropped. The Israelis call it *Operation Kadesh*. The paper mentions the Gulf of Aqaba, the Gaza Strip; names and places that are completely foreign to her. She tries to follow the progress of the fighting, all the different fronts, but can't keep them all straight. Everything is happening so fast, changing so quickly. There is so much she does not understand. Certain names keep recurring. Anthony Eden. Gamal Abdel Nasser. David Ben Gurion. Moshe Dayan. First the French are involved, then the British. And, near the end, the Americans and the Soviet Union.

And then, on November 5th, it is over. The Egyptians have surrendered.

Megan remembers, for no reason at all, that tonight there will be fireworks all over Great Britain. It is Guy Fawkes Day.

Chapter 63

Megan has not heard from anyone in Israel since September. She prays every night for all of them, especially for Binyamin. She has received no news. He said he would write again, but she has heard nothing more.

The suspense is agonizing. She dares not write. She is terrified of what she will hear. That he has been killed? No, no, it is impossible to think of him dead. But why has she heard nothing? Why has nobody written to her?

Must she stop fantasizing of a future with him? Must she stop fantasizing how they will travel together to Frankfurt to search for her German father, as they discussed on that Friday night walk in Jerusalem? Her curiosity about the *skating instructor* has not waned despite Henrietta's letter. If anything, the letter has piqued her curiosity even more. She wants to find out more about the man who, Henrietta said, was not *deserving* of her love.

Must she stop fantasizing how they will visit the Jewish cemetery in Frankfurt to search for the graves of her Mayer ancestors, and place a special stone on the grave of Marga Mayer for whom she was named? How, from Frankfurt, the two of them might continue on to America and visit her grandmother's family, the Kahns, in New York?

Must she stop fantasizing about the places in Israel that Binyamin said they would visit together? She had wanted to jot down the names, but he said, "Writing is one of the thirty-nine acts we are forbidden from performing on

Shabbat." So she had refrained. She is proud of the way she has managed to memorize just a few of the places: Tiberias, The Sea of Galilee (*where Jesus walked on water*, he said – was he teasing her?), Masada, Beersheba. There were other places he mentioned, but she has forgotten the names.

She tries to calm her nerves by staying busy, which is not difficult as there is so much to do, what with waiting on her Da, serving customers in the shop, cleaning the flat, helping her Mum in the kitchen, shopping for groceries.

She tries to think rationally. If he has been killed in action, would she not have heard by now? But what if he has been wounded? Or taken prisoner? Or, what if he has decided to forget about her, that their meeting was just a charming but meaningless interlude in his life?

Or, could it be that right at this very moment he is on a plane bringing him to London, to his new post as military attaché to the Israeli embassy? Could it be that at any moment he will ring her from London? Did he not say *lehitra'ot? Until we meet again?*

Or, is it God's will that she stay here in Cardiff, taking care of her Mum and Da? She is the only one they have, isn't she, the only one who can take care of them in sickness, in old age. Is this, she wonders, what is called 'poetic justice'? Did her Mum's tea leaves decree that she must do for her parents what they have done for her all of her life? Could she be responsible for her Da's stroke? Was it brought on by his anguish over her trip to Israel? And if it was, must she live with the guilt for the rest of her life?

She wishes she knew God's plan for her. Is it His plan that she remain a good Christian, that she marry Shaun after all, and raise Christian grandchildren for her parents?

If that is His plan, how can she fight it? And, what of Jesus? Can she just thrust him aside, forget about him? Wasn't it Jesus who always seemed to help her, who always seemed to answer her prayers?

And yet.

And yet, isn't she Jewish? Is she not descended from a long line of Mayers? Is she not Marga Mayer as well as Megan Rhys? Is she not Malka, the Jewish queen? Are not those the very things that Hen…, that her mother, in her letter, encouraged her, no, *instructed* her never to forget?

⤜⤛

Another week passes. It is the middle of November, the weather is turning cold, wet, and nasty, a typical Welsh winter in the making, with strong, blood-curdling winds blustering inland off the Irish Sea, and the rain lashing the window panes. Megan keeps the kitchen fire blazing constantly, piling it repeatedly with coal and logs throughout the day. Despite all of her and Glynis's efforts, the rooms feel perpetually damp. The wash hangs on racks directly in front of the fireplace but takes forever to dry; the garments always feel soggy and dank.

Megan tries to keep up a cheerful front for her parents, especially her Da. He now has a wheelchair in which he sits for hours before the fire. If they let him, he will just stare into the flames. But Megan and her Mum and the two therapists will not allow it. Glynis talks to him constantly to keep his attention focused; Megan reads newspapers to him. He especially likes her to read from the sports pages, and is now able to instruct her how to fill out his pool forms. He still loves to listen to the wireless concerts. He is definitely making progress. He now walks around the flat with his walker, is even beginning to negotiate a few stairs. He has begun to enjoy his Woodbines again, is now able to inhale, able to hold the cigarette in his hand after Megan or Glynis lights it for him.

One day, Andrew, the physical therapist, helps William down the steps into the shop, then brings down the wheelchair for him to sit in, so he can watch Megan and Glynis wait on the customers. How he perks up, how his face lights up at this welcome change in his routine! Mrs. Morgan happens to be in the shop when William comes down, and not much later Mrs. Griffith walks in. They both make a big fuss of him, and he, in turn, is able to make himself understood well enough to have a flirtatious exchange, an exchange that ends in laughter all around. Worn out as Glynis is, her happiness knows no bounds. After the customers leave, she doesn't stop hugging her husband. "Will, love, you're almost back, indeed. Won't be much longer before you'll be standing right here behind the counter just as you used to do, isn't that right, Meggy?" And Megan has to agree with her Mum, although she knows in her heart that her Da will never be the same man he was before his stroke.

Still, he is definitely improving. So much so, that on Sunday Megan asks her Mum if she can spare her for a couple of hours; she would like to go to church. Glynis says, "Of course, Meggy love, go by all means. It's high time we both went, indeed it is." And Megan suggests that the following Sunday she will gladly stay with her Da and give her Mum a chance to attend church. "It will do you good, Mum, just to get out of the house for a while," she says.

Chapter 64

>⚒<

Megan deliberately dawdles on the way to St. Mary's. She is well-protected against the cold and wind, wearing warm boots and a woolen muffler. Luckily, it has stopped raining, and she is able to walk slowly and leisurely, examining the window displays of the closed shops on Llandaff Road. Her head feels weighed down with confusion. On the one hand, there are the letters under her pillow, the words permanently engraved on her heart, words that prevent her from genuflecting and kneeling to the figure on the cross. Too much has happened in the last few months. Henrietta's letter and her new family in Israel have re-directed her soul.

On the other hand, how can she reject the life she has always known? How can she do that to her parents, especially to her Da in his present condition?

She has timed her arrival at St. Mary's to coincide with the conclusion of the Sunday service, hoping that Vicar Lowell will be free to talk to her.

From a distance she watches as the congregation lets out. She sees the vicar, in his cassock and surplice, standing at the main door, as is his custom, greeting each of the worshippers as they leave. After he has shaken the hand of the last congregant, the vicar turns back and re-enters the church.

She finds him in the vestry, about to remove his surplice. His face lights up at the sight of her. "My dear child," he says, coming toward her, hands extended in welcome. "It has been too long since last I saw you. I was so sorry to miss you when I came by to visit your dear father the other day. Your mother told me you were out running errands. I hope she remembered to give you my regards."

"Yes, indeed she did, Father" says Megan. "I was sorry to miss you, too. My Da is making good progress, as you must have seen."

"Indeed, I was delighted to note his progress. With God's help, and the help of Jesus, he will continue to improve."

"That is what I've come to talk to you about, Father. God and Jesus, that is. Can you spare me a few minutes?"

"Of course, my child. Come, let us sit down. What is troubling you?"

Suddenly, everything gushes out of her. Everything spills out in a flood of words that stumble over each other as she relates to the vicar all her experiences and feelings of these last turbulent months, all the changes that have gradually been taking place within her, everything she has had to conceal from her parents. She leaves nothing out, telling him of her meeting with Binyamin and his family, *her* family. She tells him of the impact her newly revealed Jewishness has had on her; how she feels this is something she must explore, cultivate and develop.

But how can she do all this without hurting her parents?

Finally, she tells him of the posthumous letter she received from Henrietta, from the lady of her dream. The letter containing her mother's last words to her. She recites from memory the translated text of the letter, word for word.

The vicar listens attentively, nodding his head once or twice. Then he sits for a long time, his head bowed low, staring at his black laced shoes. At length, just as Megan is beginning to worry that she has made a terrible mistake, he raises his head, takes her hand in his, and begins to speak.

"I hear that you are terribly conflicted, my child, and if you will pardon the metaphor, you seem to be skating on very thin ice here." He chuckles, and Megan smiles wryly at the allusion. "Perhaps it will comfort you somewhat to know that your dilemma is by no means unique." She looks at him, questioningly. "No, my child, your problem is not at all unique." He gives a deep sigh before continuing. "Let me explain. Before the war, many Jewish parents in Europe, desperately fearing what the Nazis might do, tried to send their children away to safety in England. However, not all parents were able, or willing for that matter, to part from their children. It was a terrifying time. In Germany, as you know from your own experience, the Quaker Society, and other organizations, were able to send some children to England. In Poland, and later in Belgium and France and Holland, many Jewish children were hidden in convents and monasteries for safekeeping. Some Christian families risked their lives by hiding Jewish children. Naturally, all the parents, including your mother, had every intention of returning to reclaim their children once the war was over. But, in most cases that was not to be." He sighs again. "Tragically, most of the parents did not survive the war. I have personally heard of situations such as yours, where Jewish children were adopted by Christian families, and in some cases baptized, only to discover later that they were actually Jewish." He pauses, and once again sighs, more deeply this time. "I know of a nun in Poland who decided that it must be God's will that she remain in the convent and continue her life as a nun, even after learning she was Jewish."

Megan is staggered by the vicar's recital. The vicar clears his throat. "Who could have foreseen that the war would last so long, that after the war was over so many problems and conflicts would exist for so many people? The war ended in 1945 and here we are in 1956, eleven years later, and there are still Jewish relatives searching for Jewish children who survived as Christians with their new families. I can assure you there are many young people like yourself in Europe today who have no idea that they are Jewish. Of course," he hastens to add, "personally, I'm happy for those who found kind Christian homes and comfort in the church."

"I had no idea," Megan says. "None of that ever occurred to me."

"No, I'm sure it didn't, my child. Not many people know about this sad, complicated state of affairs. Most people are still trying to put together their shattered lives. They lost husbands and sons in the war; they are still trying to rebuild homes that were destroyed in the nightly bombing raids.

"But to get back to your situation. My dear child, I cannot tell you with certainty what to do. I don't feel it is my place to do so, nor do I feel qualified. But what I can tell you is this: there is no one path to God. Undoubtedly, many of my fellow clergy would be appalled to hear me say this, but that is what I believe. Long ago, in seminary, when I was still merely a candidate for ordination, I came to this conclusion. In the end, whichever path we choose, we all arrive at the same destination, which is to worship the Almighty. If you have begun to feel your path is through Judaism, my child, by all means go ahead and explore it to your heart's content, knowing that if ever you wish to return to Jesus, he will be here waiting for you."

The vicar lifts Megan's hand, which he has been holding all this time, and joins his other hand around it, so that now her hand is securely captured in both of his. "There are only two pieces of advice I can give you," he says. "The first is that you might think about discovering and contacting other children who were sent to England before the war, as you were. Meeting them might help you to sort out your own feelings, might give you the comfort of knowing that you are not alone, and might provide you with support as you face whatever the future may hold.

"My second piece of advice is that you contact a rabbi here in Cardiff and discuss with him your newly discovered Jewish identity. I recently met the new young rabbi of a synagogue down on Cathedral Road. I have a feeling," he says, chuckling once more, "that he will be able to tell you a lot more about Judaism than I can. He seems to be a friendly sort of chap, and I will be happy to put you in touch with him.

"As to the young man you met in Israel, I will pray to Jesus on your behalf for his safety. You, my child, must follow your heart. Your parents' only desire is your happiness. I can assure you of that. Just as long as you do not cast them off, and that I know you will never do."

The old vicar gives Megan's hand one last pat, and then releases it. He stands up, and Megan is once again filled with sadness to see that, even with his cane, he no longer stands as readily and erectly as he used to; that the hands that just a moment ago held hers, are gnarled from arthritis and covered with dark blotches. He mumbles something about his aching bones, then says, "And now, my child, I must beg you to excuse me. I have some visits to make in the parish, for which I am already somewhat late."

"Thank you, Father, thank you." Megan says simply. Her heart is overflowing with gratitude to this kind old vicar, who has been a wise and comforting anchor in her life ever since she can remember. "I'm sorry to have detained you for so long." She knows she will never be able to thank him adequately.

"Go in peace, my child," says the vicar. "You know where to find me if you need to speak with me again. Now go with God."

⇒◈⇐

She walks home, suddenly lightheaded and lighthearted, her burden lifted. The relief is overwhelming. She is not alone. There are others who, at this very moment, may be awakening to a new history, to an unsuspected past.

Her unharnessed thoughts alight on the memory of the Jewish girls at Canton High School, who had to slink into the assembly hall at the conclusion of the Christian prayers and hymns, the Jewish girls whose very presence so irritated Gwen. Is it possible that those girls, too, were refugees?

She chides herself. Why has she never shown any curiosity about the other children who came to England in her transport? What happened to them? Who adopted them? Were they as lucky as she was? Had they found homes with kind, caring parents, as she had?

She vows to herself that she will seek them all out.

She vows to herself that she will seek out the rabbi the vicar told her about, and learn everything she can about Judaism, the religion that calls its Sabbath 'the Queen', the religion that has a direct path to God, the religion practiced for so many centuries by the Mayers of Frankfurt-am-Main. The religion of Henrietta, the woman who bore her, the woman who gave life to her a second time by sending her away.

She vows to herself that, regardless of her soul's journey, she will always honor and love her parents, Glynis and William Rhys.

By the time she arrives home the confusion in her head has been replaced by a profound and comforting inner peace.

Chapter 65

⇒ ⇐

The following Sunday Glynis gets dressed for church. Before she leaves, she makes sure William is comfortably ensconced near the kitchen fire, with Megan reading to him from the Sunday papers.

Megan gives him the latest football scores and amuses him with the comic strips. She is in the middle of reading an article to him about one of his favorite soccer players, whose wife has just given birth to twins, when she hears him beginning to snore. He has nodded off and is dozing peacefully, his head thrown back, his mouth slightly open. Gently, she wipes his chin.

She folds the newspaper away and goes over to the kitchen table where she has laid out papers containing information she gleaned and mimeographed on her last visit to the library. How wise the vicar is. A national organization exists, headquartered in London, whose members are Jewish children, now adults of course, who, just like Megan, were sent to England from Europe before the war. She sits down and pulls out her stationery and fountain pen. She will write to the organization to find out how she can join; perhaps they have a chapter in Cardiff. She gets no further than *Dear Sirs*, when she hears a pounding at the downstairs side door.

Reluctantly laying down her pen, she goes to the top of the stairs and looks down, but from here can discern nothing more than a bulky shadow on the other side of the door. Who can possibly be visiting at this hour of a Sunday morning when everyone is, or should be, in church? She checks her Da to make sure the knocking has not disturbed him. He is still sleeping.

Cautiously, she starts down the stairs. She is three rungs from the bottom and still unable to…. But then she stops, incapable of moving any further; her feet have become rooted to the spot. She must be seeing things. It is not possible.

Through the small glass pane near the top of the door she has glimpsed the epaulets, has recognized the insignia that months ago she memorized so well that she can visualize it with her eyes closed, would recognize it in her sleep; the insignia of the rank of major. In the Israeli army. Then she sees the face beneath the military officer's beret, the unruly mop of sandy curls. Those disquieting eyes.

With enormous effort she unglues her feet, flies across the remaining stairs. She fumbles with the lock. Her hands tremble uncontrollably.

Finally, she flings open the door.

"*Shalom*, Megan," he says. "Did you miss me?"

CPSIA information can be obtained
at www.ICGtesting.com
Printed in the USA
LVOW03s1750050418
572449LV00027B/495/P